Spectacular Praise for

MAX'S DIAMONDS

"Five Stars (out of Five)! An incredibly engaging and thought-provoking story of one man haunted by the grief of his past. *Max's Diamonds*, an excellent new work of fiction by Jay Greenfield, traces the life of a man hiding his past and a traumatic childhood. This is a story filled with secrets, lies, and an overwhelming sense of grief. … It's a place worth stopping by again, as the rich characters combine with beautiful descriptions of settings and, at times, an almost lyrical prose …. Themes of religious persecution, the consequences of lifelong guilt, and the difficulties of familial relationships and relationships created on a base of lies reside beneath the surface of this work, adding complexity as well as beauty. … It's the perfect book to read on a melancholy, rainy day, and Greenfield's obvious talent certainly makes him an author to keep an eye on."

— Tracy Fischer, *Foreword Reviews*

"A terrific read, fast-paced and darkly humorous, *Max's Diamonds* tells the story of a rootless young man determined to fashion an identify and a future for himself in defiance of the history that produced him. Part parody of the American dream of self-determination, part tribute to a bygone world defined by the claims of heritage, this riveting debut novel pits the legacy of the Holocaust against the promise of East Coast ambition to measure the conflicting moralities of mid-century American Jews."

— Eve Keller, co-author, *Two Rings: A Story of Love and War*

"Jay Greenfield's engrossing novel vividly depicts a young man's coming of age in Rockaway, a close-knit beach community in New York, during and after World War II. The Holocaust and its aftermath affect him personally through the experiences of family members. Paul, the protagonist, becomes an ambitious young lawyer, but ultimately comes to terms with his identity as a Jew through his dramatic encounter with his Israeli daughter. We could not put this novel down."

— Lawrence Kaplan and Carol Kaplan, co-authors, *Between Ocean and City: The Transformation of Rockaway, New York*

"*Max's Diamonds* is a Bildungsroman, a mystery and a multi-generational survivor's tale all at once. But above all, it's a hugely entertaining novel. Jay Greenfield has made a terrific debut."

— Leonard Cassuto, author, *Hard-Boiled Sentimentality: The Secret History of American Crime Stories*

MAX'S DIAMONDS

Jay Greenfield

ISBN 978-0-9913274-2-3

Book design by Lisa Marie Pompilio

Chickadee Prince Logo by Garrett Gilchrist

Visit us at www.ChickadeePrince. com

First Edition

JAY GREENFIELD

MAX'S DIAMONDS

JAY GREENFIELD was raised in Rockaway, New York. For several decades, he was a trial lawyer with a New York-based international law firm, where he argued in the Supreme Court of the United States, represented civil rights activists in Louisiana during 1964's Freedom Summer, and was senior counsel in several cases establishing that, under New York law, homeless families have a right to shelter. He retired early to devote himself to writing fiction. He lives in Manhattan with his wife, Judy; they have three adult children and three grandchildren. *Max's Diamonds* is his debut novel.

MAX'S DIAMONDS

Chickadee Prince Books
New York

To Judy

5 3 9 2 7

1944, 1947-1954
Rockaway

CHAPTER 1

Paul's mother told him not to look at the numbers on Cousin Max's arm. "Make believe they're not there," she said the night Max moved in with them. But when Paul awoke the next morning, the last day of 1947, he saw nothing else — 53927 glowing on a pale arm across the room. He rolled over towards the wall and pulled the blanket over his head.

"You can look. Numbers don't bite," came a scratchy voice from the other bed.

Max's English was a surprise. From the moment Max arrived last night, Paul had heard only Yiddish from his cousin and the dozen relatives and friends who had gathered to meet him. Paul understood very little aside from the sobs and the names of dead people and concentration camps. He wiggled his head out of the blanket. "I'm sorry," he said to the wall.

"Sorry for what? You didn't do nothing."

"I didn't mean to stare at them."

"Staring's not so terrible. Everyone got a number unless you went direct . . ."

Paul turned back to face his cousin. He couldn't hide — he shouldn't.

"I'll try not to stay too long," Max continued.

Paul sprang up. "No. Stay, stay. I don't mind, I won't ask anything."

Max lay still. Only his arm, neck, and head showed. Except for the purple numbers on his straight stick of forearm, his skin was the faded gray of the blanket. His neck had grooves and ridges where tendons jutted from the skin. His cheeks and eyes seemed sucked into his skull. "Max is forty," Paul's mother had told him. "Daddy's age if he was alive, but he looks eighty." To Paul, he looked older than the oldest stone in Mount Hebron Cemetery, across from the 1939 World's Fair, where, for him, Daddy breathed under the ground.

"Stare, don't stare," Max muttered. "Ask, don't ask. What's the difference?" He sat up. "You just started high school, your mother says. How old? Thirteen?"

"Fourteen."

"You don't look it. She says you're smart like your father. Next week, when I start work, I'll get up early so I don't interfere with your school. It's important you do good."

Paul resented the reminder; he would do well without urging from anybody. "Thanks," he made himself respond. "Happy New Year."

Max said nothing.

* * *

For weeks, Paul and Max said little more to each other than hello and goodbye. In the evenings, Paul would do homework or practice the clarinet or listen to the radio — anything to keep himself inside himself — while Max spoke Yiddish with his mother and grandparents in the living room. He swam two hours every afternoon with the freshman swim team and fell into bed exhausted before Max entered the room and undressed. He was usually asleep by the time the numbers were uncovered, but they followed him into his dreams — 53927 on a translucent arm bobbing in the air like a jellyfish near the Atlantic's edge; 53927 suspended from the Auschwitz entrance sign, *Arbeit Macht Frei*.

On weekend mornings, Paul would be gone before Max stirred — a Boy Scout outing, fishing in Jamaica Bay, Teen Torah Club. Anything. On school mornings, he faced the wall and feigned sleep until Max left for work in Manhattan's diamond district. When Max sat on his bed to put on his shoes, Paul knew it was five to seven. When Max sighed and tiptoed from the bedroom, it was five after. And when the door to their second-floor apartment opened and closed, he knew he could have the bathroom for five minutes until his grandfather got up to get ready for the grocery store's early customers.

But on the second Monday in March, he didn't hear Max sigh or leave the room; the only sound was the radio in the Rossini's first-floor apartment — Dinah Shore singing "Buttons and Bows." Had he fallen back asleep and missed Max's departure? Would he have time to check his math homework again? He rolled over. Max was sitting on his bed across the room, dressed and staring at him. His eyes seemed even deeper and blacker than usual, his cheeks more hollow.

Only Max's lips moved. "I know you're afraid to talk to me."

"No, that's not true."

"Like it's catching, being in the camps. But I got to ask you something."

Paul looked at the clock by Max's bed, but it was turned away from him. He might be late for band rehearsal.

"What?" Paul sat up but kept the blanket wrapped around him.

"You know when you played the clarinet last night?"

Paul pulled the blanket tighter and nodded.

"You know what you were playing?"

"It's for the band — the Spring Concert."

"The name of it!"

"Tan . . ." Paul stopped in the middle of the word, afraid his voice would crack.

"*Tannhäuser!*" Max said with disgust. "When we stood outside to be counted, they played it on the loudspeaker. *Appell* they called it, morning roll call, even though it was black outside. Hours in the freezing cold. People would go in their pants. If you moved, they shot you. If you were lucky they shot. Otherwise, the dogs. You know who wrote it?"

"Wagner," Paul whispered.

"The worst kind of Jew hater. Hitler's favorite composer."

"I won't play it," Paul said. Silently, he added: *at home.* If he didn't play it in school, they'd kick him out of band, and it wouldn't be on his college applications.

"A Nazi before Nazis got invented."

"I won't play it."

Max shook his head. "I can't ask that. I'm only here because your mother's so nice. We're not even related anymore now that your father's . . . But you and me, we're always related. I don't want to make trouble. She wants you should go to a big college."

"I won't tell her we talked about it."

"Just let me know when you're going to play it. I can take a walk. What's the band teacher's name?"

"Mrs. Heider." Max frowned, and Paul added, "She's Jewish."

Max shrugged. "The worst kind of *anti-Semitka.*"

Paul had always enjoyed rehearsing *Tannhaüser* — the solemn opening notes of the trombones and French horns, lightened by the woodwinds that seemed to dance among them like falling rose petals; a regal march made joyous by his deft fingering and perfect timing. But at that morning's band practice, instead of strewing flowers, he was standing in the Auschwitz lineup terrified he would pee in his pants. Suddenly, he heard nothing but his own clarinet and something banging. He pulled the reed from his mouth. Mrs. Heider, scowling at him from the podium, was slamming her baton against her music stand. He felt his face redden.

"Ahhh." Mrs. Heider sounded a perfect C. "Mr. Hartman is rejoining us. You came in early three bars ago." Behind Paul, a trombonist giggled until she was silenced by two baton taps.

Paul looked directly at Mrs. Heider. "It won't happen again."

That afternoon Paul skipped swim practice to prepare a little speech for Max: If his cousin didn't want him to play Wagner, he would quit the band. Max, he was sure, would tell him to play.

Waiting for Max, he practiced *Tannhaüser* in the small bedroom, the one that had been his until Max moved in and everything was rearranged: his mother in the small bedroom, Max and Paul in the large bedroom — which, in Paul's mind, was still his parents' bedroom even though Daddy had been dead for almost four years. "Temporary," his mother said, "until Max is ready to live alone." To prove it, she left Paul's pictures on the wall — Benny Goodman, the great Jewish clarinetist; Hank Greenberg, the great Jewish slugger who wouldn't play on *Yom Kippur*, even though it was the World Series; and Jackie Robinson, the first Negro to play Major League baseball. In the large bedroom he was now sharing with Max, there were no longer any pictures, only five pale rectangles that appeared a few hours before Max's arrival when his mother removed the dark-framed photographs from Czechoslovakia. "Too many gone, too many sad memories," she explained before Paul could ask. "We don't want to upset Cousin Max."

Still stung by Mrs. Heider, Paul kept practicing until his fingers moved on their own. His tone had never been better. At six PM, he went to the window and looked out of their two-family home, past the empty lot to Sixty-ninth Street, where, as he expected, Max, enveloped in an overcoat too heavy for April and a fedora that sank past the tops of his ears, was walking — almost shuffling — from the Arverne Station of the Long Island Railroad. Paul put the clarinet away and went into the large bedroom.

Max was surprised to see him standing between the iron beds, but neither of them spoke. Paul waited while Max put his hat, coat and jacket in the closet. He knew Max wouldn't remove his tie or roll up his shirtsleeves.

"I've decided," Paul began, and suddenly he saw nothing but the gray rectangle beside Max's bed where his parents' wedding picture had been — thirty-six people, the bride in white, the rest wearing black, all standing straight and looking earnest. He heard nothing except his father's voice just before they went to the beach on the day he died.

"Your mother, the prettiest bride anyone could remember, blonde like a *goy*; our parents; three grandparents who wouldn't leave no matter how we pleaded or what Hitler threatened." He had named each sister, brother, aunt, and uncle. "Over a hundred people came, but the photographer couldn't get them all in the picture, so there's no cousins or friends. But my mother, Grandma Gittel, counted, and we put back one of the cousins to get the number to thirty-six; that's twice *chai* which in Jewish is the number eighteen and means life — a lucky number."

Was Max the cousin they had added? Was he in one of the other rectangles? The one of his father's swim team at the Hebrew Youth Games? Was everybody in that picture dead?

"What's wrong?" Max knit his sparse eyebrows. "Sit on your bed. Maybe lay down. I'll get you some water."

"I'll get it," Paul said, but he couldn't move from the wedding picture that was no longer there. Everything went blank until he drank the water Max had brought.

"Why'd they want to kill all the Jews?" Paul's question surprised him.

"Good question, *yunger man*, but they never gave me an explanation." For a moment, Max's lips widened — as close to a smile as Paul had seen on his face. But only for a moment. "Who can explain? A lot of us didn't believe it until it was too late. But your father, he took Hitler at his word, what he was saying about the Jews and getting back the Sudetenland where we lived. Right after you were born, he got the three of you out, then your grandparents. The rest of us . . ." Max shrugged. "Go do your homework."

"I'm not going to play *Tannhäuser*."

"Don't be ridiculous." Max's mouth twisted in contempt. "The *goyim* run the world and you do what you got to. You beat them at their own game."

The words surged in Paul, and he felt a bolt of fierce determination. He could beat them, like Max said. Not easily, but he would try with all his might — make Max proud. Dad, too. "Come to the concert in April!"

Max's head jerked back.

"Only my mother's coming. *Tannhäuser's* the first piece, but you can wait outside till it's over. The rest is mostly Sousa. Bouncy marching music. Real American. Red, white, and blue." Paul lifted the pillow from his bed and pointed at his folded striped pajamas.

He felt Max's palm on the back of his neck. It was the first time they had ever touched. "I used to play the violin. Not too bad." Paul looked up at him and he almost smiled. "But a concert, I'm not ready yet."

He started to massage Paul's neck. Daddy had done this. But Max's palm was scaly — the opposite of Daddy's. Without meaning to, Paul stepped back, leaving Max's arm in the air, then froze; he had insulted his cousin. "Can you come to the swim meet on Saturday?" he blurted out. "It's the first time the coach entered me."

He wanted to pull the question back inside him. How would he describe his gray cousin to the rest of the team? Or explain why Max was the only one in the bleachers whose sleeves weren't rolled up?

"Thanks," Max said softly, and dropped his hand. "Maybe another Saturday I'll watch."

Paul was relieved. After this week, all the Saturday meets were away.

The next morning, when Paul opened the bathroom cabinet, Max's razor was gone. He went back to the bedroom to look under his cousin's bed. Max's suitcase wasn't there. Paul knew better than to ask questions in the morning when everybody was rushing. But, when his mother called from the store, just before six that night, he couldn't help himself.

"Where's Cousin Max?"

"It's better you don't know too much. Some of it's not so nice."

Maybe she was right. But he was almost fifteen. "You can't keep me out of everything."

"Please Paul," she said. "We're rearranging the shelves. Adding some special foods for *Peysekh* — *peysekhdike* but modern. Maybe it'll bring a customer in. Put out juice. No time for me to finish making soup."

"Is he coming back?"

"I'm sure he's not gone for good."

"What kind of juice?" The hell with them all.

Just thinking the three letters M-A-X was dangerous. It could make his clarinet screech or his schoolbooks blur. Paul stayed after swim practice to lift weights with Bobby Bartola, the team captain. "You've got heart, Hartman," Bobby told him. "Like Coach Barry says. But we have to put meat on you." He slept even deeper but, no matter how deep, 53927 saturated his dreams.

* * *

On Sunday evening, after Max had been gone for five nights, Paul heard him climb the inside stairs. Fortunately, he was in the small room and the clarinet was assembled. He began to play Sousa loud enough to drown out any discussion between the adults but, after a few bars, Max tapped at the bedroom door. *Shit*! Paul pushed the music stand next to the bed so there would be enough space for the door to open. "Come in."

Max stood in the doorway, still wearing his oversized hat and coat, carrying a black case. "This'll help you." He thrust out the case. "I bought it for you where I went."

Where had he been? Max might not answer. Or he might say what Grandpa often said — "too many questions you ask." Or, worst, he might tell him.

"Take it."

Paul obeyed, but held the case at arm's length.

"You can open it. It's not poison." Max left and closed the door behind him.

Paul sat on the bed and stared at the case. What was inside? A vampire that would spring out and latch on to his neck? Daddy's lifeguard shirt? Some kind of map that would lead him into Max's past? Whatever it was, it wouldn't be what Paul wanted from Max — to go away.

His fingers fumbled with the latch, but it finally opened. It was a clarinet. How had he not recognized the case? But it was more than a clarinet; it was a new Buffet, the best make in the world. The pathetic Bundy that Paul had just been playing — made of metal and purchased for five dollars at the synagogue rummage sale — didn't belong in the same room with it. The Buffet's tube was the blackest black he had ever seen; the keys shown like silver — maybe they *were* silver. This was no instrument for a poor boy from Arverne, an immigrant from Czechoslovakia, to play in the second chair of a public high school band — no gift you would expect from another Czech immigrant, one who had only recently survived Auschwitz.

He left the clarinet in the case and went to the kitchen. Max, still wearing his hat and coat, with a suitcase at his side, was sitting at the yellow metal table across from his mother, telling her something in Yiddish. His father had sat in that same chair with her, but he had never worn such a ridiculous hat and coat, in or out of the house. And his father usually insisted on speaking English, although Yiddish sometimes slipped in.

Paul looked at Max and said, "Thanks, I . . ."

Max turned away. "Why thanks?" his mother asked. She stood up and began folding napkins.

"He bought me a new clarinet. The best there is."

His mother, shocked, dropped the napkins in her hand. She leaned over towards Max and away from Paul. *"Far vos?"* she both asked and scolded. "Why?"

Max answered her in Yiddish, and they continued in that language as if they were alone.

Paul saw that each of them was looking at the other's eyes and nodding comfortably. He went back into the small bedroom, and put both clarinets under the bed.

* * *

The following afternoon, when he returned from school and entered the kitchen, Paul was confronted by an enormous pink enamel box, taller and wider than he was, with silver handles. After staring in amazement, he identified it by what it replaced — a much smaller yellowing Frigidaire with a humming motor on its top. Max — it had to be Max — had bought them the largest and newest GE refrigerator. Paul felt almost sorry for the rusty sink and cast iron stove which, like his Bundy clarinet, seemed shamed by its presence.

In the living room, he found a mahogany Philco radio-phonograph. It hadn't replaced anything, but it made the room seem smaller and the couch more shabby. On his mother's bedroom bureau sat a glass statuette of a deer, on his grandmother's, a nymph.

Paul's fists clenched at his side. Max was belittling the trappings of Paul's life and trying to overwhelm his mother with things his father never provided: refrigerator, phonograph, statuettes, clarinet. He wanted to smash them into shreds.

But they were beautiful. And it would be nice to have kitchen chairs that matched, uncracked plates, and glasses that hadn't once held memorial candles. Maybe even a fresh coat of paint for the big bedroom so the rectangles wouldn't show. No, that would remove the last trace of relatives who hadn't followed his father to America — except for one relative, Max, who was here in the flesh and would never leave.

* * *

Paul didn't bring the Buffet to school. How could he explain it without reminding himself of how little Daddy had left? But he practiced on the Buffet at home as soon as he was done with his homework. When Max and his mother spoke alone in the kitchen, he played a bit louder and with fewer pauses. But on the day Max returned from another trip with a silver tea service, Paul stood by the small-bedroom door to listen to his mother and Max in the kitchen. They spoke mixed Yiddish and English, and he understood the gist of what they were saying:

Who needs silver for tea?

Your father drinks tea all the time.

In a glass with a tea bag he uses maybe three times. You shouldn't. It's too much.

I want to. I'm so grateful.

Inviting you here, it's nothing. Reuben was your cousin. You're family.

That's why you should take it. Don't worry. I can afford. It's legitimate — Kosher.

I do worry. You and Bernie meeting all the time. He makes too much money too fast, and with people you got to watch out for.

Bernie, cousin Bernie — the name both infuriated and frightened Paul. The massive smug son of a bitch with the jade pinky ring and blue Lincoln was always bragging about his "associates" and looking at Paul with scorn. If he was involved, it had to be crooked. Paul put the Buffet in its case and resumed playing the Bundy in the house.

* * *

On the morning of the concert, Paul was awake, facing the wall, when Max got out of bed. He didn't hear Max shuffling to the bathroom. Instead he felt Max shake his shoulder.

"What?" Paul tried to sound as if he had just woken up.

"Sit up, please."

Paul sat up. Max, wearing the underwear he had slept in, was as gray as on the morning they first spoke. His hands were at his sides and, below his elbow, Paul could only see the last number — "7".

Max spoke deliberately. "I want you should do something for yourself. Not for me." He pointed his index finger at Paul; the nail was yellow. "For yourself."

"What?"

"For yourself, tonight at the concert you should play the Buffet especially for Wagner." Max held up his hand to stop Paul from speaking, although Paul had nothing to say. "Show the Nazis we own it now and that we play it on the best instrument in the world."

Before Paul could respond, Max turned toward the bathroom. "I'll play it," Paul called out to him. Max stopped. "I didn't before because the other kids would think I'm a show-off."

"Don't worry about nobody else." Max turned to him with a small, pleased smile. "You play good for a fourteen-year-old. Soon, when you relax, you'll get *neshome*; I think in English you say *heart*. Like my kid sister Malke. She played the flute."

Malke, another cousin, a new one, never mentioned before. Maybe she was the one added to the wedding picture to reach thirty-six.

"Treblinka," Max added. "Shot trying to escape."

Paul lifted himself out of bed. "Please come to the concert."

"Next year maybe. Definitely if you got a solo."

Paul silently hummed the triumphant *Tannhäuser* march as he strode up the steps to their apartment but, when he entered the kitchen and faced the new pink refrigerator, the melody faltered. It stopped when he opened the door to the large bedroom. Max was sitting on his bed, expressionless.

"Are you okay?"

"So you played the Wagner?"

Fuck you, Paul thought. *You told me to.* "Yes."

"And everybody applauded?"

Paul said nothing. The applause had been surprisingly heavy; several people had stood.

"A lot of Jews there?" Max asked.

"I guess so." From his seat on the stage, Paul had tried to distinguish Jews from Gentiles. Probably three-quarters of the audience was Jewish. He had searched for bare arms, but found only a few, and none had numbers.

"Just three years." Max shrugged. "You played good?"

"Okay."

Max nodded. "More than good, I'm sure."

Paul took the few steps to Max's bed. If Max didn't put his hand on his shoulder, he would reach out for Max's shoulder. His father had hugged Paul often. Sometimes, he kissed him on the lips, leaving his son both pleased and embarrassed.

Paul couldn't suppress his excitement. "You were right. I played better with the Buffet. Mrs. Heider told me it's an instrument for a serious musician. They're gonna start an orchestra — only classical. She wants me to try out."

"So, try out."

"I don't know. I'd have to quit the swim team and practice music a lot more. And then I still might not make it."

Max squeezed both of his shoulders. He was surprisingly strong. "Fishes swim."

My father swam, Paul almost replied, but then he saw the light-shadow of the swim-team rectangle. His father didn't have a medal around his neck. And he, himself, was just a skinny kid who tried hard. A varsity letter in swimming was no more than a prayer. But with the Buffet, All Queens Orchestra was possible — and it would look so good on his college applications.

"Will you help me?" Paul blurted out.

Max's hands dropped from his shoulders.

"You don't have to help . . . I shouldn't have . . ."

Max wasn't listening. His cheeks seemed to have disappeared into his skull. His cousin, who had survived the unimaginable, looked as if he would decompose in front of him.

"Help you play music?" Max asked himself softly. And then, even more softly, "Like I used to help Reuben?"

Paul didn't understand. Reuben, his father, hadn't played any instrument.

Suddenly Max stood tall and pulled his round shoulders back. "Yes! I'll get a violin, and we can play together."

"Would you really?"

"And I'll give you a key for a box."

Paul didn't understand.

"Only me and my partner know about it. I want you to have my share in case I . . . I . . . For yourself. Nobody else."

Max was scaring him. The rectangles on the wall began to pulse. "I'll explain tomorrow when we're not so tired."

Things had to slow down. Paul had to get away from the rectangles and think. What would his father say? Whatever Max was doing on his trips, whatever Max wanted to do for him, couldn't be *kosher*, especially if Bernie was involved.

"Thanks," Paul said as nicely as he could. "Thanks, but you don't . . . Let's just play music together for a while."

Max's head drooped. "No, no," Paul added nervously. "I mean nothing's going to happen to you."

"You better go to sleep," Max said and left the room.

The next evening, Paul once again stood beside the small-bedroom window. He saw Max make the turn onto Seagull Avenue, and, as Paul had hoped, his cousin was carrying a violin case. He went to the kitchen door at the top of the stairs, resolving to act as if last night's conversation had never taken place; whatever Max offered, he would accept it gratefully.

"I quit the swim team," he announced before Max opened the door fully. "Can we practice tonight?"

Max walked past Paul toward their shared bedroom. Paul's mother stopped stirring the soup. His grandmother, no taller than his mother, but much rounder, began scrubbing a pot furiously. The bedroom door clicked shut.

"What's wrong?" Paul asked. He wondered what Max had told them about getting a violin or about their talk last night.

His grandmother dropped herself into one of the wooden kitchen chairs. His mother stirred faster and spoke softly. "He's tense about playing. I don't think he's played since before the war — maybe eight, nine, years. They had this group he used to play with. They're all gone. Four people — Clara, his wife, she played the viola; his sister Molly, the flute . . ."

Not Molly — Malke, Paul wanted to correct her. *A real person with her own name.* But if he said anything, they would ask questions.

"Malke not Molly," Paul's mother corrected herself. "I'm getting her confused with the seamstress, Molly Klein, who played the oboe. Maybe five people, not four . . ."

Paul's grandmother interrupted, pausing every few words to tap her forehead. "You forgot Max's brother Aaron, the pianist. Nice boy, real talent. You never knew him."

A brother, Paul thought. *Gone.* He had always wondered what it would be like to have a brother; he couldn't imagine how it would feel to lose one.

"Shhh," his mother said. She pointed to the closed bedroom door. "Of course I knew his brother. If you knew one, you knew both. But his name was Asher. He was the one . . ."

Paul started to repeat the names to himself — *Clara, Molly, Malke, Aaron, Asher.* Would they ever stop?

"Can I go ride my bike? I'll be back by supper. The table's all set."

"Sure," his mother said. "You can be a little late."

He rode down Sixty-ninth Street, past the beach block where he had last seen his father, and made it up the boardwalk ramp in one pedal thrust. There, he turned right, towards Playland where Daddy had taken him every summer; towards the bridges over Jamaica Bay leading to Brooklyn on the way to the city; and, most important, past the beach at Seventieth Street, where Daddy and he had gone on their last day. But that was nearly four years ago, and Max was here now, not Dad. He pedaled as fast as he could, riding without hands and opening his mouth wide so that the wet salt air poured into him. From time to time he closed his eyes, first for ten turns of the pedal, then twenty-five.

At Playland, he stopped to look at the deserted amusement park. The fence surrounding it seemed higher than ever. The coils of barbed wire at its top were a surprise. Had they been there in the past? Which fence was higher, Auschwitz or Playland? Was either electric? A ridiculous comparison, but there *was* something morbid about the canvas-covered Whip and Navy Dive-Bomber rides, the boarded-up Hall of Mirrors, and the absolute silence save for the waves crashing behind him. The roller coaster, rickety in its shadows and emptiness, was even more frightening than when he had ridden it with Dad on the Labor Day before he died. But, Paul reminded himself, it was now April — time to start painting and polishing for the opening next month. The work had actually begun. Past the Navy Dive-Bomber, at the Kiddy Rides, half of the olive green mini-tanks had been replaced with shiny mini-cars. And a new picture was being painted over the House of Fun — Bozo the Clown in place of three pigs with the faces of Hitler, the Emperor of Japan, and Dracula the Vampire.

Yes! Paul thought. The war is over. The United Nations had voted to make Israel a country. Music would help change Max. They'd play together tonight and more tomorrow and even more the next day. Paul would learn music from a real musician, and Max would learn America from a real American. Whatever Max wanted to give, Paul would take; whatever he wanted to say, Paul would listen.

Paul pedaled home even faster than he had pedaled away. He left his bike outside the house, and ran up the outside steps, two at a time, to the first floor porch — the Rossini's porch. Then, by holding onto the banister, he ran up the inside steps three at a time. At the top, he heard his grandfather speaking behind the kitchen door.

"Yener fidl hot zikher gekost toyznt dolar."

Paul isolated the English-sounding words — *Fidl, toyznt, dolar* — and translated without thinking: A thousand-dollar violin! His mouth popped open. How did Max pay for *der fidl* and all the gifts? *Don't guess!* Paul ordered himself. Whatever he imagined would be wrong, and he'd go crazy in the process. Or he would learn, and it would be too horrible to live with. The important thing now is the music.

He opened the door and froze. The kitchen table he had set for five people now had four places. His mother was where she had been when he left — stirring the soup.

"Cousin Max went for a walk," she explained. "He said he'd eat in the delicatessen."

Paul remembered Max's words from last night — *I want you should have my share in case* . . . "Why'd you let him go?" he asked.

Nobody answered, but Paul felt the solemn gaze of all three — his mother at the stove, his grandparents at the table, Grandma covering her mouth, and Grandpa stroking his small white beard while pleading with his usually angry eyes for Paul to do something. Paul would do something. He was the only real American and the only one who spoke English without an accent. If he did nothing, they would ask Bernie to come over and Bernie would shove Paul aside.

"I'll call the delicatessen," he said.

"I already did," his mother answered. "They didn't see him and they're closing up."

The bike, Paul thought. Arverne was small, and he could go up and down its streets in a half hour. But only kids rode bikes.

"Is there somebody he might be visiting?"

"Who visiting?" Grandma moaned. "He don't know nobody to visit. You were right . . . We shouldn't have let him go."

"Then I'm going to call the police."

"No police," his grandfather shot back at him. "Police mean trouble."

"But Papa," Paul's mother pleaded, and the three adults launched into an argument in Yiddish. Paul didn't search for recognizable words. When he walked into the living room, the kitchen became silent, as if a plug had been pulled. Emergency numbers were taped to the side of the phone.

"Hundredth Precinct," a tired voice answered.

"My name is Paul Hartman and—"

"Say that name again! Spell it."

Paul sat on the threadbare couch. The Philco before him looked like a prop in a comedy. After some transfers, there was a new voice on the line. "This is Captain Kiley." The grim tone was all Paul had to hear. "Is this the home of Max Hartman?"

"Yes."

"Is his wife there?"

"His wife died," Paul barely managed to say. Chairs moved behind him.

"Are you a relative?"

"I'm his cousin, Paul Hartman."

"I'm sorry to give you bad news, but your cousin is dead. Drowned in the ocean. A colored guy saw him walk out on the jetty and jump in." The captain paused as if surprised by his own brusque announcement. "I guess he couldn't swim," he continued gently. "Somebody will have to come down to Rockaway Beach Hospital tomorrow morning to identify the body."

Choose, Paul ordered himself. Be the helpless kid who watched his father die, or be a man. "I'll come," he declared to Captain Kiley. "What street was the jetty on?"

"Sixty-fourth," the Captain answered.

The street number was a relief. Paul had pedaled in the other direction. He couldn't have saved Max's life. Dad's either.

CHAPTER 2

Paul turned from the telephone expecting his mother and grandparents to be looking up at him questioningly, but all three of them were bowing their heads at the kitchen table, his mother and grandmother crying softly, his grandfather muttering to himself.

"Max is dead." His voice cracked slightly, but he wouldn't let himself cry now or later. "He jumped in the ocean off the jetty at Sixty-fourth Street." Paul took a careful breath. "By coincidence, I was on the boardwalk blocks away from him, pedaling in the opposite direction."

Nobody seemed surprised by the news.

"He committed suicide," he said firmly. His mother bit her lower lip; his grandmother moaned "*Oy Gevald;*" his grandfather didn't react.

"The ocean!" his grandmother said with surprise. "*Arayngeshpungen inem yam,*" she explained to her husband. "He hated the water — thought all this *shvimen* was foolishness — *narashkeit.* I don't understand. How could he do it?"

"Only fishes swim," Max had said to him — and he said it only last night. Paul took two steps to the doorway between the kitchen and living room. "Su-i-cide," he said slowly. His boldness shocked him. "Suicide! Horrible! Isn't anyone surprised?"

"*Sha! Ganug shoyn!*" his grandfather demanded.

"Have *rachmones,* Paulie," his grandmother said. "Surprised the ocean, yes, but . . ."

"Sit down, Paulie," his mother said, suddenly composed.

He sat, but he kept his hands on his lap so she couldn't hold them.

"Surprised?" she asked. "Maybe yesterday surprised. But after some of the things he told me last night and just before he went out, maybe not so surprised."

She pulled her lips between her teeth and closed her eyes. Was she waiting for Paul to ask what Max had said? Waiting to imply that Paul could have saved Max's life just as he could have saved Daddy's? Paul would not ask.

"We tried to stop him from going out," his mother said. I stood in front of the door, but he just slid by me. So I called Cousin Bernie and asked him to go look for him."

Bernie! Paul thought. He'd take command and order Paul to his room, just as when Daddy died. Paul stood as tall as he could. "I told the police captain I would go down to identify the body tomorrow."

Somehow, Paul's hands had gone to the table, and his mother was holding them. "Don't be foolish, Paulie. A grown up should go. Let Bernie talk to the cops. He has friends there."

The phone rang in the living room. "Bernie!" his grandmother said, raising her head in hope. Paul's mother rushed to answer it. "Bernie! Thank God! Max *iz geshtoarben*. Drowned. Jumped off a jetty. The police told Paulie." After a brief silence, she shouted into the kitchen, "Bernie wants to know who you talked to at the police."

"Captain Kiley," Paul answered, looking away from her.

She repeated the name, and then shouted, "Bernie says good."

Fuck Bernie. Kiley couldn't turn back the clock and make Max alive.

His mother said something in Yiddish that Paul didn't try to understand. Then she switched to English. "What do you mean, don't go no place? Where would we go, Bernie? Tell me. But hurry over, please."

"Nu?" Paul's grandmother asked, when his mother stepped back into the kitchen.

"Bernie says we shouldn't talk to anybody. He thinks —"

"Dos kind," Paul's grandmother interrupted, turning towards Paul and raising her head.

Don't run from Bernie, Paul urged himself. The sleazy bully, tan during the winter from his frequent trips to Florida, had traded beds with Paul's mother — Mom's and Dad's maple bed for the metal beds Max and Paul had slept in. He rarely missed an opportunity to allude to his never-named "associates" or his robin's-egg-blue Lincoln made to order "to match Ruthie's eyes," or to assault Paul with a wisecrack: "How's the little scholar boy? Still grinding away?" "How's it hanging? Got hair there?" Once, he even pinched Paul's cheeks.

Only a coward would run. But if he stayed in the kitchen they'd ask him to leave — or they'd go to this grandparents' bedroom in the front and talk in a whispered Yiddish. Did he want to know what was happening? No, yes, and maybe.

He rose from his chair, went to the small bedroom, closed the door, then stood by the door and listened to his mother and grandparents discuss the funeral in Yiddish. Minutes later, he heard Bernie climbing the inside stairs, each step a conquering thump. His wife Ruthie's high heels clicked slowly behind; she'd be out of breath by the third step. The kitchen door opened, and the adults all spoke together —*"Shreklekh,*

shreklekh"; "Gevald"; "You did what you could" — until Bernie swept their voices away.

"Enough! We can't afford being emotional."

A chair scraped and Cousin Ruthie sighed loudly. "Word can't get out what really happened," Bernie said. "There'll be news articles; people will get in trouble."

Max would want him to be there, Paul thought. He opened the small bedroom door and took a step into the vestibule that separated the kitchen from the two back bedrooms. Five pairs of eyes stared at him. Bernie seemed to dwarf the GE refrigerator.

"I'm just going to get one of my books."

Quickly, Paul went into the big bedroom, but, before he could grab a book (any book), he saw the violin case in the center of Max's bed. *Der toyznt dolar fidl.* Why shouldn't he see it? Max wanted to play music with him. *Der fidl* and the Buffet were a team.

The case opened easily. The violin glowed, but what glowed even more was a white envelope tucked under the handle. It was for him from Max. Bernie could seize it in seconds.

Paul stuffed the envelope in his pocket, closed the case, grabbed his history book, and returned to the small bedroom without looking into the still silent kitchen. He held the envelope up to the desk light and made out a key and a piece of paper inside of it. But Bernie was only a few feet away. Paul rolled the envelope up along its length and, with the clarinet cleaning brush, pushed it up the Buffet tube as far as it would go. Max would be pleased with his cunning.

He went to the door again and heard his grandmother: *"A shande. Dos —"*

"Shande! Disgrace is just the beginning," Bernie declaimed. "We all know there was something funny about Max. All those gifts from a guy who was just . . . I'm not supposed to tell you, but Max wanted me to help him sell some diamonds. I tried to get him to give me specifics, but Max was not exactly a trusting guy, and I learned almost zilch, *gornisht.* I got the impression he was going to tell you more, Ida."

Was his mother whispering or was she just silent? Finally, he could make out her voice, but only barely. He pressed his left ear against the door, put a finger in his right ear, and closed his eyes. "He told me a lot of things. You can't even imagine. About the camps, his brother, his son. About hiding the diamonds and other stones too, in boxes in different places. Keys for the boxes. I can't repeat—"

"Don't repeat," Bernie said, as if to soothe her.

"Don't repeat, darling," Ruthie echoed even more soothingly. "It's nobody's business how he died. Let me make some tea."

Paul told himself to go in there. But what would he say if he did?

His mother spoke again, and now her voice shook. "Suppose the police ask me questions? Isn't the law I have to tell them?"

"No police, no law," his grandmother retorted. "For Max, the law was kill Jews."

"Why make the government rich?" Ruthie asked. Her voice was even more high-pitched than usual. "You want to keep working like slaves in that crummy grocery? Until an A&P makes you close? What about Paulie's education?"

Paul stepped back from the door. He would tell them not to worry about his education. He'd work harder, get better activities, win a scholarship. Or go to one of the City colleges — what Daddy was planning for himself.

But it would be hypocritical to make his speech and not tell them about the key. And if he told them, Bernie would take the key and call him a thief; his grandfather would call him a *goniff*; his mother and grandmother would be disappointed. Besides, if there were a newspaper article saying Max committed suicide, kids would stare at him in school, shun him. And if the key helped him find the diamonds . . . ? He tried to imagine a life with money, but couldn't.

He lay down on the bed and put his mother's pillow over his head.

"Paul." His mother's voice surprised him. She hadn't knocked, just as she hadn't knocked on the day Daddy died.

"What?" he said through the pillow.

She pulled off the pillow, but Paul remained flat on his back. The red-eyed woman above him could never have once been the prettiest blonde-like-a-*goy* bride anyone had ever seen. She was a plain Jewish housewife, as drab as those who shopped in their grocery — no makeup, nondescript brown hair, a shapeless gray dress (the same one she wore behind the grocery counter) and a blue apron (shorter and thinner than her white store apron).

"I don't know what you heard. We tried to talk low, but Bernie gets excited."

Paul didn't stir.

"Forget poor Max drowned. We're gonna tell everybody it was a heart attack like . . . " She took a few deep breaths and began to cry. "Like Daddy."

"Okay."

"There would be trouble if somebody finds out. So don't tell anybody. Bernie spoke to Captain Kiley and the cops will go along."

"Okay."

"Dead is dead. No difference how. Do you want to stay home from school tomorrow?"

"No."

"That's better, so there won't be more questions. But if somebody asks you what happened to Cousin Max . . . like when they asked about . . ."

"Heart attack," Paul said, but he knew nobody would ask. He had never mentioned Max to anyone.

They changed sleeping arrangements again that night. Paul went back to the small room, his mother to the big room. Just before going to sleep, he returned to the big bedroom for his pajamas and found that *der toyznt dolar fidl* had disappeared from Max's bed. *Good riddance.*

In the morning he brought the Bundy to band practice. When he returned home from school, his mother met him at the kitchen door and handed him the Buffet case. *Oh my God!* Paul thought. *She found the key.* But as soon as she spoke, he realized she hadn't. "It'll look funny if you don't take this one to school. Besides, Max would want you to play it. But if anybody asks how you got it, tell them Cousin Bernie."

Paul managed not to sigh in relief until he was in the small bedroom with the door closed. The key couldn't stay inside the Buffet but, no matter where he hid it, they would find it. Maybe he should just confess, give it to his mother and ask her not to tell anyone. But then he'd be her junior partner in whatever sleazy thing they were doing, and she'd never stop calling him Paulie. Besides, the diamonds could help him pay for college. Tomorrow, during Max's funeral, he'd figure out a better hiding place and come up with a plan of action. If he kept his mind busy, he wouldn't have to pay attention to whatever Rabbi Pordy said.

The funeral was a graveside service, eighteen people standing around a hole in the ground — *chai,* half the number in the wedding picture. Only the six who had been in the apartment on the night of Max's death knew how he had died. The other mourners had been told the heart attack story: "A drunken *shvartser* found his body on the boardwalk." None of them questioned it.

Although the rabbi's shirt collar curled and his pot belly jiggled, his voice exuded decency and commanded respect. "Max Hartman died twice in the Lodz ghetto: First when the Gestapo shot his wife for trying to bring their son to a doctor and, again, a few days later, when typhus took the boy's life. He died more every day in Auschwitz and every day since when he remembered." *Yes,* Paul thought. *You understand; my mother gave you the basic facts.*

But the rabbi wasn't through: "God finally freed him from his suffering." *No, no,* Paul thought. *God didn't do anything good for Max or anybody else with the numbers. He certainly didn't give him a heart attack. My mother lied to you, and I let her.*

After the service, Rabbi Pordy took Paul to the side, and said, "This must be rough on you, particularly after losing your father. Four years, isn't it? You can come to *shul* to say *kaddish* even though he's only a cousin. After all, there's nobody left to say it for him. We have a *minyan* every morning and evening, and we can talk after."

"I'll come," Paul replied, and meant it. While he couldn't recall a word from his talk with Rabbi Pordy at the time of Daddy's death, he remembered that the rabbi had made him feel like a mourner in need of consolation and not just a child to be pitied and otherwise ignored.

But on the way back from the cemetery, squeezed between his grandparents in the back seat of Bernie's Lincoln, he realized he couldn't meet with the rabbi tomorrow or ever. What would he tell him about Max's death, about the key — the truth or a lie? And whatever Rabbi Pordy said or did in response, Paul wouldn't like it. He would throw away the key. It stank. Dad would want him to get rid of it.

* * *

As soon as the few guests left the apartment, Paul put the envelope in his pocket and rode his bike down Sixty-ninth Street towards the beach. He would walk out on the jetty, say *Kaddish*, take the key from the envelope, and let it follow Max. Then, without reading a word of the note, he would rip up the paper and scatter it into the waves. But, which jetty? The one on Sixty-fourth Street where Max had drowned, or the one on Seventieth where Daddy had given him swimming lessons? Not Sixty-fourth, he quickly decided. That would be throwing Max's gift back at him.

On the boardwalk, he turned right, away from Max, and pedaled with his eyes closed and his hands in his pockets until he estimated that he had gone one block. He then put his hands back on the handlebars, stopped the bike, and opened his eyes. Perfect. The steps to the Seventieth Street beach and jetty were at his side.

He had never before walked more than a few feet out on the jetty, and he was surprised how slippery it was. He considered returning to the beach to take off his shoes, but that meant more time for somebody to see him and call the police. He held his hands out to the side for balance, and carefully maneuvered around the sea moss. Halfway up the jetty, where the wood was as slippery as the moss, he stopped. You don't say *Kaddish* by yourself on a jetty. He might slip into the swirling water and, while he could swim forever in calm water, these waves might be too much for a skinny kid.

He ripped open the envelope, and took out the key. It was surprisingly thin and long. He tried to picture the box or safe into which it fit. Big or small? Iron or steel? And where was it? Maybe the folded paper in the envelope would solve the mystery.

The waves were growing bigger. One leaped over the jetty a few feet ahead of him, spraying him from head to foot. The next one would drench him. The one after that might knock him into the ocean. If he threw the key, he might lose his balance. Without a silent word or thought, he let the key drop into the water. For a moment, he tried to follow its path, but the Atlantic's gyrations made him dizzy, and he carefully turned around.

Nearer the beach where the water was calmer, he stopped to dispose of the note. He didn't want to read it, but couldn't resist unfolding it. What harm could there be since he no longer had the key? There were numbers separated by dashes — the combination for a safe? — but he skipped over them. Below the numbers were a name and address. Two words jumped up at him before he could close his eyes. He ripped the paper in half and kept ripping until he couldn't make the pieces any smaller. Then, he opened his eyes, satisfied himself that, like Humpty Dumpty, the note could never be put together again, and scattered the bits of paper into the water. But the words that had jumped up from the note were engraved in his mind — "Greenberg" and "Montreal." He thought of the photo on his bedroom wall of Hank Greenberg, the great Jewish baseball player, and next to it the picture of Jackie Robinson, who had played for the Montreal Royals before coming to the Brooklyn Dodgers.

On the following weekend, at his mother's urging, Paul went with his Boy Scout troop on a two-night camping trip to Camp Alpine in New Jersey. When he returned, most signs of Max were gone — clothing, toilet kit, glass statuettes, silver tea service, alarm clock. In addition, the big bedroom had been painted, erasing the reverse-shadows of the photographs from Czechoslovakia. Still, Paul felt his cousin's presence. His musty smell seemed to pervade the apartment. It even followed Paul to the basement where he went to store his camping equipment although, so far as Paul knew, Max had never been down there. Most noticeably, the Philco and pink refrigerator remained, seeming bigger and brighter than when Paul had left for Camp Alpine. And, of course, there was the Buffet.

"I don't understand," he said to his mother while they were sitting at the kitchen table sorting laundry for him to drop off at the laundromat the next morning. "You got rid of Max's gifts except for the two biggest."

"Who needs reminders of so much sadness?" she said to him. "But Bernie thinks if they go too soon, it'll look funny, like we're taking down monuments Max put up to himself." She dropped her voice and lowered her eyes to the laundry. "Maybe if we locate what Max wanted us to have, we'll move, and find an excuse to get rid of them then."

Desperate to change the subject, Paul started to describe some of the birds he had seen in Alpine, but his mother interrupted. "Max said he was going to give you a key. And a note explaining how we would find something. Did he give them to you?"

Paul felt waves from the Atlantic cresting before him. He resisted the urge to swallow, and said "No" as casually as he could.

"We looked everywhere, even in the clothing we were boxing for the Hebrew Aid Society, even in his underwear, but couldn't find nothing."

Paul was holding two of his grandfather's soiled boxer shorts. Why couldn't that grumpy bastard take care of his own shit?

"Paulie."

"Don't call me that." He was being disrespectful, but she deserved it.

"Are you sure he didn't give you anything? I mean besides the fancy clarinet."

Paul stood up, raised the underpants above his head and flung them down at the table. "If you think I'm lying, just say so."

"No, no. I know you wouldn't lie to me." Her voice was too soft, almost obsequious. "You're like Daddy that way." She reached out for Paul's hand but he moved away from the table. It wasn't the first time he had lied to her face, and she hadn't believed him then either.

CHAPTER 3

Dad or Daddy? Paul couldn't decide on the name to use in his head, let alone what to call him. Should he take his hand or not? That one was easy, although the temptation was great. Ten years was too old, and next month he'd be eleven.

It was June 9, 1944, three days after D-Day, the Allied invasion of Europe, the beginning of the end for the Nazis. The calendar said spring, but Paul lived in Arverne, a beach town in Rockaway, and, for him, there were only two seasons. Summer started when the summer people began to arrive from the Bronx, and it ended when they left just before or just after *Yom Kippur*, the tenth day of the Jewish month of *Tishrei*, which was usually close to the day New York City public schools opened. The remainder of the year was winter.

The air became damper and saltier as Paul and his father walked down Sixty-ninth Street towards the Atlantic. At Rockaway Beach Boulevard, which separated the all-year houses from the summer houses, he heard the crashing ocean waves. He wanted to run ahead toward the beach with his head pulled back and his mouth wide open, but Daddy would tell him not to act like a little kid, and his mother had warned him, "Don't let Daddy get excited — his heart."

Summer had arrived. The stores that had closed for the winter were open or opening. In Mayer's Kosher Butcher, which had been boarded up for months, whole unplucked chickens hung from the ceiling and a sign, scotch-taped to the window, urged:

SEND A KOSHER SALAMI
TO YOUR BOY IN THE ARMY

Past the Boulevard, on the long treeless beach block, protective boards were coming off the wooden rooming houses and stucco bungalows. The rooming house abutting Mayer's was being painted yellow by two thick-armed men chewing cigars. A bright sign — black and red letters on a milk-white background — hung from its wraparound porch:

ROOMS
WEEK — MONTH — SEASON
Weekend Rooms for Soldiers — 10% Discount
Kitchen Privileges — Semi-Private Baths
Rockaway 5-4250

On the other side of Sixty-ninth, the trim on the bungalows had been recently painted green. Unlike the winter, when the street was lifeless except for aimlessly wandering boys and lethargic dogs, a handful of cars were parked in front of bungalows and a smaller handful of people were sitting on bungalow porches behind American flags.

Paul and his father reached the fourth bungalow from the beach where a summer family was moving in. A thin mattress was tied to the top of their flat-roofed black Ford. Sitting on the sidewalk was an ironing board and a huge metal washtub with a hobbyhorse inside. How did all this stuff get there? The car was too small. Loud voices were coming from inside the bungalow — an argument in Yiddish.

His father's square face soured in disgust. His bent nose — broken in a mountain climbing accident decades earlier — crinkled. "I'd like to go in there and shake them by the neck," he grumbled. "English! Speak English. Get out of the ghetto. This is America where—" His father stopped speaking. He looked pale.

His heart! He should take one of the nitroglycerin pills that were always in his back pocket wrapped in toilet paper. Paul should do what Mom had told him: "Call the police."

But his father wasn't holding his chest or breathing fast. He was frowning at the bungalow window. Behind it, a bald old man with thick white eyebrows and a whiter beard, wearing a black skullcap and the black suit of the Ultra-Orthodox, was hanging a small rectangular banner against the pane. Red trim, white background, a gold star in the middle — it meant that his son or, more likely his grandson, had been killed in the war.

"Oh my God!" Paul's father said. "Here I am making a speech about America, and they . . ." Gently, he pushed Paul past the bungalow.

"Three days after D-Day," he said a few steps later. "Three days after thousands stormed out of the water onto Normandy beach, I'm going swimming at the other end of the Atlantic."

His father often bemoaned the fact that he was a civilian, and Paul knew how to answer. "You tried to join," he said — a plea as much as a reminder. "You were thirty-two with a wife and a child," repeating the words of his mother.

"And a bum ticker that made the recruiting sergeant laugh at me."

His father had told him twice what had happened, using nearly the same words each time. Now, as his father grew more breathless and began dragging his feet, Paul heard again how his father tried to enlist in Army counterintelligence; how he told the recruiting sergeant about his four languages, his athleticism, and his knowledge of the Czech countryside and of people, both Jews and Gentiles, who would want to join the resistance; how the sergeant looked at his medical records and laughed; and how he had then gone "straight to the Bulova Watch factory near the 1939 World's Fair" and gotten a job designing precision clocks for Navy submarines. By the time his father finished — "I bet some of my clocks were in D-Day" — he was gasping for breath.

Paul doubted that American submarines were used in the invasion. "Maybe we shouldn't go in the water," he said. "It'll be cold."

"Did your mother tell you to say that?" He didn't wait for Paul to answer. "Don't worry, the air's warm. Hot air, cold water — that's when it feels best."

"Maybe we won't be able to find a private place to change under the boardwalk."

His father laughed. "Nobody'll see anything they didn't see before."

Paul had to say it. "Your heart."

His father laughed again, this time in a more deliberate way. "If I did what the doctors said, I'd have sat still behind the family jewelry store until the Germans came to arrest us."

After they put on their bathing suits under the boardwalk, they sat at the line on the beach where the sand turned from white to brown and from dry to moist — the Atlantic's final advance before it pulled back from high tide.

Paul wanted quiet so he could look at the pattern of the shells and driftwood washed up on the damp sand, but his father talked almost without pause. He wasn't usually like this. "The whole family thought I was a worrywart wanting to drag you and your mother over the ocean because of a little madman from Austria. Later, we tried to help them get out but, except for Bernie and his father, it got too late too soon."

The Jews were not fighting back enough, he said. "We need more Warsaw Ghetto uprisings. You should follow the war news, Paul."

Paul liked the sound of his birth name. It was so much more grown up than Paulie — what everybody else in the world except his teachers called him. He would start reading the *Journal American* his father brought home from work.

Paul picked up a large clam shell and started digging a hole in front of his foot. "Sure, in America, there's plenty anti-Semitism," his father went on, "but it's not in the air like in Europe. Segregation, discrimination against the Coloreds . . . Terrible, but all that's going to get better after the war. And the opportunities!" Paul dug faster. "Oh my God, the opportunities. You can get the best education free at the City colleges. Once the war's over, I'm going to figure out a way to go at night — be an educated man. And you. With *your* brain, the sky's the limit."

Paul's hole was filling with water. He put his feet into it and left them there even though the water was cold. If he fidgeted, Dad would think he wasn't listening — and he was.

"You'll see — all the opportunities. Oh my God, the opportunities." Daddy seemed to be getting tired again. "Are you okay, Paulie?"

"I'm cold. Maybe we should go home."

"Not yet. I want to see if you remember breathing and how to coast a wave."

He got himself up, and Paul followed him into the ocean. It was cold, very cold, but his father didn't seem to mind, and Paul wouldn't say anything. One dive into a breaking wave and his teeth began to chatter. Two dives, it wasn't so bad. Three dives and he hardly noticed the cold. He tried to duplicate his father's crawl, but he swallowed salt water and allowed the tide to pull him towards the shore. When the water was at his waist and he could plant his feet solidly on the ground, he stood and watched his father swim away from the beach. His body was so straight — muscles from his shoulders all the way down his back; his stroke was perfectly smooth; nothing turned except his head, taking air in at the ocean surface, breathing it out below. But suppose he got chest pains? There was no lifeguard, and Paul couldn't save him. *Come back,* he wanted to scream, but he was Paul, not Paulie. And then, as if his father heard the soundless cry, he turned and swam slowly towards the beach. He stood when the water was at his neck and, panting as if he could never breathe fast enough, struggled to Paul on his feet.

"Why don't we go back?" Paul asked.

"Don't be ridiculous." His father ran his fingers through Paul's wet hair. "I haven't taught you anything."

"Mom said I shouldn't stay in too long or go over my head."

"Mom said I should listen to the doctor and stay in Europe."

"There's no lifeguard."

"I used to teach lifeguards."

I tried, Paul told himself. "Watch me," he shouted, and threw himself towards the shore along with a cresting wave. He barely moved the length of his body.

His father, now breathing more evenly, was at his side before the next wave crested. He pulled Paul's hands above his head. "Reach for the sky, press your fingers together like an arrow," he told his son. "Now, catch this wave that's coming when I say, 'Go!' and make your body a torpedo aimed at a Nazi U-boat. Like I showed you last year." On the first try, Paul reached the beach.

They went to where the water was at his father's shoulders, over Paul's head, and Paul lay in his father's arms. "See what you remember," his father said, and it all came back. Paul straightened his body, put his head in the water, turned it ninety degrees to the right, inhaled through his mouth, sealed his lips, turned his head ninety degrees to the left back into the water, exhaled through his nose, and then repeated the whole process. Again and again. "Smooth, smooth," his father exhorted. Paul felt ready to leave his father's arms and do an Australian crawl straight out past the jetties like a real swimmer.

Then his father's arms weren't there. It was only Paul and the freezing Atlantic. He sank, rose back to the surface and, with his father trudging alongside him, dog-paddled toward the shore. He wanted to ask what had happened, but his father's face was the color of a whitecap.

Slowly, they made their way to their clothing. His father sat down — almost collapsed — against one of the cement poles that held up the boardwalk. Paul's mother's voice rang out instructions: *Don't waste time. Give him the nitroglycerin in his pocket. Then find a phone and call the police. Tell the operator 'Emergency!'*

Once the nitroglycerin was on his father's tongue, Paul ran towards the boardwalk stairs. But before he reached them, his father's voice, weak but insistent, came from behind him. "Paulie!" Paul kept going. "Paul!" his father called again. He stopped.

"Don't go away," his father said in a slightly stronger voice. "I feel better. The nitroglycerin is working. I'll be okay and we'll walk home together."

How could he leave him? Daddy might die before he got back — die all alone. And if he lived, he would never take Paul swimming again.

His father looked a little better but only a little. They dressed in silence.

They slowly climbed the steps from the sand to the boardwalk. Paul couldn't leave him here. He tried to guide him to a bench, but his father shook his head. "Just let me catch my breath," he said, pausing twice to gulp air.

Gradually, his father's breathing slowed and he was able to speak without gasping. "I don't want to look helpless in front of the whole world three days after D-Day — in front of the old man with the gold star." He managed to pull his lips into a grin. "We won't even tell your mother. Why give her one more thing to worry about?"

By the time they reached Sixty-ninth Street some of his father's color had returned. His brow, however, was wet. Was it the Atlantic or perspiration? "Maybe we should ask somebody to drive us home."

"I'm fine, I can walk."

His father took Paul's hand. Little kid stuff, but the hell with it. The hand was cold and damp, almost slippery. *Pull loose*, Paul ordered himself. *Run to one of the bungalows for help.* But it was only three days after D-Day.

More cars were now parked on the street. Next to one of them, beyond the gold-star bungalow, a bird-like woman was taking towels from the trunk and piling them on the arms of a freckled-faced girl not much older than Paul. Maybe he would meet the girl on the beach when school was over or next summer or the summer after that when they wouldn't be too young. Maybe she'd move from the Bronx and become an all-year-round girl — his girlfriend.

Suddenly, his father's hand became a limp icicle. His other hand was at his chest.

His father was standing, then sitting on the sidewalk, then lying on his back. Paul, driven by the sound of his mother's voice — *I told you not to go, I told you* — slid his hand under his father's behind, feeling for his pocket and the other nitroglycerin pill, but people appeared from nowhere and pulled him away. "No Sonny," one of the pullers said in a deep Yiddish-accented voice, "you shouldn't disturb him."

"My mother said . . ."

"No, Sonny.

He was swarmed, then almost carried away from his father onto the gold-star porch and pushed into a wooden rocking chair alongside the washbasin with the hobbyhorse. He could see the birdlike woman kneeling next to his father holding something under his nose. The freckled-face girl was running towards Rockaway Beach Boulevard. People were shouting in English and Yiddish. The old man with the gold star stood on his porch with his back to Paul and shouted loudest of all, switching between the two languages. *"Neyn neyn er zol zikh nit aveklevan.* He shouldn't lay down. Give him some *schnapps. Mayn eynikl iz geven a* medic in Sicily — a corporal." The old man pointed at the gold star and, for a moment, everyone became quiet.

Paul stood up and shouted: "No whiskey. There's nitroglycerin in his back pocket." The birdlike lady turned from his father and shouted back, "No, too much nitroglycerin is no good. I got something better in a suitcase." She stood and ran up the street. The argument resumed.

A man's voice: "Elaine's calling the ambulance from the phone in the butcher."

A woman: "Better she should get the doctor next to the train station."

Then the siren and, almost immediately, his father was on a stretcher being lifted into the ambulance. Paul tore towards his father. "Daddy! Don't take him without me." He tried to climb in behind the stretcher, but a man in white pushed him into arms that held him tightly.

"Calm down, Sonny," a new voice ordered. "It's not good for your father, your being such a nuisance."

Siren shrieking, the ambulance started. Paul broke free and ran after it. "Wait!" he shouted, but when the ambulance turned left towards Rockaway Beach Hospital, he accepted the fact that he couldn't catch it and kept running straight up Sixty-ninth Street towards home. He would slow up after he passed the last bungalow so that he wouldn't be out of breath when he gave the news to his mother.

But the line of bungalows never ended and the boulevard had disappeared. Footsteps, growing louder and nearer, were chasing him. "Help!" he cried out — then opened his eyes. His mother was shaking him.

He knew where he was — in the new bed Daddy had picked out with him and paid for with Grandma Gittel's insurance money — but he didn't know when he had run from the street into the dream. He didn't even know what day it was. Then it became all too clear. It was four days after D-Day; the night before Daddy's funeral; the night after Bernie had told him, "Can't you go in your room and play — stop upsetting your mother?"; a day after the ambulance pulled away from him.

She was wearing the silk nightgown his father had given her on their last anniversary. "You were shouting in your sleep."

She stopped shaking him, but remained bent over with her hands on his shoulders. The top of the nightgown was loose, and Paul saw her breasts — delicate baby eggplants like those Mr. Rossini, the landlord downstairs, grew in his victory garden, only hers were pink and shivering. Paul looked up at a spider web in the corner of the ceiling. "I'm sorry."

"It's okay. I couldn't sleep, thinking about tomorrow, and *shiva* for a week and then the hard part begins." Her hair was in ten or more little circles that were held together by bobby pins. Ruthie had insisted on setting it before she went home.

She released Paul's shoulders but he didn't move, and she lay down next to him.

"Your room looks so nice with the furniture Grandma Gittel's insurance bought. It's a shame she didn't get a chance to see it, but at least Daddy did. If we waited . . ." She started to cry. "I'm so worried about money, Paulie."

Paul, he thought. But not now. Maybe after *shiva*.

"I know you're only ten."

"Nearly eleven."

"Too young to understand money. But who else can I talk to? Cousin Bernie . . ." She frowned. "He just bosses me around. My mother worries more than me. She says she and Grandpa should move in with us from the Bronx and we'd all buy the little grocery store where old Mr. Karp used to yell at the customers before he died."

A terrible idea. Grandpa never said anything nice to him — even hello. His breath smelled of garlic.

His mother cried harder, and the mattress bounced. Paul slid nearer the wall. "We could sell my furniture, and you don't have to get me a bicycle for my birthday."

She cried still harder, and then she laughed. "Oh, Paulie, Paulie, you're so sweet, just like your father."

The blankets moved, and she was under them. Paul turned on his side away from her, and pressed himself against the wall. He felt her slide towards him and then turn on her side. Soon, her breasts would be touching his shoulder blades.

"You're my little man, the man of the house now." So many people had been telling him that before ignoring him. "You're all I got. We got each other. But that's enough." She sighed, and he pictured her nipples pressing against the nightgown. Some day he would be bigger than she was. "Daddy would want us to stick together, Paulie."

In almost one motion, without a thought, he turned his body and flung the blanket from the bed. Seconds later, they were both standing, she at the side of the bed, he at the foot.

"Paulie, what's wrong with you? I know you're upset about Daddy, but—"

"Dad, not Daddy! Paul, not Paulie! I have to go to the bathroom." He was out of the bedroom before she could say anything.

He sat on the bathtub rim until her bedroom door closed, and then went back to bed. Moments later, she opened his door and stood in the doorway.

Everything about her was different. She wore her shapeless robe and, underneath it, a long flannel nightgown. The bobby pins were gone, but she hadn't combed her hair out, and circles of hair were scattered over her head with pieces of scalp showing between them. She sat on his desk chair and stared at him. He didn't try to stare back.

Finally, she spoke. "I wasn't going to ask you, at least not for a while, but everyone says I should." Her voice was as cold as her eyes were hot. Paul pulled the blanket up to his chin. "Did Daddy seem sick before . . . before he . . .?"

Paul was braced for this — relieved to be confronting it now rather than to fear it forever. "No, he was fine. When we walked past the bungalows, he just said his chest hurt, and then he sat down."

"Are you sure?"

The questions had to stop before she had ammunition to blame him. "Yes, I'm sure."

"Did you see him take a nitroglycerin?"

"No."

"Did he tell you he took any?"

"No."

"There was only one in his pocket. He always carries at least two."

Paul shrugged.

"Were you with him all the time?"

"Yes . . . . No, no. Not all the time. When he was getting dressed under the boardwalk, I was by the ocean digging a hole with a clam shell." *I did dig a hole.*

"Did he . . .? He always . . ." The fire in her eyes had gone out. "He told me he wanted to have a man-to-man talk with you about the war, America, school, those kind of things. Did he tell you anything like that?"

"No."

"Are you sure?"

"Yes." Paul closed his eyes and kept them closed until he heard his mother moving in her own room.

CHAPTER 4

A month went by and Paul did not hear or say the name Max. His mother and grandparents, when he could hear them, spoke in Yiddish about the store or relatives he barely knew. To the extent he was included in any conversation having to do with anything beyond chores, he responded to questions about school or he summarized the day's *Journal American* article on the new Jewish state, Israel, which was being simultaneously born and attacked by the armies of five Arab countries determined to destroy it. "A pogrom to end all pogroms," his grandmother predicted, but Paul was bold enough to disagree: "Not this time. Jews are becoming good fighters." He imagined his father and himself as Haganah soldiers, rifles across their chests, patrolling the dusty streets of Jerusalem.

On most nights, after Paul went into his own room, his mother and her parents, sometimes with Bernie and Ruthie, would withdraw into the grandparents' bedroom at the front of the apartment and remain there for over an hour. He was sure that they were talking about Max's diamonds. Only the diamonds could explain the extension phone they installed in the front bedroom. Who had ever heard of such a thing in Arverne? He was glad to be excluded. But, every day the Buffet reminded him he was not through with Max.

* * *

On a morning in late May, soon after Israel declared its independence, Paul found his mother waiting for him in the kitchen, standing by the door to the stairs, wearing her best clothing and her most valued possession — the brooch her grandmother had given her as a goodbye gift when she left for America. The navy blue dress that had once curved along her body now hung loose. The veil from her black hat covered half her face but the latticework emphasized her worry lines. She wore lipstick and rouge — almost as much as Ruthie. A suitcase was at her side.

"I have to go away for a couple of days. Rochester." *Not Montreal*, Paul thought. *Good.* He slid his hand down the cool pink refrigerator door. "If I'm not back by Saturday," his mother continued, "you may have to help out in the store."

"Sure."

"The store." She shook her head in resignation. "I'm thirty-six years old, and if I don't get out of it soon, I'll be an old lady at forty. Daddy wouldn't recognize me." Her grim eyes seemed to bore through the veil. "The Bible says God sent ten plagues to Pharaoh because he wouldn't let the Jews out of Egypt, but one plague, a small grocery store with Grandpa the boss, would have done the job."

She had never spoken to Paul in this way. He suspected she was preparing to question him about the key, and if he asked her nothing, she would be more suspicious.

"Why are you going?"

"Don't worry about it!"

How could he let that go unanswered? "Don't treat me like a baby."

She parted her lips to speak, but they trembled. Then tears. "Paulie! Paulie!" She seized Paul's hands. Her fingers were cold, but not as icy as his father's had been when he collapsed outside the gold-star bungalow.

"I'm sorry, Mom, but . . ."

"Don't be upset. I'm not telling you because it's better for you if you don't know too much."

He squeezed her hands. "Mom, I'll be fifteen in July."

His mother raised her veil and looked directly at him. The tears blurred her rouge. Her voice, unlike her eyes, was now calm. "I guess sooner or later you have to know some of it."

She paused, giving him a chance to stop her, but he was afraid of anything he might say.

"Okay." She looked over Paul's head at the top of the refrigerator. "Max had this cousin on his mother's side, Jacob or Kobi — Jack in America — who settled in upstate New York. I knew him a little when we were kids in Teplice." She looked back at Paul. "Jacob was the Godfather for Max's son; a nice guy; a survivor too. For a while, he went out with Max's sister, Malke, but that ended after the world gave Hitler the Sudentenland and she joined the Communist partisans. They wouldn't take Jack because he wasn't Red enough."

Max had mentioned Malke — a flutist shot trying to escape from Treblinka. But if Paul told that to his mother, she would respond with a question — *What else did Max tell you?*

Still, he had to say something. "Did she die?"

"Of course."

His mother lowered her voice. "Anyway, Max came to America with diamonds. How he got them, how many, I knew enough not to ask." Paul nodded, understanding. "He wants us to have them — particularly for your college."

Paul could feel his heart pound.

"They're in different places with different keys, and the only one who knows how to find them is Jack. He's the only one Max trusted except for me, and Max wanted to protect me from knowing too much. Bernie helped sell some diamonds, but Max didn't trust him." His mother moved her hands in cadence with her words. "He would've trusted you if you were older, but he wanted you protected, too.

"Anyway, we kept looking for Jack, but we got no place because the name we had was Jacob Rosenzweig, what he was in Europe, and his name here is Jack Roth."

Not Greenberg, the name on the note in Max's violin case. *Good.*

"Finally, Jack called us yesterday — he had just heard Max died — and I'm going up to see him and learn about the diamonds so you can go to a good college and maybe we can get rid of the store."

Paul had to change the subject before he blurted out something about the missing key. "I didn't know Cousin Max had a son."

She took a napkin from the table and blew her nose. "He said you reminded him of . . ." She blew her nose again. "Reuben — same name as Daddy. They're both named after Max's grandpa who's Daddy's grandpa, too."

"Is Little Reuben alive?"

She looked at Paul in disbelief. "Nobody's alive. Nobody. You and I would be dead too except for your father."

"How old was he?"

"He was born in nineteen thirty-eight when you were five, and he died when he was five."

"Was Max going to teach Reuben music?" Paul was startled by his own question.

"He started violin lessons when Reuben was four."

Paul barely managed to drop himself onto a kitchen chair.

"Paulie, what's wrong?"

"Max got the violin because of me. I made him think of Little Reuben."

"Don't blame yourself," she said curtly. "There are a lot of survivor suicides."

"I know, but if he hadn't bought the violin —"

"*If, if, if!*" she broke in. Paul saw fury in her eyes. "Don't make yourself so important and miserable." She pointed down at him. "I'll tell you something I swore I'd never tell anyone — not even Grandma. But you have to promise it's between us only."

Paul didn't want to know.

"Will you promise?"

"Yes."

She sat down at the table. "On the night before . . . you know, on the night before." Paul nodded. "Max told me all about the camps. It was new things — worse than I had ever heard. He told me what people did to stay alive — things he and his brother did. I tried to stop him, but it was like a dam broke. He gave me some keys for diamonds in case something happened to him but, except for telling me about Jack, no information. He said he'd tell me everything someday soon but there was something else he had to say first. Then . . ."

She looked directly at Paul and waited until he looked at her. "Then Max asked me to marry him. He had a diamond ring in his pocket."

A horrible taste rose up to Paul's mouth as if he hadn't brushed his teeth in days.

His mother caught her breath. "But what could I . . .? How can you love, even be with . . ." She stopped and swallowed slowly. "Do you want me to tell you everything Max said?"

Yes or no? Paul couldn't choose and, if he did choose, he wouldn't be able to speak. Then, almost miraculously, he heard the horn sounding from the robin's-egg blue Lincoln. Bernie and Ruthie must be taking his mother to the train station.

Saved, Paul thought. He told himself that when his mother came back, he would talk to her as little as possible.

* * *

She called the next day during dinner. Paul's grandmother answered the phone in the living room. "Yes, operator, we'll accept . . . Ida! *Vu bistu? Ikh hob bakumen a shrek.*"

His grandfather went to his grandmother's side, and she held the phone so they both could listen. After a few moments of nodding, they turned their backs to Paul. His grandfather whispered a question in anxious Yiddish; his grandmother shrieked, "*Oy Gevald!*" and spit over her shoulder three times. Paul winced.

Questions and exclamations shot from his grandparents. Here and there Paul understood the meaning: "*Vifil diamantn?*" — How much diamonds? "*Ver nokh veyst?*" — Who else knows? "*Behalten? Vu behalten?*" — Hidden? Where hidden?

When the questions finally subsided and his grandmother called him to the phone, her hands were shaking.

"Mom, how are you?"

"I got good news," she said, but she sounded more anxious than happy. "There's a lot of diamonds, but it's complicated. At least there's money for your college. You can go out of town like you always said you wanted. For law school, too, if you want, or even medical school."

He would ask this question now or never: "Shouldn't you tell the government?"

Paul's grandfather leaned against the Philco.

"Why?" his mother asked.

"Isn't that what the law says to do?"

His mother and grandmother answered him at once. "What good was law for Max or for Jack who they made a slave?" said his mother through the telephone. "No trouble, Paul. Please, no trouble here; Jews had enough in Europe," his grandmother pleaded in his free ear.

What would his father do? *Who the hell knows!* He could hear his mother breathing.

"Mom, are you okay?"

"I'm tired . . ."

"Do you want me to come up there?" It was a preposterous offer, but shouldn't he help his widowed mother?

"That's sweet, but Jack and I have things under control." She made a sound that resembled a hiccup. "I don't know how much to tell you."

"Tell me what I have to know."

"Have to? Only one thing: You can trust Jack. Max did, and I met some people who knew him in the Grosbatten Camp." Paul wondered whether Jack was with her, telling her stories about a camp he didn't want to imagine? "Jack's a real *mensh*," she said. The two of them must be together.

"Is that all I have to know?" Paul could almost see his mother cringe, but the hell with it.

She waited for Paul to apologize, but he said nothing. "I don't know details, and I won't give you all that I know," she went on, "but you need to see the big picture."

Stop! Paul silently screamed.

"Lots of diamonds, but they're in locked boxes in different places, maybe four, five places. Some in banks. Some with people. Some we think we have keys for. Some we're not so sure. Max made it all a puzzle," she cleared her throat, "and not everybody involved is in love with him. And then, when they're found, you have to sell them slowly and only a few at a time to get a decent price. Jack thinks we can track them all down, but it's a slow process."

"Who had these diamonds before Max?" he asked, but he didn't want to know.

"They were lost." His mother's voice was cutting, conclusive.

Again, there was a silence Paul wouldn't break. When his mother finally spoke, he could barely hear her. "It's too late, Paul. The boat sailed, and we're on it."

"I didn't get on a boat."

"Maybe yes, maybe no." Now she was louder. "One more thing. There's another box that Max had a partner in." His mother paused for emphasis. "A joint box in Switzerland that takes two different keys to open. Maybe it has the most of what they hid, and the partner can sell it quickly in Europe for a fair price. The partner has one key, and if we can put our hands on Max's key, we can get out of the store before it kills the three of us."

Was the partner Greenberg? Did he live in Montreal? "You have to stop asking me!" Paul realized he was shouting. "I told you I don't have a key," he said in his normal voice.

"I didn't ask you anything." She let Paul feel the sting of her words, and then continued, "Jack is sure that if we can just get the Switzerland box, there'll be plenty for your college like Daddy and Max always wanted. Did he tell you anything, Paulie?"

Paul felt rage overwhelming him, a giant swelling wave that he could neither swim through nor coast — rage at everything and everybody but, most of all, at his own solitude. "Mom, don't call me Paulie . . ."

"I'm sorry, but—"

"Let me finish." He felt his mother go surprisingly silent. "I don't want to use Max's diamonds to go to college. Max didn't say anything about them to me, and I don't want you to tell me anything else."

There was a long silence, the longest of the evening, until his mother finally said, "Okay, Paul. Let me talk to Grandma."

* * *

On the evening his mother returned from Rochester, while she and Paul were alone at the kitchen table paying the store's bills, Paul told her he would "like to work in the grocery during the summer." He couldn't imagine a worse prospect, but he had to atone for his harshness during their telephone call. Besides he had no choice. They needed him there to handle the summer surge in business.

His mother leaned over the table and kissed him quickly on the cheek. "I appreciate it. Last summer everyone we hired quit because of Grandpa or got fired because things were missing. Every day a different aggravation." She smiled and, for the first time in God knows how long, her eyes almost twinkled. "I didn't mean what I said about God's curses on Pharaoh," she said to Paul. "The store's not worse than a lot of other jobs and nothing could be worse than the last curse on Pharaoh — killing the first born." The twinkle in her eyes was gone but, at least, tears hadn't taken over. "Daddy would be so proud of you, Paulie, and now you're starting to get so big." Her tears were close. "Don't come to the store before your last test is over. The egg man's sister teaches in the high school, and she told him you could be first in the class."

"Not that high," Paul told her, but he told himself that he could be third in his class, possibly second, if only he could keep Max and the diamonds out of his thoughts.

CHAPTER 5

Paul had liked the grocery when they bought it soon after his father's death but, after working there for three days, he agreed with his mother that it rivaled God's ten plagues on Pharaoh. When he entered it, the summer light disappeared, blocked by the cans and handwritten sale signs in the never-quite-clean window, and the ocean air was swallowed by the smell from the pickle barrel, an odor that, over the years, had gone from mouthwatering to repulsive. The floor always needed sweeping; the cooler always needed cleaning; and no matter how careful he was, when he carried eggs up from the basement, one or two shells would crack. If his frowning grandfather spoke to him, it was either a reprimand ("You break too many eggs.") or an order ("Stand straight by the register.").

Worst of all were the ultra-Orthodox women who arrived late in the afternoon — dour Yiddish-speakers wearing ill-fitting wigs, square-heeled shoes and black everything. The worst of the worst were the two with deep eyes and weary voices — Max-In-A-Dress, Paul named them. Survivors? Thank God they all wore long sleeves, no matter what the weather. But on a very hot afternoon, the taller Max-In-A-Dress pushed up her left sleeve and Paul saw numbers. He told himself not to look — what his mother had told him on the day Max arrived — and then, just as with Max, everything except the numbers disappeared. The first digit was a pale purple five — same as Max's. The second was four — different. A bottle of milk slipped from Paul's hand but, fortunately, didn't break. By the time he picked it up, the woman's sleeve was down. Without being asked, he spent the rest of the afternoon cleaning the basement.

That night, he couldn't sleep. Each time he closed his eyes, he saw Max's 53927, then the woman's 54 plus three Xs for the digits he hadn't caught. He focused on the Xs — a thousand combinations of numbers, a thousand people. If each of her Xs was zero, 54000, her number would be only 73 more than Max, and she and Max were probably on the same transport. If the numbers were all nines, 54999, they probably arrived on different days. No, there could have been over a thousand people on a train. More went to the gas chambers on many days, often directly from the train and unnumbered. Besides, men and women might have been numbered separately. And maybe other camps used numbers.

Paul sat up in bed. He had to escape the grocery. He thought of Broadman's delivery bike sitting in the alley between the grocery and Broadman's Fresh Produce. It hadn't been used in weeks, ever since, as Broadman put it, "Some customers said the delivery *shvartser* scared them and smelled funny." Paul would make deliveries on the bike for both Broadman and his grandfather, and he'd do it in the afternoon when Max-In-A-Dress shopped.

His mother objected — "You'll have to stay later to stock and clean," — but Paul persisted — "It'll get more business. Stein doesn't deliver. I'll make tips I can save for college."

"Don't worry about college," his mother replied. "Max provided for that. You'll have to raise the bicycle seat, you've gotten so big."

Now wasn't the time to remind her he didn't want help from Max.

That afternoon, he put crayoned "Free Delivery" signs in both store windows, and Paul's grandfather announced to the woman with the numbers, "Missus, you want it delivered? For nothing. You can even call your order in. No *shvartser*. My grandson, Ida's boy, will do it. You don't have to worry if he comes in your apartment."

To Paul's relief, she answered, "*Neyn; der man shloft.*" Paul wondered whether her sleeping husband also carried numbers.

* * *

The thick front wheel of Broadman's bike was half the diameter of the rear wheel; the large wire basket hanging from the handlebar could hold six bags. The pedals were a part of Paul and, whether the basket was empty or full, he controlled the bike easily. Two heavy turns and he could reach full speed; a measured turn backwards, engaging the rear wheel brake, and he could bring the bike to a smooth stop in less than a yard. Riding on the summer blocks, he sometimes slowed to catch the *kibitzing* from the pinochle (men only) and mah jong (women only) games being played on the porches. On the winter blocks, where the porch games didn't begin until after supper, he weaved through the children on the street and threw pleasantries at the people he knew. When a street was mostly empty, as was often the case, he would take his hands off the handlebars and wave them over the basket, conducting a symphony in his head. Most of all, he liked deliveries near the ocean where the salt air whipping past him drove his legs faster and made thinking impossible.

A new customer called for a delivery. "Sixty-eighth Street, beach block, second floor in the brown house around the corner from Stein's," Paul's mother told him when she put the phone down. "You'll hear somebody practicing the flute."

As he approached the house, Paul heard Tchaikovsky's "Waltz of the Flowers." A professional flutist, he thought; good enough for a recording.

He stood at the door, the bag of groceries in his hand, and waited for the music to stop. Why let a ringing bell interrupt something so beautiful? But the flute went directly from the "Waltz" to Ravel's *Bolero*; he imagined a dark-veiled woman inside, dancing snakelike for King Solomon. As he waited, the music grew closer until it paused, and the door opened.

Through the screen, Paul faced a slender girl in a white sweater, with long jet-black hair and a silver flute at her lips. She resumed playing. It wasn't the veiled woman he had imagined, but it could have been her younger sister. And while he wasn't King Solomon, he could ride a bike better than anyone in the world. When she was through, he put the bag down and applauded.

She bowed. "You're Paul Hartman, a sophomore at Far Rockaway High School. You might be a first clarinetist next term, but you're not playing as well as you used to."

Amazing.

"I'm Sibyl Pine. Same grade. I live in Neponsit, but I go to private school in Brooklyn, and I'm in the New York Youth Symphony. My grandmother lives here."

Neponsit — the rich kids in his honors class came from there. "Sibyl? What kind . . ." He managed to stop himself.

"S-I-B-Y-L," she spelled slowly. "Soft 'i'. An ancient prophetess."

Jewish? Paul wondered. She must be, if she had a grandmother who lived here. He picked up the bag of groceries. "Should I carry this upstairs?"

"Don't you want to know how I know these things about you?"

"Magic, I guess."

"I said prophetess, not witch. Do you think I'm a witch?"

Paul almost dropped the groceries, but he saw she was smiling. Even though the screen door, her brown eyes sparkled. Her teeth were straight and shiny. "I think . . . " He felt himself getting an erection and lowered the bag to cover it.

"My aunt is Arlene Heider."

Impossible! The high school band conductor everyone feared. She couldn't have a family — certainly not a mother on Sixty-eighth Street or a niece who glowed.

"We sat here yesterday watching you ride by on your bike, waving your hands like a wild man." Sibyl stepped back and jerked her hands up and down and from side to side — not at all the way Paul pictured his orchestra conducting. "My aunt says she couldn't believe it was you. In school you're so quiet and serious, especially since the spring concert. You're nice and you're shy she said, and you blush when girls talk to you."

Paul felt his face redden. "Should I bring the bag up?" If she said *yes,* he was sure to make a fool of himself when he got there. A *no* meant goodbye forever.

Her face flushed, too. "Yes, bring it up," she mumbled. Then, suddenly, she put the flute across her eyes. "No. No, no, you better not. My grandmother's asleep."

Her neck was long and white. "Let me bring it up. The pot cheese can spoil."

Sibyl opened the screen door, grabbed the bag from him and ran up the stairs.

He was stunned, but managed to call through the screen after her, "Sibyl, are you okay? What's wrong?"

He heard a door slam and he rang the bell.

"Go away," she called from above him. "You'll wake my grandmother."

His head tilted up, he walked backwards down the stone steps trying to see whether she was at the window. All the venetian blinds were shut.

He pedaled away slowly, delivered the two remaining orders and started back along Rockaway Beach Boulevard keeping his eyes on the front wheel — past Seventieth Street, where he had dropped the key in the ocean; past Sixty-ninth, where the ambulance had taken Daddy away; past Sixty-eighth, where he had just met Sibyl. But at Sixty-sixth Street, a half block from the store, he recalled walking out on the slippery jetty to throw Max's key in the ocean. *Hartman's got heart*, he told himself. His father volunteered to parachute behind Nazi lines.

He stood up from the bike seat, made a U-turn in the middle of Rockaway Beach Boulevard, and pumped past Sam's Sweet Shoppe, Lubov's Kosher Fresh Fish, Housewife's Delight Laundromat/ Cleaners, through a red light, to the brown house around the corner from Stein's Superette. He slammed the pedals backward, braking the bike with a screech, and ran up the stoop steps. The door leading to the upstairs apartment was open, and Sibyl was again inches from him, behind the screen, holding her flute.

"I saw you racing down the Boulevard. I was afraid a car would hit you. Are you okay?"

Paul tried to catch his breath. "Yes," he managed.

"I'm sorry I ran up the stairs. I—" She pressed the flute to her chest, deepening the cleft between her breasts.

"I have to get back to the store. I . . . I just wanted . . ."

"Yes?"

"Do you want to go on the boardwalk tonight? There are fireworks." Paul's words surprised him. He hadn't been on the boardwalk since the night Max drowned.

"I'm supposed to go home."

"Can you sleep over at your grandmother's?"

"Do you want me to?"

"I'll be here at seven-thirty."

She opened her mouth to speak but then closed it and raised the flute to her lips. "Can you play 'Waltz of the Flowers'?" Paul asked. Sibyl nodded. "But wait till I'm on the bike, or I'll never get away from the screen door." She nodded again.

With two long strides down the steps and another across the sidewalk, he was back in the bicycle seat. "Now!" he sang out, and the flute responded. He raised his arms in a flourish and began peddling a huge figure eight in the street, leaning the bike far to the right, then far to the left, in three-quarter waltz time. After two figure eights, he shouted, "Seven thirty," and rode by her house as fast as he could.

* * *

They walked silently until they were on the boardwalk and Sibyl turned east, toward Sixty-fourth Street where Max had drowned. Paul took her elbow and pulled gently in the opposite direction. She followed but asked, "Why not that way?"

He couldn't tell her — not on the day they met. "It's quieter this way. It'll be easier to get a bench." Paul surprised himself with how easily the explanation came. It was almost true.

They found an empty bench under a lamppost and sat down. The boardwalk rail looked silver under the light. The ocean waves were close to the shore and pure white. Beyond the waves, the Atlantic was even darker than Sibyl's hair. He slid closer to her, and she asked him when he started to play the clarinet.

They lobbed meaningless questions back and forth — "How long have you been playing the flute?" "Is my aunt a good conductor?" — until Paul could no longer stand it. "I'm sorry I acted surprised by your name. I never knew a Sibyl."

She laughed briefly. "You would know a Sibyl if you lived in England. My mother didn't want me to have a Jewish name — anything Jewish. Last year we had a Christmas tree."

Rich Neponsit Jews trying to act like Christians. Pathetic — it wouldn't work. He didn't dare reply. "When you ran up the stairs, I didn't know whether I'd said something wrong or you were worried about the pot cheese spoiling."

"Pot cheese?"

"The pot cheese your grandmother ordered — that I was delivering."

Sibyl looked puzzled. Then she arched her thin eyebrows as if it were now all clear. "If I tell you something, you promise you won't get mad?"

"No. I mean yes. I promise."

"I want everything honest between us."

"You can tell me." Paul wanted to take her hand, but if he did, she might stop speaking. *I want everything honest, too*, he thought of adding. But would that be an honest thing to say?

"My grandmother didn't order anything. She was at the Senior Center playing canasta. I just . . ." She turned her head from him and faced the beach, her black hair now a curtain between them. "The groceries . . . That was only an excuse to meet you after my aunt said you were so nice." Paul could hardly hear her. "The flute's my only friend, my mother says."

Paul kissed her hair — so lightly that he wasn't sure she felt it. He couldn't define the smell. It was neither soap nor flowers, nor something in between — just smooth and wonderful.

She turned her face to him, but kept her eyes on the ground. "Maybe I shouldn't tell you this."

Paul took her hands. "You can tell me anything."

To his surprise, she began to laugh. "I didn't even know what pot cheese is. I heard my grandmother talk about it, and I wanted the order to sound convincing. After you rode away, I threw it in the garbage outside."

He had to kiss her on the lips — she wanted him to — but there were too many people around. Without either of them saying a word, they got up and walked hand in hand.

At Seventy-fourth Street, a block past the stores, where it was a bit less crowded, she led him to the only empty bench in sight. They sat, and Sibyl held out both her hands. Paul took them gently, and they each turned then towards the other.

Now, Paul instructed himself, *kiss her as soon as these two old ladies go by*. But one of the women said, "If only Israel was there when the Nazis . . ." and Sibyl shuddered.

"I hate it when people talk so much about that. It gets me depressed."

Not now, Paul told himself — don't tell her anything. She won't understand — she has a Christmas tree.

Sibyl moved closer. "Tell me your biggest secret — something you never told anybody."

Max. But he had to kiss her first. "I have to think about that."

Sibyl squeezed his forearm. "I'm sorry. I didn't mean to upset you."

"No, I'll answer." He didn't pause for a breath. "I was the last one in my family to see my father alive."

Sibyl gasped. "I'm sorry. I didn't know. You didn't tell me."

"How could you know? We only met each other a few hours —"

Sibyl nodded. "Will you be able to go to a private college or will you go to one of the city colleges?" she asked, and then suddenly seemed flustered, just as she had when she had run up the stairs with the groceries. "I shouldn't have asked."

"My father left insurance for me to go to a private college," Paul quickly responded. A total lie, but a private-school girl from Neponsit wouldn't want a poor Arverne boyfriend who planned to attend a city college. And he still hadn't kissed her.

"The Youth Symphony's playing Friday night at Town Hall in Manhattan. My parents are driving. Do you want to come?"

His lie had worked. "Absolutely. Do you want to walk on the boardwalk tomorrow?"

She lifted her head and, without checking whether anyone was looking, they kissed.

Seconds later, the first THOOMPF and whistle of a firework rocket pulled them apart. The rocket launcher, Paul realized, was at Rockaway Playland, twenty blocks to his right, where he had stood while Max had drowned in the blackness before them. The whistle became a

Boom, and the firework's red and yellow stars reflected in the Atlantic. The reflections didn't reach Sixty-fourth, but they might during the grand finale. If they lingered here until then, he would look the other way.

They sat in silence, his arm around her, her head on his shoulder, until, after the fourth firework burst, she put her lips against his ear.

"Now it's my turn to tell you my biggest secret."

"You don't have to."

She sighed into his ear and made it tingle. "My father gambles a lot."

"I'm sorry."

"And he makes up stories . . . about . . . about everything."

I mustn't do that. "I'm sorry."

"And he has a girlfriend." She pulled his hand off of her shoulder, held it, then dug her nails into his palm. "You wouldn't do that, would you?"

He slid his mouth against her ear. "Not if you were my wife."

She kissed his neck and a shiver ran down his body from ears to toes, and then up again. Before next week's fireworks, he would tell her everything, and she would convince him that he wasn't to blame for the death of his cousin or of his father.

* * *

He kissed her goodnight at her grandmother's house and ran the half mile home, stopping at each corner to try clicking his heels together in the air, like Ray Bolger, the Scarecrow in *The Wizard of Oz*. With every corner, he came closer to success. In front of his own two-family house — the one they would soon leave — he was sure he could do it. He crouched, jumped as high as he could, and finally got his heels to touch and part. It was far from a Ray Bolger click but, still, the perfect end to a perfect day. He ran up the stoop, then tiptoed up the inside stairs.

He edged open the kitchen door quietly and saw his mother sitting at the kitchen table looking at her watch. It was long past her bedtime.

"Will you be too tired at work in the morning?" she asked him.

Paul's elation disappeared. "No. Will you?"

His impertinence came naturally now, and his mother ignored it. "Cousin Ruthie called. She and Cousin Bernie saw you on the boardwalk with this girl they don't know. Bernie wanted to go over and talk to you — make some wisecrack — but Ruthie wouldn't let him. She said you were too busy."

He wanted to keep quiet, but couldn't. "Ma, I like this girl."

"That's nice. Fourteen, fifteen's not too young. I loved your father when I was twelve."

He could trust her. She did know about things like this. "Her name is Sibyl, but she's Jewish." He sat down across from her. "She said she wants everything honest between us."

His mother seemed puzzled. "Of course you should be honest, but who talks that way? That's for advice columns in the papers." She smiled, which surprised him. "I used to read one every day in the Jewish paper, *The Forward*, when we first came here, but then your father said we should only read English papers." Her smile broadened; he could tell she was thinking of his father. "He certainly had opinions."

"I want to tell her about Cousin Max."

Even as Paul said it, he realized he wanted no such thing — at least until he was sure Sibyl was serious about him. She was a Neponsit girl with an English name, a private school and a Christmas tree.

His mother's lips went from a smile to an oval of shock. "Tell her! Are you *meshuga*? Crazy?" Almost hysterically, but softly, she began telling him why the secret had to be kept. Paul shut his ears to her, though he heard her say the word "jail" at least twice. He put up a few words of resistance, but did not make his most telling argument — *Wouldn't Daddy be ashamed of us?*

Finally, when his mother seemed close to tears, Paul said, "OK. You win." He started to stand, but her eyes urged him back into the chair.

"Just give me a minute," she said. "I stayed up to talk to you about something important. I'm not upset you stayed out late. I know you'll be able to work tomorrow. Even Grandpa doesn't complain since you started the deliveries."

She seemed to search for words. "It's about . . . I can't tell you what a gentleman Jack's been. He could have taken advantage, but he did the opposite. And, like Max, he's got nobody. When the Russians freed him he was an eighty-six pound skeleton, a slave, a human shoveling machine in a hell owned by Olymp. And his nephew in Rochester, the one he works for in the jewelry store, he treats Jack like he's got a disease. So, Grandma suggested we invite him for a few days. We got the beach and the ocean and the air's so good."

In what room? Paul wondered. There was no answer he wanted to hear.

"You wouldn't mind if we switched rooms like when Max came and the two of you share my room? It's only for this weekend."

"Does he know how Max died?"

"He knows more about Max than we do."

"Does he know how he died?"

"He might have figured it out."

"Did you tell him?"

"Yes," she answered.

"I thought it had to be secret from everybody."

She closed her eyes, then opened them. "Jack's not everybody. He's done so much for Max and for us. He survived the camps."

Always that. Paul got up quickly and started towards his room.

"Please Paul."

He did not look back at her. "You know I always do what I'm supposed to."

* * *

The suit, the fucking suit! The words hit him as soon as he closed his eyes. He sat up in bed. Should he wear it to Sibyl's concert? The answer, he realized, was inevitable.

The suit had been on his bed, dark like an undertaker, when he came home from his first day of delivering groceries on Broadman's bike. Next to it was a pair of black winged-tipped shoes, too shiny for an undertaker, two white shirts and two ties, one red and one blue. The label said "Allen's, Woodmere and Coral Gables," stores that were more expensive than any in the Rockaways. The money must have come from Max's diamonds. Ruthie must have helped his mother pick everything out. He had thanked his mother, and told himself he would never wear any of it. When the summer was over and she expressed her gratitude for his work in the grocery, he would tell her that he was returning everything to Allen's and that he wanted to own nothing, absolutely nothing, connected to Max.

But now, it was either Max's gift or the two-year old *Bar Mitzvah* suit he had worn at Max's funeral — pants ending above the ankles, a jacket that barely buttoned, and a white shirt with frayed cuffs. The only thing missing would be a sign around his neck proclaiming, *POOR IMMIGRANT BOY.* Not the way to dress for Sibyl's concert or to meet her parents. He lay back down and fell asleep quickly.

* * *

The grocery had few deliveries on Friday afternoon, when the Orthodox families prepared for *Shabos*, so Paul went home early to get ready for the concert. He showered, shaved his barely visible fuzz, and laid out his wardrobe on the bed. Except for underwear and the black socks he had bought with tip money, all of it was from Max. So what! Max would want him to look good.

He should smell good also, but there was no deodorant or mouthwash in the apartment. There never had been. Even the soap they bathed with, whatever its name, left you smelling like a scoured kitchen sink. So, on the way to the bus, Paul stopped in the drug store and bought a small bottle of Listerine Mouth Wash, a product he knew from radio jingles, and a smaller bottle of Pine Aftershave, a product he chose because Sibyl's last name was Pine. He gargled, splashed his face with the aftershave, splashed his hands and neck, and then splashed his face some more. It was an investment and a celebration — their first real date (their two walks didn't count), his first orchestra concert, and his first visit to Neponsit. He smelled his hands with pleasure.

But the pleasure didn't last. The instant he put his dime in the Green Bus's glass coin box, Paul became painfully aware of the new suit. Nobody else was dressed nearly as nicely. The bus driver rolled his eyes mockingly and then pinched the bottom of his nose. Paul breathed in and, instead of salt air, smelled nothing but aftershave — he had splashed on too much. He sat in the empty last row of the bus, where the seat ran from window to window, and focused on Rockaway as it rolled by him.

Sibyl lived on One-hundred-forty-fourth Street, the last numbered street before Riis Park, the Marine Parkway Bridge, Fort Tilden and, finally, Breezy Point where only white Christians lived and Jews couldn't get past the gate. At the tip of Breezy Point, the Atlantic met Jamaica Bay. All eleven miles of Rockaway peninsula were part of New York City but, unless it was a clear day and you could make out the Empire State Building over the bay, Manhattan could have been on another continent. Paul slid over to the right window and decided to count the number of times he saw that emblem of the city.

The Green Bus crept west along Rockaway Beach Boulevard from one ethnic enclave to another, each with its own name and post office. Paul was never more than a long block from the ocean and a half mile from the bay. Still, he made no sightings of the Empire State in Arverne, his town, where the poor Jews lived alongside a few poorer Italians, or in Hammels where the colored people lived on dusty potholed streets in what could only be called shacks. He expected a sighting of the building in Irish Town, where the peninsula narrowed and the summer population explosion — Irish instead of Jewish — was as dramatic as in Arverne. And there it was, just beyond Playland and two blocks of bars flying Irish flags. He craned his neck to the right, looked up Ninety-ninth

Street and was able to see the world's tallest building. When he got off the bus, he would celebrate with a Ray Bolger leap and heel click.

As the bus inched to One-hundred-sixteenth Street, Paul's excitement peaked. It was a wide shopping street with stores, bars and restaurants going from the boardwalk to the bay — in Paul's world, the only street on which there was both a Jewish delicatessen and an Irish bar, a *kosher* butcher and a pork store. More important, Rockaway would now become dramatically nicer. From One-hundred-sixteenth Street until One-hundred-forty-fourth Street — from Rockaway Park to Belle Harbor to Neponsit — the two-family houses would give way to one-family houses, the summer beach blocks would become all-year-round beach blocks, the homes would be bigger, the lawns trimmer, and the population would go from mixed Irish and Jewish to mostly Jewish — Jews who belonged to Conservative or Reform congregations and went to private summer camps and out-of-town colleges. Without straining his neck, he could again see the upper half of the Empire State Building with its long spire shining in the late afternoon sun; it was twenty miles away, but he felt he could touch it. Out the left bus window, he could see the Atlantic. If only he could stop smelling like a whorehouse.

Seconds later, Paul was off the bus and in Katy's Luncheonette where he ordered a Coke, left it on the counter and went to the bathroom to wash himself furiously. Now came the hard part — getting to Sibyl's house, which was twenty-eight blocks away, by six-fifteen, in nineteen minutes, before the Pines left without him. The next bus wouldn't arrive for fifteen minutes, and the only possibility was scout's pace — fifty steps jogging, fifty steps fast walk.

By the third round of fast walk, he felt perspiration on his lips — two blocks later, he felt it under his arms. What a choice — stink or be late.

When he reached Sibyl's street, he saw her standing by a black Cadillac a block away from the Boulevard, looking at her watch. He was a minute late. He began to run full steam, but that was too undignified, and he went back to a fast walk.

"You said you'd be early."

How could he tell the truth, that he had to leave the bus to wash away the smell of Pine aftershave? "There was an accident near Playland and the cops stopped all traffic. I finally got off the bus and ran." Perspiration from his brow was burning his eyes.

"My mother didn't want to wait." Sibyl rolled her eyes. "She says I'll be in a mood if my warm-up's rushed. I told her I wouldn't go without you. Welcome to the Pines."

Sibyl's parents were in the car with the windows wide open. "Get in," her mother said. She sat perfectly straight in the front passenger seat and looked ahead without moving.

Paul climbed into the car and encountered a man's hand extended from the front seat. He shook it. Mr. Pine's fingernails were perfectly shaped and clear. He was as tan as Bernie and as thin as Max, with stiff black hair combed up into a teenage pompadour.

He grinned at Paul and said, "Sibyl tells me your last name is Hartman. Are you related to Chickie Hartsman? Only one letter difference. He owned the Emerald Club and was a buddy of mine; I supplied him with customized matches and novelties. I hear you're a smart kid."

"He's not related, Maurice," Mrs. Pine said. "Tell him about your friends later. It's Friday and there will be a lot of traffic."

She sounded like the Wicked Witch of the West. No wonder her husband had a girlfriend.

Mr. Pine put the car in gear and gave it gas. "A lot of celebrities came to the Emerald and I knew them all — Eddie Cantor, Glenn Miller, Harry Houdini, Abe Simon, who was the top Jewish heavyweight and would've taken Joe Lewis if he wasn't recovering from pneumonia." He looked over his shoulder at Paul and nodded.

"Maurice, you're driving! Look at the road."

Mr. Pine turned to Paul and laughed. Paul had never met a man with such white teeth or sweet breath. He would never again gargle with Listerine.

Sibyl sat inches away from him, staring at the flute case on her lap. Paul wanted to move closer, but he was afraid the Wicked Witch would order him out of the car.

* * *

As soon as the Cadillac stopped in front of Town Hall, Sibyl ran towards the stage door. Looking at her husband for the first time, Mrs. Pine said, "I told both of you we should have left earlier. Park by yourself, Maurice. I don't think they'll let me save you a seat."

Paul, too humiliated to speak, followed her into the concert hall. He pointed at three empty seats near the wall and said, "Mrs. Pine" — his first words to her.

She stopped, looked and frowned. "Bad sight lines, but what can you expect when you arrive so late. Take the farthest in and he can sit between us. I'm sure you'll want to hear about his night club friends and novelties."

Paul did what he was told.

Twenty minutes later, when the concert was scheduled to start, Mr. Pine, slightly breathless, smiled his way past the people in their row. Paul wondered whether any of the Pines had noticed that, in his new suit, he looked exactly the same as the boys in the orchestra.

"Amazing — I met Chickie Hartsman on his way to the Copa," Mr. Pine said to Paul.

Talk to him, Paul instructed himself. *He's nice to you.* "The flutes are in the first row, to the right of the cellos. Sibyl's in the center."

"Second chair," Mr. Pine said bitterly, "although she's the best. That tall girl got first because her father's a big shot banker, but they're moving to Boston, and I'm going to have a connection on the new board."

"Maurice," Mrs. Pine hissed.

She was answered by an oboe tuning A and by some "Shhs" from behind them.

* * *

With the opening note of Grieg's *Peer Gynt* Suite, Paul realized that he had never before seen an orchestra perform. He had played in a high school band, but that was different. At home, his mother and grandmother occasionally turned on WQXR, and sometimes they talked about musicians they had known in Europe, but they never actually discussed music. The Philco dominated the living room but, aside from some Dvorak seventy-eights that had come with it, their home had no records. The phonograph hadn't been played since Max's suicide and, when they moved in September, it would be Bernie's.

Mr. Pine stood up as soon as the Grieg ended and intermission began. "I'm meeting Chickie for a quick drink to discuss some new business venture," he said to Paul and began to squeeze his way towards the aisle. Once there, he called to his wife over the heavy applause, "I'll pick you up out front." She ignored him.

Paul looked over the empty seat at Mrs. Pine who was applauding tepidly, and he told her what he had planned to say to her husband: "The flute solo was good, but not as good as if Sibyl played it."

To Paul's surprise, she turned to him. "Perhaps, but Willa Turner is a fine young woman, and Sibyl would be better off developing some friends like her. That's why I took her out of the public schools."

Paul could think of only one response — *Fuck you* — but as he searched for something less final, the Wicked Witch excused herself "to go to the powder room."

* * *

After the concert, Sibyl and Paul stood alone in front of Town Hall waiting for her father while Mrs. Pine talked to Willa Turner and her parents at the corner of Sixth Avenue. It had become chilly, and Sibyl handed Paul her flute case and hugged her shoulders. He started to remove his jacket, but she shook her head no. "If I wore it, my mother would say something nasty." She wrinkled her nose and made a grunt-like sound. "I hope they weren't too awful."

"No. I really enjoyed it." He fought the temptation to touch her. "You were terrific."

She kicked him gently in the shin. "You couldn't single me out if you tried."

Paul smiled for the first time that evening. "No, but I'm sure you were terrific."

"Sibyl," her mother called from the corner, waving at her daughter to join them.

Paul felt the fury and shame of being left by himself. But Sibyl didn't move. "Aren't you gonna go?" he asked.

"And leave you here alone?" She spoke between almost-clenched teeth. "My mother's been trying for months to get me to become friends with Willa even though she's a junior at Brearley and hates me because I'm a better flutist and Jewish."

"What's Brearley?"

Sibyl unclenched her teeth and tilted her head up at Paul. "It's this very snobbish private girl's school. Maybe the most snobbish in New York. They don't take Jews."

"So why does your mother want you to be friends?"

"That's the whole idea. Doesn't anyone in your family want to be friends with the Protestants?"

The question was almost absurd. Aside from the colored kids in school and a few teachers, he couldn't recall ever knowing a Protestant. Lots of Catholics went to his school — Italian, Irish, a few Poles — and the Rossinis lived downstairs. Was Jimmy Savitas, the Greek kid he learned Morse code with in the Boy Scouts, a Protestant or a different kind of Catholic? He must know some Protestants. But who cared?

"I never thought about that," he told Sibyl, but she wasn't paying attention. Her mother was striding towards them; her father was honking the horn in front of Town Hall; and a chauffeur was helping Willa Turner into a limousine.

* * *

"That was inexcusably rude, Sibyl. I'm only trying to help you make suitable friends."

"Don't make friends for me. Willa doesn't like me."

"You shouldn't be afraid to expand your horizons."

Mr. Pine jerked the car from the curb. "Give the kid a break!"

Paul realized that, for the three of them, he wasn't there.

He sulked in silence, along with the Pines, until they were driving across the dark Brooklyn marshes and approaching the lights of the Marine Parkway Bridge which would take them back over Jamaica Bay into Rockaway. Soon, he would be on the Green Bus to Arverne without having touched her. The suit, the shave, the Listerine — all a waste.

Something stung Paul's hand. Sibyl was pinching him. "Shh," she mouthed. She raised both her hands and soundlessly fingered the melody in "Waltz of the Flowers." She had given him the score two days earlier, and he had stayed up late practicing it. Fingering an imaginary clarinet, keeping his eyes on hers as headlights flashed by, he joined her in a silent duo.

"Sibyl!" Paul and Sibyl dropped their hands.

"They're just fooling around Evelyn," Sibyl's father said with a forced laugh. "Leave them be. It's late, Paul. Do you want to sleep over?"

Paul flinched. He had no idea what to say.

Mrs. Pine looked out the passenger window — the first time she had moved during the drive. "Don't be ridiculous, Maurice. They're too old for boy-girl sleepovers."

Sibyl and her father responded together. "Mother!" "Evelyn!"

Mr. Pine scowled at his wife. "How many empty rooms do you need?" He turned to Paul. "You can stay over whenever you and Sibyl go out, if it's okay with your parents."

With effort, Paul managed to say, "Thanks, but I have to work tomorrow."

* * *

Climbing the stairs to the apartment, after a grim bus ride to Arverne, he told himself what his mother had told him when Max moved in — *Don't look at the numbers, not even at his arms.*

How do I control my eyes?

Control them.

He opened the kitchen door, prepared to see the survivor but, instead, his eyes froze on his mother's new pink fingernails — almost the color of the refrigerator. They were spread out on the kitchen table like a winning gin rummy hand. She hadn't painted her nails in years, probably not since Daddy died. Her crisp yellow dress, which he had never seen before, was much brighter than her daily dresses. Her usually flat hair was fluffy and appeared a bit lighter. All the fruits of Max's diamonds.

"Paul dear," his mother sang, "this is Jack Roth, Mr. Roth. I told you about him."

Jack stood up and held out his hand. Paul stole a glance down from the man's face. On Jack's left forearm, where Max's numbers had been, Paul saw only some thin pale hairs. But what about the arm extended toward him? Maybe in Jack's camp, unlike at Auschwitz, the numbers were tattooed on the right arm. He looked. Nothing there either. Paul took Jack's hand. "I'm glad to meet you."

Jack's grip was firm, but not too hard. "Call me Jack. I heard good things about you." He had a Yiddish accent, but it was milder than Max's.

Did he look like a survivor? Unlike Max, Jack stood as straight and tall as his own father, and he was probably twice the weight of the eighty-six-pound skeleton rescued by the Russians. He eyes held sadness, but, unlike Max, his cheeks hadn't been permanently hollowed.

"I appreciate your inviting me to visit," Jack said. "The air here is so much fresher." He sounded as if he were reading from a script in a language he didn't understand. "Everybody says you do good in school and the store. That's nice."

Paul's mother looked up at Paul almost pleadingly, but he couldn't speak. Everything inside him had frozen.

"Jack brought one of the new model Kodak cameras," his mother finally said. "They make it in Rochester. Very advanced. We can take it to the beach on Sunday and he'll show us some of the techniques he learned from some of his Kodak customers." She stood and broke into an eerie smile. "How about some nice iced tea?"

The harder she tried, the more immobile Paul became. "The tea sounds good," he managed, "but I better go to bed. Saturday's a busy day."

"Don't forget," his mother said. "You're staying with Jack in the—"

"I remember."

In the middle of the night, Paul woke and turned his head just enough to see the other metal bed. It couldn't be. The white bedspread on Jack's bed — or was it Max's bed? or Bernie's old bed? — was folded under and then over the pillow, as smooth as it had been when Paul had come in the room. He strained to hear — hoping for Yiddish from the kitchen, afraid of anything from the small bedroom. There was only silence.

He was sure he wouldn't be able to fall back asleep but he closed his eyes and, when he opened them, it was light. A figure inhabited the other bed. Jack? Max? Daddy? The milk-white arm hanging down the side had something on it. A bruise? A number?

Paul shot up, drenched in sweat. He forced himself to check the other bed. It was Jack; the rusty hair left no doubt. Thank God it was almost time to get up.

* * *

During his lunch break, Paul called Sibyl and asked, "Can I sleep over tonight?"

"Any night. My sister says she's never coming home again, and my mother's afraid I'll do the same thing if she doesn't let you sleep here. She even apologized for being so awful yesterday. Bring the Buffet. We can play a 'Waltz of the Flowers' duet."

"Okay, but first let's go to the outdoor movie on the boardwalk — *Anna and the King of Siam*. A real date." He'd use the tip money he was going to put in his college savings account.

After the movie, he called his mother from the Pines' empty kitchen, and told her he would be sleeping over.

"Is it all right with her parents?"

"They invited me."

"Jack will be disappointed. He thought we'd all go to the beach tomorrow, take pictures with the new camera, and then go to Bernie and Ruthie's for a cookout."

Paul could hear Mrs. Pine upstairs, opening and closing doors nosily, purportedly getting Paul towels. She might be in the kitchen any moment. "We're playing music tomorrow."

"Jack will be hurt."

"It's my one day off."

His mother didn't answer, and Paul heard Mrs. Pine starting down the stairs. He had only seconds to get off the phone. *Speak*, he silently pleaded with his mother. If they didn't say goodbye before Mrs. Pine came in the kitchen, he'd have to hang up.

His mother said nothing, but Mrs. Pine shouted from above, "I don't think he should use Lisette's pillow. I'll get another one from the attic." Her footsteps clicked back up the stairs.

"Mom," Paul whispered into the receiver. He didn't know what he would say next, except that he wouldn't apologize and wouldn't go home.

His mother whispered back: "Okay. I guess you have to live your own life."

"I can meet you and Jack on the beach in the afternoon."

"Only if you want. It's up to you."

Mrs. Pine's anger infused the house. She stripped the sheets from Lisette's bed in two violent pulls, complained to her husband about making her waste the beautiful afternoon at the wedding of some "*nouveau riche* rag merchant," spoke to Sibyl in a saccharine voice, and ignored Paul's offer to help straighten up. Finally, the four of them stood in the vestibule saying their goodbyes. "Don't forget, dear," Mrs. Pine said to Sibyl, "Aunt Dotty has to go her principal's party, and I told her you'd be on the beach at one-fifteen to watch the children."

Mr. Pine winked at Paul. "Forget? It's the third time you reminded her. They're only going to play a duet. I'll ask the Klicksteins whether they heard it."

When the Cadillac's engine started, Paul realized he was afraid of what would come next. "Let's practice."

"Practice what?" Sibyl replied. "Don't look so frightened. I set things up in the basement and opened the windows facing the Klicksteins. My mother really will ask them whether they heard 'Waltz of the Flowers'."

When he looked at the Pines' finished basement Paul knew he would have trouble playing "Waltz of the Flowers." The room was too intimidating — wood paneling, wall-to-wall carpeting, puffed-up couch, flowered easy chairs, even a television set (the first Paul had seen in a private home), and a Philco radio-phonograph console more imposing than the one Max had given them.

Paul sat at the music stand; the score he had been practicing was waiting for him. Sibyl sat next to him, with no stand or score. She nodded her head and they began to play. After a few bars, Paul took the clarinet from his mouth.

"What's wrong?" Sibyl asked. "You didn't make any mistakes."

Paul shook his head in disgust. "The right notes but no feeling — like a player piano. You really love it — you can hear it in the music — but I just make correct sounds."

Sibyl seemed embarrassed. "Willa Turner said something like that before she became so unfriendly. All I wanted since I was a little girl was to play music. When I stopped going to the Brownies so I would have more practice time, my mother said I was freaky."

She lifted the flute. "Listen to the music. Dance with it inside yourself, enjoy it without thinking, like when you ride your bike."

They played together for a while, and then Sibyl signaled to stop. "Better, but you're not letting the feeling take over. Try it again and, no matter what I do, you keep playing."

They went back to the beginning and, after a few bars, Sibyl stood up. Without missing a note, she began waltzing around the room. Her skirt flounced out, her hair swayed as she turned in small graceful circles. Paul swayed with her. There was no longer a *one-two-three, two-two-three* beat in his head, only the flow of her curved body.

Still dancing, she lowered the flute and called out over his clarinet, "Dance along with me, but don't stop playing."

He had never danced a waltz, but his feet and fingers moved together. His body swayed with the music they were making. Without touching, they glided around each other, past the television, the Philco, the puffed-up couch, around the room, again and again.

When they completed the piece, Sibyl turned a dial on the Philco, and an orchestra began "Waltz of the Flowers" all over again. They played along with the orchestra and kept dancing. And then they put their instruments down, and danced in each other's arms. And then they were on the couch.

With Sibyl in his arms, Paul was skimming ocean waves. He could somersault in the wave or just coast. Either would be perfect, and everything was new — their tongues twirling around each other with the music; her breasts pressing against him and then in his hands; smooth skin with wonderfully large brown nipples feeling even better than they looked.

The Philco began to repeat the same bar of music. Suddenly, Sibyl was at the console and the music stopped. She pulled down her sweater. "We have to have an understanding." Paul pushed himself up off the couch. "I don't . . . Not all. . ." she stammered. "I don't want to go all the way. I promised my mother . . . ." She looked at him pleadingly. "You'll respect that, won't you?"

"Yes," Paul managed to say. He was relieved.

Sibyl came over, kissed him quickly, and fingered a few bars of "Waltz of the Flowers" on his forehead. "Now, let's play something else so the Klicksteins can give a good report."

"Play what?"

"What about Wagner's *Tannhäuser* — near the beginning where the woodwinds take the melody? My aunt said you played it beautifully at the concert — that you know it by heart."

Without hesitation, Paul reached for the Buffet.

CHAPTER 6

Both Paul and his mother spent most weekends away from Arverne — Paul at Sibyl's house where he and the Wicked Witch avoided each other, and his mother upstate with Jack. "We're seeing people about . . . you know what," she explained to Paul.

The day before Paul's senior year began, his mother called from Rochester. "Jack and I got married this morning. I wanted you to be the first to know."

Paul wasn't surprised but he couldn't speak. Squeezing the phone, he looked at the radiator and discovered that the picture of his father had blurred. Or was that Max's picture? No, it was only a vase of cloth flowers. His father's picture was in his mother's bedroom. Or had she put it someplace else? There was no picture of Max anyplace.

"We just decided. Get it done quick right here in Rochester so Jack doesn't miss work." Barely stopping for breath, she recounted the details — rabbi, place, just two witnesses, their plans to buy the jewelry store where Jack worked "using some of what Max . . . you know." Then, almost desperately, "I'm not leaving you, Paulie." He closed his eyes and tried to concentrate. "There's a nice room for you here, but you can stay in Arverne if you want to finish high school in Rockaway and keep seeing Sibyl. I'll make sure you have everything you need for your education. You know that Max . . . Say something, Paulie. Paul!"

He knew what he had to say. "I'm glad. Really glad. Congratulations. *Mazel tov.*"

"We'll fix the room up nice." She was crying. "And Jack's nice, too."

The talk had to end while he could still control his words. "I want to graduate with my class. Do you want to talk to Grandma?"

"Don't rush me off all the time!" Was she hurt, angry or both? It didn't matter. Paul wouldn't discuss her marriage.

"I've got two more things to say," his mother went on. "First, bring Sibyl up for Thanksgiving. We'll have a good time."

"I'll speak to her," Paul said as pleasantly as he could. He knew they wouldn't go.

"And the other thing . . . I want you should have . . . Daddy would want . . ."

Whatever words she was searching for, Paul doubted he could handle them. "Let's talk about it later. We've covered a lot today."

"No, no, it's something you'll like." He could picture her nodding. "There's a Pet Evaporated Milk carton in the cellar, on the table near the burner, with all the pictures Daddy and I had. I'm sure you know what I'm talking about. Ruthie's going to ship it to me, but first I want you to take whatever you want, even the wedding picture from Teplice that you used to look at with Daddy."

Suddenly, for the first time in years, perhaps since Daddy's death, Paul wanted to hug his mother. "Thank you," he managed to say. "I'll look at them today."

"Now you can get Grandma."

"I really hope you and Jack will be happy."

* * *

Paul had discovered the carton of pictures on the day the family moved. Whenever he had encountered it in the basement, he had looked the other way. But today, he went through the photos carefully. At the top were the ones from his parents' bedroom wall, those his mother had taken down the day Max arrived. He paused at the wedding picture; in its center the earnest groom who had become his father and then left him, and the "blonde-like-a-*goy*" bride who had also left him. (What color was her hair for the new marriage?) He remembered his father telling him that, for luck, there were exactly thirty-six people (twice *chai*) in the picture, and only one of them was a cousin. Paul counted them out, but didn't search for a face that might be the young Max.

He would take only one of the pictures from the wall — his father's swim team at the Hebrew Youth Games. But when he examined the framed photo, he wasn't sure he wanted it. As he remembered all too well, four of the fourteen swimmers, but not his smiling father, had medals around their necks. His father must have lost. Then, why the hell was he smiling? Did Paul want to remember his father as a young man without a medal? Would he love his father more if he had a medal? How could he be such a shit?

He searched the bottom of the carton for more pictures of his father. Two curled snapshots were nearly perfect except that the black and white had faded to brown and gray — Daddy holding little Paulie on a pony, and his father, younger than the earnest groom, in a bathing suit with a whistle around his neck, standing confidently, hands on hips, before a lake. The word "Wasserretter" running across his bathing shirt could only mean lifeguard.

The next photo so stunned Paul that he dropped it back in the box and then raised it slowly. It was an almost all-brown snapshot of five emaciated men, each wearing a tattered prison uniform and holding a shovel. "Befreite Olymp Sklaven — Grossbatten 4/45" was scrawled across the bottom. Jack had been a slave of Olymp; "a shoveling machine," according to his mother. The man in the center, the only one standing straight, must be the eighty-six pound survivor who was now his stepfather. Had his mother placed the photo in the box to remind him what Jack had been through? Did she want him to take it? He wouldn't. Still, he had to learn what "Befreite Olymp Sklaven" meant, and he wrote the words on the back of the Paulie-on-a-pony picture. Two days later, he consulted the German-English dictionary in the school library and confirmed his tentative translation: "Freed Olymp Slaves."

Paul wouldn't mention the survivors' snapshot to Sibyl. She would be annoyed he brought this Jewish darkness between them, and he would be tempted to reveal Max.

He would tell Sibyl about his mother's marriage, but not just yet. That morning, her father had moved into his girlfriend's apartment, and her mother was hysterical. Sibyl wanted to spend as much time with her as possible, which Paul understood to mean don't come over. He could almost hear her say: *Be thankful she found someone nice. I wish I could live with my Grandma.*

He spent the rest of the day exhausting himself by running on the boardwalk and swimming in the Atlantic. Luckily, school would start tomorrow.

* * *

The Columbia admissions application arrived on November 2, 1950, one day after an enormous army of Chinese "volunteers" reversed the tide of the Korean War and drove American and South Korean forces into a disorganized retreat. The *Daily Mirror* headline was one word: "**ROUT!**" Below it was a picture of four bedraggled GIs, their faces wrapped in brown scarves, trying to push a 105 millimeter howitzer through knee-deep mud.

He was tempted to throw the Columbia envelope into the garbage. How could he apply to college when his country — the country his father was ready to die for — was losing its new war, and when Stalin (who, according to the *Journal American*, had orchestrated the Korean War) was arresting Jews on trumped-up charges of "anti-Soviet activity"? He should enlist and make his father proud — be done with Max, and escape both his deceptions of Sibyl and her increasingly volatile mood swings. And if he joined the Marines, his uniform and hand-to-hand combat training should shut Bernie up forever.

The idea was crazy for more reasons than he could enumerate, including the fact that he didn't want to lose his life to a Chinese bayonet. Moreover, because he was only seventeen, he would need his mother's permission to enlist, and he wasn't going to ask her for anything. But in July, when he turned eighteen, he wouldn't need anybody's permission.

He plucked the application out of the Columbia envelope and found the item that concerned him: "24 — If admitted to Columbia, will you need financial aid to attend? ____ YES ____ NO. (If yes, a scholarship request form will be sent.)"

Paul couldn't check either Yes or No. If he checked Yes, Miss Warren, the School's College Advisor who reviewed all applications, would tell her friend, Mrs. Heider, Sibyl's aunt, and Sibyl would learn that Paul's father had not left insurance to pay Paul's college tuition — that he had left nothing and Paul had been lying to her since the day they met.

And checking Yes didn't guarantee a Columbia scholarship. While his grades were probably high enough to overcome the school's quota for Jews, a scholarship was something else. There was surely no shortage of poor New York Jewish boys, as smart and determined as he was, who wanted financial aid from the city's most prestigious college. He could lose the competition, just as his father had lost the swimming competition.

If he checked No, that meant money from Max's diamonds and all that went with it, including having to call his mother and relive the sight of Max's key as it was swallowed by the Atlantic Ocean.

Queens College, an excellent public commuter college, wasn't a good option either; it would both reveal his lie to Sibyl and condemn him to four more years with Grandpa. The least awful choice might be to do nothing and let himself be drafted, or to join the Marines.

And then a third option presented itself: One week after the Columbia application arrived, his mother came down from Rochester, unannounced, to visit Ruthie who was, in his mother's words, "having an operation for a woman's problem. Keep it confidential." While his mother was in the living room, speaking Yiddish with his grandparents, Paul saw her address book on her bedroom bureau. As if a light switch was suddenly turned on, *Greenberg/Montreal*, names on Max's note, flashed in his head. Without pause, thought or guilt, he went into the bedroom, opened the address book, found a K. Greenberg on Rue Lavoie, Montreal, and wrote the phone number on his palm.

A plan seemed to formulate itself. He would call K. Greenberg and report that on the night Max died, he had showed Paul a key and had told him that on the next day he would give him that key along with an explanation of how to use it to obtain diamonds for his education. Paul would tell K. Greenberg that Max had then put the key in his pocket, and it now must be at the bottom of the ocean. (The story would have bits of truth in it.) In return for lending him the money for Columbia tuition, Paul would furnish K. Greenberg with an affidavit (a word he knew from *30 Days to a More Powerful Vocabulary*) that a Swiss lawyer could use to recover the contents of the Swiss deposit box. A wild idea, but he would refine it. Faced with the Columbia application, he had to try.

The next day, he went directly from school to Central Avenue in Far Rockaway and changed a twenty dollar bill into coins at a bank he had never entered before. From there, he went to a phone booth in the Far Rockaway Long Island Railroad station and placed the first long distance call he had ever made.

"Hello, who is this?"

"Is Mr. Greenberg there?"

"My husband's dead. Who is this?"

An obstacle — but easy to overcome. "I'm a cousin of Max Hartman who knew—"

"That *mamzer*! He murdered my husband! How dare you call me — you, another Hartman?"

A greater obstacle, but Paul was the son of a man who taught lifeguards and the roommate of a man who survived Auschwitz. Just last summer, he had saved two women from drowning. He could get Mrs. K. Greenberg to go along with his plan. "Max died over two years ago."

"I hope he suffered. You speak Yiddish?" Her accent was thicker.

"*A bisel.* Only a *bisel.* English is better."

"Yiddish is better for cursing. Hell is too good for Mr. Max Hartman." He could hear her angry breathing. The phone booth became suddenly hot. "What do you want from me?" she continued. "I don't know details. None of us talk details about those terrible things, not even me. And thanks to Kalman, I spent the war hidden by nuns."

"Did you know . . . ?" Paul told himself to keep quiet.

"Did I know Max? He's lucky I didn't. Kalman thought Max would get him killed by the SS in Auschwitz — Max was their pal —

and, then after the war, by the anti-Semite Polack partisans. Or maybe Max would kill him himself so he wouldn't have to share nothing."

Not the Max I knew, Paul assured himself. But he knew nothing about the Max he knew — nothing about any of them. But only quitters quit.

"Can I come up to see you?" he whispered into the receiver although there was nobody who could hear him. "I think there's a box in Switzerland where Max — "

"No box!" Mrs. Greenberg screeched. "A box killed him!"

"I don't understand."

"One box is enough!" She paused and then repeated "Enough!" stretching out the "F" sound at the word's end. "The police — the Royal Mounties no less, but not on horses — arrested my husband because, as a favor, Max got Kalman to rent a bank box in Kalman's name because Kalman had Canadian immigration papers and Max didn't. My husband, whose got a soft spot for every *gonnif* in the world, particularly if he's Jewish or Irish, does it." She paused and Paul pictured her dabbing her eyes.

"Then," Mrs. Greenberg continued, the agitation in her voice mounting, "the Royal Mounties show up to lock him up and ask questions about the box. They tell us there's smuggled diamonds in it. We tell them we don't know from diamonds and Kalman was just doing Max a favor with the bank. The truth! On my mother's grave, the truth."

Paul searched for words to stop her, but found none.

"In the middle of the questions, he tells them he's got a chest pain but they don't pay no attention. An hour later . . . " She paused, weeping, and blew her nose. "The Nazis and Auschwitz didn't kill him, but your beloved cousin Max and the Royal Mounties did."

Mrs. Greenberg seemed to be waiting for a response, but Paul could think of nothing except the thumping of his heart. Finally, Mrs. Greenberg spoke again. "What's your name? Where — "

Paul tried to hang up, but his hand shook so badly that he kept missing the receiver cradle. Finally, he used two hands and succeeded.

* * *

On the Green Bus returning from Far Rockaway, Paul berated himself. His plan was a desperate kid's fantasy that could put a spotlight on Max's diamonds and land his mother in jail. Max wanted him to use the diamonds for college. Why fight it?

How did Max get the diamonds? Paul wondered. He surely didn't find them at the end of a rainbow. *No!* Paul ordered himself. If he questioned any relative, did research or let his imagination run loose, his life would be consumed by the diamonds' history while the Columbia dilemma remained unresolved. The facts, if he could ever learn them, would make things worse — perhaps drive him crazy.

He needed another phone booth where he wouldn't be seen or heard, and he settled on the Long Island Railroad elevated station at Sixty-ninth Street in Arverne. From the bus, he went directly to the LIRR concrete platform which was the highest structure for blocks. Once on it, Paul realized that by turning in a circle he could see most of the places — ocean, boardwalk, houses, grocery store, Playland — where the defining deaths, lives, and longings of his seventeen years had occurred. He resolved to look only at the phone booth and his shoes. After Mrs. Kalman Greenberg, all that mattered was to get away from everyone and every place that had made the Columbia application a Hobson's choice — as far and as soon as possible.

Jack answered the phone: "I-J Jewelers."

Why hadn't he anticipated this? "It's Paul."

"I don't think you should talk to her now. She's too upset."

Paul tensed. Did Jack know about his call to K. Greenberg? He should have anticipated that as well. "She's my mother." Paul looked around and saw a thin Negro man on the platform. Was he the one who had seen Max jump? He'd have to speak more softly. "You have no right to stop me from talking to my mother."

"Maybe you should remember more often who she is."

Jack had never before spoken to him harshly. Ever since the night they first shared the big bedroom, their conversations had been an exchange of platitudes.

"Look," Jack said in a softer voice. "We — your mother and me — we just got off the phone with Frieda Greenberg."

Paul managed to say, "Who's she?"

"Okay, we'll do it your way, so just listen. Frieda's dumb, mean and angry — *beyz vi a kishef-makherin* — and you shouldn't talk to her or anybody else about the diamonds without speaking to me first."

"Can I speak to my mother?"

"She'll just cry and, whatever you say, you'll make her more miserable. Frieda already did a job on her. Why don't you just tell me why you're calling, and I'll speak to her when she's calmer. I'm not a monster, Paul. She wants what's best for you, and I want what she wants."

Strange — the phone booth in the Far Rockaway station had been an oven, but this one was a refrigerator. "I know you're not a monster, but this is between my mother and me."

"Will you tell her you didn't speak to Frieda Greenberg?"

Paul swallowed. "It's about . . ." He couldn't complete the sentence.

"Do you want to ask whether she can help you pay tuition for a private college?"

Paul couldn't tell whether he was furious, appreciative or both. "You read my mind."

"Why else would you call Frieda?" Jack paused, then continued. "Don't answer. It's best not to talk about it now. Frieda thinks the police are tapping everybody's phone. In her mind, there's only one police force in the whole world; it includes the Royal Mounties, FBI, Gestapo, Scotland Yard, KGB, and its main job, all the police every place, is to get the Jews — even in Israel where they arrested her husband on some phony smuggling charge, she says. She's crazy, but sometimes I wonder."

"Tuition."

Jack made a sound somewhere between a cough and a laugh. "I'm getting off track because the answer's not what anybody wants."

"Please!"

"Your mother wants to help you; this I promise." Paul pictured Jack nodding his head slowly. "Believe it or not, I do too. But there are problems. One guy's suspicious of us. Another may be trying some blackmail. Plus we have to make the jewelry store modern."

Paul had to know: Money for Columbia tuition or not? Even bad news was better than uncertainty.

Jack saved him from having to ask the question directly. "Even though Max made everything so hard, and Frieda — please don't talk to her no more — and Frieda's such a pain in the *tuchas*, I think your mother and me will work everything out and you'll get what you need. I really do. But if I was you, I'd make another plan too."

Paul made another plan — the Marines.

* * *

He called his mother on the day after Thanksgiving, intending to say nothing about Max, Jack, Daddy, diamonds, money, or college. That left only talk about Sibyl, turkey and their standard blather — unless of course, she volunteered the news that could determine the next four years of his life. He told her that the dinner at Sibyl's Aunt Dotty's "was very nice," although Sibyl had sat at the table silently sulking, stirring herself to talk only when she answered a question addressed to Paul — "Columbia, I hope; he's a shoo-in, but he won't talk about it." — and then returned to her silence.

Finally, his mother dropped a hint. "Would Sibyl consider the Eastman School of Music in Rochester? It's supposed to be good for flute. Then, if you went to the University of Rochester here, you wouldn't have to pay room and board. The four of us could be like a family."

Paul counted to seven, to keep his alarm out of his voice. "She wants to study with Charles Crowell at Juilliard. She says he's the best flute teacher anyplace."

"So you want to go to Columbia?"

"I hope so."

She waited a few moments before responding. "Jack's making progress, but you don't need specifics. It's long distance and expensive. Is Grandma there?"

* * *

On December 31, which marked the third anniversary of 53927 being branded inside his own head, Paul sat in his room completing the Columbia application — everything except Item 24: "Will you need financial aid?" Maybe his decision to check No, which left him at his mother's mercy, was too hasty. He could check Yes and tell Sibyl that his mother and Jack had used his father's insurance money for the Rochester jewelry store. He could go on to "explain" that as the money was no longer there, he was applying for a Columbia scholarship. But one lie demands another. *That's terrible,* Sibyl might say. *Did you tell them they had no right?* Bullshit begets bullshit, and things were already too complex.

He hammered the top of his head with his fist and, when the room stopped spinning, checked No. He'd bring the completed application to his college advisor on January 2, the first school day after vacation. If he waited any longer, he'd only agonize more. His mother would give him the money. She had to.

Nevertheless, when she came to New York in January and he told her he had applied to Columbia, she stared blankly over his shoulder and, in a flat voice, said, "That's nice. You deserve to get in."

Is that all? Paul wondered. Wasn't she his mother?

In March, when he called Rochester to wish her a happy birthday, she asked if he had "heard from any colleges."

"I got an acceptance from Columbia today."

"That's wonderful. Daddy would be so proud."

"I'm going to tell them yes."

She didn't respond right away, and Paul silently pleaded with her: *Please! Can I go to Columbia or should I join the Marines? Answer me — I'm your only child.*

She finally spoke. "That's good. It's a fine school. Nice campus."

"Mom!"

"Maybe . . . There shouldn't be any problem." Some life had returned to her voice. "We still don't have all of it . . . . You know, everything from Max . . ."

It was her birthday and he couldn't prod her any more. Besides, there would have been plenty of money if he hadn't thrown the key away. He made a fist to pound his head, but then opened it; his head already hurt.

"Max wanted a private school for you."

Paul felt his mother looking directly at him. She was still beautiful. "And we should get ourselves straightened out soon. But, just in case, can you still apply to Queens College?"

"I'll get an application."

* * *

He didn't send for a Queens College application, but he did go to the post office to pick up a Marine Corps recruitment brochure. He knew, of course, that nice Jewish boys didn't become Marines, but that was a reason to enlist. And Korea was as far away as he could get.

A long folding table at the side wall of the post office held several piles of brochures, fliers and forms — Army, Navy, Coast Guard, Passport Applications, Special Delivery Mail, "Rodent Prevention," "Dangerous Plants." The two neatest piles were Marine brochures. One showed a Marine sergeant standing as tall and straight as a human could stand and wearing a dress blues uniform that seemed glued to his skin. Behind his head in bright red letters was the word "READY". Across his waist, was the invitation:

JOIN
U.S. MARINES
1775 * * * 176th Anniversary * * * 1951

If he stepped forward as the sergeant's urged, he would be part of an elite fighting force that had served his father's chosen country from its very beginning — so much more than an immigrant boy from a Yiddish-speaking home.

The cover of the other brochure was much less colorful. Against a brown and gray background that reminded him of the Olymp slaves' snapshot, a young man in a brown tee shirt grimaced in pain and determination. The message was spelled out in block yellow letters —

WE'D PROMISE YOU
SLEEP DEPRIVATION,
MENTAL TORMENT,
AND MUSCLES SO
SORE YOU'LL PUKE
But we don't like to sugarcoat things
MARINES
(The few and the proud)

He could do it. "Hartman has heart," Coach Barry had said, and Paul would ask the coach to let him participate in the afternoon physical fitness program he ran for real jocks. Paul would be in perfect shape before boot camp began. If he did well there — and he would — they might even ask him to go to Officers' Candidate School. Bernie wouldn't dare pinch the cheek of a Marine lieutenant. Even his grandfather would look at him with awe.

The nearest recruiting office was in Far Rockaway. He could speak to the recruiters today. But what would he say? That he might join in four months if his mother didn't give him money for Columbia? Marines aren't tentative. They want men who act, not agonize. He put the brochures back on the table, taking care to keep the two piles as neat as he had found them.

* * *

Paul vowed not to raise the subject of college with his mother or Jack. Either she would do what Max wanted for him or he would enlist in the Marines on July 19th, the day after his eighteenth birthday. The Army Recruiting Sergeant had laughed at his father when he tried to enlist, but the Marines would welcome Paul. He would tell nobody until he was on his way to boot camp at Parris Island. No apology, no explanation. He would visit a prostitute as soon as boot camp ended. Enough of the *everything but* that had restrained him with Sibyl.

His birthday came and went without word from his mother about tuition, but he deferred enlisting until September. Columbia was still possible, and the summer was too enjoyable to disrupt. He and Sibyl had returned to the Berkshires — Sibyl as a Tanglewood student, Paul as a lifeguard at a nearby resort. On their first night there, he told her (untruthfully) that he had sent Columbia his tuition deposit; from that point forward, her funks abated and her passion (subject to *everything but*) soared.

A month before Paul was scheduled to start Columbia, his mother called him at the Lifeguard Shed.

"I'm not supposed to get calls here. I can't talk, but I can listen."

"I think we worked it out. We had problems at the store — modernize or close up — and then . . . This man who was helping . . . you know. He got sick. So Cousin Bernie — "

"Maybe we shouldn't talk on the phone."

"You're right. I'm sorry. But Bernie's been so helpful . . . He can give you what you need until we have the cash."

Paul closed his eyes. Over the past few years, fat Bernie had become muscular Bernie, more powerful than anyone in Coach Barry's fitness program, oozing wealth from his diamond pinkie ring to the weight room he had installed in his basement. In June, at a cousin's funeral, he had told Paul, "Only *schmucks* need college to get ahead. Good friends and respect are better. But I guess you want to impress your girlfriend. She's spooky, but she's got sweet little tits."

Paul brought the telephone mouthpiece to his lips and spoke softly, "I don't want to get involved with Bernie."

"Can you wait till I come down for *Yom Kippur*?"

Paul did some quick calculations. "If I buy used books and get enough private swim lessons, I should be able to make the deposit and first tuition payment. But that's all."

"Maybe we could go to *shul* together. Rabbi Pordy still keeps the men separate from the women, but it would be nice if we walked in and out together."

"You're not going to give me money in *shul*, are you? On *Yom Kippur*?" Paul felt the nastiness of his words. "I'm sorry Mom. It's just . . . the whole thing."

"Max wanted you to have a good education." She sounded as if she had taken offense. "Whatever he did, it's nothing compared to what they did to him. We're only trying to give you what you deserve."

* * *

Paul and his mother spent all of *Yom Kippur* in synagogue on opposite sides of the *mekhista*, the curtain separating men from women. He wondered whether he would have gone if it meant sitting next to her.

An hour after sundown, while the two of them were alone in the kitchen breaking their fasts, his mother handed him an envelope. *Thick,* Paul thought; *cash, not a check. Good.*

"There's everything you need, plus some. It shouldn't get delayed again."

"Thanks." Paul stuck the envelope inside his shirt and looked directly at his mother. She looked younger than when she had moved to Rochester, but her sad eyes reflected a life of accumulated losses — a young husband she had loved since childhood, the home of her youth, most of the guests in her wedding portrait, a son who kept his distance, a suitor who killed himself after she rejected him. "Thanks," Paul repeated. "After I said *Kaddish* for Daddy, I said it again for Max, even though neither of them believed in it."

"So did I. It's a prayer for the dead, but you say it for the living, too."

She put her hand against his cheek. It was cold, but he willed himself to stay still. "It's cash," she whispered. "This man who was hiding the box for Max just gave it to us when he realized that Jack was Jacob Rosenzweig. Jack won't talk about it, but he helped some of the other prisoners even though it could have cost him his life. If you want, Bernie can give you tips on how to handle it so the government don't ask questions."

Paul closed his eyes, "Ma, please. *Yom Kippur* just ended."

His mother stroked his cheek again. "I don't blame you for not wanting to talk to Bernie. God knows what he's doing."

The phone rang in the living room, and Paul nearly jumped from his chair. It was Sibyl. Her father's check for the mortgage payment had bounced. "Please, Paul," Sibyl urged. "My mother's taken a strong sedative, and I'm afraid to be alone with her."

"I'll come over now."

"Don't say anything to your mother. In fact, don't let my mother know you know."

"Sure." Another deception, but this one was easy and harmless.

"Bring your clarinet."

Back in the kitchen, Paul stammered for an explanation to give his mother, but she just waved at him. "Make your bus. I can tell it's important. One thing, though, before you go."

Paul braced for a toxic revelation about Max or Bernie or Jack or Frieda Greenberg, maybe even his father. "What?"

"The money's still under your shirt. Hide it someplace safe."

Suddenly, he felt the envelope of cash clinging to his skin. The envelope, he realized wasn't touching his skin — it was between his dress shirt and his tee shirt. But that made no difference. It was part of him.

CHAPTER 7

At eight a.m. on September 13, 1954, an hour before Paul's first class of his final year at Columbia, he heard a knock on his door. "Phone. Your girlfriend." Sibyl had never before called this early.

As he walked to the pay phone in the dormitory hallway, Paul thought back to the call from his mother one day before the first class of his final year at Far Rockaway High School when she reported that she had married Jack and would live in Rochester. Today's call could be worse. Sibyl might deliver the ultimatum he feared: Commit to marriage or say goodbye. He wasn't sure he loved her, but he was desperate for her passion; he wasn't ready for a lifetime commitment, but, without her, he had nobody. And he no longer had a home — not even Rockaway.

Two days earlier, he had gone to the Arverne apartment to pick up some clothing and had made the mistake of arriving while his grandparents were there. Grandma greeted him effusively. His grandfather, without a word, went into the living room. Grandma shrugged helplessly and followed him.

Almost immediately, the old man began berating her in Yiddish, and Paul fled to his bedroom. But he hadn't escaped. The volume and vehemence of the tirade escalated and, like a tidal wave, slammed through walls and doors. Paul had made no effort to understand the Yiddish, but then his grandfather, suddenly and surprisingly, switched to English.

"Your grandson, he just takes; not even thank you. Too good for us. Soon he'll stop being a Jew. Tell my darling daughter — if she is my daughter — tell her that while she runs away to make sure she has a man on top of her — "

"*Shvagg!* Shut up!" a voice roared, and Paul realized it was his own voice. He knew what he wanted to say — *I hope she's not your daughter because then I wouldn't be your grandson.* He would say it to his face. If only he could say it in Yiddish.

He had one foot in the living room when his grandmother stumbled forward and clutched his shirtsleeves.

"Please, Paul," she pleaded with both her voice and eyes. "Grandpa don't mean it. He loves your mother — you too — but he don't know how to show it. And he never got used to America. In Europe, he was — " Paul put his arms around her and she buried her head in his chest. "Here, greenhorns . . . safe from the Nazis, but lost." Her voice was muffled by his shirt. "Ashamed of how we speak English. Ashamed to speak Yiddish — our language — if there's *goyim* around. And soon, Family Foods — a supermarket like they have in Far Rockaway with fancy lights and big advertisements . . . We'll have to take from your mother even more."

As she begged, Paul looked past her head to lock eyes with his grandfather — an ancient man, his face and beard yellowing, standing by a streaked window staring at nothing. The lost ghost-like look of Max. As long as the old man lived here, Paul wouldn't return.

Now, in the hallway of the Columbia dorms, he lifted the phone to his ear, but waited for Grandpa's image to dissolve before saying, "Hello."

"I'm sorry to call so early, but I had to get you before you get totally wrapped up in your honors thesis." Sibyl spoke crisply, emphasizing each consonant. "Something has come up and I have to talk to you this evening. We can meet at the gallery downtown where I'm playing." Before Paul could reply, she went on. "It can't be on the phone, it can't wait, and it can't be sooner." She took a breath. "My mother wants me to go with her to the lawyer in the morning — take sides in the divorce. She says she'll have a breakdown if I'm not with her. I have a forty-eight-year-old child, and I'm not even engaged."

"Sure," Paul said. Any other answer might bring on the ultimatum.

"I'm sorry, but I'm committed." She paused and then emphatically said, "No! I want to play. Women painters and sculptors are taking a stand, and I want to be part of it."

"What do you mean, taking a stand?"

"It's an all-woman show in one of the Tenth Street galleries — cooperatives set up by artists who are trying new things and can't get into the establishment galleries uptown. Women artists especially. One of them, Danielle Donat, was Brancusi's best student. Remember, we saw his sculptures at MOMA last Fall? Shiny surfaces."

"Yes," Paul answered, although he remembered the art less than his own concern. Charles Crowling, Sibyl's flute teacher, had just announced that he would be leaving Juilliard to return home to London, and Paul feared she would follow him. Although he had a physics quiz the next day, Paul had stayed with her until the museum closed, reminding her by his presence of his devotion and the good life they shared in New York.

"Well," Sibyl continued, "I met Danielle a few days ago. She said Brancusi never lifted a finger to help her career, but he helped some male students who weren't as good. She said the co-op's showing work by up-and-coming women artists like her and by more established women artists such as Lee Krasner — she's the wife of Jackson Pollock. Danielle feels that Lee put all her energy into Pollock at the price of her own art. And then he showed his appreciation by sleeping with everybody in sight."

"What's the address?"

* * *

The Ten/Four Gallery was, as Paul expected, located at the corner of Tenth Street and Fourth Avenue. Taped above the elevator buttons was a mimeographed flier —

OUR ART — OUR STATEMENT
Emerging Women Artists

Five women were named, including Krasner and Danielle Donat. After class, Paul had gone to the Fine Arts Library where he looked at photographs of Krasner's and Brancusi's works. There were no photographs of Donat's.

The small elevator inched upward. What the hell was Sibyl going to tell him? It couldn't possibly be good news.

When the elevator door opened, he stepped into a different world — one framed by high white walls and a floor so varnished he could slip on it. Sixty or so people milled around — from disheveled grad school students to Wall Street brokers; from a woman with unshaved legs wearing combat boots to an Audrey Hepburn look-alike wearing almost nothing. Most held paper cups of wine; several were nibbling cheese cubes on toothpicks; only a few were looking at the art. As he wound through the crowd looking for Sibyl, the number and diversity of the paintings cheered him. On the wall behind him, big blobs of primary colors; on another, straight-edged black and white geometric figures running in and out of each other, almost ready to break loose from the canvas. He recognized Lee Krasner's work on the opposite wall, and felt drawn to an enormous painting (maybe part collage) that had been reproduced in one of the contemporary art textbooks he had skimmed earlier in the day — a few subtle colors and shapes, mostly vertical strips of brownish pink, woven together into a complex yet soothing whole. He wondered what made it beautiful.

A flute played in the far corner, a classical piece he had heard but couldn't identify. Something was missing in the music. Paul listened carefully and realized what it was — no *neshome*. The tone and rhythm were fine, but there was none of the indefinable warmth that marked Sibyl's playing. Please don't let it be her. He went toward the music, but the flutist was blocked by the back of an enormous man in a checkered flannel shirt. Paul seized a cup of wine from the tray floating by him and finished it in one gulp. The flannel back swayed with the melody, and Paul saw Sibyl playing with wide-open eyes.

He moved closer to her, but so did the giant who seemed far more interested in the flutist than her music. Two women alongside the giant chattered in loud whispers. *Shut up*, Paul wanted to tell them. *Don't you hear her playing?* The giant turned. He was at least six-and-a-half feet tall with a reddish beard that ended halfway down his barrel chest. *Paul Bunyan.*

One of the women — a little thing in a tan gabardine skirt — tittered. Paul silently urged the giant to seize her by the waist and lift her, King Kong style, into the air; maybe even devour her in three big bites, gabardine and all, so Sibyl could see what a brute he was. The giant, however, merely put his finger to his lips, and the women left. Sibyl nodded in gratitude, but her eyes remained as lifeless as her music. Paul went to the man's side, directly in front of Sibyl, and mouthed "I love you." She looked at him as if they were strangers.

When Sibyl finished the piece, the giant beat his hands together. Paul stepped between them. "Are you okay?" he mouthed, but she didn't seem to understand him. "I can see something is wrong," he said. "What did you want to tell me?"

"Not here. Not now."

Paul gripped her forearm. "What's going on? You said . . ."

He felt a weight on his shoulder, and then a vise squeezing it. "Is he bothering you, Sibyl?" The giant's voice was surprisingly high-pitched.

Sibyl stood and took Paul's hand. The vise disappeared. "It's all right, Boris. I invited him here. We've been going together since high school."

Ignoring the giant, Paul asked her, "Are you okay? You were playing without moving."

She looked at him in both surprise and anger. Paul had never before criticized her playing. Then she whispered in his ear, pausing every few words to catch her breath. "I was offered a job with the Thames Woodwind Ensemble in London, and I can probably study at the Royal

Academy. Reginald Smith, the conductor, wants me to rehearse with them in New York and go back with them on Sunday. I have to let them know by noon tomorrow."

Whoa, Paul thought. *Slow down*. The black geometric forms, now free of their frames, were whizzing by his head.

Sibyl tugged at Paul's sleeve, and said to Boris — "We'll be back in a few moments." She led Paul to the opposite end of the gallery where they stood among shiny sculptures that resembled the work of Brancusi but, to Paul, weren't as gripping. Obviously, a poor imitation by Danielle Dorot. No wonder Brancusi hadn't promoted her career.

Who is that big guy? Paul wanted to ask but knew better. "Tell me."

Reginald was Boris's cousin, Sibyl told him, and both of them had heard her play at Juilliard. "Reginald said I should study at the Royal. With Crowell there, it's the best place for flute. He says I should make the move right away because one of his flutists is pregnant, and I would be a good replacement. He joked that I even have an English name so I'd fit in fine." A strand of her long hair slipped from her back to the front of her shoulder, and she began to pull on it as if it were a church bell. "Boris came from Seattle to see his cousin and hear the Thames. He'll lie about my performance here — say I sounded even better than at Juilliard." She seemed close to tears.

"You never told me about any of this."

"I started to yesterday, but you just were all caught up in telling me how Professor Bassiter wanted you to teach college instead of going to law school."

He saw Sibyl reflected in one of the sculptures — her curves were longer and gentler in the metal, her hair blacker. He closed his eyes, but his longing for her deepened. "I'll be a better listener, I promise. But what about us?" He opened his eyes and saw that hers were closed.

"It's all so undecided. You keep saying you don't know what to do next year."

"Sibyl darling," he made himself say. "It's only September." She didn't respond, and Paul decided to play a trump card. "What about your mother? Would she be okay with you in England now that your father may move in with whatever-her-name-is?"

Sibyl opened her eyes. They, too, had become darker. "Her name is Holly. My mother says I should go — learn from her mistakes."

Not a trump. A joker.

Boris materialized, looking at his watch. "Danielle says your playing is lovely."

"Reginald says that lovely is praise for a cucumber sandwich," Sibyl retorted.

Paul had never seen a cucumber sandwich, and he doubted that anyone in Rockaway, even Sibyl's mother, had ever eaten one.

"Time for more Bach," Sibyl continued. "Introduce yourselves." She gestured at the two young men. "Paul, clarinet, my boyfriend, I think, but he doesn't like making things official. Boris, piano, Reginald's handler." She turned and strode back to the music stand.

Before Sibyl had taken two steps, Boris asked, "What did she tell you?"

"She told me Reginald offered her a job."

"More than a job," Boris said sneeringly. "A career plan any serious flutist would grab."

As Paul struggled for a response, Boris looked into the crowd and clapped his hands. "Oh my God, Lee's here. Everyone thought she'd stay in Springs because she was so upset by Jackson's boozing and screwing. Maybe de Kooning will show up. His wife's a painter too."

Paul recognized Krasner from the clippings. She was a *mieskeit* (one of the few words in his Yiddish vocabulary), a poor, ugly Jewish girl from Brooklyn whose parents couldn't afford an orthodontist or a nose job.

"You're surprised by how she looks?" Boris let out a high pitched laugh, almost a cackle. "Maybe if she had her teeth fixed, Pollock — "

"I'm here to see art, not teeth."

Boris lowered his head, reminding Paul who was bigger. "You're not here to see art. You're here to string Sibyl along so she misses the best opportunity she may ever have." He frowned, stood up straight, and walked towards Krasner.

Paul looked at Sibyl across the room, pointing her flute at the floor and clicking the keys rapidly — something else he had never before seen. The pull of London against their years together. The pull of music — "all I ever wanted," she had told him — against . . . Against what? Quickly, he made his way through the crowd.

He spoke into her ear. "Nothing's undecided. I want to go to law school, but I want to marry you first."

As if he hadn't spoken, Sibyl raised the flute to her lips and began playing Bach. She sat straight, moving only her fingers. Paul dropped to his knees — the hell with how it looked — and pleaded, "*Neshome*. Feel the music."

She kept playing and sat even straighter. "I love you," Paul whispered. "We can get married in December, during Christmas vacation."

Sibyl rose, and he did too. Where would he go for Thanksgiving dinner if she left him? Where would he sleep during Christmas break? "You can be a wife and a performing musician," he murmured to her, careful not to say *mother*. "If I go to Harvard, you can go to the New England Conservatory. Most of the Tanglewood musicians are from Boston."

She closed her eyes and began to sway. Without missing a beat, she switched from Bach to "Waltz of the Flowers."

The inevitable — what they had both wanted from the very first grocery delivery.

Paul stepped back and listened as she completed the piece. She put down her flute and kissed Paul on the forehead. "Danielle told me to go after this set. The place is so crowded, nobody can hear the music anyway."

Minutes later, they were in the elevator kissing, held together by a passion Paul hadn't felt in months. When they reached the ground floor, she pulled him out of the building and toward Fourth Avenue, her hair floating behind her.

"Wave for that taxi on the corner," she shouted. "I don't want to let go of you, and I can't wave with my flute case."

A taxi stopped, and she pushed him in. "Seventeenth and Seventh, across from Barney's," she told the driver.

"Where are we going?" Paul asked.

"Danielle's new apartment," Sibyl answered breathlessly. "She's driving to New Haven."

"I thought you wanted — "

"That was then. Now it's really happening."

Again, things were moving too fast, but this time they were taking him to where he wanted to be. He felt desperate — for the license; the fucking (finally!); their own address, separate from families they couldn't bear; and a partner who would always be there. She slid his hand under her skirt and up her thigh. Her underpants were damp.

* * *

Over the years, they had brought each other to climax many times in various ways, but it was nothing like this. There was no word to describe it. *Before*, the gradual peeling away of the world. *During*, a joyous tension mounting beyond where it could mount any further and then, after mounting still more, exploding into release before exploding again. *After,* a peace beyond his comprehension. Two people could not have been closer. They were literally joined below the waist in love, flesh of my flesh, bone of my bone, as Adam and Eve had been before they were separated — separated so they could join together again. Lying in a half-furnished apartment that smelled of fresh paint and promise, alongside a young woman who had shared with him the greatest pleasure he had ever experienced and who would accompany him through life, Paul decided that there must be a God. Random selection could never have produced something this wonderful.

But the real world continued to exist. In the morning, while Paul dressed, Sibyl sat in bed with the blanket pulled up to her neck, telling him about the Thames conductor: "Reginald Smith. Remember the name — a genius. He'll have a major orchestra before he's thirty-five. Sleeps around, but it doesn't interfere with his musical judgments. He never tried a thing with me. Just offered me a job out of the blue."

Paul tied his shoelaces tightly. "You're not sorry about London, are you?"

"You're better for my music than Reg or the Royal."

Now it's Reg — and he'll be in New York for five more days. The previous evening, she had switched, in a matter of seconds, from a controlled Bach to a sensuous Tchaikovsky. Over the next few days, she could switch again, and fly off to London. She often switched sides between her parents. ("He treats her like dirt, and I'm going to help her squeeze him dry." Or, "She's a cold conniver, and I'm going to be there for him.") Her motives mystified him. But last night!

A diamond ring, Paul thought — *and right away*! Seal the engagement before Reg could make a move. That, of course, meant being more beholden to Max and his mother, but he had made that choice years ago. And, once things were settled, he would tell Sibyl everything.

* * *

That afternoon, he called the Rochester jewelry store from his dorm phone booth and told his mother, as soon as she answered, "Sibyl and I are getting married in December."

"You're smart to do it soon," she said immediately, "before she joins some orchestra in Timbuktu or her mother manages to make trouble between you."

So much for the joyous *mazel tov* he had been anticipating. And she wasn't through: "If you're married in law school, you'll be able to concentrate better and get better grades. One of our customers — a big lawyer here — said it's still hard for Jewish boys to get a good law job, even from the best schools, unless they have top grades. And Bernie says if you're married, he can practically guarantee you won't be drafted."

"Keep Bernie out of it. I'm not getting married to stay out of the Army."

"Of course not."

"Or to get good grades."

"Of course not."

"I'm getting married because . . ." Paul had to think. He couldn't mention Reginald or his self-willed exile from the Arverne apartment. "Because I love her."

"Of course that's the reason."

"Isn't that why you and Daddy got married?" Paul demanded.

To Paul's surprise, his mother paused before answering. "Yes, but that was special and I was *meshuga*." Paul could hear her laughing to herself. "I loved him since I was a little girl, even before there was a Czechoslovakia. I cried at his *bar mitzvah* I loved him so much. Grandma said she would lock me in the cellar with the potatoes if I kept carrying on. She was afraid I would make a scandal. Maybe I shouldn't tell you all this."

How had he lived with her all these years and understood so little about her?

"Paul," his mother said tentatively.

Her tone made him suspicious. "What?"

"I think you should give her a nice diamond engagement ring."

She had a hidden agenda. "Sibyl doesn't want one."

"Don't be ridiculous."

"She doesn't." He *was* being ridiculous, but he couldn't help himself.

"Every girl does. I told Daddy I didn't want one — the only time I lied to him — but he had absolutely no money. If he thought I wanted one, he would have pawned Grandma Gittel's false teeth. Put it on Sibyl's finger before they hand her a ticket for Timbuktu."

How could he respond when she was reading his mind — and was so right?

"You know, Sibyl and me," his mother continued, "we talk. Women need other women to talk to. I've got Grandma and Ruthie, but she's got nobody — certainly not her mother."

"I know."

"I can't give you exact words, but I get the feeling she was tempted by some music group that wants her. Not in Timbuktu, but not in America either."

No time to think, and nothing to think about. "Can you lend me money for a ring?"

Before she spoke, Paul knew what his mother would say.

"Why buy? We got diamonds. Why sell one of ours to buy another that's not as nice?"

The phone booth was suddenly a box — like the pink GE refrigerator — and Paul was about to be trapped inside it. When Paul first placed the call, the booth had no particular odor, but now it was beginning to give off Max's smell of mold. It wasn't a coffin, Paul assured himself — too narrow and vertical — but the smell was leaving him little air to breathe.

"It's my ring for her," he nearly pleaded.

"Sure it's from you, but use one of the diamonds Max left." He could picture her at the other end of the phone: palms up, nodding her head while she spoke, as if she were trying to explain fractions to a slow child. Paul had not expected this. Money from Max's diamonds for tuition was one thing, but Max's diamond on Sibyl's finger for life? "Let me think about it."

"You don't need to think, Paulie," his mother said. "I know the perfect stone for Sibyl — very fine, but not big and showy. Nicely mounted. Refined like her."

Why not? Since Max gave him the Buffet, he had benefited from the diamonds in a variety of ways. "Thanks. When can I get it? The people from Timbuktu are still in New York."

"You can have it on her finger tomorrow. Maybe today. Ruthie has it in Woodmere."

"Ruthie?" he questioned, and then exclaimed, "Ruthie!"

"Oh my God!" His mother inhaled loudly. "I didn't mean to tell you."

Again, he anticipated what she was going to say, but he couldn't articulate it, even silently. "Is this the ring . . . Max . . . you?" He couldn't compose the question.

"There's nothing *wrong* with it." She stretched the word "wrong," turning it into a sob, and then began to speak rapidly, as if she were afraid Paul wouldn't let her finish. "He wanted to give it to me on the night before — the night I told him I couldn't marry him. I tried to say it nice, but it was still no. How could I say yes when . . . So many reasons."

Paul had to say something that made sense and consoled her. "You couldn't have imagined he would kill himself," he said, realizing as he spoke that it was easily imaginable. "You couldn't say yes just because . . . You can't marry somebody you don't love." But even after their six years together, even after last night's ecstasy, did he love Sibyl?

She spoke in a calmer voice. "When I finally went to bed on the night he died, I found the ring under my pillow with a note. Two words: 'Remember me.' This would be remembering." She inhaled, cleared her throat. "He would be happy to have a real musician wear it. And such a fine girl. Ruthie took the ring because she was afraid I'd flush it down the toilet."

"Did you want to flush it?"

"Never!" she nearly growled. "I owed Max to remember. Even when we needed money so bad to buy the store in Rochester and fix it up, Jack wouldn't consider selling that."

Jack! He had enough of his mother's love life. "Mom, forget about it. It's ghoulish. I appreciate that you want to help, but Max's ring is no way to start a marriage after we spent six years hiding him from her."

She didn't respond right away, and Paul couldn't contain his anger. "I wanted to tell her about him and about the diamonds on the day we met!" He worked to lower his voice; anyone walking in the hallway might hear. "When I came back from the boardwalk, you told me I couldn't . . . that people, including you, could go to jail. Do you remember?"

"Like yesterday," she whispered. "You wanted to tell the truth from the very beginning — like Daddy would do. I should've listened, but they all worked on me."

Paul opened the phone booth. He thought of the girl with the flute behind the screen door — of the young woman adjusting pillows last night so he could get right to the sweet spot.

"Someone wants the phone." Nobody was in sight, but he was too close to saying, *Yes Mother, they did work on you, and then you worked on me!*

"I have an idea," she said. "When are the people from Timbuktu leaving?"

"It's England. Sunday."

"Oh my God, Paulie, we have to move fast. That flute teacher, the one she thinks is so wonderful, who went back to England — "

"Charles Crowell."

"Crowell. He's in New York now giving a lecture and then going home. Sibyl told me."

Paul grasped her plan before she spelled it out. It was perfect: Get the ring on Sibyl's finger before Crowell, pied piper-like, could tempt her to England. Then, when the Brits were back home and Sibyl was immersed in wedding logistics, the two of them, mother and son, would tell her everything and convince her of the truth: Paul had resisted the deceptions from the beginning, but reluctantly went along in order to protect his mother.

Welcome to the family, Paul thought. "How angry do you think she'll be?" he asked his mother, fishing for reassurance.

"Not at you. She loves you, and I gave you no choice. Maybe at me she'll be mad, but not for too long. She wants a good woman friend — even a mother. Not as much as she wants you for a husband, but I'm part of the package too."

Paul had to get into the fresh fall air and run in joy along the Hudson River.

*   *   *

Two hours later, Paul, clutching the small box delivered by Woodmere Taxi, ran the three blocks to the I-House where Sibyl and other Juilliard women lived under supervision. Sibyl was alone in the sitting room waiting for him. When she saw the box, she exclaimed, "Oh my God! Is it . . .?"

"Yes."

She threw her arms around his neck. "I never expected . . . How did you . . . ?"

"Don't ask questions. Just enjoy it."

They sat on a small green Victorian couch and, together, picked at the flowered wrapping paper. Suddenly, Paul realized he had no idea what the ring looked like or where he supposedly bought it. No problem; Sibyl would believe whatever he said and, in a few days, she would know the whole story and love him all the more.

"I should have brought it unwrapped so I could kneel and put it on your finger."

"You still can." Her eyes and mouth opened wide together. "It's beautiful."

It was beautiful, an oval like her face. Paul knelt to put the ring on her finger, and saw that it was too small. He tried anyway, but it got stuck at Sibyl's knuckle. Why hadn't his mother thought of that? She owned a jewelry store.

"What size did you tell the jeweler?" Sibyl asked laughingly.

Paul, remaining on one knee, answered without hesitation: "I just drew a little circle. Let me have it back, I'll get it enlarged."

Sibyl jumped up and walked past Paul toward the staircase. She raised her left hand high. "Maybe in a few days. Today, you're not getting it off my finger."

"Where are you going?"

"To get some soap and try to push it where it belongs." Sibyl climbed a few stairs, and then stopped. "Give me five minutes so I can tell my mother I told you so."

* * *

Ruthie called the following afternoon to tell him that his grandmother had just died. His mother was, she said, "too upset to talk yet." Too upset to tell her son, Paul thought, but not her mobster cousin's wife. He wouldn't call his mother either.

There had been a chest pain Grandma called "indigestion," a sudden collapse, and death before the ambulance reached the hospital. Quick, as had happened with his father. He wished he could cry for her, but he knew he wouldn't. Grandma had always been kind to him, particularly when Grandpa had been awful or when Paul sat alone in the kitchen after his mother had moved to Rochester. But how could he cry for his grandmother when he hadn't cried for his father?

"She was a nice lady, Paulie, your grandmother was, and she loved you. It's a big loss for you, and I'm sorry."

He could feel her anguish. Ruthie, with all her makeup and jewelry, was more than the often plump, always pretty, woman a few steps behind Bernie. She was a nice person — and a separate person from her loud-mouthed, bullying husband. "Thank you," he managed to say.

"Everybody expected him to go first," Ruthie continued. "Your mother's upset, really upset, Paulie. It's not just she lost her mother, but your grandfather's saying she killed her and abandoned you by moving to Rochester, and he wouldn't go to the funeral if she did."

"She has to go."

"Bernie told the old man he'd have him put in an insane asylum right away — Today! — if he didn't behave. He said it in Yiddish, even though he hates Yiddish, like your father did, but he wanted to be sure there'd be no misunderstanding.

"The engagement!" she suddenly exclaimed. "*Mazel tov*!" She sang the Yiddish words. "I should have mentioned that first. Jewish law says that if a funeral parade and a wedding party meet at a crossroads, the funeral should stop so the wedding can go first." This was news to Paul.

"So," Ruthie continued, "even though the funeral's this week, I want to talk first about the wedding." Paul grew apprehensive about what was coming next although he had no idea what it might be. "I wish you'd let Bernie and me throw you a big wedding or at least a medium or small party," Ruthie said. "Jack and your mother will kick in. Nobody will know who's paying what so Sibyl's family won't be embarrassed. In our house would be best. Don't answer now unless the answer is yes because I don't want Bernie and you getting madder at each other."

Paul knew that the answer had to be *No thanks*, so he remained quiet, and Ruthie spoke again: "I know the story of the ring. Your mother told me on the night Max died. And I learned the two of you now plan to tell Sibyl the whole Max story."

"Yes," Paul said trying to match her stern tone. "If not now, when?"

"If not now, when?" Ruthie slowly repeated. "That's the third part of a three-part statement by the great teacher Hillel, but I'm not going to debate Talmud with you because you don't know anything."

Paul was surprised. Ruthie had more religious education than he had realized.

"But since you brought up Hillel, I'll tell you the second part of Hillel's statement: 'If I am only for myself, what am I?' You asked, 'If not now, when?', I'll tell you when Paulie: Never!" She let the word sink in before repeating it. "Never. Too many people can end up in jail. I wouldn't have sent the ring if I thought you were planning something so stupid."

Paul had to get out of this conversation — to think about Grandma, not Hillel or Bernie. "I'm not going to talk to anybody about any of this for at least a week, or until *shiva's* over and we figure out what to do with Grandpa." The sentence exhausted him.

"Not 'we', Paulie. You left the family a long time ago except to take money."

Hearing "Paulie," the baby name, uttered with such contempt, gave him the strength to hang up.

* * *

Grandma's death meant funeral, relatives, talk of the past, and the risk that Sibyl would hear the name Max while Reginald and Crowell were still in New York and the ring was too small. Any response to a one-word question from her — *Who?* — could make her reconsider.

On the night before the funeral, when the family received visitors at the Riverside Memorial Chapel in Far Rockaway, Paul managed to steer Sibyl away from anyone who might mention Max's name. After the funeral, at Bernie's house, he stood at the long buffet table trying to keep Sibyl in sight while listening to a distant cousin fume about Germany. ("We dropped the atomic bomb on the wrong country.") He tensed when Ruthie appeared and, saying all the right things to the distant cousin, pulled Paul away. "Don't stare at Sibyl so hard," she said in a low voice. "Your mother and I are making sure she doesn't hear what she shouldn't hear. Why don't you go in the den and do some schoolwork? I noticed you brought a briefcase."

Kicked out of my own grandmother's funeral reception, Paul thought, but it was better than trying not to stare at Max's ring or his grandfather's scowls.

Two walls of the den were covered, floor-to-ceiling, with bookcases: one wall with fiction, and one nonfiction. Classics, Paul saw, and probably never opened. He ran his eyes over the titles and was surprised by how few he had read. He started to pace the length of the room, from the fiction bookcase to the largest globe of the world he had ever seen. "Shit," he muttered, and turned to repeat his steps.

"What are you shitting about?" Bernie had appeared in the den without Paul realizing it. He stood over the globe as if everything shown on it were his. "Stop feeling sorry for yourself. You got the world by the balls — marrying a classy girl, getting a Columbia degree, probably going to a fancy law school."

Maybe it was time to rejoin the family, Paul thought — join as an adult member about to be married. "Maybe you're right," he said.

Bernie looked taken aback that Paul agreed with him. He ran his hands over the globe. "I'm sorry about your grandmother," he said hesitantly. "My favorite *tante*. She was always nice to me when I was a wild kid in the old country, getting thrown out of school twice a week. When I bought her pearls for her last birthday, she said, '*Far vos* pearls? Nobody's taking me to the prom. I'd rather you give me your gun so I can throw it away.'"

Paul, smiled at his cousin. "What did you tell her?"

Bernie didn't return the smile. "Nothing. I couldn't tell her that when you do what I do, you just can't up and quit." Bernie clenched his fists. "How she and your mother put up with that *mamzer*, your grandfather, for so many years is beyond me.

Paul agreed, but made himself say, "Don't talk that way. He's still my grandfather."

Bernie looked at him with disgust. "Do me a favor and don't tell me how to talk in my own house." He stood to his full height and folded his arms. It was the old Bernie. "We have to get clear about the ring." Paul tried to stare back, but failed, and Bernie continued. "Your mother had this crazy idea, even before you met Sibyl, that she wanted your wife to wear the ring Max wanted her to wear. I can't explain what makes no sense. But she realizes now that no matter what she told you, she can't tell Sibyl anything about Max."

But I can tell her, Paul said to himself. Then he heard himself saying it out loud.

Something slammed against his chest and, before Paul realized what was happening, Bernie had shoved him into a wing chair and was standing above him. His cousin's shoulders bulged against his white-on-white monogrammed silk shirt.

"Listen, you little Ivy League shit. If you blow this whole thing and get your mother even more upset and get Ruthie and me involved, I'll personally break all four of your limbs."

Screw you, Paul thought, and tried to stand up. He braced for a fist but, to his surprise, Bernie stepped back. Paul let himself drop back into the wing chair.

"Look, Paulie." Bernie's lips were trembling. "I'm not going to give you my life story, but your mother's important to me. In 1938, just after *Kristelnacht*, she and your father helped get my father out of Germany. It was practically impossible — fucking Roosevelt didn't want more Jews — but, thanks to them, we managed it, and my father died of old age looking at the ocean in Miami Beach instead of a gas chamber in Auschwitz. I don't forget that."

"Okay, I'll just tell Sibyl that I had a cousin who survived Auschwitz and . . ." Paul stopped in mid-sentence. *And what?*

Bernie looked at him in wonderment. "You don't understand. You know how to take school tests, but you don't understand squat. Yeah, you'll just tell Sibyl, and she'll just tell one person, and that person will tell one, and soon everybody'll know. And her father — "

"What's he have to do with it?"

Bernie shook his head slowly. "You mean you've been going with her since you were in short pants, and you don't know the story with that *putz*?"

"I didn't know you knew him."

"I knew Maurice Pine when he was Morris Pinkus." In pantomime, Bernie spit on the floor, just as Grandma had sometimes done. "It took me a while to connect him with such a classy daughter. Sibyl, no less. But then the phony la-di-dah iceberg wife and the English names all fit together." He spun the globe.

"What's he have to do with the ring?"

"Nothing unless you start talking. The guy's got a dick for brains. He's usually in debt up to his eyeballs and, trust me, the lenders don't like not getting paid. If your future father-in-law knew the whole story of that ring, he'd lean on us — even some polite blackmail."

"His daughter's engagement ring?"

"He'd cut off her finger for it if those guys got mad." Bernie glared at him. "But maybe you'd like that. If she only had nine fingers, she couldn't leave you for an orchestra."

Paul leaped from the chair. He knew the bigger man would flick him away or beat him to a pulp, but the Warsaw ghetto uprising was also hopeless.

"Paul! Bernie! Don't argue," his mother implored from the doorway. "I've got enough to handle with Papa."

Paul studied his mother. Her black dress was too big for her. The gray that had been gone from her head was back at her temples. Her fingers were thin enough to wear Max's ring as it was.

"I'm sorry, Paulie." She spread her arms, but Paul couldn't move. "I was going to tell —" She stopped speaking. Sibyl appeared in the doorway, the diamond glinting on her finger. It *was* beautiful. Paul would get it enlarged tomorrow.

.

5 3 9 2 8

1958-1959
Foley Square

CHAPTER 8

Of the 394 lawyers in his graduating class, Paul had the second best job — he would be a law clerk to Federal Court of Appeals Judge L. Clayton Webster, widely considered the ablest appellate judge in the country. The best job would have been clerking for a Supreme Court Justice, and that would be Paul's job the following year if Judge Webster recommended him to Justice William Brennan, as he probably would if Paul proved himself as good a clerk as he knew he could be. After a stint on the Supreme Court, he could become either an associate at an elite law firm or a tenure-track assistant professor at an elite law school. Because of the exploding demand for able lawyers and the increasingly large percentage of Jews near the top of their classes at the major law schools, many firms once closed to Jews were now beginning to hire them. One of those firms had made Paul an offer after a twenty-minute interview in Cambridge. And last spring, at the *Harvard Law Review* banquet, the dean had pulled Paul aside and said, "You have a contagious love of the law, and I hope you'll consider teaching. If we don't have a spot, I can help place you with one of our competitors."

Not bad for a poor Jewish boy from Czechoslovakia by way of Arverne. His father would be proud. Max would think his money well invested.

It was the third week in August 1958, and Paul's clerkship was scheduled to begin after Labor Day, but he couldn't stop himself from visiting the courthouse. "I just want to get the feel of the chambers," he told Vivien, the judge's secretary, when he phoned. "I want to see the Court of Appeals Library, one of the courtrooms, and my office too; figure out where I'll put my pictures." He hoped these pictures would soon include Little Reuben, who was as yet unconceived, and whose mother-to-be wasn't ready to give up her diaphragm. Paul didn't tell Vivien that he wanted a chance to luxuriate in those rooms before he threw himself into the job and luxuriated in nothing.

Halfway up the Foley Square courthouse steps, he recognized the back of a slight balding man by the glass entrance doors. The fringe of blonde hair belonged to Tyler Martin, one of Judge Webster's outgoing clerks, who had been a year ahead of Paul at law school. The man's clothing — blue blazer, chinos and white buck shoes — was Martin's Harvard uniform.

The sight of Martin cooled Paul's enthusiasm. During the 1956-1957 school year — when Paul was in his second year, and Martin his third — they had encountered each other almost every day at the *Harvard Law Review* offices in Gannet House and, aside from an occasional unsmiling nod, Martin had never acknowledged Paul's presence. And it wasn't just Paul whom Martin ignored. About half the *Review* editors were Jewish, and Paul couldn't recall Martin having talked to any of them about anything not related directly to the *Law Review*. Unlike other Gentile editors, Martin entered Gannet House in the company of only Gentiles, he left only with Gentiles, and he took no part in any of the Gannet House breaks — brown-bag lunches, touch football games, the daily arguments about recent Supreme Court decisions. To top it off, he took a post-clerkship job with Knox and Black in Boston, one of the few remaining firms that explicitly excluded Jews.

Martin opened the door for an elderly woman, and Paul immediately turned around and started down the stairs. He felt ridiculous, but he suspected that if Martin saw him, he would conclude that Paul was a brown-nosing Jew scouting out the premises and trying to get a leg up on the other new clerk. Martin wouldn't say anything unpleasant, but he would silently sneer when Paul tried to explain why he was there.

Paul told himself he would laugh at this someday, but right now he wouldn't tell anyone, particularly Sibyl, who was annoyed that he was engrossed in a job that hadn't yet begun while she was engrossed in fixing up their new Brooklyn Heights apartment. But why was Tyler Martin going in the courthouse? Vivien had told him the outgoing clerks were on vacation.

Paul stopped at the bottom of the steps. He was being paranoid. The world is changing, becoming more of a meritocracy. Ty might feel that it was Paul who had been the unfriendly one at law school. *Think Dad, not Max*, he urged himself. Besides, Ty's presence could allow him to enjoy shark-fin soup. He started back up the steps.

It was almost lunchtime, and he could already taste the shark-fin soup at Min Lo's, a Chinatown restaurant he and Sibyl frequented before they moved to Cambridge. Since the soup was served for only two or more customers, lunch with Ty could turn the good day into a splendid one.

Vivien, a fireplug of a woman with a reputation for bullying clerks, gave Paul a businesslike handshake and showed him his office. It was little more than a cubicle half-filled by a wooden desk that could have once belonged to Abe Lincoln, but Paul liked it. Its window looked out on Foley Square, and the freshly painted walls would be a good background for his diplomas and for his photographs of the Volume 71 *Law Review* editors and his father's swim team. The framed photo of Sibyl — the one that captured her contented smile as she brought her flute to her lips — would sit on the radiator cover.

He returned to Vivien's desk near the hallway door, and asked where Ty Martin's office was. "We were at law school together, and I saw him coming into the courthouse," he told her. "I thought both of the outgoing clerks were on vacation."

Vivien pointed to a closed door at the end of the hall. "There's an expedited appeal." Then she closed her lips tightly. *Nosy Jew*, Paul imagined her thinking.

He went to Martin's office and knocked softly. There was no answer, so he knocked a bit louder. "Yes," a resigned voice responded. Ty sat at his desk reading a book entitled, "Introduction to Metallurgy." The Princeton seal on his blazer told Paul to come no closer. Who the hell would wear a blazer in this heat — at his desk no less? And why was he reading a book on metallurgy?

Fuck shark-fin soup. Paul would come up with an excuse for standing in Ty Martin's doorway and then get out of the courthouse.

Ty put the book face down on his desk, stared at Paul, and said nothing.

"Just came up to look around," Paul said. "I didn't expect to find anyone."

"Don't you start after Labor Day?"

Paul felt fury at Martin and at himself. How the hell had he allowed someone with a last name for a first name and a first name for a last name put him on the witness stand? "Is there some rule against my looking at my office?"

"Are you asking me a serious question?"

Paul had no reply that wouldn't make him seem foolish or to be spoiling for an argument. But standing silent in the doorway or walking away in a huff would also be foolish, and he asked, "What are you working on?"

"It's confidential," Martin said, looking beyond Paul's shoulder. "An expedited appeal and Judge Webster needs my memo quickly."

Paul realized that he was breathing through his mouth in anger, just as Bernie sometimes did. Without saying anything, he left Martin's office, closing the door behind him.

For a moment, he wondered what to say to Vivien on his way out, but Vivien wasn't in sight. He noticed a tabloid newspaper on her otherwise empty desk. It was the *Boston Post* opened to page 6, and he read the top headline upside down:

JUDGE'S SON ARRESTED
IN HIT-AND-RUN

Drunk Driving Charged

He went directly to the elevator, afraid that he would surrender to the temptation to read the article right there, and be caught doing it. But, at the out-of-town newsstand near the Municipal Building, he bought the *Boston Post* and read the article on the subway home.

It began, "The son of a federal appeals judge who refused to stop the execution of Commie spies Julius and Ethel Rosenberg was arrested for drunk driving and leaving the scene . . ." Paul skimmed the middle paragraphs, but read the final paragraph twice:

> Robert Webster is law clerk to Chief Justice Richard Story, Jr., of the Massachusetts Supreme Court. Neither his father, Judge Webster, nor Chief Justice Story would comment.

Paul knew from the press release issued by the Court of Appeals that his fellow incoming clerk, Richard Story III, was the son of the Chief Justice of the Massachusetts Supreme Court and a direct descendant of Joseph Story who, in the early nineteenth century, was one of the two greatest United States Supreme Court Justices, as well as a professor at Harvard Law School. *Surprise, surprise.* The two WASP judges were scratching each other's backs. You take care of my son, I'll take care of yours. Jews wouldn't dare be so obvious. Maybe Story III had a lock on the Supreme Court clerkship with Brennan, but nothing would stop Paul from being the best law clerk he could be and giving Judge Webster no principled choice but to recommend the clearly superior candidate. Fuck Webster if he chose to be a hypocrite — Paul would still beat the *goyim* at their own game, even if they fixed this round. America is opportunity.

* * *

That afternoon while Paul was alone in the apartment unpacking books, Judge Webster called. "I'm sorry to bother you before your clerkship formally starts, but Vivien said you were up in the office and seemed ready to go." His voice was the foghorn Paul remembered from their interviews.

"I am," Paul said, trying not to sound too eager.

"We're in New York for a day, and plan to go back to Vermont tonight. There's an expedited appeal that Ty Martin — I think you know him — has started to work on . . ."

Paul didn't want to speak without thinking. He grabbed a thin volume of T.S. Eliot's *The Waste Land*, put it into his mouth and bit down on it hard. Finally, that anti-Semitic poet would serve some practical purpose.

Judge Webster continued, his foghorn now lightly muted: "And there's something we should discuss before I ask you to take it on. Can you come in?"

Paul put *The Waste Land* on the floor and said, "Yes."

He left Sibyl a note: "Judge W wants to see me on an emergency. Save most of the boxes for me to unpack. Love you--P." He knew this probably meant the disruption of their plans to spend time enjoying New York before their new jobs began, but Sibyl shouldn't mind. They had just taken a two-week vacation in the Berkshires, and she would agree that he couldn't begin his clerkship by turning down an emergency appeal.

* * *

Judge Webster's office was massive, somewhere between the size of Bernie's den and living room. But, unlike Bernie's leather den furniture, which was smooth and shiny as if on display in a showroom, these couches and chairs were dull and cracked, their seats and backs curved by years of lawyers sitting in them.

In shirtsleeves and a vest, Judge Webster looked even more imposing than Paul remembered him — easily identifiable as the Columbia football player he had been in the twenties — with snow white hair brushed back and a Mount Rushmore face.

"Come in," the judge boomed. He pointed to one of the chairs, and Paul sat. Between them, the canyon of desk was bare but for a yellow pad and a large white envelope. Reading upside down (for the second time that day), Paul saw that the envelope was from Crane House

Sanitarium, Bedford, NY. *The judge's son,* Paul thought. *They're putting him in a sanitarium.*

"Are you settled in your new apartment yet?" Judge Webster asked.

"We're making progress."

"In Riverdale, I think Vivien told me?"

"Brooklyn Heights."

"Very nice area, I understand." The judge crossed his arms and put each thumb under the opposite suspender. Then he uncrossed them and put each thumb under the near suspender.

Paul was usually uncomfortable with small talk, and had never had any with a man like this. "What case do you need me on?"

The judge shook his head quickly, as if he had been suddenly woken. "It's a patent case. From a commercial point of view, maybe the most significant one we've had in years."

Paul could feel his heart speed up.

"A new process for making steel — produces a better product at a lower price. Invented in Germany. I was going to ask Chip Story, your co-clerk, to work on it. He's a chemist, and he'll be up to speed on the technical issues."

This explained the metallurgy book Ty was reading. Paul told himself to keep quiet.

"I mentioned it to Chip at his wedding breakfast last week," Judge Webster continued. "Same church where Puck — Mrs. Webster — and I were married." He cleared his throat. "But now Chip has to delay starting his clerkship. Nancy broke her hip on their honeymoon — in Wyoming and she can't travel. Can you believe it? He wants to be with her until she's mobile."

The bonds between the Story and Webster families were tight. "When is the appeal being argued?"

"Right after Labor Day. After the jury found the patent valid and awarded thirty million dollars in damages, the trial judge entered an injunction prohibiting the defendant from using the steel-making process covered by the patent. That meant shutting down a refurbished steel mill outside of Buffalo. If the patent is no good, we've got to lift the injunction soon and let those people go back to work. It can't wait for Nancy's bones to heal."

"Are the papers here?"

Judge Webster looked at the desk, then at Paul, then back at the desk. "Ty Martin has them, and he's started work on the appeal."

Martin was obviously trying to keep the important case from him, but Paul couldn't show any emotion.

"When . . . After," Judge Webster mumbled. The granite face on Mount Rushmore seemed to be softening and rounding. "Ty said that . . ." The judge stopped in the middle of his sentence. Paul could almost feel the man's discomfort.

The judge pulled back his shoulders and the boom returned to his voice. "Ty thought you wouldn't want to work on it and, because of the emergency, he volunteered to take it on — extend his clerkship until Chip came in. He reminded me that you were born in Europe, and that some of your family — "

Out of both pity and anger, but mostly anger, Paul broke in, "Just because some Germans killed Jews, lots of Jews — millions — including my relatives, doesn't mean I can't be objective about a patent on a German invention — can't do my job as a law clerk." He wasn't sure he believed what he had just said, but he would believe it once he thought about the matter.

The judge had begun to nod while Paul was speaking, and now he kept nodding. "That's what Chip said you'd say. You're right. You should decide whether you wanted to handle the Olymp appeal."

Olymp! Paul was afraid his heart had stopped beating for good. *Befreite Olymp Sklaven.* He saw nothing but the mostly brown snapshot, each skeleton nearly as narrow as his shovel. The man in the middle was, like it or not, his stepfather.

"Olymp?"

The judge looked at Paul solemnly. "A German company with a bad war record. Do you think that might impede your objectivity?"

Paul had every reason to be biased against Olymp, and the ethical rule was clear: Bias or the appearance of bias disqualified him from working on a case involving Olymp. But how can you beat the *goyim* at their own game if you take yourself out of that game — if, unlike Ty and Chip, you're the Jew who can't work on every case?

"I can be objective."

"They used Jewish slave labor. Their principal owners were convicted of war crimes."

"Should that disqualify me?"

The judge visibly twitched. "Of course not. I owe you an apology. Ethnicity can't determine who works on what case."

Right, Paul told himself. But the problem was more than ethnicity. It was Jack's enslavement. Should he tell the judge and let him decide?

"I'm glad you're willing to step up to the plate," the judge continued.

He couldn't mention Jack now and handicap himself even more.

"How do I get the papers?"

"I'll ask Ty to bring them to you, bring you up to date on his research too."

The judge ran his fingers over the white envelope from Crane House Sanitarium.

"Thanks," Paul said and quickly left.

* * *

He had planned to wait in his office with the door closed so that Ty would have to knock and he, like Ty, could wait before answering. But instead of playing a pointless game of spite, he went to the library and asked for the leading treatise on patent law. When he returned with Volumes 1-3 of Chisum's *Patents*, the papers in *Olymp v. Anvil* were on his desk. At the other end of the hallway, the door to Ty's office was open and the desk was empty.

Paul closed the door to his own office quietly and, before sitting down, flipped through the briefs until he found what he was hoping for: Both sides and the trial judge agreed that the patent at the heart of *Olymp v. Anvil* was for an invention made in 1953, eight years after the war and Jack's liberation. Paul put his mind to work: Whatever Olymp did to Jack during the war was long before the invention and shouldn't be the basis of bias against it. Therefore, Paul assured himself, there was nothing wrong with his working on the appeal.

Paul recognized that his reasoning might be specious, but it was too late to change course. He had told Judge Webster he could work on the Olymp appeal, and he couldn't let that bastard Martin get the better of him. If he agonized any more, he wouldn't have the time to do the outstanding job he had to do.

He sat down to read the briefs.

* * *

He came home to their new apartment at ten, and he saw a stranger sitting on the couch amidst unpacked cartons. Sibyl had cut her hair.

His wife sat as if posing for a portrait, waiting to be seen, and Paul was aghast. The silk mane that had so drawn him to her on the day they met was gone. What hair remained seemed dry, less black. There was nothing to stroke. Under her white cashmere sweater her curves were still evident but, without the ebony background of hair, they were less dramatic.

"I like it," Paul made himself say. "It's just such a surprise."

"I wasn't sure you'd notice."

Paul slammed the hallway door shut behind him. "That's so unfair!"

She was close to tears, he realized, and, he squeezed himself into the only empty space on the couch. Two cartons separated them. She apologized; he apologized; she cried; he put the interfering cartons on the floor and licked her tears. Her neck was as smooth and cool as ever.

"Its way overdue," she said. "I'm sick of looking like the girl musician from central casting. I should've done it when I changed schools."

Her abrupt switch from one of the world's greatest and most selective conservatories to (in her words) "a garden variety ed. school with no real musicians, particularly in the so-called music department," was a subject Paul had always tried to avoid. It was her choice to leave the conservatory, Paul regularly reminded himself. He had never suggested it — never even hinted at it — and it had surprised him even more than her newly shorn hair. Then why did he feel he had wronged her?

* * *

Two years earlier, on the day Paul completed his all-important first year law-school exams, Sibyl had simply announced, "I've switched from the New England Conservatory to the BU Education Department."

"This is out of the blue," Paul had said.

"It's done. I'll teach music in a high school and conduct a student orchestra just like my Aunt Arlene." Sibyl's grandmother had agreed to pay for everything, including private lessons, she told him. She had already registered for summer courses.

Paul, who had been lightheaded from the sudden loss of exam adrenaline, didn't know how to respond. He did know that words were required, but all he could manage was, "Why did you wait so long to tell me?"

Her answer had shaken him: "I would have talked to you about it, but that would have interfered with your round-the-clock studying. Or maybe it wouldn't have, and . . . I don't even want to think about that."

Then, without being asked, she had given her reasons. "I know I'm a very good flutist, but that's not enough. I'd never be more than second chair in a second-rate ensemble. Never a featured soloist or even a performer where it mattered. Instead, I'd make bus trips to cities I'd never want to live in and stay in depressing motels with paper cups in the bathroom."

When she finally said what he wanted to hear — "And what about children and a normal family life?" — her voice was without affect. When she said what he didn't want to hear — "I was sure you really didn't want me to be a full-time performing artist" — she ignored his protestations.

Throughout their remaining two years in Cambridge, each of them tried to assure the other that Sibyl would always be a performing artist, "a real musician."

— "You'll find a serious group to play with."

— "I can play music I'll be proud of at weddings, even children's theater."

— "Your aunt played when the Royal Ballet was in town. She found it very fulfilling."

— "They're always putting quality groups together for film shoots."

They tried hard because, Paul admitted to himself, they knew they were failing.

When Paul came home from school, he would often find her either sitting silently or else dancing around the apartment while playing a waltz on the flute — but never "Waltz of the Flowers." The dinners she prepared were frequently extreme: One night she might serve canned spaghetti and peaches, and on the following night boeuf bourguignon and caramel soufflé. Her lovemaking was either passive or voracious — rarely tender or playful. He began to suspect that she was faking orgasms.

Late in Paul's final semester, when she was offered a job in New York City's High School of Music and Art, Sibyl suddenly seemed happy. "There really is no public high school like it anyplace," she had exulted. "Margaret Kettle, the Chair of the Woodwinds Department, called me to say how delighted she was. It's subject to funding, but that shouldn't be a problem. There are real musicians on the faculty; Margaret was with the Metropolitan Opera orchestra until she got pregnant. And kids who want to be real musicians. It'll be like teaching me."

* * *

Paul wondered how Sibyl would react to the disruption of their plans for the rest of August — fixing up their apartment together, going to the beach in Rockaway without letting anybody in their families know, and visiting New York tourist sights they had never quite gotten to. But, whatever her reaction, he wouldn't tell her anything about the appeal, even its name. Eventually, it would be public information that Judge Webster was on the Olymp matter, and Sibyl might then mention Jack's enslavement. But she might have forgotten the name of his enslaver — she was repelled by Holocaust details — and "eventually" was a while off.

Paul slid next to her on the couch and took her hands. "When I'll be free to talk about the case, you'll agree it's a genuine emergency. How can I start the job by saying no?"

"Did you ask whether the other new clerk could do it?"

"He just got married and his wife broke her hip. Pretty badly it turns out."

"That wouldn't stop *you*."

Paul jumped to his feet and looked down at her. "That's not fair! Don't you think . . ." He stopped abruptly. Sibyl was smiling. "Why are you smiling?"

She pulled on his hands, and he returned to the couch. "Lighten up. Paulie." She only used that name teasingly. "It amuses me how predictable you are. I told Margaret that once you saw your office, we'd never take a boat cruise around Manhattan."

"No, we will — "

"Let me finish." Paul sat back and listened. "Believe it or not, I'm busy too. After I got your call, I accepted a two-week job in *The Boyfriend*, filling in for a flutist whose mother is dying. Then I went out to cut my hair. Margaret got her beauty parlor to stay open late."

"I'm glad about the job," Paul said. "And once I get done with this appeal, I won't leave you home alone."

"I know you mean it, and that it's not going to happen. I want to do more with my life than wait for you to come home."

Paul took her hand and kissed it. The engagement ring — Max's ring — brushed his cheek. He closed his eyes and said, "You'll do a lot more."

Sibyl slid onto his lap. "But there is something you have to do."

"The answer is yes." Paul put his hand under her sweater.

"Give me something to look forward to. Margaret invited us to the Halloween party she and her husband give every year. October 18th. It's early this year because they're going away for her brother's wedding."

Sibyl took a pen from her pocketbook and wrote "10/18/58" on Paul's right palm. "We should come up with a special costume."

October 18, Paul computed, was eight weeks away — an eternity. The argument of the Olymp appeal was two weeks away. "We'll figure out a great costume in all that time," he said, "but right now my mind is someplace else."

"So is mine."

* * *

Although Ty Martin had been looking at a metallurgy book, the Olymp appeal could be understood and decided without any knowledge of chemistry. The main issues were the identity of the inventor, infringement (whether the defendant, Anvil Metal, used the steel-making process covered by Olymp's patent), and what damages Olymp suffered. Paul researched these matters thoroughly and wrote a memo showing that, on each point, Olymp had introduced strong evidence in its favor and the trial judge had given correct legal instructions to the jury. "The verdict for plaintiff Olymp should be affirmed in all respects," he concluded.

He also concluded that he had not violated any ethical principle by working on the appeal. He had shown that he could be fair to a German company, even a Nazi slave-master, whose patent, when upheld, would give it a lawful monopoly on a revolutionary steel-making process — the key to a gold mine. Despite what had happened to Max and Jack, despite the Holocaust, he could — and did — fairly analyze and apply the law.

But Paul's memo to Judge Webster went beyond the correctness of the jury's verdict. He suggested that the Court of Appeals opinion also review the law concerning patent damages and consider whether the established principles have to be refined for a case such as this one where Olymp's patent would revolutionize an industry.

Under the patent statute, Olymp was entitled to collect a "reasonable royalty" from anyone who used its patented invention. But how was this reasonable royalty to be computed? In instructing the jury on this question, the trial judge faithfully parroted standards spelled out in earlier cases. Those standards, however, made little sense in the Olymp case because Olymp's groundbreaking invention was only just beginning to be used by manufacturers. The problem was compounded by the trial judge's instructions being laden with economic jargon that few, if any, of the jurors could have understood. Paul proposed that the Court of Appeals opinion include a revised standard for computing reasonable royalty that would make sense in this case. Parenthetically, Paul reminded Judge Webster that in the summer before he entered law school, he had assisted a Harvard Business School professor writing a book on business valuation.

He realized, of course, that he was reaching out for a major assignment that would allow him to shine — one that would show him to be a creative thinker uniquely equipped to be a Supreme Court Clerk. Was he being a pushy Jew? He wouldn't ever consider that question. If he were a passive Jew, Richard Story III would roll over him. If his father had been a passive Jew, Paul would be dead.

With Sibyl playing eight shows a week, Paul was able to work over the weekend and at night, and he finished the memorandum on the Tuesday before Labor Day. Judge Webster called him from Vermont on Wednesday.

"A fine job. Most law clerks are reluctant to question established standards — to say that the emperor's not wearing clothes. But how confident are you that you can come up with something workable that doesn't further confuse the law on reasonable royalty?"

Paul was ready for the question. "Based on my research over the past few days and at the B school, I think it's doable. But, until I try, I can't be sure."

"Interesting. I'll discuss it with the other judges after the oral argument. In the meantime, take a breather. Soon, with Chip's starting date up in the air, you're going to be very busy. Why don't you come up to our summer place in Vermont for the Labor Day weekend? Come tomorrow before the other guests so we can discuss your suggestion. Not full time work — you'll still have most of the weekend. Bring your wife. I think you told me she's a musician. Oboe, right?"

Paul was shocked by the invitation, but he managed to reply, "Flute."

"It's not necessary, but my wife would love it if she brought her instrument. Puck had a brief career as a pianist before she became pregnant. Do you play anything?"

This was a double blessing from God. Sibyl's temporary job was ending tonight and, at her urging, he had begun playing the clarinet again.

* * *

The Websters' "summer place" was a castle with two stone guest cottages set on three acres of lawn. It faced west, overlooking a pristine, private beach, Lake Champlain, and the densely wooded New York shoreline. Acres of pine separated it from any neighbors. Paul and Sibyl were given a cottage twice the size of their Brooklyn Heights apartment. The two couples had dinner on the beach — a leg of lamb roasted in the sand, and the best red wine Paul had ever tasted. After demitasse and cognac, the men and women separated. Paul and Judge Webster stood over the glowing coals smoking cigars while the judge described the practical problems in implementing *Brown v. Board of Education*, the Supreme Court decision finding segregated public schools unconstitutional. Whatever the problems with Judge Webster's son — and Paul knew nothing beyond the *Boston Post* article — they had no impact on the judge's demeanor. He was still the Mount Rushmore icon — the great man imparting wisdom.

"Consequently, we could end up with more segregation than there is now. Did you take a course with Lionel Trilling?"

Paul's stomach jumped at the abrupt transition. What was going on? "Yes."

"You're lucky. I was long gone from Columbia when he came. What did you read? Let's sit down."

For the next quarter hour, they sat on a bench — a tree trunk split along its length — and discussed Proust and Joyce, wandering between characters and scenes, without any agenda. The judge's voice no longer boomed and, at times, he came close to sounding wistful. Paul wondered when they would get to Olymp. The case hadn't yet been mentioned but he didn't see how he could change the subject — and he wasn't sure he wanted it to change.

"Lionel got me interested in Yeats," the judge announced, and began to recite a Yeats poem from memory. Paul recalled the poem, but its name escaped him. Why was this man, someone who had achieved everything, trying to impress him?

Well before the poem's end (Paul remembered that much), the judge stopped reciting and his voice dropped. "Lionel was the first Jew to get tenure in Columbia's English Department, and it was a messy squabble." So that's where the judge was going. "It was the mid-thirties, and my father, who was a trustee, was one of his big supporters. Plenty of alums weren't. The three of us and sometimes a few others would meet in my father's apartment to talk strategy, and some of the meetings evolved into a mini-tutorial on Yeats. Best course I ever had. We were going to organize a letter-writing campaign but, after my father spoke to President Butler, Lionel's tenure was rammed through."

The subject had to change. Paul wanted to overwhelm Judge Webster with the quality of his work, not kiss his ass for being nice to Jews, provided they were as brilliant as Trilling, which he certainly wasn't.

"I never knew that," he said to Judge Webster.

"The world is changing."

And in favor of Jews, just as his father had predicted, but Paul wasn't yet ready to discuss this with the man who could help him benefit from those changes. He felt relieved to see Sibyl approaching with Mrs. Webster. (He couldn't even think of her as "Puck.")

From the moment he had met Judge Webster's wife, Paul had been struck by her sad beauty. She was a trim, well-shaped woman with blue-tinted white hair and green eyes that seemed to have been dimmed. She looked serene, but Paul suspected it was a mask — a suspicion confirmed by frequent but unpredictable twitches in her jaw and neck. Throughout the evening, she and Sibyl had spoken to each other softly, often nodding understandingly. He recalled what his mother had said on the day he gave Sibyl Max's diamond ring — *A woman needs a woman friend.*

"Paul," Mrs. Webster said, "would you care to play something with Sibyl and me? I brought Wagner's *Siegfried Idyll* in an arrangement for flute, piano, and clarinet. It's one of his few chamber pieces, and it's beautiful."

Wagner! Paul couldn't play Wagner and he couldn't refuse to play him without ruining the visit. "Yes," he made himself say. The cognac and cigar smoke numbed his head.

"We'll get our instruments," Sibyl said.

"No, I'll get them," Paul replied and pushed himself up from the bench. He needed time to think. "You save your breath for the flute."

"We'll be in the living room," Judge Webster ordered.

On the walk to the cottage, Paul reminded himself that he had played Wagner in a high school concert with no objection from the living Max. *You do what you have to.* But with Judge Webster as the entire audience, Max in his mind, and Wagner's score on the music stand, his clarinet would squeak. He would leave the clarinet in the cottage and say that he had forgotten to take any reeds. *Freudian slip; I guess I didn't want to ruin a duet by real musicians.* Afterwards, when he told Sibyl he was too nervous to play, she would laugh and say he was ridiculous.

*   *   *

Mrs. Webster replaced the Wagner —"Two can't play a trio" — with a Bach Flute sonata that Sibyl knew well. Good, Paul thought; he had never been told Bach was anti-Semitic.

He sat in an uncomfortable, low-backed chair and listened. Mrs. Webster's playing was workmanlike, the level Paul might have reached if he kept at it, but Sibyl was mesmerizing. Paul forgot the chair and felt the flute melody inside of him – a calm patch of ocean with gentle white waves on which he floated until, at crescendos or allegros, the waves flowed through him and he felt their tremor. Had Sibyl gotten better or had he not paid attention to her music?

Mrs. Webster lifted her hands from the keyboard. "Go on, dear; I just want to listen."

Sibyl played Bach by herself for ten minutes without anyone speaking. Mrs. Webster was crying. Embarrassed, Paul looked away and saw Judge Webster frowning in disgust. Then, for no apparent reason, his always ruddy face paled, his frown disappeared, and his jowls dropped farther down his cheeks. Paul shifted his eyes to Sibyl. He tried to picture her with her long hair restored, and wished he had urged her to stay at the New England Conservatory.

The silence continued after Sibyl put down her flute. Finally Mrs. Webster spoke: "That was . . ." She shook her head slowly. "You are an artist." She blew her nose. "I hope . . ."

Judge Webster broke in. "That was beautiful, Sibyl. Maybe we should turn in. Paul must be exhausted from all the work on the patent appeal."

Paul picked up his cue. "I am, but I'll be able to talk about it in the morning."

"A short meeting," Judge Webster replied. "Mostly to discuss the damages issue. Your memo was convincing, although I'm keeping my mind open until the oral argument is completed. Afterwards the two of you might like to take a crack at croquet. Puck is a champion."

Mrs. Webster winced, but quickly turned it into a smile.

* * *

There was no croquet. When Paul and Sibyl came to the main house for breakfast, they were greeted outside the door by one of the women who had served dinner on the beach. (The Websters hadn't introduced any of the staff and, although some had been called by first name, Paul couldn't attach a name to this woman; he promised himself that if he did beat the *goyim* at their game, he wouldn't act like them.)

"Morning, Mr. and Mrs. Hartman," she said. "Lovely day we're going to have." She had a slight Irish accent, and either her round cheeks were excessively ruddy or she was blushing. "Judge and Mrs. Webster are very sorry, but the judge's sister got suddenly sick in Maine. She's alone and they have to run up and see her before her doctor leaves for the weekend. They said you could stay and enjoy the place as long as you like. I'll make sure you're well provided for. John can fuel up a boat if you'd like to go out on the lake."

"Thank you, Edna," Sibyl immediately replied. She took Edna's hand. "That's very kind of you, but there's work that needs to be done at our new apartment. Thank the judge and Mrs. Webster and all of the staff who've been so welcoming. Ask Mrs. Webster to call me when she gets back to the city if she'd like to play some duets with me."

Paul, annoyed with himself for not knowing Edna's name, annoyed with Sibyl for declining the invitation without consulting him, and grateful to her for offering to play duets with Mrs. Webster, held out his hand to Edna but, instead of taking it, she handed him an envelope. "A note from the judge. I'm sorry we won't be spending more time with you. The music was beautiful. I'll bring some breakfast to the cottage. The eggs were laid this morning."

"Thank you for that too," Sibyl answered, then turned to walk towards the cottage. Paul wanted to read the note on the spot, but he just followed.

"Read it!" Sibyl demanded, as soon as the cottage door closed. "Whatever it says, it will make you work for the rest of the weekend."

"What are you so angry about? Why are you turning down an invitation to us as if I'm not there?"

Sibyl threw the suitcase on the bed. "We don't have enough time for me to give you a full answer and, anyway, I'm not sure you'd understand."

Easy, Paul warned himself. Things could get out of control. He opened the envelope. The handwriting was barely legible, but it was Judge Webster's and he'd have to master it.

Paul:

Sorry we had to leave so suddenly.

Chip Story called. Nancy had a setback, and he's not sure
when he can start. You'll have to pick up two appeals I
was holding for him. Vivien's leaving the records and
briefs on your desk. Under the circumstances, you have
plenty to do, and we should probably put aside the
damages issue we discussed. *Olymp* can be decided
without reexamining established precedent.

LCW

No! Paul resolved. He wouldn't put aside an opportunity to do
something exceptional. He held the note out to Sibyl and said, "See, I
don't have to work over Labor Day."

Sibyl waved the note away. "I don't think the great man would
want me to see his private note to his prodigy. Let's get out of here."

* * *

They drove without speaking, east on the Websters' dirt road and south
on Vermont 16, two straight empty lanes flanked by pines. From the
corner of his eye, Paul saw Sibyl's expressionless face — a *mannequin*,
he thought. She clenched a wide brimmed straw hat in her lap. Unnerved
by the silence, he said, "You didn't have to offer to play duets with Mrs.
Webster. I appreciate it."

Sibyl responded in a listless voice: "I offered because I like her,
and she's a competent pianist. I feel sorry for her too. They're having
some problem with their son."

A yellow light went on in Paul's mind. He didn't want her to learn
that he was a snoop who read a *Boston Post* headline upside down on
Vivien's desk. "Would Mrs. Webster want you telling me what she told
you?"

Sibyl shrugged. "I don't know why not." Her voice had no
energy. "It's in all the newspapers — drugs, hit-and-run, jail. The judge
blames everything on her. Then he washes his hands of their son — says
let him rot in jail. Then he wants to direct everything and get the bum to
knuckle under. There's no sick sister." She paused for emphasis.

"Webster hasn't spoken to his sister in years. They've probably gone to Boston to try to deal with the mess."

"You sound so cynical. This isn't like you." Paul realized his sanctimony was feigned and distasteful, but things were complicated enough.

"Maybe you're right, but I can't stand him: Always has to be in charge — the way he frowned when he saw how much his wife was moved by the music, then raved about her croquet skills as if she were a trained monkey. And why do you have to fawn on him? Sure, in the music world people fawn all the time. It was a required course at Juilliard. But there are limits."

"This *really* isn't like you." Paul had never been so angry with her. "I get ahead by good work, not by fawning."

She looked at him and her face softened. "I apologize. That man just sets me off. You do get ahead by good work — and lots of it."

They drove in silence, but without tension. Paul turned on the radio, and Sibyl said, "Judge Webster wasn't my only reason for wanting to leave." Paul turned the radio off, and Sibyl continued. "There's this senior at Music and Art, the first flutist in the orchestra — Vera Arnum, a remarkable talent. She's auditioning for the Young Mozart Competition in Vienna. Margaret wants me to coach her. She thinks Vera will respond better to me than her regular teacher, who's a rigid battle-ax. Now I'll have some time this weekend to work with her."

"Why didn't you tell me? We didn't have to go to Vermont." Paul reached out for her hand, but she slipped hers away and looked out the car window.

"Are you kidding? You were so steamed up about the invitation and my playing with Priscilla, it would have been cruel — like putting a pin in your balloon."

"Priscilla?"

"Her real name, not the ridiculous nickname that your idol branded her with."

"Don't start with Judge Webster again! I won't apologize for being ambitious."

They were driving through a shaded area, and Paul saw Sibyl's reflection in the passenger window. Her face was no longer that of a mannequin but it was whiter than usual. "Paul!" she shrieked and threw her arms across her eyes. Paul jerked his gaze towards the road. Twenty yards directly ahead of them, two bicyclists in bright orange cycling shirts were pumping their way up a long hill. Paul slammed on the brakes and barely managed to swerve around them. He checked the rear mirror to confirm the cyclists were all right. Then he erupted.

"Damn it! I can't concentrate on driving if you're just going to attack me through Judge Webster."

He checked the mirror again and saw the cyclists — now diminishing orange specks — behind him. Sibyl rolled down her window, leaned out and threw up.

There was a bald spot at the top of the hill, and Paul pulled over. Sibyl was gasping for breath and repeating, "I'm sorry . . . I'm sorry."

The car was clean, but Sibyl's straw hat was a mess. Paul helped her out and sat her gently in the shadow of the car. He cleaned her hat with water Edna had given them for the road, and sat down beside her. *Pregnant?* he wondered, but didn't ask. Using both hands, he fanned her with her now clean, but damp, hat.

If she were pregnant it must have happened on that Saturday in July when the principal of Music and Art called to tell her that the funding had come through for her job. "Let's commemorate with a baby," Paul had said, and Sibyl answered with her usual response: "Let's wait. Let me take the job, get some teaching experience on my résumé first, or I'll never work." Nevertheless, when they came home tipsy from a celebratory dinner, and Paul brought her to climax with his tongue before she had taken off anything, even her panties, she had laughingly acquiesced when Paul said, "Please no diaphragm for just once." They never discussed that evening because they both knew that the baby they might have conceived would be one more impediment to the career she wanted so badly.

Did he want her to have a career? Over their ten years together, she had never asked him that question, and he had never asked himself. She was a musician – her choice since childhood, her role to define. But he knew what he wanted now – for Sibyl to feel better, for the birth of Little Reuben in early 1959, and for enough peace of mind to write the best draft opinion Judge Webster had ever seen, including an analysis of the law on patent damages.

He fanned harder and, when some color began to appear in her face, he could no longer control himself. "Is it . . .? Do you think . . .?"

"Maybe. I'm late. I'm seeing the doctor next week."

Paul felt an urge to kiss her, get up and dance around the car, do cartwheels. He had never done a cartwheel, but he was sure he could.

"If it's a . . ." Paul stopped. Sibyl was staring straight ahead.

"Maybe I'm not pregnant," she said, and then said nothing — the worst silence yet.

"You won't have to give up your music."

Sibyl half closed her eyes. "I already gave it up."

There it was, out in the open. Should he remonstrate with her, tell her she had a great job at a great school, that she'd find a group to play with? That would only make her point.

"Are you thinking about Mrs. Webster giving up her career?" A stupid question, Paul realized. Priscilla Webster didn't approach Sibyl's level of talent.

"I'm not thinking of anything. My mind doesn't go all the time, like yours." She looked directly into his eyes and then looked down. "Can we spend the whole weekend together?"

"What about Vera Arnum?"

Sibyl smiled. "Maybe I'm as bad as you."

"Not quite, but you have potential."

CHAPTER 9

The Olymp appeal was argued two days after Labor Day. Paul sat behind the three-judge panel in the corner next to the robing room where, immediately after the argument, the judges would meet and reach their decision. He took copious notes, pleased that every point made by the lawyers and every question asked by the judges had been covered in his memo.

Late that afternoon, Paul looked up from his desk to see Judge Webster, in shirtsleeves and red suspenders, enter his office. They hadn't spoken since Vermont. "Our deliberation took no time because we all agreed with your memo," the judge said before Paul could stand. He filled nearly all of the space between the desk and the door. "I'm writing the opinion. When you do your draft, adhere closely to the first part of the memo, but forget about reexamining the reasonable royalty standard. You're needed on other things. Chip's starting date is still in the air, and you'll have to take on one or two more of his cases."

Paul was prepared for this, but didn't want to seem too prepared. "I think it's possible to do it all. The royalty issue grows right out of the work I did at the B-School in Fifty-five." He held up some typed pages. "This is the memo on the copyright case. It only needs proofing." Then he tapped the legal-sized pad on his desk. "That's most of the memo on the Oyster Bay eminent domain appeal. It's going quickly because I edited a law review note on the subject."

Judge Webster looked at the ground and sucked on his lips. "Okay. You know what you can handle. But there's no longer any need to rush in *Olymp v. Anvil*. Anvil's been enjoined from making steel by the Olymp process, and that's as it should be. Our opinion will simply turn a preliminary injunction into a permanent one, and give some guidance on damages for the future."

"Fine," Paul said, as casually as he could. "And thanks for the wonderful time we had in Vermont. How's your sister?"

The judge opened his mouth a bit, and his bulldog nose crinkled in confusion. Then his mouth opened wider in sudden understanding. "False alarm, but my wife insisted on running up there. Sorry it upset your weekend. We came back that night — you should have stayed."

Sibyl was right. The "sister" crisis was a lame excuse for dealing with whatever mess their son was in. "I'm glad everything's okay."

Without another word, the judge left the office but came back almost immediately. "I'm giving you a lot of work." He nodded in agreement with himself. "It can't be helped, but make sure you get home some evenings. You have a lovely wife — and very talented."

"I will, but Sibyl's home less than I am." An exaggeration, but not a big one. Between teaching, coaching Vera and helping Margaret organize a woodwinds concert, she seemed to be building a fulfilling career in music, which eased Paul's concern about his many hours out of the house.

"Puck says she may be . . ." The judge paused, apparently searching for a word he felt comfortable with.

"She's seeing the obstetrician next week."

"Are you going with her?"

"Of course." Until the judge's question, Paul had been planning to be in the office.

"Good. It's important that . . ." As if a bell had gone off, the judge snapped his shoulders back. "When you get to the reasonable royalty issue in Olymp — don't give it top priority, but when you get there — cite some reputable economists. Make it clear that we're not creating a new rule out of whole cloth."

The judge disappeared, and Paul immediately called Nat Rosen, a friend from Columbia who worked at the NYU Law Library, and arranged to have a carrel in the library stacks. He could work at night without anybody from the courthouse knowing it.

* * *

Sibyl was coaching Vera on Sunday, and Paul went to the office to start on one of the cases originally intended for Chip Story. The work went well, and he left in the early afternoon. Tomorrow evening, he would go to the "Secret Dungeon," his private name for his carrel at NYU, and begin serious research on reasonable royalty, but the rest of today was free. Sibyl would be home soon — perhaps she was there now — ready to spend hours in bed with him. They would have time to walk on the Promenade along the East River and marvel at the Manhattan skyline before getting dressed for the wedding of Sibyl's Juilliard roommate.

Climbing the subway stairs towards Borough Hall, a classical temple of a building that seemed misplaced in downtown Brooklyn, Paul emerged into gray silence. The buildings around him — Borough Hall, the Post Office, the Brooklyn Federal Courthouse, the State Courthouse, the Motor Vehicle Bureau, a few stone office buildings that must have been there in the nineteenth century — were ghost-like in their emptiness. Except for a few seedy men scattered on park benches, Cadman Plaza, the narrow green triangle of urban park stretching from Borough Hall, seemed to have been vacuumed clean for the Lord's Day.

A thin man in a wrinkled cream-colored double-breasted suit got up from one of the benches, waved to Paul, and approached him. He was too dressed up to be a bum, but he had the forlorn look of a vagrant. It wasn't until they were a few feet from each other that Paul recognized a shriveled version of his father-in-law.

Paul squinted at Maurice in the gray light. Wasn't he living in Florida?

Maurice gripped Paul's jacket sleeve. "I have to talk to you."

Paul pulled himself free. "Let's go to our apartment." So much for his afternoon plans.

"No, no, not there." Maurice shook his head rapidly. "I don't want Sibyl to see how much I've changed."

Paul looked at him and silently agreed. Was it two summers ago or three that they visited Maurice in Florida after he moved in with Faye? Since then, the older man's body had stooped and his tan face had yellowed. Bags hung from his eyes. He needed a better fitting hairpiece, one not so shoeshine-black.

Paul pointed at the row of mostly empty benches lining Cadman Plaza, and Maurice again shook his head no. "Sibyl might see us when she gets out of the subway."

"How do you know so much?" Paul immediately regretted his harsh words. On the day in 1948 when he first met Sibyl's parents, Mrs. Pine had greeted him with disdain, but this sad wreck had invited Paul to sleep over. "I'm sorry, Dad, but I'm rattled by your being here."

Maurice pointed to Borough Hall. "Let's talk there. We'll be dry and nobody will see us."

Paul was surprised to discover that it had started to drizzle. He followed Maurice up the steps, past the Grecian stone pillars, and into the shadows of the Borough Hall portico.

"I'm in trouble, Paul . . . Big trouble . . . I owe a lot of money to people you don't want to owe money to. They don't fool around." He sounded like a Mickey Spillane novel.

"Mobsters?" Maurice ignored the question, and Paul asked, "What happened?"

Maurice raised his head. "You don't want to know."

"If it's important to you, I do."

"I borrowed money for business from . . . forget from who."
Maurice lowered his head again. "The banks wouldn't lend me more, and
I had no other choice. It looked like a sure thing — brandy and gourmet
delicacies from Spain. With all the Puerto Ricans coming here and soon
the Cubans who will be pour in once Castro kicks out Batista, we were
sure they'd lap up the good Spanish stuff. Start in Florida, then go
national. But there was trouble with the licenses, which meant I needed
more money for *schmearing*. The interest started out triple what the bank
charged — vigorish they call it — and went up when I missed a payment.
Then we found out the people who spoke Spanish wanted their fancy
foods to be French."

Maurice grabbed Paul's arm again. "You won't tell Sibyl any of
this, will you? She's all I got. Her sister won't even speak to me."

"I won't tell her."

"I started to play the ponies at Hialeah. I had tips and went big
time." Maurice scowled. "They played me for a sucker." He started to say
something more, but stopped.

"You lost?" Paul asked as gently as he could.

"The same guys who lent me money for the business," he
mumbled. "More vigorish."

My first client, Paul thought; I'll help him. "Is there anything you
can sell?"

"My soul, but I already sold it." Maurice broke into a half smile.

"Faye — doesn't she have money?"

"Tons, but it comes with conditions."

"Conditions?"

Maurice frowned. "She got me into the mess — the Spanish
importing, the vigorish. What she wants is the two of us should take over
what her husband did before he got sick . . . with Cuba and . . . forget the
details. What she *really* wants is she should take over and I would take
the risks. I walked out on her last week."

Somewhere near the Brooklyn Bridge, a siren wailed. Paul willed
himself to focus on solving Maurice's problem. "Bankruptcy!" he
shouted, over the siren.

"What?"

"Under the Bankruptcy Code, if you file a petition for personal
bankruptcy, you should be able to discharge all your debts."

As Paul spoke, he realized he was being ridiculous.

Maurice agreed. For the first time, he stood straight. "This isn't a Harvard Law School test." He shook his head. "These guys don't know petitions. They want their money."

Paul had to keep trying. "Have you spoken to Bernie?"

Maurice sighed. "Bernie spoke to me. I owe him too, but he's not pressing like the others. They do business together, but he's not one of them." He stepped closer to Paul and dropped his voice. "He explained how you could get me out of this."

"Me? How?"

"You're not supposed to know this, but he told me to talk to you."

"I assumed you . . ." Paul considered what he was about to say — *I assumed you wanted legal advice* — and cut himself short. "There's nothing I can do."

"Sure there is. It's simple." Maurice spoke quickly. "Your judge is deciding the Olymp case. Just tell me how it's going to come out. Olymp's stock will go up if they decide its patent is good, down if it loses, vice versa for the other company. It's like having next month's newspaper. They told Bernie that if I pass that on, my debts are canceled. I'll never ask you for anything again."

Paul was too stunned to speak. His wife's father was asking him to violate his oath and irrevocably defile the legal career he had barely begun.

"No one will ever know," Maurice said.

I will, Paul thought. *And Bernie.* "It was only argued a few days ago."

"I know. Bernie's got friends in the courthouse. They told him you were sitting near the judge's bench and writing everything down, and that the judges had their secret conference when they decide who's going to win. They even told him what time you left the office today." Maurice hunched his shoulders. "Bernie knows everything except what they decided."

Paul fought to keep his hands still. "You're asking me to commit a crime." Maurice began to tremble. "Think about it, Dad. It really is a crime."

"Think about *what*!" His voice was low, but the last word — *what!* — was almost a bark. "It's vigorish on vigorish, and every day I don't pay, it goes up. *That's* what I think about!"

Paul knew he had to say no, and that he couldn't say it.

"Paul, please. They might . . . Remember Lou Farr, the Knish King?"

Paul nodded. In the summer of 1954, a few weeks before he proposed to Sibyl, he had saved Farr's mother from drowning and had then refused to accept a thick envelope of cash from the King's chauffeur. (*Lifeguards don't take tips for saving lives*, he had told himself. *My father wouldn't have.*)

"He told me he wanted you to take his daughter out, but you wouldn't because you loved Sibyl so much."

Paul cursed himself. He should have taken out the Knish Princess and accepted Farr's money, freeing himself from both Max's diamonds and Sibyl's family. "What about Farr?"

"They broke his knee-caps. And Lou owed less than me."

Why not tell him? Who beyond Maurice and Bernie would know? Too many people, Paul realized. He, himself, would know, which meant that his father would know, which meant Reuben Hartman's American dream would be sullied. Max would know, and he'd be disappointed in the skinny kid in whom he had invested his diamonds. (Or maybe Max wouldn't be disappointed.) And beyond them, the scores of WASP judges on the walls of nearly every Harvard Law School lecture hall — gilt-framed portraits of red-robed, white-wigged, somber-faced Englishmen who resembled nobody from Paul's childhood — would know.

Three years earlier, as he entered Harvard Law, Paul had been inspired by Dean Richards' orientation speech, particularly the closing words: "The law is a noble calling; be worthy of it." With just a few words to Maurice, *Olymp will win the appeal*, Paul would never have a noble calling. When he saw Ty Martin, he would have to turn away.

Maurice pressed his palms together. "You know who's going to win. Just tell me."

This tormented man — the father of his wife, the grandfather of their soon-to-be-born child — looked ready to collapse at his feet. But Dean Richards had urged him to teach law.

"Why don't you go to the FBI?" he asked. "I'll go with you."

Maurice sighed and looked at Paul as if he had two heads. "By the time the feds find a crime — if they even try — we may both be dead."

"Give me till tomorrow to find a solution," Paul urged. If Reuben Hartman could volunteer to organize resistance behind Nazi lines, the son of Reuben Hartman could find a lawful way to help his father-in-law.

Maurice pounded the air with his fist. "Olymp's the only solution. Please!"

"I'm leaving." Paul started down the Borough Hall steps and, without stopping or turning, said: "I'll come up with something. I promise."

* * *

Turning from Cadman Plaza onto Court Street and then onto Montague, the street that led to his home, Paul tried to think of people who might be willing to lend Maurice money. He had rescued people from drowning; he had, as a friend, coached two or three Columbia students in courses they were close to failing; he had done favors for a variety of people who were struggling with government regulations or forms. Surely, some of these efforts could be converted to cash. He ran names through his head, but quickly gave it up; each prospect fell somewhere between inconceivable and comical.

Why not simply go to Judge Webster and tell him the truth? The judge certainly knew someone in the Eisenhower Administration who could make sure that the right people would meet with Maurice and him, and keep both of them safe.

But how much truth? Should he tell the judge that Maurice had unlawfully solicited confidential information? Could that fact start a trail of investigation leading back to Max? To his mother and the cash for his tuition payments? Could it lead to jail?

In 1955, before law school began, Paul had reviewed only one of his new textbooks with care — "Criminal Law." Within an hour, he had identified more than a half dozen criminal statutes his mother might have violated every time she lied to government officials, searched for Max's diamonds or sold them. Twenty more minutes of reading had satisfied him that while he, himself, did little more than take money and keep his mouth shut, he could be indicted as her aider and abettor and, perhaps, as her coconspirator. That was enough to know and, while he worked slavishly in all of his other courses, he did the bare minimum in criminal law and received his lowest grade in his three years as a law student.

He would push Maurice from his mind for a few moments and, instead of going right home, he would walk to the Promenade at the end of Montague, stare at the East River, and think. Water always soothed him, the drizzle would reactivate his mind and he would come up with a solution.

He welcomed Montague's Sunday silence. Everything seemed closed except China Dragon near the corner of Henry Street, half way to the Promenade. The electric dragon hanging over the restaurant door flashed from red to blue to green and then disappeared for a few moments before reemerging as red, a procession of lights like the Fun House in

Rockaway Playland. Paul walked faster. The sooner he reached the Promenade, the sooner Maurice's problem would be solved.

A familiar, large blue car passed him and parked just before the China Dragon. Just as he couldn't flee Ty Martin, Paul couldn't flee Bernie on the street leading to his home. He slowed to his normal walking pace but he was soon at the Lincoln.

Bernie rolled down the window. He wore a skintight polo shirt that was almost as dark as his tan, along with aviator sunglasses darker than both. His biceps bulged. Paul glanced at the backseat, expecting to find Maurice, but Bernie was alone.

"I told him to wait for me at the diner on Fulton, but I don't know if he can sit still that long. He's scared shitless, and you didn't do much to help him."

"We'll think of something," Paul said.

"Sure you will. Come in the car so we can talk."

"There's nobody in sight."

"Fuck you. Stand there and get wet."

The dragon turned blue, and Paul saw that the Lincoln's upholstery, like the car's body, was also blue. But the blue of the car was lighter, the blue of an ice-cold lake. Blue wasn't Bernie. Brown was. Those muscles were. He wondered whether he could outrun Bernie. Maybe, if Bernie started to get out of the car, he could go into China Dragon and call the police. But the police were Bernie's friends; ten years ago they helped him hide Max's suicide.

What would Max do in this situation, a matter of survival his cousin must have faced regularly in the ghetto? Stupid question: Max hadn't escaped.

"Your father-in-law's in deep shit," Bernie said. "He owes money to people who get unhappy when they're not paid. I'm one of them, but I'm his solution, not his problem. Morris, Maurice — whatever you call him — is *meshbokhe*, family; his son-in-law's mother is my favorite cousin. I'm amazed you'd turn your wife's father down when he's so desperate. Families don't operate that way." Bernie raised his dark eyebrows. "I'm even more amazed you're working on the Olymp case. Did Jack ever show you the pictures when he was liberated?"

Paul managed to shake his head no. He had found *Befreite Olymp Sklaven* by himself. But he didn't need a picture to know that he had reason to be biased against Olymp, that it was unethical for him to work on the appeal, and that his crazy ambition had made him a bigger jerk than Maurice.

"For a while, I figured you might have gotten on the case to stop the Olymp Nazis. They're about to achieve one of Hitler's dreams — control of the world's steel production."

"A clerk doesn't have that kind of power."

"But then I realized you're not that kind of guy. Your father would have figured a way to fuck Olymp, but not you."

Paul wanted to punch Bernie in the nose, but he knew he would end up lying in the gutter with his cousin's well-shined loafer on top of his throat.

"I was even more surprised this Jewish judge, Weinstein, was on the appeal."

"Feinstein."

"His half-brother was killed at Treblinka. A lot of people think he's out for revenge, and that if he wasn't one of three judges, it would be a sure thing for Olymp. A friend of mine in the clerk's office told me that there's a lot of trading favors in that court and that your boss and the other guy are going to go along with whatever Feinstein wants."

Paul wished he could tell the bastard he was wrong. Judge Feinstein usually deferred to Judge Webster, and all three judges were going along with Paul's memo. Maybe he could at least tell Bernie that he didn't know what he was talking about. But Bernie might be trying to trick him.

"Can you lend Maurice money to pay off the debts? I would if I had it."

Bernie raised his eyes upward. "I'll bet."

"Will you help him?"

Bernie's hand shot through the open car window and seized Paul's wrist. His grip was tighter than Maurice's — not strong pain, but enough for Paul to understand he couldn't pull away. "Let me explain something. I'm not part of the mob. I'm just a reliable Jew boy they do business with because I'm too smart to cheat them. They respect me. I try not to do muscle, but they know I can take care of myself. If I act soft-headed — if they think I'm a pussy — it's over. Why do you have to make a big deal out of something so simple?"

"You want me to commit a felony."

Bernie's grip tightened. "I take an awful lot of crap from you, Paulie. Since you've been a little kid, you look at me like I'm a leper. Ruthie and I offer to make you a wedding, and you don't even give us the courtesy of an answer. You never thanked me for all I did to get you the cash from Max's diamonds. You probably never thanked your mother. If it wouldn't upset her, I'd slap you silly. She tells me you didn't interview at any of the Jewish law firms even though they got the smartest lawyers around. You're ashamed of what you are."

Answer him, Paul told himself.

"Felony!" Bernie spit over Paul's shoulder. "Spare me the sermon. You've been taking stolen goods since high school. There must be a dozen people out there, including your boss, who know who's going to win and are trading Olymp stock in their Aunt Tillie's maiden name. Ask Sibyl if she wants these guys mad at her father."

Paul didn't want to imagine how Sibyl would respond. "It's complicated."

"I'll make it simple. You know what I'm asking you is right." The dragon turned green. "There's ten thousand in cash for you — I got it in the car."

That was it! "Up yours!" Paul snarled. He wrenched his hand free and stepped back out of Bernie's reach.

Bernie's face went frighteningly blank. "Have it your way, but whatever happens will be on your shoulders. And keep your trap shut or Maurice won't be the only one hurt."

Sibyl! The baby (if there is one). "I won't tell anyone."

* * *

In bed that night, lying beside his wife, and more than a bit drunk after the wedding, Paul exhorted himself to think like a lawyer. He had to assume the truth of what Maurice had said — better to be conned by his father-in-law than be responsible for his murder or maiming. There was no time to waste. How could he get money for his father-in-law? Lots of it, he assumed, but he'd focus on the amount after he identified the source.

Only a few hours ago, Maurice had told him Faye wasn't an option. Paul would accept that as a given. Just last spring, at Sibyl's graduation from BU, Lisette, Sibyl's sister, had told Paul: "Our father would be better off dead than marrying Faye. From the frying pan into the deep fryer — worse than the fire. Leo, her husband was a crook who knew how to work with the boys, and she's a bigger crook who doesn't know. Plus she's involved in some wild parties that even our over-stimulated father finds creepy."

Paul needed creative options. The first that came to mind wasn't that creative and had become impossible. Lew Farr, the Knish King, had told Paul to call if he ever needed anything. "I got friends," Lew had said, sounding like Bernie, but Lew's friends had broken his knees.

The second and most feasible creative option was Danny Lee, the heir apparent to a Hong Kong merchant bank who had a dorm room next to Paul's at Columbia and whose freshman philosophy grade went from F to B after Paul began critiquing his papers. At graduation, Danny's father, with his son at his side, had told Paul: "Danny says he would have flunked out his first term without you. I hope that if the need arises, you'll let us show our gratitude." Paul would call the Columbia alumni office and track Danny down.

The final creative option underscored his desperation: Rabbi Pordy. This decent man, who had conducted both his father's and Max's funerals and who knew how to listen, had, like Paul, moved up from Arverne and was now the Senior Rabbi at a prestigious synagogue on Manhattan's East Side. Paul could tell him the basic facts (which need not include Max), and do whatever the rabbi advised. Granted that would be avoiding moral responsibility, but that, of course, was what Paul wanted.

Close to dawn, Paul fell asleep. When he awoke at ten, he found a note from Sibyl.

> I tried to wake you, but then decided to give you the rest you'd never give yourself. Please forgive me (joke, I hope).
>
> Forget about meeting me at Dr. Kale's. I have to run back to school as soon as he's done. I'm going with Vera to the Young Mozart Competition audition, and I won't be able to make supper, but you'll probably stay in the office anyway.
>
> I'll call, — S

Damn her! If she had woken him, he could have gotten Danny's address from the Alumni Office this morning. Now, as he had to go to the obstetrician's office — he told Judge Webster he would — he couldn't get to Columbia before mid-afternoon.

* * *

He arrived at the obstetrician's office a few minutes before Sibyl's appointment, but Doctor Kale had taken her early. Two pregnant women were in the waiting room. One, who appeared ready to give birth instantly, looked exhausted. The other glowed. He and Sibyl were entering a new world. They had to do it together — if she would only allow it — if he would only allow it.

When Sibyl emerged, her expression conveyed nothing. He got up to greet her, but was reluctant to speak in front of the pregnant women. She spoke first: "I told you it wasn't necessary to come." She walked by him and he followed her into the hallway and onto Madison Avenue.

Paul stepped alongside her. "Stop galloping. What did he say?"

She slowed her pace, and looked at him. "I'm pregnant." She could have been reporting yesterday's weather.

Then and there, Paul decided: He would tell Maurice the Olymp outcome. Otherwise, his father-in-law could be hurt and Sibyl might have a miscarriage. He stepped in front of Sibyl and made her stop walking. "Aren't you glad?"

"I think I . . . I know I am, but right now, I'm overwhelmed."

Paul felt his face drop. "Let's have lunch to celebrate."

She raised his hand to her lips and kissed it. "I'm having lunch with Margaret and Vera's outside teacher, the battle-ax. She thinks Vera shouldn't audition for the Young Mozart yet; she has several years of eligibility left and shouldn't start out as an also ran."

Good. No lunch meant Paul would have more time to locate Danny Lee.

Sibyl kissed him like she meant it. Euphoric about the kiss and the baby, Paul went to the phone booth at Ninety-sixth and Madison and called Marilyn Helft at the Columbia Alumni Office. During his last term of college, after Marilyn's husband died, Paul had continued the swimming lessons for her Down's Syndrome son without fee. Marilyn said she would be glad to help locate Danny Lee, but couldn't get to it until tomorrow. "My top priority then," she said.

Wonderful. He'd tell Maurice that something promising was in the works.

* * *

Sibyl called Paul at the office three hours later. "My father and Faye are getting married. Tomorrow. No kidding. Faye's got pull in Florida, and a lot of things were waived."

Paul felt a wave of relief so strong he could coast it to a distant shore. Then he remembered that Faye's aid came "with conditions"— terrible conditions according to Lisette. He couldn't let Little Reuben's grandfather have to choose between his kneecaps (or worse) and Faye.

"Should we fly to Florida to talk to him?" Paul asked. He had no idea what he would say there, but he'd come up with something.

"Faye offered to have a private plane bring me down to the wedding," Sibyl said, "but the OB vetoed it. Daddy wants to talk to you. Do you know about what?"

Thank God, Paul thought. He had to end this before Sibyl asked more questions. "No. Did you tell him about the baby?"

"Let me get used to the idea first. It's been a big day. Vera's not going forward with the audition, and Margaret's very upset. She thinks that maybe she and I should visit Vera's mother. So you should eat out, but don't get home too late."

"I'll call your father now."

He called from the lobby pay phone so there would be no way of tracing the call to him.

"Maurice?"

"Yeah, I'm back. You didn't tell Sibyl anything that happened, I hope?" He sounded anxious, but not as desperate as when he ambushed his son-in-law at Borough Hall.

"No. I told you I wouldn't, and I keep my word."

"Forget everything. I didn't talk to you yesterday, you didn't see Bernie."

"What happened?" Paul asked, and immediately realized he had violated one of the cardinal rules of trial practice: When you get what you need, don't ask another question.

Maurice spoke softly, pausing every few words to catch his breath. "I didn't bullshit you, not a word, except I didn't tell you Bernie set up the whole thing." Maurice seemed to gasp. "But I've graduated from Bernie. Faye made a deal for me: We're going to do some work for the guys I owe. And I made a deal with her. We're going to get married right away so she's respectable and they can have charity dinners in her honor again." He grunted or chuckled. "Next to her, Bernie's a newborn lamb."

Paul looked around the marble lobby. The United States Courthouse in Foley Square was, except for the Supreme Court, the most important courthouse in the country. He shouldn't be having this conversation. But how could he face Sibyl if he didn't try to save her father?

"You don't have to do this. Tomorrow, I expect to be in touch with a super-rich friend who might be able to help you. A legitimate loan."

"Talk to a friend?" Maurice laughed sadly. "First make sure he paid up his life insurance. You too. Forget it. Once I told these guys I would help them, I can't renege. That's not how they operate. You could deliver the money this second, and it's too late."

Paul felt relief and then shame for feeling relieved. "I didn't turn you down. I just wanted time to think."

"You could've fooled me. Would it have killed you just to tell me what I asked?"

Paul couldn't answer.

"Don't worry about it," Maurice said, with condescension. "I'll do what I have to." Paul felt the pathetic man's contempt and, although he didn't know what he could have done differently, that he deserved it. "You just go be the American success story. Only don't treat my daughter like she's a mop. She didn't sound happy being alone so much."

"I'm heading home soon."

Paul had planned to spend a late night at the Secret Dungeon, but he put off the Olymp research and arrived home at eight. Sibyl was asleep.

CHAPTER 10

Paul was determined to be through with Maurice — not even to talk about him until Reuben's *bris* or Ruby's naming ceremony. But when he came home the next night and found Sibyl sitting up in bed and staring at him, he felt compelled to ask whether the wedding had taken place.

"This afternoon," Sibyl answered. "Lisette went. She wasn't going to go, but he told her that Faye's children were coming, and he started to cry."

"What did Lisette tell you?"

"Horrible," Sibyl shivered. "Faye's children were as crass as their mother, but not nearly as shrewd. The bride wore a jewelry store, and the groom was dazed with tranquilizers — almost asleep." Sibyl wiped her eyes with her pillow case. "They're going on some kind of business honeymoon to Cuba, but Lisette's afraid the real business is smuggling."

"I'm sure Lisette's exaggerating," Paul replied, although he feared the truth was worse.

To his relief, Sibyl dropped the subject and described a Mozart sonata she would be performing at a bridal shower for Priscilla Webster's niece. "Should I let her pay me?" Sibyl asked.

"Absolutely. You're not a relative and, with a baby, we have to think about saving."

But later that night, after Sibyl was asleep, he realized that money was not his primary concern. He wanted their children to be proud Jews, as he and his forebears had been for thousands of years — Jews who, like him, would want both to beat the *goyim* and to live with them, but not to join them. If Sibyl, who had grown up with Christmas trees and an anti-Semitic mother, became too close to the Websters, it might be tempting and easy for her to slide away from Judaism completely and to take their children with her. Boundaries must be set and maintained, and Sibyl's performance at the shower was one of them. She must play as a paid professional, not as the intimate friend of the family matriarch.

* * *

He arrived in the office the next day to find a letter from the *Columbia Law Review* accepting for publication his seminar paper on school desegregation orders. The article would virtually guarantee him a job at a top law school if that's what he wanted — perhaps even Harvard or Yale. He walked, almost ran, with the letter to Judge Webster's office like a little boy with a good report card. But why not? The judge was delighted and asked for a copy.

After leaving the judge's office, Paul turned his head and pantomimed spitting over his shoulder twice. It was a Jewish superstition intended to ward off the evil eye and to prevent good luck from turning into bad luck. *Narishkeit*, foolishness, but why not?

Someone saw the pantomime — a man his age, but thinner and taller, with high cheekbones and silky blond hair, leaning against the wall outside Paul's cubicle. It had to be Richard Story III, or a character from an F. Scott Fitzgerald novel, or both.

Paul felt his face turning red, but this wasn't the time to be apologetic or weak. "I guess you're Chip Story and you're wondering why I mimicked spitting over my shoulder."

"I am Chip, but I'm not wondering. I assume it's some kind of superstition." He sounded the way Franklin Roosevelt would have if FDR had grown up in New England.

"My wife is pregnant."

"Congratulations. Nancy and I are newlyweds and that's overwhelming enough."

Chip smiled, but Paul disbelieved the sentiment and shrugged. Chip's hair was combed straight back, without a part, like Judge Webster's; his eyes were light green, like Mrs. Webster's. He looked past Paul and said, "Judge Webster spoke to me last month about working on the Olymp case because of my chemistry background, but Vivien says you're doing it."

"I started on it a few weeks ago," Paul said as matter-of-factly as he could.

Chip's eyes returned to Paul, but he was blinking. "Do you want to switch cases? It's a subject I'm interested in, and I've got a habeas case that's up your alley. The judge won't mind."

The switch, Paul realized, would be a gracious escape from a case he shouldn't be working on — no more *Befreite Olymp Sklaven* — but this smooth aristocrat must have an agenda. And Judge Webster might conclude that Paul was getting cold feet on the royalty issue.

"No thanks. I've got a lot invested in it. Can I come to you if I have any technical questions?" he asked, telling himself he'd die before he did that.

"Of course."

A few minutes later, Chip reappeared and knocked at the door even though it was open. Paul recalled Ty's cold "Yes" in response to his own knock, but Ty was a shit. "Come on in. You don't have to knock."

Chip took one long step to Paul's desk, and held out both his hands, palms up, "Look, we're going to be working together for a year, and this is no way to start."

He bore no resemblance to Ty Martin, except for the blond hair, and Martin had only a thin semi-circle of that. "I agree." Paul stood up and they shook hands.

Chip squeezed Paul's hand. "Let me introduce myself formally; I'm not Ty Martin."

Chip's words took Paul's breath away for a moment. Then he squeezed back. "I'm glad of that. And by the way, neither am I."

Chip half smiled. "Look, Paul, you've got to be p.o.'d about Ty trying to preempt you from the Olymp case, but I had nothing to do with it." He sounded sincere, but so would any good con man. "All I know," Chip went on, "is that just before my wedding, Judge Webster told me he had a patent case involving the interaction of metals and that he was holding it for me because there might be chemistry issues I'd find interesting. That's his idea of wedding banter."

Again, Chip half smiled at Paul, but Paul tried to look blank.

"The judge never mentioned who the litigants were," Chip said. "Then he tells me, after Nancy's accident, that Ty started to work on it on his own because it was Olymp that owned the patent and you were a refugee from the Nazis. It was the first time I knew Olymp was involved or knew anything about you except that you were supposed to be a smart and nice guy."

"Thanks."

"I told the judge you should decide whether you have to be disqualified." Chip nodded. "He almost choked. He's not used to anyone disagreeing with him, especially his best friend's son."

Was this bullshit? Paul hoped not — their year together would be long — but he would assume nothing. "What was Ty trying to accomplish?"

Paul sat down behind his desk, and Chip sat on the window ledge.

"To curry my favor, maybe. I never could stand the guy."

Since Chip was blunt, Paul, too, would not measure words. "I assumed he was trying to help you get Judge Webster's recommendation for the Brennan clerkship. Was that paranoid?"

"That question's beyond my competence, but it's based on a false premise." Chip smiled. "Ty knew I had told Judge Webster I'm going back to get my doctorate in chemistry after the clerkship." He looked down at his hands, then up again. "I'm clerking for the same reason I went to law school — I promised my father I'd give it a try. Anyway, even if I did want to compete with you, you'd win. You've got a better record, and Judge Webster favors Harvard grads."

Paul was somewhat relieved, but not yet ready to trust him. "Judge Webster's son is clerking for your father, and you're clerking for his father."

Chip looked directly at Paul. "Yes, there's back scratching. Lots. My father did a favor by giving Rob Webster a job he couldn't do and didn't want. Some favor. And Judge Webster did my father a favor by giving me a job I can do and don't really want. But that doesn't mean Judge Webster is going to recommend me for a Brennan clerkship that should go to you."

"What do you mean your father gave Rob a job he couldn't do?" Paul asked, then wondered whether Chip might consider him a nosey Jew. But what's wrong with trying to understand the man you're working for?

"I guess you don't know Rob Webster. I do. At Devon, the families and headmaster elected me his big brother, despite the fact that Rob's older than me and already had a big brother. Rob's mission in life is to disappoint his father, who is easy to disappoint."

Chip described how the Websters' stormy father-son relationship had culminated in August when Rob, after being arrested for drunk driving, refused to voluntarily commit himself to a psychiatric hospital unless his parents first left Boston. "The sentencing judge said voluntary commitment or prison. If he was a poor Irish guy from South Boston, it would have been the Navy or jail. A Black kid, prison, period. I had to leave Nancy, who needed almost everything done for her, and come back to take him to the hospital. Judge Webster was wild — worse than when Rob's brother joined an ashram in India."

"I don't think I want to know all this."

"Everybody knows it."

Paul knew some of it, but not because he was part of that *everybody*. He knew it because he read a newspaper upside down when he saw it on Vivien's desk. He got up from his chair and sat next to Chip on the window ledge. "I don't understand why Ty . . ." He stopped himself because he did understand. "Anti-Semitism?" he asked.

Chip dropped his chin "Yes. And trying to ingratiate himself with me. And jealousy. You seemed to enjoy law school so much and are in line for the Brennan clerkship." He gave a quick smile. "We WASPs are losing our grip — faster at Harvard Law School than at Princeton. It wasn't what he had grown up expecting."

Chip slapped Paul on the knee and eased himself from the window ledge. Paul remained there still. Maybe Chip should take over the Olymp case after all. But then, Max's voice intervened and asked how he could trust someone who looked like that.

* * *

Judge Webster and Paul began to meet most afternoons, sometimes into the evening, sitting side by side in front of the judge's desk. (The judge's meetings with Chip were less frequent and shorter; Paul would not let himself speculate about the reasons for this.) They would first review memos and revise draft opinions in Paul's cases. Then, more often than not, the judge would push the legal papers to the side and, as in Vermont, discuss literature: Yeats' poems, Eliot's "The Love Song of J. Alfred Prufrock", and novels by Dickens, Hemingway and Austen. On a rainy evening, about two weeks after Maurice's marriage, the judge, out of the blue, asked, "What are your long-range career plans?"

Webster had suddenly gone from Elizabeth Bennet to Paul's ambitions. Where would he go next? Paul had to be careful.

"After I clerk, I'll probably go to one of the big firms. Then I'll decide whether I want to make a run at partner or teach." He wouldn't mention his hope for a Supreme Court clerkship.

The judge stood and put his hand on Paul's shoulder. The warmth of the touch radiated down his arm, but then he nearly shivered with fear.

"You know I expect to recommend you to Justice Brennan for a clerkship next September, after you finish here."

Had the judge squeezed Paul's shoulder? Paul forced himself to sit still and dug his fingernails into his palms. "Thanks. I . . . ."

Judge Webster started pacing behind Paul. "I'll be doing Justice Brennan a service."

Paul looked ahead over the judge's desk at the charcoal portrait of Chief Justice John Marshall, and sat as straight as he could. "Thank you."

The judge stopped behind Paul and again put his hand on his shoulder. "You're wise to go to one of the large firms after Brennan.

Whether or not you teach, there's no substitute for the real world. But, before you take a job, you should talk to me."

"I'd like that."

The judge walked around to his desk chair, gripped it, let it go, opened his desk drawer closed it, and sat down. "It's a hard thing to say . . ." He was facing Paul but speaking to his own hands. "I've never discussed this with . . . with a Jewish clerk before."

Paul willed himself total self-control. "You mean that some firms don't take Jews? I understand that."

"I'm ashamed of having been a partner at one of them. Fortunately, the prejudice is breaking down. Not for any high purpose, mind you. The big firms need to hire the best young lawyers, and more and more of them are Jewish." The judge raised his eyes to Paul. "You'll get any job you want, but that doesn't mean you'll stand a fair chance of making partner."

"Things are changing," Paul said. He didn't know whether he believed it.

The judge's fingers drummed the desk. "Most firms will say the right thing, but some aren't ready for more than a token Jewish partner, if that."

"I think I'll be able to figure out who's not playing it straight."

"Don't count on it. We old guard types are experts at vagueness." The judge smiled to himself. "When the Supreme Court clerkship starts, call me. At that point, I should be able to give you some real-world advice."

Judge Webster was being so kind, offering to act as his personal guide through the *goyim*. The Olymp draft opinion, Paul vowed, would be even better than he had planned. Wisely, he hadn't ceded the case to Chip. "Thanks." Paul struggled for words to express his gratitude more fully, but he feared his emotions and simply added, "I appreciate it."

"It's the least I can do. How's Olymp coming?"

Paul looked directly at Judge Webster and said, as casually as he could, "You'll have a draft the week after next."

"Early November will be fine. You can't ignore your other cases." After a brief pause, the judge added, "Or your lovely wife."

Paul welcomed the deadline. As hard as he was working, he was making little progress. The cases and articles he read seemed to swim before his eyes. He read one case with great care before remembering that he had read it two days earlier and had returned it to the library because it had been harshly criticized in the book he had worked on. His outlines of the Olymp opinion — particularly the section on damages — were both disorganized and repetitious. He asked himself why he was having these problems, but then decided that self-analysis would be a pointless waste of time. Only a firm delivery date would focus his mind. He stood up to leave and, out the window, saw only fog; unlike most days, not even a trace of the Statue of Liberty. He would work at the Secret Dungeon tonight.

* * *

Neither Judge Webster nor Chip came in that Friday. Paul, of course, knew better than to mention this to Vivien or anyone else in the courthouse. Why initiate a conversation that might show him to be a nosey Jew? He would wait to tell the news to Sibyl. The week had been stressful and, at breakfast, they had promised each other to go to bed early and not to mention the Websters or jobs until after they made love. But, at six in the evening, when Paul was ready to leave the office, Sibyl called.

"I'm at the Websters', spending the night with Priscilla. She took a tranquilizer and is lying down. It's almost like what happens with my mother except this husband does real harm. I might as well tell you what's going on since you're going to be around people involved in it."

Paul didn't want to know more. The Supreme Court clerkship was his unless something happened to make Judge Webster reconsider. And that something was more likely to occur if the judge and he became involved in each other's life and history. But he dared not stop Sibyl.

"Go ahead."

"Rob Webster left McLean Hospital. That's near Boston. His father wanted a New York hospital, but the District Attorney insisted on Massachusetts. He just walked out — disappeared. The judge blamed it on Priscilla for being so soft on their sons, making them irresponsible weaklings." Sibyl sounded close to angry tears. "Then he chartered a plane to fly him to Boston and hired private detectives to find Rob and get him back in the hospital before they threw him in jail again. He told Chip's father to get Chip up there to help the detectives. One good thing, though: You can work in the office tonight without worrying about me being alone."

"That's so unfair," Paul said angrily, but he knew she was right.

* * *

At eight on Monday morning, Chip was waiting for him in the courthouse lobby. There were shaving nicks on his face. He seemed exhausted. "Mort

Lazan and I switched clerkships. He's clerking for Judge Webster now, and I'm clerking for Judge Feinstein. We already moved our stuff."

Paul was taken aback. Whatever happened that weekend had destroyed the son-for-son clerking agreement. Judge Webster now had two Jewish clerks, which was probably a first for him, and might mean competition for the Brennan clerkship.

They went to an empty table in the fifth-floor cafeteria. "I knew what would happen and shouldn't have gone to meet them," Chip said. "The director of the detective agency, Judge Webster, my father — they wanted me to tell them everything Rob told me and then help them find him. I'd be a junior G-man with a badge like *Dick Tracy Comics* used to sell. I told them I promised Rob to keep everything he said confidential, and I had to honor that promise."

Why was Chip confiding in him? Paul, himself, had never confided in anybody. If he unburdened himself in return, uttered the word *Max* or *diamonds* or even *Jack*, he might be unable to hold back the memories and feelings he had kept to himself for over ten years. Once the dam broke, his brief friendship with Chip could end before it had a chance to grow.

"The detective worked on me while my father and Judge Webster sat there simmering. The guy patronized me — almost patted my head. The hospital was better for Rob than the street or jail, he said, and if I was really a friend, etcetera, etcetera. All I could think about was the last thing Rob told me: 'Don't let them get me back in my father's clutches.'"

"Let's get coffee," Paul interrupted. Rising in him was a fury he needed to quell — fathers who made their sons turn on them, sons who couldn't appreciate their fathers. Didn't they understand what they were missing?

Their coffee cups in front of them, Chip began describing "Stag Weekend," during which his father, Judge Webster, and three or four of their friends would spend the Veterans' Day weekend hunting at the Websters' or his father's country house.

Paul wondered whether Chip was off on a tangent. "Stag weekend?" he asked.

"Only an anthropologist could explain it," Chip said, with a bemused smile. "Everybody's male, even the help. No women on the place for anything. Everybody brings their sons who are old enough to hunt, but this year Judge Webster had no sons to bring. So right there, in front of the detective, my father suggested that Judge Webster invite you. Webster said maybe, and asked me if I would speak to you. I told them that was a terrible idea; a substitute son would only underscore the absence of his real sons." Chip paused for a moment. "I said it more delicately than that — at least I hope I did. This shook them up even more than my refusal to help the detectives."

"Thanks," Paul said. "I'd have a hard time saying no, and a harder time saying yes."

"Except for telling him I'm not going to practice law, this refusal to help them find Rob is the first time I didn't do what my father wanted." Chip's voice dropped. "When did you stop listening to your father?"

Paul closed his eyes. "My father died when I was ten." Before Chip could respond he added, "I guess I've always done what he wanted." But that wasn't so, Paul acknowledged to himself. His father wouldn't have wanted his only son soiled with Max's diamonds, even if they paved his path to Columbia and Harvard.

Chip winced. "Wow! I'm sorry. I guess . . ."

"So, Mrs. Lincoln," Paul said, "did anything else happen at the show?"

Chip almost smiled. "The two of them and the detective stormed out. Who would dare say no to them? When I got home, Judge Feinstein and Mort Lazan called together to ask me if I would accept the trade. I had to say yes because I couldn't go on working for Webster and I couldn't just quit and dump my caseload on you."

"Thanks again."

"Nancy said I was right."

"You were."

"Thanks, buddy."

* * *

Back in his cubicle, after saying goodbye to Chip, Paul finally had to admit the obvious fact he had been trying to hide from himself: He was blocked on the Olymp opinion — Jack and Max wouldn't let him write it. The two survivors — the slave and 53927, the one who had married his mother and the one who wanted to — had pulverized the mental discipline that had propelled him from a delivery boy in Rockaway to the cusp of a Supreme Clerk clerkship.

He told himself he should view them as inspirations, not obstacles: If Max and Jack could survive the Holocaust, he could write a good draft. He assured himself that he wasn't giving a windfall to a corporate war criminal. The Olymp before the Court was neither owned nor managed by enslavers. In fact, in 1950, three years before the invention of the steel-making process that was at the center of the lawsuit, it had been pardoned for any war crimes. He was only doing what courts must do in a government bound by the rule of law. Nevertheless, when he confronted the blank page in the Underwood and thought, *Olymp*, a watermark appeared on the otherwise blank paper — *Befreite Olymp Sklaven*.

How could he clerk on any court if he allowed a blank sheet of paper to freeze him? How could he be anything if he lost the determination that defined him? Although Sibyl and he had promised each other to spend more time together, he couldn't come home for dinner until the job was done well. Yet, he couldn't just take a leave of absence from their ten years together, particularly with Little Reuben growing inside her. He had to make up for the time away. Crawling into bed beside his slumbering wife at one in the morning, after fifteen hours of dropping pages in the wastebasket, he emptied his mind and saw the remedy to their being apart so much — Margaret's Pre-Halloween costume party. They'd go as Pinocchio and Geppetto. Who would be the rebellious puppet and who would pull the strings? They would answer that question together and, with humor, lighten the gloom growing between them. He fell asleep immediately.

"Yes!" Sibyl exclaimed joyously when Paul proposed the costumes at breakfast. "And I have to be Pinocchio; I'm the better dancer and you're the better manipulator." Paul didn't like the sound of that, but let it go. She wanted to make both costumes, but he insisted it be a joint effort — he would construct Pinocchio's wooden nose and the puppet guide. Within a day, however, he realized he'd never find the time, and he sought out Oscar, their building's assistant custodian. For thirty dollars, Oscar agreed to make the nose and guide, and to back up Paul's story that Paul had built them in the basement on Tuesday night while Sibyl was at a school concert and Paul, in fact, was in the Secret Dungeon. Paul felt sick when Oscar winked at him, acknowledging his deception.

* * *

On Wednesday, three days before the party, he managed to push Max and Jack out of his head, and the Olymp draft finally began to flow. After the NYU Library closed, he went to an all-night diner off Washington Square to complete the first half. But when he read his work at home the following morning, he found he had written a twenty-page theoretical essay, replete with economic jargon unrelated to the real world.

On Friday morning, he ripped up Thursday's draft because it read like the "Boy Scout Manual on Edible Plants." For the first time, he worked at the Secret Dungeon during the day. By six, he was confident that, when revised, what he had written would be a useful guide for determining a reasonable royalty for a patented invention that could revolutionize an industry. It was consistent with both economic theory and judicial precedent; it was clear; and trial judges could easily explain it to juries. He would finish it in his Foley Square cubicle on Saturday, and then type the final version on his Underwood. He celebrated by going home for dinner, practicing the Pinocchio puppet dance with Sibyl, and making love with her.

Sibyl rolled on top of him when they were through. In the past weeks, her breasts and hips had rounded. He slid his hand between their stomachs. "Where's our baby?"

"I'm glad we're going as characters who need each other and work together," she replied.

"So am I," Paul said, but his mind had gone back to footnote 9 of the latest draft which distinguished running royalties from flat royalties. Could it be cut?

* * *

Paul loved his cubicle — the old wooden desk that commanded nearly half the space; the fortress-like Underwood that filled nearly half the desktop; the piles of books, briefs, and trial records on the floor in each corner, one pile per appeal except for Olymp which had three. The diplomas and certificates on the wall reminded him that he was fulfilling the hopes of his father and his cousin. The picture of Sibyl on the radiator would, at the Supreme Court, be replaced by a picture of her with Reuben. Maybe, by then, her hair would be long again.

He loved his office the most on Saturday mornings, when he often had Judge Webster's chambers — half the thirtieth floor — to himself. He didn't have to wear a suit or wonder whether Judge Webster would resume the late afternoon meetings he had abruptly terminated after Chip began working for Judge Feinstein. (Although he had enjoyed them, Paul wasn't entirely unhappy that the literature discussions had ended. Unlike his work with the judge on particular appeals, he was never quite sure of the ground rules for these discussions.)

Even lunch was better on Saturday. At 12:30, Paul and several other Court of Appeals clerks — enough to fill one or two large tables — would walk to a restaurant in Chinatown that prepared special dumplings and a surprise soup for them. After lunch, as sated as he might be, he would be reenergized by the work on his desk.

On this Saturday morning, however, the day of Margaret's party, he was appalled by yesterday's draft. He had read an important Supreme Court decision too broadly, he had mischaracterized the discussion of damages in Anvil's brief, and he had relied too heavily on an economics treatise that had recently been criticized by a Nobel Laureate. Judge Webster, who had never had cause to question Paul's accuracy or thoroughness, could lose confidence in him. Worse, the judge might accept Paul's work and submit an opinion that would be rejected by the two other judges on the appellate panel or criticized in law reviews.

He looked at his watch and began to perspire. It was now or never. More time in the Secret Dungeon would only produce more angst. He swung his chair towards the window, leaned back, and ordered himself to think like a lawyer: Define the problem that was snarling his legal brain, lay out his options, evaluate them, and *act*. He swung the chair back and rolled a piece of paper into the Underwood:

Problem

Because of M, J and 6,000,000 others, I'm unable to draft a good opinion.

Options

(1)   Tell Judge W everything.
(2)   Stop the crap and do what you have to.
(3)   Panic.

He typed Xs over Option Three until there was nothing but a thick, black undecipherable line. Then he studied Option One and revised it to read: "Tell Judge W everything about Olymp enslaving Jack." That was enough — Max and Maurice were irrelevant history.

He should pick up the phone this second. Wasn't that his duty, especially since Judge Webster had been kind to him? The judges on the walls of Harvard Law School — the legal forefathers he shared with Judge Webster — demanded nothing less. But none of them had survived the Nazis. And none ever needed the foresight to escape to a new country with a wife and infant son. He had to be guided by the actual men in his actual life. Option Two — "Stop the crap and do what you have to" — was *his* survival.

Parts of yesterday's draft, perhaps more than half, could be salvaged. But first, his head had to be swept clean of everything except the discrete issues in *Olymp* v. *Anvil*. A brisk walk toward the East River, away from Chinatown, a quick sandwich where nobody would know him, and a brisk walk back would do it.

He strode through the courthouse lobby and out the revolving door, eyes straight ahead, trying not to see whether the other law clerks were gathering for the Saturday Chinese lunch. At the concrete pillars atop the long flight of courthouse steps, Paul realized he had forgotten his jacket. Too late to go back. Besides, it was remarkably warm for October. Several people weren't wearing jackets. The gray-haired man at the foot of the steps wasn't even wearing a long-sleeved shirt.

As Paul descended the steps, something pulled him toward the man in short sleeves — something on his arm. Was it a tattoo? Paul looked at the man's face and saw Max.

CHAPTER 11

No, it can't be. He's too old. But it's ten years later. And how can you tell the age of someone who looked 80 when he was 40? It *is* him — sunken eyes and cheeks, rat-gray pallor.

Halfway down the steps, Paul saw that the man's tattoo was a number. But his mother told him not to look at Max's arm.

He grabbed the railing and tried to study the man's face, but nothing would stay still. He made it down to the fourth step. The number was paler than he remembered and higher up on the forearm. The first digits were *five three* — the same as Max's. The courthouse steps seemed to slide away from him.

"You don't need to stare." The accent had traces of Yiddish, but it was different from anything Paul could recall hearing. "It's five-three-nine-two-eight — one more than his. I'm his brother Asher, your cousin."

The temperature seemed to plunge — colder than at Brooklyn Borough Hall.

On the evening Max drowned, his mother or grandmother had said that Max had a brother Asher, or was it Arnold or some other "A" name, who played the piano and died with everyone else. "Do you play the piano?"

Asher looked at Paul quizzically. "Not for twenty years." He raised his left hand. Each of his three middle fingers pointed in a different direction; all were horribly gnarled like the fingers of the witch in Snow White. "I got your pal Max to thank for this, too."

Paul squeezed the railing.

Asher climbed the three steps up to him. He was a few inches shorter than Paul. Max had been a few inches taller, but Paul had grown since Max's death.

Asher pulled on Paul's arm. "Let's eat lunch. We got a lot to talk about."

Paul let Asher lead him, keeping his eyes on their moving feet — Asher's square-toed shoes with brown frayed laces, his own shiny black loafers with pointed toes. After a while, Asher maneuvered him through the door of an unfamiliar luncheonette and into a booth.

They sat facing each other, Paul with his back to the door. Asher's white shirt was dull from too many washings, just as Max's shirts had been. But Max's shirts had long sleeves covering his numbers. Asher's arms were bare but, thank God, they were at his side, the numbers out of sight below the Formica table.

"I don't want to eat. Just tell me what you want, and let's go."

"A real tough guy, huh?" Asher winked and put his arms on the table. Paul gazed over Asher's head at the jukebox.

"You can look. It's only numbers."

Paul lowered his eyes to Asher's forearm and stared. It wasn't as difficult as he had expected. 53928. Max plus one. He spoke deliberately: "I thought . . ." And then he felt his throat go dry.

"They all thought I was dead, and I was, except my body. You should have seen your mother's face when I showed up in Rochester. I hadn't seen her since her wedding in Teplice. Max and I played there for a wedding gift. He was on the fiddle, never a real violin player, and me, the accordion — they didn't have a piano." Asher smiled briefly. Same crooked teeth as Max. "And I hadn't seen Jack — he's my second cousin on my mother's side — since my sister Malke broke up with him. I only wish I could've surprised Max too. Except I might have killed him before he opened his mouth."

Paul tried to ignore what Asher had just said about Max. He focused on the numbers. The brothers must have arrived at Auschwitz together and been sent to the left, for tattoos and slave labor, instead of to the right, for gas and immediate death.

The waitress, heavy and expressionless, stood above them, holding two menus.

"Two tuna fish sandwiches, two coffees," Asher said.

"I don't want tuna fish," Paul said, although that was what he often ate for lunch.

Asher looked up at the waitress. "Okay. Give him a menu."

A mistake — the menu might shake in his hands. "Okay, tuna fish." Asher winked again. "No, make it roast beef on rye — very rare." The waitress concentrated on her order pad and wrote slowly. "A Coke instead of coffee."

Asher shrugged. "Whatever I say, you say different."

Paul looked right at the numbers. "Don't play with me. Just tell me what you want."

Asher leaned over the table until his head was barely an inch from Paul's. His breath smelled of garlic. "I don't play games, *tatele*. If I did, I'd be dead in Poland." Asher sat back in his seat. "Malke's in jail."

"Where?"

"In Russia. Be patient — you'll learn. You got to help me get her out — her kid, too."

A legal problem, Paul thought, and, unlike Maurice, probably one he could solve thorough the law. He'd discuss it with Judge Webster and, together, come up with a solution. "What do you want me to do?"

"She's in this prison for politicals — Lubyanka — on some Zionist plot they cooked up. Next, Siberia, the Gulag, maybe worse. They're after the Jews. Soon they'll start killing us again or make jail so terrible we kill ourselves — clean up what Hitler missed."

No, Paul thought. It *was* like Maurice. Asher would also ask Paul to disclose the outcome of the Olymp appeal but, instead of invoking the specter of harm from American mobsters, he'd warn of harm from Russian anti-Semites.

"I thought things had improved since Stalin died."

Asher looked as if he wanted to spit. "You sound like the Jews before the war. Don't want to see nothing till it's too late. Stalin was one of a hundred million Russian anti-Semites."

Stalin was Georgian, Paul thought, not Russian, but it made no difference.

"Stalin dying didn't keep my sister out of Lubyanka. Khrushchev making a speech about Stalin being a killer, that didn't change nothing. They're still after us, only now it's sometimes possible to get some out."

The waitress approached with the food. Asher stopped talking. Paul's roast beef was on white bread, not rye, and it wasn't rare.

As soon as the waitress left, Asher pushed his food to the side, and Paul did the same. Asher lowered his voice into gravel. "I know Russia. That's where they took me after the war, where my sister Malke, the idealist, found me. She wanted to go there to make the world a paradise for workers — strawberries and cream for breakfast. I got out as quick as I could."

South Africa, Paul thought; maybe Australia. Asher's accent was clipped English plus Yiddish. Later, when Malke was safely out, he would ask Asher what he had been afraid to ask Max — *What was Auschwitz like?*

"Are you listening?"

Paul tried to sound indignant. "Of course."

"This is no game," Asher whispered. "With fifty thousand dollars, I can get her and her kid out. Maybe to America — to Israel for sure."

Maybe Asher wouldn't ask about the Olymp outcome. Maybe he would make a naïve plea to a supposedly rich American cousin. "I don't have fifty thousand dollars. Not even a thousand. I just graduated from law school."

"What you got's worth a lot more than that."

A precept from the dean's orientation speech echoed in Paul's head: *If you receive a corrupt proposal, ask yourself what you have done to make someone think you might be receptive to that proposal.* Paul knew what he had done: He had survived — lived a safe and good life as a Jew in America while Jews in Europe were killed for being Jews. He had spurned Max's generosity and then accepted his legacy of tainted diamonds. And there was more. He hadn't reported Bernie's and Maurice's criminal requests — he hadn't even told them *no* in unambiguous English. To the contrary, by telling Maurice, "I didn't turn you down," he had invited another try. All this was enough for several corrupt proposals.

"I don't understand," Paul said in the most neutral voice he could summon.

Again, Asher leaned across the table. "Don't act dumb. You can save a Jew, your cousin, her kid — two Jews — by giving me the key you got from Max. That should get us more than enough. The rest can be divided, but nothing for me."

It's not the Olymp case. *Thank you God.* "I don't know what you're talking about."

"Tell it to Frieda Greenberg."

Fuck you God. "Yes, I spoke to Frieda Greenberg." He looked directly into Asher's bloodshot eyes. "She just carried on about how she hated Max. Nothing about keys."

"You'll know soon why she hated," Asher retorted. "It's a big club, the people who hate Max because of what he did to them."

Paul realized he was breathing deeply and slowly through his nose. The bastard was goading him. He would have to defend Max, the dead man who had helped him so much. But how could he defend anybody when he knew nothing and had just been caught lying?

"I don't have the key. On the night Max died . . . ." Paul told Asher about the violin case on Max's bed and what he found inside it. "I walked out on the jetty, just like Max, and threw them after him."

As Paul spoke Asher nodded steadily, then slowly said, "Ab-so-lute-ly." He stressed each syllable, making it clear that he meant *Bullshit!*

"If you don't believe me, I don't care. The key and the piece of paper with the numbers — I assumed it was a combination for a safe deposit box — are at the bottom of the ocean off Rockaway Beach. The paper said Greenberg and Montreal, and that led me to Frieda."

Asher finally stopped nodding. "Forget the numbers. We know them. They're for a Swiss bank account. A Zurich lawyer found them out for Jack years ago." He jutted his chin. "But you need two keys for the box in Switzerland. Frieda gave me one." He pointed to his left back pocket. "You got the other. Your mother, Jack and Frieda managed to get everything Max and Kelly hid except for the box in Zurich."

Paul's head jerked, "Kelly?"

"Frieda's husband, Kelly Greenberg. Nice guy. I'll explain the name later." Asher started to smile, but stopped. "Seven different boxes spread over America and Canada. They sold the diamonds they could get their hands on, and now all the money's gone. Most of it went to you and your mother and to the store in Rochester which never did too hot, and the rest of it to some *gonif* who got Frieda to invest in oil wells with no oil. All that's left is what's in the Swiss box, which is plenty, and the diamond on your wife's finger."

Paul clenched his teeth. That bitch — yes, his mother, that bitch — had told Asher that Sibyl was wearing Max's ring. A few words from Asher to Sibyl, and Paul's marriage could end.

"Why are you looking so mad?" Asher raised an eyebrow.

"Who told you about the ring?" Paul locked his eyes on Asher's.

"What's the difference who told?"

Paul felt his jaw move in and out, and made no effort to stop it.

"Okay," Asher finally said, "I'll tell you so you can hear the story of how Max got the diamonds. Maybe then you'll find the key in the ocean."

"I'm waiting."

"Okay." Asher ran his tongue over his lips. "Jack said they made from one of the diamonds your engagement ring, and as soon as he said it, he realized he shouldn't have. Your mother got hysterical, and they both made me promise I wouldn't use it for a threat."

"You just did."

"No, I didn't." Asher fixed his eyes on Paul's; they were as dark and deep as Max's eyes. "I respect Jack and your mother too much to tell anyone about the ring."

The bastard seemed to mean it, but who could trust him. "Tell me what you want to tell me. But I can't give you what I don't have. And Max never told me about the diamonds."

Asher interlaced his fingers tightly until the crooked digits grew purple. "Stop making me for a fool. After what Max did to get those diamonds, he wouldn't die without making sure you and your mother could get what he wanted for you."

"Nobody ever told me where the money came from."

Asher looked up at the ceiling. "From the sky it came, like the manna God gave the Jews in the desert." He lowered his head. "Look *Peretz*." Paul was surprised to hear his Hebrew name, and Asher forced a smile. "You went to *Talmud torah*, didn't you? You know something about your religion?"

Stop toying with me, Paul wanted to scream, but he only nodded.

"Did they teach you that the Talmud says if you save one life it's like saving the world?" Paul nodded again. "The life is my sister and my nephew — both your cousins. Aren't six million murdered Jews enough? Do you have to make it six million plus two?"

"Stop toying with me!" Paul realized he was shouting. He lowered his voice. "If I had the key I'd give it to you, but I can't give you what I don't have, and I have to get back to work."

He started to get up, but Asher snarled, "Stay! Listen," as if he were commanding a dog, and Paul sank back into the seat. Three booths away, the waitress and an old woman stared at them. Paul raised his chin toward them, but Asher spoke louder. "They can listen. Everybody should know." The old woman hid behind the menu, and the waitress turned away.

Asher's voice dropped. "I'm not going to let my sister die the way your beloved Max left me to die in the Polish mud so he could run off to steal diamonds. I don't tell the whole story to nobody, but maybe, if you listen, you'll stop the ocean *narishkeit* and give me the key."

Paul pictured Max — the face in front of him minus a few years — handing him the Buffet, telling him to try out for his high school orchestra, talking softly to his mother in the kitchen. And later, making Columbia and Harvard possible — even providing the ring for his marriage.

"Tell me what happened."

Paul braced himself. Asher took a bite of his tuna fish sandwich and chewed it. Paul picked up his roast beef sandwich, then put it down.

The waitress was over them again. "Is something wrong with the food?"

"No, he isn't too hungry," Asher answered. "Bring me some fresh coffee and an apple pie à la mode. Chocolate." He nodded toward Paul. "Bring him too."

Asher chewed another small piece of sandwich and waited until the waitress was behind the counter. "We expected the worst, but not so bad as what happened. The thirst dried up your eyeballs. The stink! You don't know how much a person can stink. Worse alive than dead."

Asher sucked in air, then exhaled it slowly. "I'll start with the Lodz Ghetto. That's where Jews got collected till they put us on a transport to Auschwitz — both in Poland, of course. Transport!" Asher made a short gurgling sound. "A boxcar train they packed us in to ship us — the kind they used for cattle. Everybody says six million killed, but nobody wants details. If you weren't there, you don't ask, and if you was, you keep it inside."

Asher was right. Over the years, Paul had known several survivors — Max, Jack, the Berkshire Inn gardener who helped him with the rowboats and canoes, the grocery store customer with numbers on her arm. But, except for a few words from Max, none of them had alluded to the Holocaust, let alone recounted a single experience. In seemingly endless Columbia dormitory discussions of seemingly countless subjects — McCarthyism, the Korean War, Jim Crow, Buick tail fins, Elizabeth Taylor's breasts — the subject simply never came up. The Jews didn't want to think about it, and the Gentiles didn't want to embarrass them.

"We always stuck together, Max and me, and we were gonna keep sticking. But Max was in a daze. Just a few days before, both our wives . . ." Asher shut his eyes tightly. "The four of us had a double wedding." He opened his eyes which seemed to have grown even redder. "The Gestapo shot them both in the street when they tried to take Max's son to a doctor after curfew. For some reason, the Gestapo let this *kapo*, this Jewish policeman, take the boy back to the house. He would have been better off if they killed him with his mother."

Max's son! His mother mentioned him to Paul in 1948. "Was his son named Reuben?"

Asher nodded.

"Was he alive when you went on the transport?"

Asher shook his head no.

"How did he die?"

"Why are you asking?"

"My mother wouldn't tell me."

"I don't want to tell you, neither. Of all the things that happened, that was the worst." Asher scraped his lips with his teeth, then stopped and sat up straight. "But I will tell you so you don't think I'm hiding anything. It was maybe two days after they shot our wives. Reuben had typhus, but we had to leave him alone in this room we all shared because there'd be no food or water if we didn't go to work. I told Max to stay, and I'd find a way to get some extra food, but he wanted to try and see the doctor to get medicine." His narrow shoulders dropped.

"When we got back at night, there were rats on the cot chewing at Reuben's face. Maybe a quarter of it was gone."

Paul put his head into his hands.

"He was still breathing but couldn't make a sound. He died a couple minutes after we got there."

Paul felt a fatigue so great that he lacked the strength to collapse. Asher looked at him but didn't seem to see him. "Do you know how old he was?"

Paul couldn't answer.

"How old?" Asher repeated.

"Five," Paul whispered.

"Five. Did I tell you enough?"

They both sat still and silent. Then, Asher took a long swallow of water. "After that, Max just gave up — like a straw man he was. Maybe it explains what he did later. I don't know. I'm not judging or trying to understand. Just telling."

You are judging, Paul thought. "Go ahead, if you can," he said.

"I can. Don't worry." Asher cracked the knuckles on his right hand. "I want to be fair. Max saved my life at the transport." He paused, waiting for Paul to ask the details.

"How?"

Asher described how he dragged Max to the boxcar and pushed him in. "Otherwise, the Ukrainian guards would have clubbed his head in." But Asher then slipped on some garbage and fell on the ground just a few feet from one of the guards. The guard raised his club and Max pulled Asher up and got them both the car. "All of a sudden he was his old self. It could've meant his life, but that's how close we were.

"In the train," Asher went on, "Max goes back into his daze, but at least he listened to me. We took turns sitting on each other's shoulders so that one of us could breathe fresh air through the crack at the top of the boxcar. The trip was almost a week and, at some point, Max went from a straw man to a dishrag. I kept slapping him so he didn't die. And I'll tell you the truth: When the guy next to me passed out on his feet, I took the sausage from his pocket and gave Max half. But the sausage turned out to be bad. Max shit in his pants and threw up all over himself. He was a mess, and I was sure that when we got to Auschwitz — by this time everybody understood everything — they were going to send him right to the gas. By then the sausage guy was dead, lying on a pile of bodies in the back of the car. His clothes were pretty clean, and he was Max's size, so I just undressed him. Some old lady started screaming at me — respect the dead, that kind of stuff — and I told her I'd kill her if she tried to stop me.

She knew I meant it. Anyway, I took a kerchief from one of the dead women and cleaned Max a little bit. Then I put the sausage guy's clothing on him — except Max kept his own hat, which you'll understand later — and gave him some candy I found in the pile. Finally, the train stopped at Auschwitz — I could tell from the dogs barking and the bright lights and the Germans shouting orders. But mostly I could tell from this sweet smell of dead Jews burning."

The waitress brought the pie and coffee, and Asher kept talking.

"I could see when they opened the boxcar that it was organized pretty much the way these underground guys told us in Lodz. You had to strip on the platform and give them everything you had. You were too scared to be cold. Then they made a selection depending on whether you looked strong enough to work. If the SS doctor pointed right, you went straight toward the sweet smell — the gas and ovens. If left, you could live a little longer.

"Max looked like death, and I knew that the only hope was the plan we made when our wives were still alive. Before we stripped, I pulled Max over to this big SS lieutenant — Strummer, I learned later — and slipped him one of the diamonds I had hidden and also the HRD Antwerp certificates we both had showing we were trained jewelers who really know gems — diamonds in particular. Strummer understood what the certificates meant. Then I gave him our caps and told him there are good diamonds inside the lining. The caps had every diamond from our Teplice jewelry store — some we didn't really own, but that's rules for a world without Nazis. Before I knew it, Strummer stuffed everything inside his jacket. He said something to a guard and, a few minutes later, we both got sent to the left, even though Max couldn't stand without me holding him up.

"I won't tell you what it was like there — and we had it better than most because of Strummer. We started hauling rocks, *shvartsorbet*, but then they made us *sonder kommandos*. You know what that is?"

Paul shook his head no, although he thought he knew.

"When the gas is finished, you pull the bodies out. Not easy because they're piled up against the locked door trying to escape, and most of them have gone in their pants, except they weren't wearing anything. Then . . ." Asher's steely eyes had gone dull. "Then . . ." He lifted his coffee cup to his lips and put it down without drinking. "Then we pull out their gold teeth and look up their *tuchasas* to see if they've hidden anything. Later we go through the shit on the floor. The Germans don't want to lose anything valuable.

"Some guys went crazy doing this work. One, Fenichel, who slept next to me on the bunk, he threw himself against the electric fence and got fried on the barbed wire."

Fenichel. Paul had read the name recently. He had heard and said it. But that was all he could remember.

"Then one day, like a miracle, Max is his old self. He and I become the best workers. When one of the guards — crazy even for an SS — said he wanted skin with tattoos for a lamp, Max and I volunteered."

Afraid he might howl, Paul pressed his lips together.

"What's wrong with you?" Asher demanded.

"That's enough," Paul managed to respond.

"Enough for what?" Asher's crooked fingers scratched the table. "It's not nice like being a big shot clerk for a judge? But that wasn't the worst — in Auschwitz, no matter what happened, there was always something worse."

"Why do I have to know all these details?"

Asher ate a forkful of pie and ice cream. "I never told anybody some of this, not even Malke, but I'm telling you now so you'll help her because it's the right thing to do, especially since you got so much from Max. But I'll do what I have to do to get the key from you — even turn your mother over to the FBI."

"What has she done?"

Paul, of course, knew the answer. Although on the night of Max's suicide he wasn't aware of the legal terms, he had instinctively realized what he would later learn as a law student — that his mother's lies to the government about the cause of Max's death and what she had received from him were crimes. Every time she sold a diamond and gave Paul the cash, they were each, according to the Federal Criminal Code, "engaging in acts in furtherance of a conspiracy."

"You're the smart lawyer. You tell me the crimes."

Attack, Paul told himself. "There are none by her."

Asher's eyes narrowed. "Look, Sonny, I don't bluff. I checked with a lawyer this morning, and he said she did all kinds of immigration and tax crimes. Just the kind of thing the Jew haters in the FBI would like to get their hands on."

"Who's the lawyer?"

"Ben Fenichel, the brother of the guy who threw himself on the electric fence. He has an office on Vesey Street. He knew how close his brother and me were in Auschwitz."

Paul remembered: Ben Fenichel, who had taught securities law at Brooklyn Law School, had been disbarred as part of the settlement of a fraud case brought against him by the Securities Exchange Commission. The law clerks had discussed it at last Saturday's Chinatown lunch.

"He's been disbarred," Paul told Asher. "Not a lawyer anymore."

"Fenichel says it's all politics, but he still knows law and what's a crime."

"So do I. And I also know that the government can't prosecute you if it waits too long. Ask Mr. Fenichel to tell you about the statute of limitations."

Asher sat back. "Okay, I won't argue with you." He put his hands on the table and stretched them open. The fingers on his left hand were even more crooked than Paul had realized. "I like your mother. She gave me two thousand dollars and told me she doesn't think there are any more diamonds in America or Canada. I believe her, but I'm going to do whatever I have to do to save Malke with the diamonds in Switzerland. I'm sorry."

Paul couldn't stop him. One visit by Asher to any of a dozen government agencies — even an anonymous letter — could mean the end of everything he cared about. He didn't know the story of Max's diamonds, he wasn't sure he wanted to know it, and he couldn't believe whatever Asher would say. But, he had to listen.

"Tell me what you want me to know. I won't interrupt."

Asher eyed him, then wiped his brow. "After the gas, we worked on the ovens. These details you can do without."

Thanks, Paul thought.

"That wasn't too long because of what I told Strummer: We knew diamonds and had certificates. He got us jobs in the warehouse where they sorted out what the people brought. Much better. I told you that when the boxcars pulled in, they took everything you had, stripped you bare — eyeglasses, even false teeth. We sorted the clothes, Max and me, but our real job was to help Strummer and the two SS animals who were stealing with him. Whatever the SS took from the prisoners was supposed to get shipped back to Germany, but Strummer didn't see why they couldn't take a bit for themselves. So, when nobody was around we would inspect stones that Strummer and his guys took and tell them whether something was real or a good fake. If it was real, they'd swallow it and, when they got outside the gate, they crapped and dug it out. Strummer didn't want to lose nothing, so he got us these jeweler tools. If it was too big to swallow, we'd cut it up if we could."

Asher snorted, "SS. The supermen of the super race. So super they shit diamonds."

Paul cringed. Asher didn't change expression. "A fortune they swallowed. In return, we didn't become ashes, and Strummer got us extra rations. Everybody else got two pieces of moldy bread a day and a soup that was no better than dishwater. We got three pieces plus some scraps the dogs didn't want. While this is going on, Kelly Greenberg shows up. Max and me knew him when he was Kalman, before he became Kelly. He was a *kontrabandist*, smuggler in English, and a *zasser* or *passer*; somebody who if you steal something he buys it."

"A fence."

"Yeah, fence. It was the Greenberg family business, smuggler and fence, like jewelry was our family business. What all of them were really known for is that they didn't lie or cheat. You'll see how Max took advantage of all that."

Asher described how, before the war, Kelly expanded his operations to include arms smuggling. "He was the best at that. The *Irishers* who wanted to get free from the English were his biggest buyers, and they gave him the name Kelly as a joke, but he kept it. Well, when Kelly got off the transport, he was prepared like we was, and he gave Strummer a newspaper article about him and his family. It was in Yiddish, but Strummer had plenty of translators. The next thing you know, Kelly was working in the warehouse too, keeping the inventory books. His real job was telling Strummer who he could talk to outside to get the diamonds into Swiss banks or hidden someplace safe and telling him how to do business with these guys. He even wrote introduction letters in Yiddish with code words so his friends will know he was working together with Strummer.

"Max and Kelly became real close, talking all the time, and they came up with this idea. They told Strummer before they told me."

Paul stared at the melting ice cream. For some strange reason, he was hungry — ravenous. He wondered how long they had been sitting there.

"Wake up, *Tatele*," Asher almost sang. "You're like Max in the cattle car. Pinch your cheek. This is important for you to know."

Paul ate a spoonful of ice cream.

"Okay. Strummer loved music. Like a good Nazi, Wagner most of all. He played records in the warehouse and they played it over the loudspeakers when we would line up in the dark for roll call. *Appel* they called it. Max and Kelly saw there's a whole lot of musical instruments in the warehouse that people brought on the transport — violins, clarinets, trumpets, everything. Don't ask me how, but there's even a tuba. The two of them told Strummer he should start a prisoner orchestra. Live music would help when the transports come in and the people might not cooperate with the SS making the selections — who gets a number tattooed, who becomes smoke. A Jewish orchestra would help them fool themselves a little longer.

"I don't know who had the idea first — Max who thinks he's a musician or Kelly who can't tell a flute from a herring, but wants to save his brother Shlomo's life." Asher tapped his own head, "Shlomo's missing something up here. Not smart enough to be a *passer*, but he plays the drum pretty good so long as he doesn't have to read too much music.

"Strummer tells them to handle everything, and they start by making Shlomo the drummer and Max the conductor and first violinist. Max never conducted nothing before and, while he's a pretty good fiddler, they got first-rate violinists there. One guy, Arnold Meltzer, was assistant concertmaster in the Paris Symphony, but he ends up in the gas."

"Gas?" Paul questioned. "I thought that was when prisoners arrived."

"You thought! You thought because you didn't want to know — like most Jews." Asher paused to let his words sink in.

"The SS made selections for the gas all the time, not just from the trains. You were afraid every morning that they would call your name at the *appel*. Max said he had nothing to do with Meltzer being in the selection, but he's lying."

"How can you say that?

"Don't be a fool," Asher answered. "Meltzer gets selected the day after he said he wants to play in the orchestra. Max even takes Meltzer's violin. Strummer doesn't realize it's worth maybe twenty thousand dollars. But even he, *chazer* that he was, couldn't swallow it."

Paul saw the violin case on Max's pillow. "Did Max keep Meltzer's violin?"

"Nobody kept nothing. It was enough to keep alive."

Asher recounted his pleas to become part of the orchestra, and Max's poor excuses for refusing him. "At last," Asher continued, "I'm about to give him a piece of my mind when he tells me what's what. My brother, whose life I saved, says to me, 'Strummer told me Meltzer's in tomorrow's selection.'"

Outside, a horn blared. Paul turned and saw through the window a smiling young woman sitting in a Buick convertible waving at someone. Sibyl was prettier and, tonight, when their costumes were the hit of the

Halloween party, she would be smiling too. Whatever happened with Meltzer, if it did happen, was long ago. "The orchestra?" he asked Asher.

"Just a dozen players and, in spite of Max, it's pretty good. They play on the platform when the transports come in. Something by Schubert when they're from Austria, and Dvorak for the Czechs, and for the Hungarians, Bartok. It gets everybody calmer before they die. Sometimes, in the evenings, they play for the guards. Some mornings, they play at the lineups while we stand there for hours, freezing in the dark. Mostly Wagner — *Tristan* a lot; *Tannhäuser*, too. Max finds a tuba player for the deep bass notes. You know it?"

Paul heard the long opening notes of the tuba and trombones in *Tannhäuser* as he licked the Buffet's reed in preparation for the clarinets' entrance at the Far Rockaway High School concert. Max had told him to play. But did he have to play so well — or enjoy it?

"You know it?"

"What could Max have done?" Paul felt himself shaking.

"I'm not passing judgments, and I was no angel. I heard there were angels there but, maybe except for Kelly, I never met one who stayed alive. Let me just tell you what he did."

"Go ahead." Paul tried to empty his mind and just listen.

"The orchestra gets put in the barracks with the *kapos*. They get a stove and an extra blanket, and they practiced indoors while we froze. No dogs at their ankles or getting slammed by rifles. In our barracks, we're stacked up on boards, three men to a board, three levels high, like boxes of toilet paper in a warehouse, and for them it's two and two."

Paul's wondered how many men were in Asher's barracks? How many digits on their arms? The prisoners were stacked nine high so it all depended on how many stacks. Probably three or four stacks on each side. Normally, he would be able to do the computations in his head but, facing Asher, he could not. For months, he had tried not to see the five digits on Max's arm from across their bedroom but, in the barracks, the digits, would have engulfed and devoured him. If he survived a single night, he would be crazy.

To Paul's surprise, the waitress was holding the check over the table. Asher grabbed it, and Paul said, "Let me pay."

"I'm not looking for a free sandwich." The waitress hurried back to the counter.

"By now everyone knows the war's almost over," Asher said. "We hear the guards talking about the Russians a few days away. American planes all over the sky. But the transports keep coming, most now from Hungary, and everything gets speeded up, like they're afraid some Jews might not get killed. More diamonds getting swallowed. We're still sorting clothes in the warehouse. What for? Who's gonna wear them? But it's keeping me alive.

"A week or so before the death march, Kelly and Shlomo disappear. 'Gas?' I ask Max and he says, 'Don't ask too many questions.' Later that day, when they blow the horn sending us back to the barracks for roll call, Max tells me I should stay in the warehouse. I tell him he's crazy. You get shot on the spot if you miss roll call. Max says trust him — he's gonna save my life and make me rich. He's my brother, so I stay."

"As soon as everybody's gone, Strummer comes in, and they tell me this plan they got. I can see it's Max's idea." Asher wrinkled his forehead. "In a day or two, they're gonna empty the camp and start marching us west so the Germans can surrender to the Americans instead of the Russians. No picnic the march, Strummer says. Anyone who can't keep up gets shot. Strummer makes a pistol with his hand." Asher imitated the gesture. "And he puts the barrel — his index finger — between my eyes. Ridiculous for an SS officer whose business is killing Jews, but it scares me."

Asher made a pistol with his hand and pointed his index finger at the ceiling. Paul waited for Asher to aim at him across the table. Only a finger, Paul assured himself, but his mouth had gone dry. Finally, Asher opened his palm. The gun was gone. Paul reached for his water glass.

"Strummer goes, but first he says that Max will tell me their plan and, if I listen to my brother and don't do something dumb, I'll keep alive and come out a rich man. Rich I don't care. I just want to live long enough to kill Strummer."

The plan, Asher said, was to help "Strummer and his boys" smuggle more diamonds and gold out of Auschwitz — "stuff that was too much to put in their stomachs." These would be sewn into the linings of prisoner shirts the brothers would wear. Max, Asher and Strummer would be at the back of the march and, when they reached a crossroads three kilometers from the camp, where there was a statue of Mary and Jesus, Max would make believe he collapsed, Asher would kneel next to him, and Strummer would fire some shots at them. The shots would miss by a bit but the brothers would act dead. When the death march was out of sight, they would go to a farmhouse Strummer had described where they would be hidden for a few days until the war was over. They would then leave with one diamond each, and the farmer would shoot them if they tried to take any more. Max and Strummer had a deal that if Strummer was tried for war crimes "and we testify he saved Jews, we'd get some more diamonds."

"Did you trust Strummer?" Paul asked.

"You're being ridiculous again. The only thing I was sure was that everybody would double cross, and that Max had his own plan which would get him the most and maybe put me out of the picture."

Paul assured himself that this wasn't the Max he knew — but then, he admitted, he didn't know Max.

"For the first time since I go in the cattle car, I think I'm not gonna make it. I'm not sure I want to make it. For what after all this?" Asher pulled a napkin from the dispenser. "Max must see it in my face because, just before the guard comes to take us back, he pinches my cheek like I did to him in the cattle car, and he tells me, 'I'm gonna save you like you saved me.' He tells me he figured out a way we can keep the diamonds they're gonna sew in our shirts plus some of the diamonds the SS shit. Whatever he's scheming, I'm sure it's not gonna work, but I say all right because, if I say anything else, he'll get Strummer . . ." He rolled the napkin into a tight ball. "I don't want to think about it — to die knowing my own brother killed me."

Asher threw the napkin ball, against the table. "What else could I do?"

And what else could I do? Paul silently repeated Asher's question. *Turn my mother in? Tell Sibyl the truth and risk losing her?*

"The death march," Asher continued. "Ten steps out the gate, and you wanted to be back in the camp." Asher's voice slowed. "The mud was a foot thick and it took all your strength to lift your foot up and put it down. It got through the holes in your boots into every cut and sore, so cold it burned. Weather? There was no weather — you could only feel and see your feet. Growls from the dogs, *Schnells* from the guards, rifle butts in your back. And, just as Strummer said, everybody who fell got shot in the head.

"I figure the hell with it; I'll just fall down and die before Max figures out some way to kill me to get the diamonds in my shirt. And, all of a sudden he's there, holding me up pushing me ahead. And then — I couldn't believe it — he gives me a chocolate bar. 'From Strummer,' he says. 'Eat it — just a little bit further. You're gonna be rich if you don't give up. Rich! Rich!' *Meshuge*, my brother, but I eat the chocolate and keep pulling my feet from the mud.

"A couple more steps, this guy in front of me grabs for the guard's gun. Maybe if more of us would've done that, it would've been better, but that's another story. Before I understand what's happening, the dog leaps at the guy's face and bites his nose right off. And then the guard shoots him in the head. A piece of his skull falls on my shoe and something sticky — it wasn't blood — hits me in the face, but I don't do anything except walk around the body. The dog's lapping up the stuff pouring out of the guy's head, and I tell myself I'm not gonna fall down. The dog's tongue gives me more strength than ten chocolate bars.

"It's crazy, but the more I go, the stronger I get. And then, all of a sudden, Max is telling me the Jesus-Mary statue is right ahead. He's gonna fall and I should kneel down next to him. Out of nowhere, I start thinking about the Purim story — you know, when Mordecai tells Esther she's got to let the King of Persia *shtup* her in order to save the Jews, and Esther says she doesn't want to, and Mordecai comes right back and tells her, 'Maybe God made you for this.' I start to think maybe God made me for this — to carry diamonds that came out of a Nazi's asshole — and, for the first time in I can't tell you how long, I laugh. Max tells me to stop or they'll shoot me, and I calm down.

"Max tells me to look ahead at the signpost next to the statue where Strummer's standing. That's where it's gonna happen. I see the names of towns on the signpost — lots of letters and no vowels. Then I look at Strummer, something I tried not to do since the day I gave him the diamonds in our caps. He's a big guy with jowls and a pockmarked face. More than anything, I want to kill him. Not just because of all the Jews he killed, but because he and the SS — all the damned Germans — made me and my brother into animals.

"Max and me slow up so we're at the end by the armored cars. When we get to the crossroads, Max says 'Now!' and he falls down. Strummer gets his pistol out and without thinking, I go to grab it. Suddenly, I got all the strength in the world. I even got a plan. I'm gonna kill Strummer and run into the woods. If I can't shoot the dogs before they get to me, I'll shoot myself.

"But all of a sudden, I get tripped from behind, and I fall in the mud. I don't have to look who tripped me, but I see Max anyway. There are some shots — two go in my arm they tell me later — and it hurts so bad I forget the pain in my feet. But at least I feel warm.

"Strummer's shouting at the guards, '*Schnell, schnell!* Keep moving. Only two more dead Jews.' My face is in the mud. I'm part dozing, part not dozing, and I hear the armored cars go by. And then it's quiet, and I hear birds. I had forgotten all about birds. It must be sunny.

"And then I hear Max. He's lying in the mud near me. 'Asher, Asher, are you alive?' I'm afraid to make a sound or move a muscle. In a second there's no more sun, and I feel him over me. He's ripping off the back of my shirt, where the diamonds are. I open one eye and see he's raising a rock over my head.'"

Paul was shaking.

"Don't ask me how, but I pull air into me and manage to say 'Curse of Cain.' When we were little kids, we were so close in age — only ten months — we were in the same class at *Talmud torah* and, when we studied Cain and Abel, we decided that's the worst curse in the world — to know you killed your brother. The next thing I know is Max is running into the woods with the back of my shirt, and I pass out."

Asher seemed to be dissolving into his vinyl seat. His eyes — two deep black dead pools — were directed at Paul, but they seemed aware of nothing. "The last time I saw my brother."

Paul had to collect himself. Soon, but not today, he would analyze that story and try to convince Asher that Max probably saved his life and the lives of the orchestra members as well — that the rock he saw in Max's hand was the hallucination of a starving man who had just been shot. But how do you discuss Auschwitz — argue about it — with someone who had been there? "What happened next?" he asked.

"Next!" Asher grunted a cynical laugh. "Next means time, and time stopped in Auschwitz. Next for me or for Max? I'll start with me because I was there."

Asher said that he lay in the mud "for a day, maybe more." When the Russian troops went by, he was unable to make a sound, but a cart ran over his hand, and the pain gave him the strength to scream. Moments later, a Russian officer leaned over him and asked in Yiddish, "*Lebstu nokh? Are you alive?*" Asher answered, "*Lebedik? Ikh veys nisht.* Alive? I don't know." The officer told him he was a doctor, and Asher went unconscious.

The doctor, Leon Barsky, brought Asher to a field hospital and then, after the war, to a hospital near Leningrad where he tried, with little success, to repair Asher's fingers. "Then," Asher said, and broke into a real smile, "then he shows up with Malke, in a Russian officer's uniform no less. She's a major, with medals all over."

Paul interrupted, "Max told my mother she was dead — that the whole family died."

"He wished, so he wouldn't have to face nobody. Leon found her. She was famous." For the first time, color bloomed in Asher's face as he spoke of Malke's heroic deeds as a partisan, particularly blowing up a bridge with a German troop train on it. "Her husband died in the explosion. You don't hear about Jews like them. Only those who went to the camps. Most Jews think too much. Malke and the others, they fought."

Paul wanted to remind Asher of the Warsaw Ghetto uprising, but he couldn't think of a second example.

Eventually, Malke and Barsky who were both true-believer Communists — Malke changed her name to Josefina after Stalin — were married and had a son named Reuben. "Named after everybody," Asher explained, "but mostly Max's son who died in Lodz. My idea. You shouldn't curse the son for the sins of the father."

Asher went to Palestine (which had not yet become Israel) and got a job in Haifa making boxes. "I wanted nothing to do with jewelry or music. I just wanted to keep apart from everybody and try to forget — most to forget Max." But another Auschwitz survivor recognized him and told Asher that his brother was in Tel Aviv selling diamonds on the black market, and that Kelly was also alive, and was wanted by the British for smuggling guns to the Haganah.

"It was then," Asher said, "that I decided to kill Max, and I buy a gun. I don't want revenge, but I'm thinking the new Israel that's going to be born, the whole world, would be better without Max in it. Kelly smuggled arms past the British, Malke blew up bridges — this would be my contribution."

Paul thought of the submarine clock his father designed when the Army wouldn't take him. You do what you can. But designing a clock is a far cry from killing your brother.

"But then I think Curse of Cain. I got to get to someplace Max will never be, where I'm not going to meet anybody from anyplace I ever was. I know somebody who knows somebody, and I end up at a mine in the middle of Australia. Perfect. For the people there, Jews are Bible stories, Auschwitz they never heard of.

"It wasn't far enough," Asher said to himself as much as to Paul. "Leibel Barsky — Malke's brother-in-law, Leon's twin — suddenly appeared in the middle of Australia and told me that Leon was one of the Jewish doctors killed by Stalin when he took over killing Jews from Hitler, and that Malke was one of the famous Communist Jews they threw in Lubyanka. She's been rotting there five years."

Asher looked straight at Paul. "With fifty thousand U.S. dollars, Leibel says, he can get Malke and Reuben out of the country. Otherwise, it's only time before they make it so miserable for my sister that she kills herself. Or they pick up where Stalin left off. Leibel's got a letter from Malke, and I can see he's legitimate.

"So I tell Leibel I got nothing, but Max had these diamonds and he should go ask him for some. Then, for the first time, I learn my brother's dead. I'm glad so I don't have to worry I'll kill him. I learned Kelly died, too, in a Canadian prison, and for this I feel bad.

"Leibel knew about the diamonds. He and Kelly became friends in the British prison. He thinks Frieda Greenberg and Jacob Rosenzweig can tell me if there are any left. So I decided to go see them.

"I start with Frieda because the fare is cheaper to Canada, but mostly because Kelly would have told her the truth and Max, I'm sure, lied to your mother. Frieda, who's very friendly, tells me the whole story."

Double hearsay, Paul thought — what Kelly told Frieda told Asher told him — and inadmissible in court. Any one of the three — or all three — could be lying or mistaken. But what else was there?

The hearsay report was that Strummer smuggled Kelly out of Auschwitz in the bottom of a truck that was taking dead prisoners' shoes to "someplace" Asher went on to say that Shlomo was also in the truck "because Kelly wouldn't go without him. That's a real brother. Still, Shlomo died in the truck, probably from typhus."

Asher pulled another napkin from the dispenser and tore it to shreds. When he spoke again, his accent was more Yiddish. "After the war, Kelly, Strummer and the other SS thieves were supposed to get the diamonds that Strummer hid with Kelly's friends, and they'd divide it in some way — that's if one of the SS *mamzers* didn't kill the other guys first.

"The truck leaves Kelly at the farm near the crossroads, and when Max shows up he convinces Kelly that the two of them should become partners, take the diamonds in the shirts, find the others hidden on the farm, and then locate the diamonds Kelly's friends smuggled into Switzerland — in other words, fuck the SS. Kelly at first doesn't want to do this because, even though it's the SS, a deal's a deal. He's crazy that way, Frieda says, like his whole family. But Max works on him; he tells him he owes it to Shlomo, and Kelly says he'll go along.

"Then, one-two-three, things happen." Asher held up three crushed fingers. "One, Max kills the farmer and his wife. Self-defense, he tells Kelly, because they're Polack *anti-semiten* waiting to kill them. Two, they find a lot more diamonds hidden on the farm. And three, the Jewish underground shows up and Kelly volunteers to smuggle guns into Palestine. Frieda tells me Kelly only wanted to help make Israel independent but I think he's also scared to stay with Max. Max and Kelly make a new deal. While Kelly's smuggling guns, Max will collect the smuggled diamonds — Kelly will tell him where and how — and they'd divide them when things calm down. Kelly gives Max letters to show the people holding the diamonds."

Paul wondered whether, after hearing all this, he'd be able to work on the Olymp opinion or play Geppetto at Margaret's party. "I have to get back to the office."

"You have to save Jews. Reuben's seven years old." Paul closed his eyes.

"Max collected the diamonds, and the three of them got together in Montreal. It looked like Max was living up to their deal, including putting diamonds in a two-key box in Zurich; one key for Max, one for the Greenbergs. But it turned out that some of the stones Max gave the Greenbergs was fake — good fakes, but fake. Max hid his diamonds in different places in America and Jack tells me they're all gone, mostly used by you and your mother. Frieda's good diamonds are gone too. That leaves Zurich and the key you got."

"You're not going to believe me, are you?"

Asher ignored Paul's question, and described the Sunday dinner his mother had served in Rochester. They were Paul's favorite childhood foods. "Not even my wife made rugelach that good," Asher said abruptly.

"I told them the whole diamond story. Some of it they already knew from Max and Frieda, although Max told some lies, and I asked them for the second key for the Zurich box. Jack — in my head, he's still Jacob or Kobi — won't talk about the key in front of your mother. It gets her too upset, and she's afraid you'll get upset too if anyone asks you again. Meanwhile, she's just sitting there crying."

Asher's face went from gray to red, and his eyes which had been deep in their sockets seemed to lunge forward. "Upset, I tell them." Without seeming to realize it, Asher switched to Yiddish. "*Vos rheds tu narishkeit? Malke ken shtarbin.*" Paul didn't need a translation — *shtarbin* is death. Malke can die.

"Jack tells me I should tell you the story. He's sure you got the key and, even though you seem mad at everybody who knows about the diamonds, you'll do the right thing if it's Malke's life or death. Your mother just sits there quiet — she doesn't disagree."

Damn her, Paul thought. *She still believes I have the key.* She wasn't on his side. She never was.

Asher put his hands, palms up, on the table. "So here I am."

Paul couldn't simply repeat *I don't have it.* If he who saves a single life saves the whole world, then what is he who causes a death? The key was gone, but he could save Malke's and Reuben's lives by finally answering Maurice's question — Who is going to win the Olymp case? He could tell Asher what to do with that information.

"Don't look so scared. You remind me . . . "

Paul slid out of the booth and stood in the aisle. There was laughter at the counter. Two teenage couples were sitting there. The nearest to him, a thin girl, had Sibyl's long, black, long-gone hair. They looked Jewish and must have relatives who were Holocaust victims. Then why the hell were they laughing?

Asher's hand reached out for Paul's arm, just the way Bernie's hand had reached in front of The China Dragon, but this time Paul stepped back from it.

"Sit down," Asher demanded. "I gotta know today." The laughter stopped.

Paul put his hands on his hips and bent over towards Asher. "Auschwitz didn't give you the right to boss me around." He tried to lower his voice. "How do I know you're not blaming Max for what you did? Rushing me so I can't think? I'll call you tomorrow." He moved towards the door, looking ahead, but he felt the teenage couples staring at him.

* * *

Was Foley Square east or west? North or south? There were street signs, but he couldn't make them out. A taxi swerved around him, and Paul realized he was in the middle of the street. He waved the taxi down.

"Federal courthouse, Foley Square."

"That's only three blocks."

"Take me anyway."

"*Meshuge,*" the driver mumbled.

The hack license hung under the meter, and Paul looked at the name — "Kaplovitz, Stefan." Probably a Russian Jew. He looked at the driver's picture. Older than Max and Asher.

"Where were you during the war?"

The taxi stopped abruptly. "Mister, that's none of your business. Get out."

"I'm sorry, but my cousins were . . ." Paul couldn't finish the sentence.

After some silence the driver said, "I'm sorry, too," and started the cab. "What happened to me in the war is too long a story for three blocks."

Paul saw no numbers on Stefan Kaplovitz's bare arms. He pictured Max's 53927, then Asher's 53928, and then it hit him: He didn't know Asher's phone number.

"Please take me back to where we started."

Again, the cab stopped suddenly, throwing Paul forward. "Now, I mean it. Get out! Don't pay me. Just get out."

The driver turned and pointed at the rear door. His index finger ended at the knuckle; the middle finger was gone. Paul jumped out of the cab.

Plan, he ordered himself as he ran toward the luncheonette. Get the phone number; go back to the office; draw a line down the center of a yellow legal pad; list the reasons to disclose the Olymp outcome on one side, the reasons not to disclose on the other.

Narishkeit! Malke blows up bridges and you write lists. No wonder so many Jews died.

It was simple: Malke and the newest Reuben might die. Fuck the WASP judges on the Harvard walls.

Asher was standing in front of the luncheonette, his arms folded, the numbers distinctly visible. Paul remembered Mordecai's admonishment to Esther: Perhaps God made you for this.

He didn't wait to catch his breath. "I know how you can get fifty thousand dollars."

Asher looked perplexed. You've got him, Paul thought. Freedom! Freedom from all of them. "If I tell you, will you promise never to contact me again?" Asher craned his neck forward. "Promise or I'm leaving." Asher nodded. "You've got to say *I agree* and that you won't contact my wife, either."

Asher exhaled slowly. "I agree."

"Or the child we're gonna have or any children after that, or even my mother and Jack. Out of my life completely. Forever."

"I agree."

"And if you get more than you need for Malke and Reuben, you'll use the rest to get other Jews out of the Gulag."

Asher nodded.

"Say it."

"I agree."

"As soon as I go, write down what I'm telling you."

"I don't have a pencil."

"You survived Auschwitz. You can get a pencil."

Asher nodded nervously, and Paul continued, but in a softer voice. "Write down Olymp will win the Court of Appeals patent case argued last month."

"Olymp! Those Nazi murderers. I don't understand."

"You don't have to understand. Tell it to Ben Fenichel, if you really know him. He'll be able to turn that information into money."

Paul repeated the message for Fenichel, and had Asher repeat it for him. "After you tell Fenichel, take what you wrote, rip it in small pieces and flush it down the toilet. Leave no evidence. Let it go where the Swiss key is."

Without waiting for Asher to react, Paul turned and started toward Foley Square.

CHAPTER 12

No regrets, Paul assured himself, as he walked the three blocks from Asher to Foley Square. He did the right thing, but there was a price: The words whispered in front of the luncheonette had made him *treyf* as a lawyer — unkosher, impure, defiled — and he could no longer clerk at the Supreme Court or teach law.

Although Paul's family had never followed all of the hundreds of Jewish laws governing every aspect of life, the concept of *treyf* had been drilled into him by six years in an after-school Orthodox *Talmud torah*, his Orthodox relatives and neighbors, and the moral condescension of so many observant Jews. *Treyf* originated with Eve and the apple. There are foods you can eat (kosher) and foods you cannot (*treyf*); foods you can mix (eggs and kosher meat — kosher) and foods you cannot (milk and any meat — *treyf*); fabrics you can wear (wool or linen) and fabrics you cannot (wool mixed with linen). And once *treyf*, always *treyf*. If a kosher hamburger becomes a cheeseburger, removing the cheese will not restore it to its kosher state. There is no absolution.

The words whispered to Asher had also cut him off from the venerable judges on the Harvard Law School walls. But they were always alien to him, and he to them—aristocrats from a country that had expelled Jews and never given them full equality. Worse — much worse — was his estrangement from the portraits of the two deceased Jewish Supreme Court justices that hung in the Supreme Court building — Benjamin Cardozo, whose book, *The Common Law*, had deepened Paul's reverence for the Anglo-American legal system, and Louis D. Brandeis, who, in addition to being a great judge, had championed the causes of social justice and Zionism.

And worst of all, if he were to become a Supreme Court clerk, would be his encounters with the living Jewish Supreme Court Justice, Felix Frankfurter, legendary professor at Harvard Law School, who made it a point to meet with all of the Court's clerks. He would take a particular interest in Paul who, like him, had been born in Europe. Every time Paul saw Frankfurter — in the courtroom, the hallways, the meals the justice hosted — he would feel the burden of having betrayed the trinity of

Jewish justices who, as much as anyone, had helped to gain respect and acceptance for all American Jews.

He would tell Sibyl about Max when they arrived home from the party glowing with the success of their costumes. He would not wait until tomorrow and certainly not until some indeterminate date in the future. Telling her *eventually* meant telling her never.

For the rest of the afternoon, he would work on the Olymp opinion. Tonight, he'd be Geppetto, moving the strings while Sibyl did her Pinocchio dance and everyone at the Halloween party applauded with delight. Later tonight, after finally breaking his silence about Max's diamonds, he would do his best to gain Sibyl's empathy. Tomorrow, back to the opinion. He'd finish it by Tuesday — an arbitrary date, but he couldn't be done with Asher, Max and the whole damned Holocaust until it was behind him. Wednesday felt far away.

* * *

Back in his cubicle, Paul put a blank piece of paper in the Underwood and began a new draft. Fourth draft? Fifth? It didn't matter. This time, his work would be flawless. He owed that to Malke.

As Judge Webster had told Paul on the day the appeal was argued, the case was routine in all respects but one. Olymp's new process for manufacturing steel was unique, novel and inventive — the test of patentability. It was, the district judge concluded, "revolutionary", and the patent issued to Olymp, the employer and "assignee" of Eric Koerner, the inventor of the process, was presumptively "valid." This meant that no steel manufacturer could use that process without a license from Olymp. The files of Anvil Steel, the defendant, showed that Anvil had used the Olymp process and had refused to even discuss a license. Anvil was, under the Patent Law, an "infringer" and was obliged to pay Olymp a "reasonable royalty" for the steel it had made by the Koerner/Olymp process. That part of Paul's draft opinion, which dealt with validity and infringement, required only a minor reworking of Paul's original memo to Judge Webster; it had been completed weeks ago.

The difficult issue, which had driven Paul to the Secret Dungeon and on which he had been blocked for weeks, concerned the "reasonable royalty" that Anvil or any other infringer — past, present or future — owed to Olymp if it produced steel by following the patented process without a license from Olymp. Because the process lowered costs and improved quality, the patent was, as Judge Webster had told Paul, a "gold mine". The meaning of "reasonable royalty" would help determine the value of that "mine."

The trial judge gave the jury instructions as to how the reasonable royalty was to be determined if they found the patent valid. These instructions correctly parroted the language of earlier cases, but they made little sense in the Olymp case. Taken as a whole, they were almost incomprehensible. However, neither side objected to them, and the jury awarded Olymp damages of $30,002,500 which was exactly half-way between the 60 million dollars which Olymp's economics expert testified was a reasonable royalty and the $5,000 royalty urged by Anvil's expert — an irrational compromise. Paul's unfinished task was to draft a section of the opinion which would review the law concerning "reasonable royalty" and provide workable guidelines for computing that royalty in future cases.

Even if Olymp had not been a brutal enslaver of Jews, and of Jacob/Jack Rosenzweig/Ross in particular, the challenge was great. Olymp's patent was truly revolutionary, it had never discussed license terms with any manufacturer, and there seemed to be no case dealing with a comparable situation. Nevertheless, in his countless hours of research and thought, Paul had identified several factors that should be taken into consideration, such as the cost savings to Anvil from using the new process, the better quality of steel produced, and Anvil's plans for marketing and pricing the new product. His draft opinion would be as good as he had originally intended.

The words flowed, the precedents fit, and his recollection of the evidence was nearly total. At five, Sibyl called to remind him he had to be home by six to put on his costume; she had promised Margaret to get there early and help set up. "She's my boss, my friend, too. Please."

This meant Paul would have to leave the office at 5:25, before he could complete the section entitled "Valuation Models."

"Why don't you bring the costumes and makeup, and we can put them on at Margaret's," he urged her. "I'll be a better Geppetto if I have this one section of the opinion behind me."

"Please, no later than eight. Six hundred West End Avenue."

Paul resolved to leave for the party at 7:15 — surprise Sibyl by being early, and make it easier to leave early so there would be time to tell her what he should have told her in 1948.

* * *

The phone rang at 7:10, and Paul laughed into the receiver. "One foot's out the door."

"It's Jack. There's something your mother thinks you should know about right away."

Jack! — the bastard who sent Asher. "Tell me. I'm in a hurry."

"Nice to talk to you, too." The sarcasm surprised Paul. "Did you see Asher today?"

Paul spoke deliberately, just as Asher had.

"You shouldn't have told him I have a key. I don't have a key." His initial anger was turning to shame. He was picking an argument with a true hero who had survived what he was afraid to imagine — and at Olymp, no less.

"I'm not going to argue with you," Jack replied, "but, for once, don't be so high and mighty. If a cousin of mine's in trouble — if any Jew's in trouble — I'm going to try to help, no matter what they teach you in all your schools."

"If I had a key, why would I keep quiet about it all these years?"

"What did Asher tell you? I realize that, to you, I'm an uneducated *nudnik*, but I know some things you don't."

"Now's not the time to talk about it."

"Did he tell you Malke's been in Israel for a week?"

Paul went cold. "How do you know that?"

"I just spoke to her."

Paul covered the phone with his hand. Otherwise, Jack might hear his anxious breaths.

Jack continued: "I got a wire today from my nephew in Tel Aviv saying she's in a resettlement town near Lebanon — a few trailers and some rocks. It took an hour to get through to her on the phone, and a few minutes later the line went dead."

Paul felt his heart pounding. Maybe Asher didn't know Malke was in Israel and, when he learned, he'd realize he didn't need the money. Maybe he'd then forget what Paul had told him — the whispered words would be harmless. But maybe Asher had conned him.

"Do you have a phone number for Asher?"

"A number!" Jack scoffed. "The tattoo's his number, he said. After this is over, he's going to live where nobody'll ever find him. The middle of Australia's not far enough."

"I've got to tell him about Malke."

"Good luck. I know he was going to tell you he needed money to help get Malke out of Russia. That's what he told us and we believed him. Maybe he believes that too. I wanted to call you before Asher showed up at your office, but your mother's always nervous about calling. Don't tell her nothing. She's upset enough by what Asher told her about Max."

"Is it true what he said?"

"True?" Jack laughed. "Who knows true? Maybe to Asher it's true. Max said some of the same things about what went on in the camp — only what Asher said Max did, Max said Asher did. True was the gas and the Nazis and everybody who's gone. It's not so important if one Jew was more desperate to stay alive than another Jew."

"Was there an orchestra at Auschwitz?"

"Orchestra, how do I know?" Paul could almost see Jack shrugging. "Asher says there was, Max never mentioned it, somebody who spent three years there told me there wasn't, somebody else said there was. An orchestra for the gas — nothing was too much for the Nazis."

"What was your camp like?"

"I don't think you want to know."

Fuck you! Paul wished he could say. If he could handle Asher's report, he could handle this. "Please tell me."

Paul expected some silence, but not as much as there was. When Jack finally spoke, his voice was strangely steady. "I was at Grossbatten where it was simple, not like Auschwitz. A small camp, like twenty skeletons, where you did slave work for Olymp — mostly shoveling coal — until you got too weak from typhus or hunger and they shot you and gave another skeleton your shovel. They didn't beat you because you were a machine. Less than a machine — the machines they oiled."

Paul read his last sentence on the Underwood: "The Koerner/Olymp process is valuable, perhaps revolutionary, and, under the Patent Act, Olymp is entitled to a reasonable royalty reflecting that value."

"That's enough details," Jack continued. "Now Olymp's making more money than ever. If they get the patent in your case, they'll make more still. Everybody wants to forget."

The call had to end. He couldn't lecture a former Olymp slave about Olymp's rights under the rule of law, particularly after his own words to Asher had violated the law. "I have to go. Sibyl's waiting for me at a party. I'll speak to you soon."

"Yeah. Enjoy."

* * *

Paul turned to the typewriter and wrote, "The determination of a reasonable royalty depends upon . . . ." Before Jack's call, the remainder of the sentence had been completed in his mind, and all he had to do was let his fingers race over the metal keys. Now, he could not summon another word.

Options, he told himself. List the options, just as he had done this morning before 53928 took him over. He knelt to search his wastebasket for the earlier list, then sprang up and kicked the basket on its side. There was only one option — *Fuck the Nazis!* Do it for Little Reuben. And for Big Reuben too — show his father that, like the Warsaw Ghetto partisans, his son would fight back. And fuck Olymp, in particular, for his stepfather and the other four scarecrows in the *Befreite Olymp Sklaven* picture. Do it now before the snapshot faded completely.

Instead of drafting an opinion that would help Jack's enslaver amass vast profits, he would summon all of his skills and energy to convince Judge Webster that Olymp's patent should be held invalid and it should collect no royalties. Judge Webster would then convince the other judges.

It would be an overwhelming endeavor. All three appellate judges and their clerks, including himself, had already drawn the opposite conclusion. It would also be irresponsible, perhaps unethical, even crazy. The lawyers for Olymp and Anvil, the advocates, were the one who were supposed to convince the judges. The law clerk's job was to assist his judge — do research, check the trial record, prepare memos, draft opinions. At most, if the judge requested it, a law clerk might give his dispassionate views as to how a case should be decided — the very thing Paul had done weeks earlier when he wrote an evenhanded memo agreeing with Olymp's position on validity and infringement, and suggesting that it might be entitled to more than the $30 million damages awarded it. But these job descriptions had nothing to do with Auschwitz or Grossbatten.

For a brief moment, Paul considered the consequences of succeeding. What would happen if he could persuade the judges that, contrary to their decision and Paul's initial memorandum, the Olymp patent was invalid? If the words whispered to Asher proved false, would Asher be in danger? Should Paul warn him? Maybe. Probably. But first he had to beat the Nazis.

It was now almost 7:30 on Saturday evening. Judge Webster would be in the office on Monday morning. If Paul's memo were completed by then, he would read it. But if it weren't . . . Paul wouldn't even address this possibility. There was too much to do.

Paul knew the final line of the memo – *For these reasons, the Court should reconsider its tentative decision in favor of Olymp*. But, to get there, he had to come up with, substantiate and write out a winning argument Anvil's lawyers had missed. It could be done because it had to be done and because he would give it his all. But it couldn't be done unless he started immediately.

Everything, especially Sibyl, had to be out of his mind except the task at hand. If he thought of her disappointment, he wouldn't be able to concentrate. Besides, her disappointment would be gone by tomorrow night when he told her the whole story, or nearly the whole story, and she appreciated the horror of granting Olymp a stranglehold on world steel production.

He called their apartment, but there was no answer and he didn't have Margaret's number. For a while, he couldn't remember Margaret's last name (something to do with a musical instrument). By the time it came to him (Kettle) and he looked the number up, it was after eight.

Sibyl didn't say hello. "Where are you? You're supposed to be here now."

"I didn't have Margaret's number. There's a crisis and I can't go tonight. I'm sorry."

"A crisis? I'm—"

"A crisis. I can't explain without breaching a confidence."

"Crisis . . . I . . . ." She was breathing angrily. "I'm sitting here like an idiot in a Pinocchio costume with puppet strings and no Geppetto to pull them."

"Cut the strings off and say you're Pinocchio after he became a real boy. Say that Geppetto had a fire in his woodworking shop."

She hung up.

He started to redial Margaret's number, then stopped. Sibyl had been the one who hung up, and she should call. Besides, whatever he said tonight would be rushed and easily misunderstood. It would be better if he gave a slow and thorough explanation tomorrow. He put the phone in its cradle.

Paul took nothing for granted. He reread the briefs, the trial judge's opinion, every word of the patent, and the leading Supreme Court decisions, looking for arguments Anvil's lawyers might have missed. The trial record was 1,697 pages, more than he could get through in one night, but he was able to focus on the key testimony and to skim the rest. At six in the morning, he put the record down and listed every possible argument that could be raised against Olymp. With one exception, each had been made and rejected; the exception was a quibble about dates that Judge Webster would brush off.

His adrenaline ebbed. The hopeless task was hopeless, and he wouldn't get revenge on Olymp. Instead, he would go home, tell Sibyl whatever came out of his mouth, and hope for her love and empathy. Then, after some sleep, he would return to the office, do his job as law clerk, and help Olymp dominate world steel production for years.

He ran his tongue along the roof of his mouth and tasted rancid ice cream. It was the last thing he had eaten — lunch with Asher, paid for by Asher. That smug bastard would look at him with contempt. *You're just one more Jew who would have gone without fighting back.*

Paul wanted to scream, but clamped his mouth shut. What good was screaming? At least Fenichel's brother threw himself against the electric fence but, if Paul did that, Olymp's victory would be certain and Asher's contempt deserved.

He would go back to the beginning, Title 35 of the United States Code, the patent statute, and march through every section until an idea came to him. The first section, section 100, defined the statute's key terms. Under subsection (d), a "patentee" was the person "to whom the patent was issued" as well as "successors in title to the patentee." In the Olymp lawsuit, the patent had been issued in 1954 to Otto Koerner, an Olymp metallurgist, for "a new method of manufacturing high strength steel in a continuous casting process." The heart of the invention was a series of steps and temperatures for cooling liquid steel. Koerner had assigned the invention to Olymp, which made Olymp the "successor in title."

Paul went right to section 102(d), commonly called the "true inventor requirement" — "A person shall be entitled to a patent unless . . . he did not himself invent the subject matter sought to be patented . . ." At the trial, Anvil had claimed Koerner was not the true inventor, and had put into evidence an article indicating that Koerner's brother-in-law, Daniel Hanson of the University of Stockholm, had come up with the basic idea in 1950. This argument seemed to be a winner until Olymp flew Hanson to America to testify, as a surprise witness, that Koerner had disclosed the idea to him in 1949 at Hanson's engagement party.

So much for Hanson. But maybe Anvil's lawyers had overlooked the possibility of another true inventor. Paul recalled a bit of Koerner's trial testimony that he had skimmed earlier in the morning. He went back to the trial record and saw that in 1944, Koerner, who had been wounded at Stalingrad and honorably discharged from the German Army, went to work at Olymp's Bernberg Foundry. When Paul had first read that several weeks earlier, he had gone to an atlas to locate both Bernberg and Grossbatten, the town named on the *Befreite Olymp Sklaven* picture, but had found neither. Still, Jack might know something about Bernberg. He certainly knew something about Olymp. It was worth a try.

Outside Paul's window, night was dissolving into gray dawn. He removed his watch and put it in the desk drawer. The telephone number that usually escaped him came effortlessly.

"Hello?" Jack answered.

"It's Paul."

"Don't you know what time it is?"

"I have to ask you some important questions."

"Your mother wants to know whether anybody's sick. Have you spoken to Asher?"

Paul spoke slowly. "Jack, please trust me — just answer my questions."

Jack breathed into the phone as Sibyl had last night. "Go ahead."

"Do you know where Olymp's Bernberg foundry was?"

"Do I know! Grossbatten and Bernberg are right next to each other. Like one place. They marched us there from Grossbatten every morning, even earlier than you called."

Paul's free hand chopped the air, but he had to speak calmly. "Do you know the process they used for making steel — sequence of steps, temperatures, how they cooled it?"

"I knew I shoveled coal into a furnace, and if I slowed up I was dead. That was enough to know. The temperature — the hottest thing I ever felt. Twenty degrees above hell. The march there in the morning, when it was still dark, like an icebox, but the hot was worse."

"Do you know anybody who knows those things?"

"The ones who know are the Nazis. We don't correspond."

"Is there anybody I could talk to who could tell me about the manufacturing process?"

"There was, but he died a few years ago. Franz Levy. He was a genius scientist — metal scientist . . . Professor . . . I forget where . . . until he got rounded up like all us plain Jews." Jack sounded exhausted. "He slept in Grossbatten, in the barracks like us, and the SS wanted to kill him — he couldn't shovel coal — but Olymp wanted his brain, so when we marched to the furnace, the scientists took him to this office and gave him something extra to eat. He did drawings and made equations for them."

"Was one of the Olymp scientists named Koerner?"

"They never introduced me."

"Do you know whether Franz Levy had any notebooks?"

"These questions, Paul, I don't enjoy answering. Even when this kid who's doing a book about it said he wanted to meet me, I told him no."

Paul slid to the edge of his chair and drummed the desk with his free fingers. "What's this guy's name?"

"He was at one of these Ivy schools. Not the ones you went to. In Connecticut, I think."

"What was his name? Did he write to you?"

"You don't let go, do you, Paulie? Guys like you survived."

A compliment. Maybe the greatest compliment he had ever received. Or was it?

"Please Jack, it's important."

* * *

Two hours after he spoke to Jack, Paul climbed to the third floor of a weary New Haven row house and rang the bell over the name "Osterlin". A young man, a few years older than he, wearing undershorts and a sleeveless undershirt, unlocked the door. Behind him, Paul could see a red butterfly chair with a gash and a racing bike without a chain. "Is David Osterlin here?" The man looked Paul up and down, but avoided his eyes. "I'm Paul Hartman, a law clerk at the Second Circuit. My stepfather, Jack Ross, used to be Jacob Rosenzweig, said you might have some information I need for an emergency research project." The man leaned on the door. It could slam any second. "I think Olymp may have stolen one of Franz Levy's inventions. I'm trying to stop it from making a fortune from that invention."

Paul pulled out his identification card, but Osterlin waved it away. He met Paul's eyes for the first time. "For Franz Levy, and to stop Olymp from getting away with more murder, I'll give you all the time you need. My Ph.D. dissertation was on survivors' guilt and I spent hours interviewing some of the Olymp slaves, especially Franz." He swung the door open.

Paul stepped into a small living room/kitchen. Nearly every chair and table had something on it — overflowing ashtrays of all sizes and shapes, 45 and 72 rpm records, a hookah pipe, even a scrawny black cat ready to spring. He smelled cat and stale tobacco.

"Excuse the chaos," Osterlin said proudly. He needed a shave more than Paul did. "I successfully defended my dissertation Friday and had a big party last night. Sit down while I put on clothes." He nodded toward a sagging couch strewn with art books, then pointed at the steamer trunk in front of it. "Just dump the books on my custom-made coffee table."

A few moments later, Osterlin spoke from a room directly behind the couch. "Tell me how Franz fits in."

Good, Paul thought, no time wasted. "A patent has to be applied for and issued in the name of the actual inventor or his assignee, which is usually the employer. Olymp claims that the inventor of a valuable patent it owns is one of its metallurgists, a man named Koerner. If that's not so, the patent is invalid. With all that slave labor, I wondered—"

"I get it," Osterlin interrupted. "Franz died last year. He just lay down and didn't get up. My advisor paid for the funeral. Besides the two of us and a rabbi, there were four people there — three survivors who didn't open their mouths and a niece who kept saying, 'I did everything I could.'

"I didn't try to understand the work Franz was doing as an Olymp slave. It was enough for my purposes that both he and Olymp thought it was important. He felt he had come up with a breakthrough, but whenever I suggested taking the next step — getting a patent lawyer, speaking to someone on the Yale engineering faculty — he just stared ahead with a blank look on his face. I'm a social psychologist, not clinical, but he was obviously depressed. I'm sounding like his niece — I did everything I could — but I was afraid that if I pushed too hard, he'd stop talking to me. No wonder I study guilt."

Osterlin came into the living room and sat next to Paul. In front of them, on the steamer trunk, he put a thick gray-covered notebook, some recording tapes, and two stuffed Redwells. "Jesus, he was a nice guy. What do you want to know?"

"What's the notebook?"

"His daily log of the work he did in Bernberg in late forty-four and forty-five. No matter what they put him through, he was a real German scientist and kept records of everything. It's in German. Can you read it?"

"No," Paul said, fighting the urge to add that although German, more than Yiddish, had been his parents' principal language in Europe, they refused to speak it in America.

"Is he bothering you?" Osterlin asked. Paul had no idea what he was talking about. "Lucifer. My cat."

Paul looked down and saw that the black cat had crawled on his lap. He swept Lucifer to the floor with his forearm and was immediately afraid Osterlin would be angry. "I'm sorry . . ."

"He's used to it. He survived an animal shelter. What are you looking for?"

Paul opened his briefcase, took out Volume VI of the *Olymp v. Anvil* Record on Appeal, turned to the Koerner patent, and showed Osterlin some graphs and equations on the patent's second page. Lucifer leaped back onto his leg but Paul ignored him. "It's Trial Exhibit One. According to Olymp, this is Koerner's invention. Is there anything like that in the notebook?"

Osterlin pushed art books to the floor. He flipped through the notebook until he came to a page with a U-shaped graph and three columns of numbers. It resembled the second page of the Koerner/Olymp patent. Paul stroked Lucifer in order to keep himself from leaping off the couch. Osterlin moved his eyes back and forth between the Record and the notebook. "Do you have the patent in German?" he asked.

"It's the next document in the Record. Trial Exhibit Two. They're counterpart patents. Should be identical in every material respect."

Osterlin turned some pages in the Record and again compared the two books. Then he put them both on the trunk. "I never saw the patent before."

"And I never knew there was a notebook."

"When, according to Olymp, did Koerner make the invention?"

"November 1950."

"Six years after Franz's notes here." He grimaced in disgust. "You don't have to understand German. Whoever wrote the patent copied it from Franz's notebook — charts, graphs, equations, number for number, line for line. Every word, too — including misspellings and grammatical mistakes. German thoroughness." Paul compared the books, and immediately saw Osterlin was right. Levy was the inventor and Koerner had copied what he had done.

"Can I borrow the notebook? I'll get it back to you in a few days."

"I don't know. I promised Franz's niece I'd give everything to this museum they're building in Jerusalem. But I think I've got photostats of the pages we compared," he said.

"I've got more stuff you might want." Osterlin pointed to the tapes. "Interviews with Levy — don't worry, in English — and transcripts of the interviews. I'm pretty sure he talks about Koerner. Let me get carbon copies that you can keep."

The bedroom door slammed and, once more, Osterlin spoke to him through the wall. "Do you think you could get Jack Ross to speak with me?"

The clock was running, but Paul had to let Osterlin talk. "I'll ask him."

"Do you know his story?"

"We're not really close."

"Well, there was a lot of tension between Olymp and the SS." Paul listened, allowing himself to sink into the couch's frayed cushions. "Olymp wanted slaves to shovel coal, and the SS wanted them dead. So Olymp came up with a compromise that was perverse even for them. They had ten shovelers, and every month they computed how much each guy shoveled. The four who shoveled the least were handed over to the SS and its mercies. The other six got another chance to compete. Rosenzweig survived longer than anybody, but nobody resented him. One of the shovelers said that Rosenzweig gave each new guy some clues on how to get more coal in the furnace and conserve his own energy. Amazing when you consider what could have happened if the new guy out-shoveled him. He received the highest compliment one survivor can give another — 'He stayed a human being.'"

Paul could not linger on that compliment or anything else. "I'll tell Jack how helpful you've been. Maybe he'll talk to you then."

And I'll show him the respect he deserves.

Osterlin came out of the bedroom and handed Paul a copy of a transcript. "Page sixteen — Franz without editing." Osterlin read aloud while Paul looked at the carbon:

"They brought in this young guy, Eric Koerner who lost a leg at Stalingrad, to help me do computations. He had an engineering degree, and he asked questions about everything. He even took my notebook at night to study, but I don't think he understood what I was doing. He was a nice boy, not a Nazi. Whenever he could, he brought food for me to smuggle to the other prisoners. They killed their own people for a lot less."

Osterlin stopped reading and said, "A good Samaritan."

"A good Samaritan," Paul repeated. "Maybe even a hero or a saint. But also a plagiarizer and not the true inventor."

Osterlin shrugged. "People are complicated. I'll do whatever you need me to. Olymp's taken enough from Jews."

* * *

On the train back to New York, Paul did an outline of his memo to Judge Webster and wrote the final two paragraphs:

In summary, there is, at the least, an open issue as to who the true inventor is — Koerner or Levy — and whether the patent is invalid under section 102(d). The trial, of course, is over and the record is closed, but there is ample authority for remanding the case to the District Court for a supplemental trial on the sole question of inventorship. While this is out of the ordinary, the facts are even more out of the ordinary, and the interests of justice would be ill served if Anvil does not have a fair opportunity to present this new evidence in the District Court.

For these reasons, the Court of Appeals should reconsider its tentative decision in favor of Olymp.

There was still a lot to do. First the rhetoric had to be squeezed out: Only objective analysis and dry prose, and no more than one reference to the "interests of justice." Then Paul had to find some of the "ample authority" for ordering a new trial under comparable circumstances. It had to exist, although he had no idea what it was.

But, before anything else, he would go home and speak to Sibyl. He wouldn't script what he would say — he would just sit on the couch, stroke her long black hair, rest his head between her breasts, and tell her of his deceptions and his love. He would ask her to wait a few hours for the details so he could finish his memo and stop Olymp from profiting further from the Jews it had helped to murder.

By the time he entered the taxi on Lexington Avenue outside of Grand Central he was close to tears. On the FDR Drive, he realized the scene in his head was impossible. Sibyl's hair was no longer long. He was too tired to think and, when the taxi drove onto the Brooklyn Bridge, ten minutes from home, he let himself doze.

A note was under the milk-glass vase on the Chippendale hallway table:

I'm leaving town for a few days or a few weeks or longer. I don't know how long. Yesterday, I was asked to audition for a symphony orchestra. I wanted to talk to you about it, but you had a crisis and I said yes last night.

Please don't try to find me. I have to concentrate on the audition.

I'll call you when I have a better idea of my plans.

I hope your crisis is resolved. Mine isn't.

S

Paul started to reread the note but stopped after the first sentence. If he focused on it, he'd never complete the memo. He put the note back under the vase and left for the office.

CHAPTER 13

At eight the next morning, Monday, Paul slid his memo under Judge Webster's door and left for home. The judge usually arrived at eight-thirty and, as soon as he read the memo, he would call Paul in and ask him why he had undertaken this independent and unprecedented investigation. Paul had no answer he could give, and wouldn't spend time thinking of one. The time had come to find Sibyl — to, at long last, put his wife at the top of his To-Do List.

Vivian called seconds after Paul entered the apartment. "The judge wants to see you now." Paul said he would come right in. After losing his wife (only temporarily, he hoped), he couldn't risk losing his job as well. There was no point in telling Vivian that he had been up for over forty-eight hours.

Vivian told him to wait in his office "until the judge is ready for you."

At his desk, Paul put a piece of paper in the Underwood. He had no idea what he would write but, if he didn't do something, his heart would hammer uncontrollably, his skin would go clammy, and acids would whirlpool in his gut. As he raised his hands above the round typewriter keys, he saw Judge Webster at his door, holding the memo with his fingertips. Paul stood up.

"Sit down." Paul sat, and Judge Webster let the memo drop on the Underwood. "What made you do this after we had reached a decision?"

The truth, Paul told himself. *Impossible* — unless he wanted to be arrested.

"I felt uneasy about the decision." Paul closed his eyes.

"You don't look well," Judge Webster said. "Do you need to lie down?"

If you fall down, they shoot you. Paul opened his eyes and looked directly at the judge. "My mother's husband — my stepfather — was a slave laborer at an Olymp plant."

The judge shivered. "I'm sorry for him," he said, in a voice as soft as Paul had ever heard him speak. Then he crossed his arms over his vested, barrel chest. "I'm sure you realize that disqualifies you from working on the case."

Paul stood up. Judge Webster still hovered over him, but it wasn't so bad.

"I have nothing to do with him." Paul struggled to keep his voice steady. "We hardly ever talk. I realize I should have told you, but what happened in the 1940s to somebody else in Europe shouldn't limit what I can do. I came to America in 1933 with my real father when I was an infant." Paul feared he was whining. "I'll resign if you want me to."

Judge Webster sighed. "Go home and lie down. You don't look well. Is Sibyl home?"

The memo seemed to be pulsing on the Underwood. Paul picked it up and thrust it toward the judge. "Don't you . . . It's right. Isn't that what matters?"

The judge took the memo. "I'll consider it. Go home."

* * *

Paul knew that if he was to find Sibyl and reunite with her, his mind had to be ruled by reason. Still, as he opened the apartment door, he imagined Sibyl there and the note gone. But nothing had changed. He sat on the hallway floor, then crossed his legs and closed his eyes as if he were meditating at a Buddhist shrine. He had to think clearly.

He had just accomplished the near-impossible and turned the Olymp case upside down. Now, he had to do something more difficult — get Sibyl back. When he located her, they would first speak on the telephone. The mixture of passion, longing, regret and anger that he felt — and that she, too, must feel — might prove too volatile and unpredictable unless she first understood that he did not fault her for leaving and that he had truly changed. He would add that he was sure she would play brilliantly at the audition and with *neshome*. No, he wouldn't say *neshome* or anything else that might evoke the Judaism she tried to ignore. He would wait for her to mention the baby.

Should he say he would live wherever she had a job? If necessary, yes. *Say anything!*

With difficulty — his thighs ached terribly — he got up from the floor, went to the kitchen and, standing in front of the open refrigerator door, ate half an Entenmann's marble cake and drank nearly a quart of milk from the bottle. Now, a few moments rest. He lay down on the couch and closed his eyes.

It was early evening when he started awake with a flashing image of what he had seen on the kitchen countertop while devouring the cake — a pencil with teeth marks and a pad of paper. He went right to the garbage pail and found a torn penciled note scattered among coffee grounds. He spread the pieces out and quickly pieced them together — "NW 217." This was a five-piece jigsaw puzzle so simple that it meant she wanted him to find her. Within minutes, a Northwest Airlines operator was telling him, "That's our new DC-7 daily from LaGuardia to Seattle, with a stopover in Detroit. No plane change. When would you like to leave?"

"Yesterday," Paul answered, "but I need to speak to my wife first."

Detroit, he knew, had a great symphony orchestra. The Seattle Symphony, if there was one, wouldn't be as good. He'd focus first on Detroit to show his respect for her talent.

From the kitchen wall phone, he called his high school clarinet teacher, who was now an officer in the Musician's Union. "Mr. Fabrizio, it's Paul Hartman."

"Paul! Call me Lou. You're a big shot lawyer now."

"I need a favor."

"Anything. I really appreciate all the time you spent with my nephew Mauro on his citizenship application, though I'm not so sure you did America a favor."

"Do you know anybody in the Detroit Symphony?"

"Lots of people, but they're all in Europe on a two-month tour."

"Does Seattle have a symphony?"

"Are you kidding? Didn't you read Walter Winchell today? No, he's in the *Daily Mirror* — not a paper for Harvard lawyers."

"What did Winchell say?"

"Seattle's got this new conductor, Reggie Smith from England. He—"

"Who?" Paul interrupted. The name frightened him, but he couldn't place it.

"Reggie Smith. He took the Thames Woodwind Ensemble from a local second-tier group to a world-class ensemble. That's why they brought him to Seattle."

Things were fitting together well — too well. Smith was the hot-shot who tried to get Sibyl to join the Thames and move to London, who forced Paul to choose between marrying her quickly or losing her, and who made it necessary to use even more diamonds from Max. Paul eased himself onto a kitchen chair. He needed to focus on what Lou was saying.

". . . packing them in, but there's a lot of extracurricular activities. Reggie's not just waving his baton. The first French horn — wonderful musician; I played with her at the City Center Opera. Old enough to be his mother. She got jealous and quit. And he has a paternity suit someplace, a harpsichord player — England I think. The union's going to make some inquiries. Conductors aren't supposed to do that."

This was as simple as Sibyl's five-piece jigsaw puzzle. The bastard was trying to fuck her. Paul had bested him in 1954 by marrying her, and he'd best him in 1958 by supporting her.

"Thanks, Lou. Don't tell anybody I asked." He hung up before Lou could respond.

Schnell wasn't fast enough. Mrs. Webster — blue-haired Puck — must know Sibyl's Seattle number. Judge Webster might answer, but that didn't matter anymore.

Mrs. Webster picked up the phone. "It's Paul Hartman. Please tell me where Sibyl is."

"I'm . . . I'm not . . . I'm not sure."

Puck was a lousy liar who didn't like to lie. "She's in Seattle, isn't she?"

"I don't . . . She . . . I promised her I wouldn't say."

"Please! I love her. She's carrying our child." In a moment, he would cry. "I'm going to change — not put my work before everything. Not like . . ." Paul made himself stop. The full sentence, he realized, would be: *Not like Judge Webster.*

Before Mrs. Webster responded, Paul recalled what he couldn't believe he had forgotten. "That big guy! I think he's related to Smith."

"Boris Kendall? They're cousins. His mother went to the conservatory with me."

It all came back — the Paul Bunyan look-alike who was mooning over Sibyl in 1954 — Smith's pimp. He wrote the name down. "He's from Seattle, isn't he?"

"Yes. Didn't Sibyl tell you that the three of us and Boris' mother went to hear Reg conduct the New York Philharmonic? It was a sensation."

"Yeah, she mentioned it," Paul said, lying. The concert must have been on an evening when he was at the Secret Dungeon. He wanted to get off the phone quickly before he said something stupid. But he couldn't control himself. "Did she go to Seattle to be with Boris?"

"She went there to audition for an orchestra," Mrs. Webster snapped. "I'm sure you know Boris is . . . is different. That's the term his mother uses."

A homo, Paul thought. Hadn't Sibyl told him that before he proposed? But he couldn't imagine the wife of the Honorable L. Clayton Webster using that word — or, for that matter, any word beyond "different" — to describe Boris' sexual preference.

"Can you give me Boris' number? That won't be breaking any promise."

She didn't answer immediately, and Paul realized he would have to go all the way. "I'm not going to urge her to come back. Just the opposite. I'll encourage her to take the job if she's offered it. If she wants to live in Seattle, I'll go there." He wondered whether he meant it.

"I'll get the number. I hope it's not too late."

Too late for what? Paul asked himself, but then a single word consumed him: *Schnell!*

* * *

Again and again, Paul gave the long-distance operator Boris' number, counted eight rings, sometimes nine or ten, then hung up. First he called every 15 minutes, then every ten, and then he stopped looking at his watch and called whenever he felt close to screaming. Shortly after two in the morning, the long distance operator said, "Sir, we tried three minutes ago."

"Please, Operator, it's an emergency. Try just once more. It's only eleven in Seattle."

"All right. But after that, I'm going to have to ask you to speak to my supervisor."

Finally, there was a voice at the other end. "Hello."

"Boris?"

"Who's this?"

"Paul Hartman." The line went dead.

Paul reached the same long-distance operator and said, "I cut us off accidentally."

Boris answered on the first ring. "Stop calling."

"Please! I just want Sibyl's number. I'm sure she'll want to hear what I have to say."

"Listen, you self-centered bastard. Sibyl doesn't want to talk to you."

"You listen, you fairy pimp."

There was a short screeching sound and then total silence. Minutes later, the long distance operator reported that "the line seems to be disconnected."

* * *

Paul left for the airport at nine the following morning. The phone rang as soon as he locked the apartment door behind him. *Calm, calm,* he told himself, but it took two rings to find the key in his pocket, and another two rings to realize he was turning it in the wrong direction. *Calm. Don't run.* But his feet wouldn't listen, and he charged into the hallway table. The table fell with him, then under him, as he hit the floor. He heard a crash and felt sharp pains explode in his forehead and knee. Around him, he could make out nothing except shattered milk glass and two table legs. Maybe Sibyl's note had vanished. He managed to get up, hop into the kitchen on his left foot and grab the wall phone.

"Hello," he gasped.

"It's me, Paul."

He sensed longing. *Thank you, God.* "I'm sorry about—"

"They took me." Her barely audible voice seemed higher than usual. She made a sound, a soft screech, that was either joy or pain. "Third chair, but it's a wonderful orchestra."

"I'll come out there. I love you."

"We're going on a good will tour to Central and South America sponsored by the State Department — ten cities, five weeks, topped off by a grand finale Thanksgiving concert in Rio. It will open doors for any audition I want."

"Is that okay with the obstetrician?"

She didn't answer right away, then said, "There's something I have to tell you."

Her tone of voice told him more than he wanted to know. "I just had a big fall in the hallway," he announced and, as he spoke, the pain shot from his knee into his forehead — or was it the other direction. He leaned against the kitchen wall.

"I'm in Seattle," she said, as if she hadn't heard him. "A clinic — really a doctor's office. The conductor . . . it's Reginald Smith, from The Thames. You remember?"

Paul slid his back down the wall until he was seated on the floor. "I remember."

"He said I looked pale, and asked if I was pregnant. It was a guess."

Paul felt as if the air had been sucked from his lungs.

"There was only an opening because one of the flutists was having a baby, and . . . " Sibyl stopped speaking. Paul could sense she was swallowing, and he swallowed along with her. "I told him no, I wasn't. I had to. I had already turned him down twice — right after you proposed and a year later when we were in Cambridge and he wanted me to fill in on the U.S. tour for a flutist who was having vertigo attacks. I didn't tell you the second time because you were in the middle of exams and I knew you had to concentrate. He liked my playing, but I'd be out forever if I turned him down a third time. I had to make my lie the truth."

Paul let go of the phone and watched it swing slowly back and forth, pendulum-like, at the end of its spiraled cord. Her voice came from the receiver, but he had heard enough.

"*Yisgadal, v'yiskadash,* Little Reuben, Little Reuben," he began and then stopped. You don't recite *Kaddish* for a fetus, certainly not while you're sitting by yourself on a kitchen floor. The gesture would violate Jewish law in a half-dozen ways. And Little Reuben wasn't dead — only postponed until Sibyl and he were together again.

Paul put the he receiver back to his ear as Sibyl was saying, "I'll never have an opportunity like this again."

"Maybe, maybe not," he said in the most even-toned voice he could squeeze from himself. "But you'll have my backing no matter what you do. How are you?"

"The doctor says I can rehearse and go on the tour. How are you?"

Air had returned to his lungs, but the air was freezing. "I'm glad you're okay."

Neither of them spoke, and Paul felt a new pain — this one in his right hand. Somehow, a sliver of milk glass had been jabbed deep into his palm. He left it there and the pain flared up his arm and into the back of his head, where it exploded his false composure. He struggled not to roar, *You killed our child — an innocent Jew.* He felt an urge to rip the phone out of the wall, as Boris must have done, fling it out the window and follow it. But then, there would never be a Little Reuben. Asher would sneer at him: *You can't even handle a single death.*

"Do you think Smith is after you?" he asked without thinking.

"After me?"

"Reginald Smith. You know. Walter Winchell's column said . . ." He couldn't finish.

"Don't you realize — don't you realize!" Her second "realize" was a three-syllable accusation. "Don't you understand what's just happened? I'm a very good flutist!"

Paul tried to picture her in the hospital bed at the clinic. Or was it a regular bed? Or the top of a kitchen table? "I'm sorry."

"There's never been anybody besides you."

"I'll be there late tonight. I won't interfere with anything."

"No, no," she pleaded, and then demanded, "Please! No! I have to give it my total effort. I think you understand that." She made a throaty sound, part laugh, part sob. "We leave in three days and rehearse all day into the evening. If Reggie finds out you came—"

Paul let go of the phone again.

* * *

An hour later, he stood before Judge Webster's desk.

"I'd like to keep working for you."

"Your eye looks terrible. Did you get in a fight?"

Paul shook his head. "It's too embarrassing to explain." Like an out-of-control fire, the pain grew and spread inside him. Inches away was the soft leather chair he sat in when they discussed cases or literature, but the judge didn't point at it and Paul wouldn't ask.

"I'm not going to lecture or warn." Judge Webster's matter-of-fact voice was frightening. Paul stared at the judge's desk, which seemed shinier than ever. "I seriously considered dismissing you, but your behavior was so out of character I can only attribute it to some transitory emotional strain having to do with Olymp."

Transitory! Paul suppressed an urge to smile.

Judge Webster went on in an uncharacteristic soft voice: "Not being Jewish or having these connections, I can't imagine what that strain must be."

He waited for a response, but Paul had nothing he could say.

"I recused myself from *Olymp v. Anvil*, and the parties agreed that Judge Malone can replace me. I circulated your memo to the new panel. No matter why you wrote it, it makes a point that should be considered."

The judge folded his hands on the desk. "I want only one assurance from you." Paul, with great effort, pulled his shoulders back. "You will not discuss the Olymp case, in or out of the office, with anyone. Not a single word."

Paul looked Judge Webster directly in the eye. "You have my assurance."

Judge Webster nodded at the leather chair, and Paul sat down slowly.

"You've really hurt yourself, haven't you?"

"I just tripped in the apartment."

"Perhaps you and Sibyl should go away for a few days."

Paul was surprised. Puck — or Priscilla, the name Mrs. Webster preferred and Sibyl used — hadn't told the judge that Sibyl was gone. And how could he act so calm when his son was a fugitive from justice? Paul both pitied and admired the man. He leaned forward. "I'm sorry to have caused you so much trouble. Nothing like that will happen again."

"I know it won't. Let's move on."

* * *

Paul stopped before his desk, and looked at the briefs and record in *Valley Mall v. Simone* which Judge Webster had just handed him. They seemed fresh from the printer — smooth covers, tight bindings, never before opened. He closed the door behind him, sat down and smelled each of the six booklets. He began to stroke the "Brief of Plaintiff-Appellant," but that seemed perverse. He turned to page 1, "Issues on Appeal." The central question — the extent to which a shopping center owner can prohibit picketing inside the mall — was particularly interesting. Three hours later, he looked up from the briefs and realized he was the only person remaining in Judge Webster's chambers.

Despite reminders of Sibyl, he went back to the apartment. She might call. There, he gobbled China Dragon takeout, cleaned up the mess from his fall, and burned Sibyl's note. That done, he could again escape into the Valley Mall papers.

Shortly before one, the "Plaintiff-Appellant's Reply Brief" slid from his hands, and Paul thought he might be tired enough to sleep. He opened the bedroom door and was immediately wide awake. Their marriage bed would be half empty; when he reached out, he would feel nothing except a puffed pillow. He closed the bedroom door, and went to the couch where every sleeping position put pressure on a part of him that hurt. He tried the easy chair, but the ottoman kept sliding away. Back on the couch, he stared at the ceiling, resigned to a sleepless night. To his amazement, he was awakened from a deep, dreamless sleep when the phone rang. Sibyl, he hoped, but it was 6:00 AM, 3:00 AM in Seattle. Asher, he dreaded.

It was Jack. "Sorry it's so early, but I wanted to get you while your mother was asleep."

Paul sat up. "I meant to call you. David Osterlin — this guy at Yale whose name you gave me — he said you did some noble things at Olymp, that you helped — "

"I shoveled coal."

"He told me —"

"He can't tell you nothing. He wasn't there. Look, Paul, we don't got time for some snot-nose professor. Asher called. He didn't know Malke was in Israel. Everybody thought she was still in Lubyanka. He's going away soon. Do you want to talk to him while he's still here?"

Fuck you! Paul thought. The shoveling saint was in cahoots with Asher, trying to learn whether the whispered information — "Olymp will win" — was still good. Like Eric Koerner, who both stole Levy's ideas and risked his life to get food to prisoners, his stepfather was a complex human being. Too complex to cope with right now.

"Do you want to?" Jack repeated.

A new voice, one without a trace of Yiddish, thundered in Paul's head – *You will not discuss Olymp with anyone.* The commandment was inflexible and, just a few hours ago, Paul had assured Judge Webster he would follow it. Asher would ask Paul whether he stood by his whispered message, and Paul, to keep his word to Judge Webster, would have to end the conversation abruptly.

What would happen to Asher if Olymp lost the appeal and its stock price went down instead of up? What would happen to the people who paid Asher for supposedly confidential information (Olymp will win) that turned out to be wrong? What would happen to Paul himself? He had, of course, been aware of these questions, but had never directly confronted them, and he wouldn't confront them now. The most important thing now was to get Sibyl back and, with her, the hope of a new Little Reuben.

"Paul?"

Paul wished he could think of a response to Jack, but whatever he might say would only make things worse. But still, he had to say something. "Tell Asher to forget I ever spoke to him." Slowly, he put the phone back on its cradle.

* * *

He had ripped up her note, but the marriage bed was there to remind him of what he had lost. He moved his bureau drawers and much of his closet's contents into the living room, laid it all out on the rug, closed the bedroom door, and resolved not to open it until Sibyl returned. Then he realized he had left his watch on the floor alongside the bed. The hell with it. He'd buy a watch at the Woolworth's on 14th Street, next to the YMCA where he swam.

Without strict discipline, he'd never survive until Thanksgiving. He would call her only once a day, only to her room, and avoid any emotionally laden subject, particularly the baby. He'd win her back with idle chit chat.

At noon, he called her room from the phone booth in the courthouse lobby. When there was no answer, he called the rehearsal hall. A breach of discipline, but he had to survive today.

It took a few minutes for her to get to the phone. "It's Paul. I hope—"

"Are you crazy? Trying to get me fired before I start?" Her loud breaths between the rhetorical questions underscored her anger. "Nobody calls a musician during rehearsals."

Schmuck! Paul cursed himself. *Pest!* "I'm sorry. Where can I get you tonight?"

"We're leaving this evening. I still have to get some shots."

"What's the first stop?"

"Mexico City. I'll call Priscilla to give you the itinerary. Please Paul, Reginald's coming in. I'll call from Mexico." The phone clicked.

Fuck you, too, he thought. After he had decided to give up the Supreme Court clerkship for her and tell her the whole story of Max's diamonds, she had presented him with a *fait accompli* from three thousand miles away and now wouldn't speak to him. Still, he had to have her back. Why? he asked himself. There were too many reasons — passion, love, loneliness, Little Reuben, habit — all of them amorphous, and any of them capable of sending him into a panic. He called Priscilla and arranged to pick up Sibyl's itinerary from the Websters' doorman.

* * *

Sibyl didn't call from Mexico City, and didn't return his call to Paraguay. He reached her in Lima at two in the morning. "Why don't you call back? I just want to talk."

"It's so hectic with all the traveling, and I feel under such pressure."

She needed him. "Tell me about the music."

She didn't answer right away, and then said, "I played well tonight, especially when the flutes were alone in Offenbach. 'Beautiful, beautiful,' Reginald almost shouted."

Paul pictured her smile forming. "What was the program?"

She began to describe the pieces, and Paul probed for details. Her words trickled until Paul asked her to sing some of the Offenbach. After humming a few measures, her words gushed forth — performers, rhythms, mistakes, the idiosyncratic personalities. Paul wondered how many years had passed since they last spoke in depth about her music.

"Play the Offenbach Reginald liked," he urged her.

"It's two in the morning!" They both laughed.

"You played the flute for me before either of us said a word, but you should get some rest. I'll call tomorrow."

"If it's Sunday, it must be Santiago. A matinee."

Neither of them said goodbye, and Paul enjoyed the silence. He couldn't remember the last time he had felt this serene. "I miss you," he finally said.

"Paul?" she responded tentatively.

"What?" He was careful not to add *darling*, but he tried to convey it in his tone.

"I'm so confused, leaving so suddenly. That's not me. It was humiliating — sitting there with puppet strings and no Geppetto."

"I can't tell you how sorry I am, how much I regret it." He was careful to make no promises for the future. "There's no excuse, but there is an explanation. Too much for two a.m. but maybe, when you have the whole story, you'll see what a dilemma I was in."

"Paul?"

He could barely hear her. "What?"

"Do you think I did the right thing? You know, with the doctor in Seattle?"

Paul lay down on the couch. He had prepared his response carefully. "Yes. If you would have asked me, I would have told you that before. I would have been with you — made it easier for you." Total bullshit, but he said it with such sincerity that he almost believed it.

"I know you, Paul, and I just . . . " She cut herself off and sighed loudly. "I appreciate that, even if you're just saying it to make me feel better. Call at six tomorrow. I'll play for you."

* * *

On each of his four calls to Santiago, her room didn't answer, and when he called Buenos Aires the hotel operator wouldn't put him through. After another day of fruitless efforts, he called Pan Am for the Montevideo flight schedule, but hung up while the agent was checking availability. If he kept being a pest, she might be through with him forever.

At midnight, six hours after his aborted call to Pan Am, when he returned to the apartment from the Secret Dungeon, the phone was ringing.

"It's me. I've been calling for over an hour."

No bullshit, he ordered himself, and he told her about the Secret Dungeon and how much time he was spending there. "If anyone in the office finds out I'm working in secret, they'll think I'm crazy, but if I can't keep busy all the time, I really will be. Where are you?"

"Montevideo, but I'm calling about what happened in Buenos Aires last weekend. Or maybe it was last week; I've lost track of time."

He lay on the couch, ready for a long talk, wondering which one of them would first say I love you. If one did, the other might repeat it, and the words could again become true.

"Tell me," he said as kindly as he could.

"I wasn't planning to call. I'm always afraid that if we talk, something will get said that will make it hard to merge myself into the music. Without that, it's sound, not art."

How could he have let her go? "Tell me."

"What happened made me think about things I never wanted to think about. And there's nobody here I can talk to. Maybe Boris, but he gets too emotional."

What the hell was it? And why was Boris involved? "Tell me."

"It started when we landed in Buenos Aires. This guy from the State Department met us and told Reginald that the sponsoring committee wanted Wagner added to the repertoire."

Paul sat up. He wanted no more memories of Max. But maybe she was becoming more Jewish and would understand, when he finally told her, why he couldn't have let Olymp win.

"Reginald called a rehearsal the next day — it was supposed to be free time — and the whole tour almost came to an end. I mean, I knew Wagner was an anti-Semite. A lot of people were, including my mother." She giggled nervously. "When we played *Tannhäuser* in my basement, did you know how vicious he was?"

"Who can remember so far back?" His pathetic evasion parched his throat.

"I got quite an education. First, Boris announces in front of the whole orchestra that he doesn't want to hand out the scores — it was the Forge Scene from *Siegfried* — not only because it's Wagner, but because a lot of high-up Nazis escaped from Europe and are now living in Argentina and Uruguay, and they're the ones who want to hear Wagner performed."

Paul thought back to the Far Rockaway High School band concert ten years earlier when a Jew — Mrs. Heider, Sibyl's aunt — chose Wagner's *Tannhäuser* as the opening piece, and the school's largely

Jewish band performed it for a largely Jewish audience. Which was worse? Paul wondered — Jews playing Wagner for Jews in Rockaway or Jews playing Wagner for Nazis in Argentina. Unlike the Auschwitz orchestra, the musicians in both Rockaway and South America were not playing for their lives.

"Reginald went wild." Deepening her voice, and giving a poor imitation of an English accent, Sibyl parodied Reginald's pronouncement that "one had to judge art independently of the artist." Deepening her voice further, she said, "Anyone who disagrees with that should leave now, including you, Boris. This is an orchestra, not the Oxford Debating Society."

Sibyl resumed her natural voice. "Three people, including Boris, got up and one of them, Lilly Auerbach, a second violinist who never opens her mouth, started to make a speech about what happened to her and her family in Poland, and she kept talking after Reginald told her to stop. Nobody breathed."

Sibyl seemed almost desperate to recount everything Lilly had said. Another Holocaust story, but one the two of them might share.

"Lilly said her whole family died in Auschwitz, although they never thought of themselves as Jews. My God, Paul, that's my family. Music was her family's only religion."

Were any of Lilly's relatives in the Auschwitz orchestra? Did Max select them as performers? Or did he consign them to becoming ashes? Or maybe Asher was lying and he, himself, was the evil conductor. Paul shut off his brain. These speculations could only make it more difficult to get Sibyl back.

"What you believed or what you did was of no consequence," he said. "All that mattered was your ancestry. One Jewish grandparent and you had to die. We all shared that."

"Boris said something similar. He spoke after Lilly, and he told how the Holocaust descended on his mother's family in Hungary. It was mesmerizing. His mother's mother was Jewish, which makes him Jewish according to Nazi law, and Jewish law too, even though he grew up thinking he was a Unitarian until his mother's Aunt, who survived Treblinka . . ."

Paul put the phone on his lap. Now was not the time for yet another Holocaust story. When he heard Sibyl say "Wagner," he brought it back to his ear.

"Boris said Wagner represents . . ." Paul again stopped listening. She would repeat the explanation Max gave him — only in proper English.

Sibyl finally paused, and Paul asked, "How was it resolved?"

"Reginald and the union delegate met with the State Department man, and they reached a compromise." She sounded drained. "We'd play Wagner only in Argentina and Uruguay, maybe Rio, and anybody who didn't want to play it didn't have to, but they wouldn't make any kind of scene. Not much of a compromise." She laughed to herself. "Only three people didn't play, and I'm ashamed I wasn't one of them, but how could I refuse after what I did to get here?"

"Don't agonize over it. I had a cousin who told me that Christians run the world and you have to beat them at their own game."

Paul couldn't believe what he had just heard. For the first time in their ten years together, he had alluded to Max. Soon she'd know everything about his cousin, as soon as she appreciated Paul's resolution to tailor his ambitions to her artistic career.

"A cousin?" Sibyl asked. "Is this someone I met?"

Paul had to be careful. All could be lost in the next few moments. "Too complicated for an intercontinental phone call."

If not now, when? he asked himself. *Dive in, and trust your instincts.* "I've resolved to change. When you come back, I'll—"

"No!" Sibyl nearly screamed. "If I think about after the tour, I'll never be able to handle the tour. Let me tell you about the Wagner."

Paul closed his eyes. There was no risk of falling asleep. "Tell me, please."

"It was terrifying. You could tell the Nazis in the audience. They were sitting together at attention, all in the same perfectly pressed dark suits and dark ties, like uniforms. Their wives were dressed like Marlene Dietrich — the little black hat pulled over their short hair, the white gloves. When it was over, the whole army of them stood up at attention and beat their hands together in unison. I was sure they would give the Nazi salute and then march me away."

Was Strummer in the audience? Paul wondered. Aiming his imaginary pistol — his thumb and forefinger — directly at Max? At Asher? At Sibyl and Paul and every Jew in the world?

The intercontinental calls had to end. Wagner would come up, and God knows where that would lead. They would talk when she returned, when he could convey the sincerity of his resolution and she would appreciate how he had been compelled to conceal Max from her.

"Maybe it would be best if I don't call again so you can focus on the music."

"I appreciate that, Paul."

"I'll pick you up at Idlewild on the twenty-eighth. Priscilla gave me the itinerary."

"I appreciate that too."

CHAPTER 14

Chip and Nancy rescued Paul from a regimen of near-ceaseless work, swimming past exhaustion, dreamless sleeps permeated with the smell of chlorine and, during the snippets of time when he was awake at home, trying not to stare at the telephone. A few days after Sibyl left, Chip called and told Paul that his "half-sister, a flutist, heard that Sibyl was going to South America with the Seattle Symphony." He invited Paul "to come over this Sunday, the twenty-sixth, for supper and to watch the Giants-Browns football game from Cleveland." Chip guaranteed that Paul would be "amazed by how exciting pro football is on TV."

Paul wore his red Berkshire Lodge lifeguard shirt to the Storys'. He wanted Chip and Nancy to see that he was more than a nose-to-the-grindstone striver. And the shirt could give him an opportunity to talk about his father.

The game was better than exciting: During his five hours at the Storys' apartment, nobody mentioned Sibyl, and Paul told of his father's attempt to join the Army Counterintelligence Corps. When he left, Nancy invited him to Thanksgiving dinner — a good reason not to go to Rochester.

Each week brought one or two invitations from the Storys — a French movie, *Mon Oncle*, at the Paris Theater, a Knicks game, the Martha Graham Dance Company. Paul wanted to reciprocate with something special and, through a scalper who swam with him at the Y, he bought three fifty-yard-line tickets for a Giants home game against Washington, and went directly from the Y to Chip's Foley Square cubicle. While he and Chip discussed the possibility of the Giants making the playoffs, Paul scanned the pictures on Chip's radiator. In one, two beanpole children, a boy and a girl, flanked an attractive woman on a beach with a lighthouse in the background. The boy was obviously Chip. All three had thin lips, light eyes and blonde hair blowing behind them. Another picture seemed to be the same three people, a dozen or so years later, with the same lighthouse behind them. Chip, now the tallest, was in the center. The second tallest, and the only one not in a bathing suit had to be his flutist sister. She was still long-legged, and it was clear from the thin cotton dress blowing against her body that her legs were shapely and her breasts small. The three of them, mother and children, at ease in this natural setting, seemed to belong there as much as the lighthouse. So different from the pictures on his parents' bedroom wall where, except for the *goy*-like bride, dark-haired and dark-clothed Czech Jews confronted the camera as if it were an enemy.

"Nantucket," Chip said, pointing at the beanpole picture. "Our mother's family has had a house there since before the Indians. That's the summer Willa became taller than me for a little while and she started to stoop. The other one's from last summer soon after Willa's son died and her husband left. We were trying to cheer her up. It didn't work."

Willa was grieving for a baby she had lost and really wanted. Paul changed the subject to lunch. That night, for the first time in years, he masturbated.

* * *

A week before Thanksgiving, Jack called him at home. "Don't hang up on me like last time. I'm calling for your mother because she's afraid to talk to you." Jack paused, but Paul said nothing. "You got to come for Thanksgiving to Ruthie and Bernie's. It's important, and I'll explain to you why."

"I'm sorry about hanging up. I'm not going to do it again — and I won't interrupt."

"Ruthie has. . . Nobody likes to say the word, and I promised your mother I wouldn't. Ruthie has the C. Like in the old country, everybody's afraid that if anybody says the word, the angel of death will show up sooner. It's in her privates. We don't say that word neither."

Ruthie, Paul thought. Always there. Always pretty. Usually smiling. Always nice to him — almost always. But for Bernie, he could have liked her. "How long will she live?"

"Too long for her own good. But, instead of sitting around and feeling sorry for themselves, she and Bernie decided to have the biggest Thanksgiving dinner ever — make the pilgrims feel like pikers. Catered, of course, all the cousins on both sides. She wants to see everybody together, just in case. Most of all, she wants your mother, who's her best friend. And she wants you."

As Jack went on, the pitch of his voice rose and fell, as if he were speaking Yiddish, which Paul found both grating and comforting. "Your mother and Ruthie, they feel bad about Bernie giving you such a hard time, and they promised nothing like that's gonna happen."

"I'll come." Chip would understand family obligations.

"Any human being would."

After Jack gave the details, Paul said what he had to. "Can I speak to my mother?"

"She's on the way to Woodmere. She's managing the whole dinner and making sure Ruthie's taken good care of. Bernie bought her a first-class plane ticket and is having a limo pick her up at the airport. First time she's flown — that's one more than me."

"I'll call her tomorrow."

"Good. She's worried about you. About Sibyl, the baby . . . you know, everything."

Reality exploded in Paul's head. There would be questions at the dinner, and he had to make his story consistent with Sibyl's. She, too, wouldn't want the truth known — abortion was a crime.

After getting off the phone with Jack, Paul considered calling Sibyl, then rejected the idea. He had humiliated himself enough. Instead, he called Mrs. Webster. If the judge answered, he would hang up.

Mrs. Webster answered, and Paul said, "I'm going to a family Thanksgiving dinner and there will be questions—"

To his surprise, Mrs. Webster interrupted. "Just say it was a miscarriage in Seattle. That what Sibyl's been saying . . ."

"That's what I'll say. I'm planning on picking her up when the tour's over."

"She's hoping you will. I'll tell her. Be gentle. It hasn't been a great trip."

"I will, Mrs. Webster."

"Priscilla."

Maybe everything would work out.

* * *

On the day before Thanksgiving, two days before Sibyl's return, while Paul was at home supervising the cleaning service he had hired for the apartment, Vivien called. It was important that Paul come in to the office right away. The Olymp opinion must have been filed.

As Paul expected, the judge's desk was empty except for a stapled multi-page document, face down on the polished surface. But, as he hadn't expected, the judge seemed tired and his right eye was twitching. His family problems were showing.

"I've written a letter recommending you to Justice Brennan."

Paul didn't react. Sibyl's return was all that mattered.

"Your memo in *Kaminsky v. Dulles* is a gem," the judge went on. "You're asking us to disagree with the Ninth and Tenth Circuits — no small thing — but your analysis of the history of passports leaves no choice. I never realized that's how our passport system evolved."

"A 1950 Ph.D. dissertation suggested it." Paul did not volunteer that he had reviewed every publication dealing with passports that was contained in the NYU main, law, and history libraries.

"Check its sources carefully."

"I will," Paul said. He already had.

"I'll be seeing Justice Brennan next week, and I'll tell him about Olymp. I'm sure he'll agree it's a once-in-a-lifetime aberration."

"Thank you," Paul managed to say. Later, if Sibyl didn't want to live in Washington or if he felt irrevocably *treyf*, he could change his answer to *Thank you, but*. He was relieved that the judge didn't offer his hand to shake.

The judge picked up the document on his desk. "You've probably guessed what this is." Paul nodded, and the judge read from the last page: "The case is remanded to the District Court for a supplemental trial on the issue of whether the true inventor was Koerner or Levine and whether the patent is invalid under section 102(d)." That was almost verbatim what Paul had written on the train from New Haven, with one exception. Paul's memo and, doubtlessly, the opinion from which the judge was reading had the inventor's actual name — Levy, not Levine. Paul wouldn't point out the error because, for Judge Webster, and maybe for the world, the inventor was just one more anonymous dead Jew.

The judge handed the opinion to Paul. "For you. Since Levine's inventorship seems beyond dispute, Olymp will probably dedicate the patent to the public so as to avoid punitive damages and minimize publicity about its war record. Still, what you did was not the way the system is supposed to work, and both of us should refuse to talk about any aspect of the case. I'll mention it to Justice Brennan — he'll probably think you did a great thing — but you shouldn't bring it up unless he asks about it."

Paul was proud. Although it couldn't compare with Malke blowing up a bridge and didn't come close to avenging the Olymp slaves, he was responsible for some small measure of justice. But, when he entered his cubicle, Asher's face rose to meet him. Paul had no idea what Asher had done with the information he had whispered. What would happen next? But if he thought one more second about Asher, he might not be able to do what had to be done — get the apartment ready for Sibyl, survive the just-in-case dinner, comfort Ruthie, win Sibyl back, and recreate Little Reuben. Until all of that was accomplished, he wouldn't read the opinion.

But he couldn't keep himself from the newspaper headlines. All three evening papers reported on the case. It was the lead article in the *Journal American* and *World Telegram* business sections. In the *Post,* half of the tabloid's front page was the headline:

NAZI SLAVE
PATENT DENIED

Olymp Stock Plunges

Paul threw the *Journal American* and *World Telegram* away before reading a single paragraph. He didn't lift the *Post* from the newsstand.

* * *

It would have been easy to go to Woodmere by the Long Island Railroad, but Paul rented a black Buick (impressive, but not showy) so he could leave immediately if he were shaken by questions about Olymp or Sibyl.

A man who could only be called a butler opened the door, took Paul's coat, and led him into the living room beyond the foyer. One glance at the guests in sight, and Paul was glad he had worn the custom-made suit he had worn to job interviews, vest and all. He had never been in this latest iteration of Bernie's mansion. Everything — paneling, light fixtures (he saw a chandelier in the distance), art, drapery, rugs — was in good taste, even lovely. It was as if the house, itself, were wearing a custom-made suit.

Bernie came over to Paul. In the two months since he had threatened Paul in front of the China Dragon, his face had become fleshier and his perpetual tan had faded. He squeezed Paul's shoulder hard, but within the range of affectionate. "Ruthie will be glad to see you. So will your mother. To tell the truth," he squeezed a bit harder, "so am I. Thanks."

"I wanted to come." Paul put his hand on Bernie's shoulder, but didn't squeeze. "I'm sorry about what's happening with Ruthie."

"Me too," Bernie said wistfully. "The C . . ." He released Paul's shoulder and took his elbow. "Let's go talk to her. But first I want you to try something special." He led Paul to a dark, wooden table from which drinks were being served, and nodded at the bartender who poured Paul two inches of liquor from a bottle Paul couldn't identify. "It's a private brand," Bernie said. "Twenty-four years old from the best distillery in Scotland. I drink it neat to get the full flavor."

The scotch slid down Paul's throat and was delicious. He took a second long swallow and felt its effect almost immediately. He had never been a good drinker, but tonight that might be an asset. He finished the drink and, as soon as he lowered the glass from his lips, the bartender refilled it. He took another swallow, but then put the drink down. Bernie might be trying to get him drunk — set things up so the Harvard lawyer would humiliate himself. He could hear Bernie's triumphant voice: *That kid doesn't respect anything or anybody. No wonder his wife walked out on him.*

Bernie's actual words took over from those in Paul's imagination. "I'm probably feeding you too much scotch. We don't want to upset your mother."

Paul's instinct was to drain the glass in front of him, then ask for another. Whatever Bernie wanted, he would do the opposite. But that would give Bernie complete control over him.

"Sleep over tonight," Bernie said. "I'd like to tell you some things about your father. Good things, but he made your mother promise she'd never tell anybody."

This wasn't the real Bernie. "Give me a clue," Paul said. "And tell me what you're after."

Bernie gripped Paul's forearm, as tight as he had at the China Dragon. His lips were close to Paul's ear and, when he spoke, Paul could feel spittle.

"What I'm after is that you shouldn't be a righteous prick like your father was at his worst. But Reuben had a best too, and I'm still trying to figure out what yours is. You did a nice thing coming here, and I want to be nice too, but you make it hard." Bernie released his grip. He pulled his head back from Paul's ear, but spoke softly.

"The winter before you were born, your father was working on a ski patrol in St. Moritz. Usually, they didn't hire Jews, but they made an exception because he was so good. Anyway, he saved some kid who had been left there by his own father. The kid was hurt, and the father was drunk and with a woman who wasn't his wife. Reuben got pictures. He knew how to play hard ball, your old man. If he wasn't so rigid, he could have made a lot of money." Bernie nodded. "Anyway, the kid's father turned out to be a senator from Kentucky or Tennessee, one of those places, very involved with the State Department — a bunch of anti-Semites who were trying to keep the Jews where Hitler could kill them.

Maybe it was gratitude or some polite blackmail about what happened at St. Moritz, but your father used this senator to get some of the family, including the three of you and my own father, into America. And then, when my father wanted to show his gratitude to the Senator, and to Reuben, too, your father gave him a big speech and made him feel like . . ." Bernie winced. "It hurt."

Paul picked up his drink and finished it. "Thanks for telling me. I'm sorry I was rude." The bartender filled his glass again, and he took a long swallow. "I'm tempted to stay and learn the details, but I'm picking Sibyl up at the airport tomorrow."

"Idlewild's ten minutes from here. I can give you a razor and anything else you need. I'm glad you and Sibyl are getting back together. You know, I speak to Maurice once in a while. He's in Cuba now, against my advice — doing something stupid. I'm sorry about the baby."

Paul's call to Priscilla had prepared him for this. "Miscarriages happen — no big deal — but neither of us wants to talk about it."

"Ruthie and I know miscarriages. It *is* a big deal." He patted Paul's shoulder. "Your mother doesn't know the pregnancy's over. Ruthie thinks Sibyl should be the one to tell her."

The scotch buzzed in Paul's head, and the room began to spin. Bernie lowered his eyes. "I shouldn't have come down so hard on Montague. I should have realized Reuben Hartman's son would get pissed off if I offered money."

Suddenly, Paul couldn't stop the scotch from speaking. "Is my cousin Asher coming?"

Bernie's eyes hardened. "He disappeared. I promised Ruthie I wouldn't say his name or Olymp to you. Or tell you it was about time you pull the Swiss box key out of the ocean. Your mother and Jack need money badly, and they won't take any more from us."

Paul was surprised to be holding an empty liquor glass. "I'm going to see Ruthie."

"Go by yourself. In the room past the chandelier. If you upset her, you're dead."

"I don't need your threats to do the right thing."

* * *

The room with the drinks wasn't the living room. It was the opening act for the real living room which was under the chandelier. Paul kept his eyes on his feet so he could focus on walking and not have to greet anyone he knew.

Past the living room was a small library-like room where Ruthie's ghost sat in a wing chair that could have held three of her. Her blonde hair — probably a wig — was swept back smoothly along the sides of her narrow head. Every bit of skin on her face seemed painted or creamed, but cracks were emerging.

Paul's mother, like a lady in waiting, stood alongside the apparition. Ruthie presented her cheek to be kissed, but Paul went to the side of her chair and kissed her lips. His mother presented her lips, and he kissed them too. "I'm sorry you're going through all this, Ruthie," he said. "I'm glad you're having this dinner." His words weren't slurred.

"I'm glad you came, Paulie," She took his hand, but her fingers had no life. "I wish Sibyl was with you."

"She'll be home tomorrow, and we'll visit you on Saturday." Paul saw that his mother's mouth was trembling. "She's doing well and the baby's fine." It was compassionate bullshit.

Ruthie perked up and said, "I told you, Ida. You're worrying about nothing."

Admirable, Paul thought. Despite her suffering, Ruthie wanted to shield her friend for a bit longer. Paul bent over to kiss Ruthie again, but his face swayed past hers.

His mother grabbed his forearm. "Are you . . .? Did you drink—"

"I'm fine. Fine."

Paul freed his arm. Had Bernie gotten him this drunk, or had he done it by himself? It made no difference — he was out of control.

"Maybe I should get a bite—"

His mother put her finger to her lips and then pointed it at Ruthie. Asleep in her chair, she seemed to have shriveled by an additional third. His mother pulled Paul into the real living room where at least thirty people were slowly rocking back and forth.

"Mom, I should go eat something."

"Just one thing. You did a *mitzvah* in coming. Maybe forty people walked in to see Ruthie, and you're the only one to kiss her on the lips. Daddy would have done that."

Paul felt an urge to hug her, but that might make the room turn faster.

"Whatever went wrong between us," he said, "it's a big part my fault too." It was more compassionate bullshit, but the scotch might soon make him say what he really felt — something that would pain them both. "Are there hors d'oeuvres before supper?"

"In the sitting room. Across from the drinks table." His mother took his hands. "But first, you have to understand something so you don't get hurt."

Paul bent, found his mother, and the spinning slowed. He might need another drink to get through dinner.

"Ruthie wanted you to sit at her table in the dining room." His mother's palms were perspiring. "But then something happened yesterday that got Bernie and Jack upset."

Paul felt nothing; even his heartbeat stayed the same. Olymp was coming, and there was nothing he could do.

"When I'm around, nobody talks about what happened yesterday. But Jack said it would be best if you didn't sit with him or Bernie — avoid arguments that would upset Ruthie. So, you'll be at one of the tables downstairs. Not really a basement. More like a nightclub."

Obviously, Jack and Bernie knew about the Olymp decision. How could they not?

"So, I'm exiled," Paul said. "If it's not the same menu, can you send a care package?"

His mother gave him a flickering smile, and then pressed her cheek against Paul's vest. "Come here Saturday with Sibyl like you promised. And tell me what's really going on with the two of you. Maybe I can help."

"Your help won't help!" Paul burst out. He stepped back abruptly and his mother nearly lost her balance. The room had become more crowded, and people were staring at them. He was dangerously close to saying what he thought — that she caused the problems between Sibyl and him by making him lie about Max and then running away with another survivor.

"You better go back to Ruthie." He headed towards the twenty-four-year-old scotch.

* * *

The scotch tasted even better than he remembered, and he turned towards the hors d'oeuvres table. The first thing he saw was a silver bowl of giant pink shrimp, each at least three inches long, in concentric mounting circles. *Treyf.* Didn't Ruthie come from an Orthodox background? Weren't some of the guests kosher? He wouldn't eat it and, tomorrow, he would become kosher. Wagner had made Sibyl feel Jewish, and they needed to start afresh.

He heaped a plate with everything else on the table, although the brown stuff looked like pork, and devoured it all with a glass of red wine. One more neat scotch for a perfect finish, but when he reached the center of the room, the floor began to tilt back and forth. He dropped himself into a love seat and was surprised to see someone sitting next to him.

"Hello cousin." The speaker was a young man, possibly a few years older than Paul, with thick curly hair as black as Sibyl's. Like Paul, he wore a three-piece interview suit. He extended his hand over Paul's lap, but Paul didn't take it.

"Are we related?" Paul was sure he sounded drunk.

The man kept his hand where it was. "I'm Walter Rosenzweig. My father was Jack Ross's cousin, so I guess we're distant step cousins."

Paul shook Walter's hand, but didn't have the strength to squeeze. Walter's fingers slid to Paul's pulse. "You're *shiker*," he said. "Crazy drunk. I'm a doctor, and I advise you to lie down."

Paul told himself to be polite. The guy was a pain in the ass but nobody, particularly Ruthie, needed a scene. "I appreciate it, but I really want to be at Ruthie's dinner."

"I understand." Walter released Paul's wrist. "I'll get you coffee and stick by you. Jack says you've got a lot going on in your life."

"I don't want to talk about Jack."

"He took your mother from you." Walter smiled, pleased with his insight. "It's an old story. I'm a psychiatric resident."

The room had steadied a bit. "Please don't try to help me understand myself."

"You're right. I owe you an apology."

"Not needed. But I might need help getting to dinner."

"You've got it." Walter smiled again; his teeth were white and even. "You know, we're *landsmen*. I was born in the Sudetenland, too." The smile disappeared. "But while your parents moved to America, mine went to Germany to take over my grandfather's creamery near Cologne. It was just before Hitler, so it turned out to be a bad move."

Paul asked what he had to: "How did you get out?" He didn't want an answer.

"Only I got out. On the *Kindertransport*. Do you know what that was?"

Paul wasn't sure, but he nodded. Now wasn't the time to learn.

"They wouldn't take my sister because she was too young, so she stayed with my parents and my grandmother. Then, in 1938, soon after *Kristallnacht*—"

"Stop!" Paul's shout shocked him. He was on his feet. "No Holocaust story. They've ruined my life." Suddenly, it poured out — a full plate of *traife*, and he followed it, head first, onto the rug.

* * *

When he awoke and the spinning slowed, Paul forced himself out of bed. He was fully dressed, except for his shoes and suit jacket. He focused only on the open door to the bathroom. He got in without wobbling, and saw a note taped to the medicine cabinet —

Paul — I left 4 pills on the 1st shelf.
Big for pain. Small for nausea.
One each before breakfast and lunch
Call me Friday. Hope you feel better.
— W

Below the note was Walter's card. He was the Lehman Senior Resident in Psychiatry at Creedmoor State Hospital.

Paul dropped the pills into the toilet. He didn't want help from a survivor who worked in a mental hospital.

He found aspirin in the medicine cabinet and managed to fall back asleep. Then later, there was a tap at the door, followed by a knock, followed by Jack sticking his head in.

"He's dressed. You can come in, Ida." Paul heard in Jack's voice a mixture of anguish and anger. He sat up. The dizziness had eased. He had no idea what time it was.

Jack stepped aside, and his mother entered the room. Her eyes were red circles. "Paulie, Paulie," she gasped, and lurched towards him. Jack seized her shoulders and pulled her back. "Asher is dead," she said.

Paul tensed his body so it wouldn't shake.

"The police called," his mother said. "Police! They want —" She began to sob, and Jack eased her onto a vanity chair.

Jack clenched his fingers into fists, released them, and kept repeating the gesture as he spoke. "I'll explain what we know, and this time you won't be able to hang up on me."

"No Jack, please," his mother said between sobs.

"I'm sorry, Ida," Jack said gently. "You need to listen, Paul, because the police want to talk to you too. We're supposed to be at the Hundredth Precinct in half an hour."

"The Hundredth Precinct," his mother repeated. "That's where —
"

"I know," Paul said. The Hundredth Precinct had notified them of Max's suicide. He wanted to go to his mother to console her, but the floor might tilt beneath him.

"Did Asher die in Rockaway?" he asked her. *What's the difference where?* he silently answered himself. *I made it happen.*

As if reading Paul's mind, Jack said, "It's not important where."

Paul's mother ignored her husband "He died on a Hundred-eighteenth Street. The apartment house across from the Jefferson Arms Hotel. Do you know where that is?"

"We don't got time for a class in maps," Jack said. "Tell him what's important."

"I passed that building every day I went to Sibyl's house," Paul said to his mother. "Her cousin's sweet sixteen was at the Jefferson Arms. It was the first time I wore a tux." He wanted to talk about the tux, about Ruthie, even about Sibyl or throwing up on the rug — anything except Asher. And she too, he suspected, wanted no more mention of Asher.

Jack's hands became fists. "One thing I gotta say, Paulie. And if it upsets you, Ida, I'm sorry."

Paul stood straight. He would take it in silence. His headache was almost a relief.

Jack breathed deeply. "I never liked Asher, even in Europe where I was close to some of his family. But, whether he jumped or got pushed, he didn't deserve to die."

Stay calm, say nothing, Paul kept repeating to himself.

"And I don't appreciate having to go to any police for anything, even if they don't have a swastika or German names." Jack glared at him, then disappeared into the hallway.

"Sit down, Paulie, you look terrible," his mother said. Relieved, Paul sat on the bed, but when his mother added, "Maybe you should go see Jack's cousin Walter," he stood again.

"Ma, just tell me what you know."

His mother wiped her eyes. "I'll try. Late in the night . . ." Her voice dropped. "You know, I can't remember if the detective said it was last night or the night before."

"Ma, please."

"You're right." She seemed to be talking to herself. "He and Frieda Greenberg were living in the apartment house. He was working at this piano repair shop in Boro Park. The owner was from Prague — Miller or Muller or—"

"Ma!"

"Stop Ma-ing me!" Paul looked away from her. "You don't *act* like I'm your mother. He fell from the fire escape! Four flights — maybe five. All right?" She began to sob.

Paul didn't know which of them moved first, but they were standing against each other by the foot of the bed. Her fingernails dug into his palms.

"The detective said maybe he was thrown." Her voice had steadied. "Somebody saw some big guys go in the building. Frieda saw the body in the alley. She called the police, called me, and disappeared. The cops asked who Asher saw, and Jack said we didn't know."

Paul had biked only to Playland, no further — twenty blocks before the Jefferson Arms. He couldn't have prevented it. No, that was 1948 — 53927, Max. This one's 1958 — 53928, Asher. And Dad was 1944 — no number. Maybe he had some indirect responsibility for Dad and 53927. But 53928 was not a maybe. That Jew, his cousin, died because of him.

"Why?" his mother asked. "Why would he jump when he and Frieda were talking about starting again, like Jack and me? And why would anyone want to kill Asher? Jack says it's got something to do with Olymp, but I don't . . ."

She drove her nails into Paul's palms. "Paulie, listen."

"You're hurting me, Ma."

"Listen." She drove her nails deeper. "Maybe you should go away for a while. Jack knows people, and Bernie knows more people. No, not Bernie. You make him crazy." She released his hands. "I have a better idea — Walter!" Her voice became more animated. "I'm sure he can get you into his hospital so that nobody outside will know you're there. He's brilliant, like you."

"I have to pick up Sibyl at the airport."

"Oh my God, the tour. Is the baby all right?" She cried again and her sobs seemed to tremble. "That's something else nobody's telling me about. Talk to Jack."

Jack appeared in the doorway. "We talked enough! Ask him if he thinks he—"

"Mom, I have to get Sibyl." The calmness in his voice frightened him. "I'll call you at Bernie's later. I will."

"Don't forget to call us unless you want to get us all arrested," Jack responded. "And don't go home first because the cops will bring you in before we can talk. And shave before you see them. Don't look like you got a hangover and slept all night in your clothes."

"You got to make things right with Sibyl," his mother said. "You're lost without her."

"And don't stay here much longer," Jack interjected. "Bernie's asleep — Ruthie had a terrible night — and he don't know about Asher yet. But I left him a note."

"Bernie gets crazy, Paulie. Jack can give you details. Don't even apologize or say goodbye. Maybe you could clean yourself up at Walter's apartment."

"Don't get Walter involved, Ida. Your son can figure out a way to wash his face."

Finally, they left. Sibyl's plane would land in four hours. If he couldn't fill that time, he would go crazy.

He saw a Nassau County phone book on the vanity table, and a new idea commandeered him. He flipped to "T" in the yellow pages. "Five Towns Tattoo" was on Peninsula Boulevard, ten minutes away. He pictured the ten digits on his forearm — 53927 above 53928— a memorial he would carry — his "Curse of Cain".

No! It would be a mockery. He hadn't earned the numbers; he wouldn't have survived; he couldn't even listen to Walter's Holocaust story. There was only one way out. Only one thing might approach what he had done to Asher and Max.

* * *

He parked near the foot of Sixty-ninth Street by the gold star bungalow where Daddy had collapsed in 1944. Even for late November, the street was desolate. Foot-deep sand blown from the beach blocked the ramp to the boardwalk. Not a dog in sight. Two of the rooming houses were not boarded up for the winter, and their windows were broken. The green trim on several bungalows was flaking; they couldn't have been painted in over a year. Arverne was rotting, yet the ocean air and the sound of the waves were immutable. He trudged through the sand onto the boardwalk, unsure whether to turn east towards Sixty-fourth Street, where Max had jumped, or west towards Rockaway Playland, the direction he had first walked with Sibyl.

He couldn't tell Sibyl the whole story. She would blame him for the deaths — Asher, Max, even Daddy, — and for forcing her father back to Faye. She might even say that there wouldn't have been an abortion if he had come to Margaret's Halloween party.

He removed his overcoat and jacket, rolled up his left sleeve and, shivering in the cold damp air, wrote his cousins' numbers on his forearm with a ballpoint pen. It was legible, but a mess. No Germanic precision or neatness, but that made his point even stronger. By the time his overcoat was back on, he was no longer shivering.

He thought of baring his arm again and writing "Little Reuben" under the numbers. But why cause Sibyl more pain?

He walked east on the beach — the suicide direction — and, at Sixty-fourth, he turned towards Max's jetty. The tide must have been higher when Max jumped, and the water much rougher. Otherwise, even Max, who couldn't swim, would have found it difficult to drown.

For Paul, a lifeguard who had pulled six people from the water, drowning required creativity. He would dive off the jetty's deep end and swim underwater away from the beach until he had no breath and his overcoat was saturated. Then, like Daddy on their last day together, he would do the Australian crawl out to sea. No stopping until he was too cold and exhausted to move his arms.

He would insure against his lifeguard instinct to swim towards safety, not away from it. Once in the water, the mere thought of the shore could turn him around and ease his body into the waves just as his father had taught him a few blocks from here. He knelt on the beach and crammed sand into all of his pockets — overcoat, pants, jacket, even vest, as much as they would hold. The ocean would turn it into mud and weigh him down. It might not be as heavy as cement, but it would add to his exhaustion and, in combination with everything else, create an obstacle even the strongest swimmer couldn't overcome.

It would be an awful death, but no worse than the Auschwitz gas, and not nearly as bad as what happened to Little Reuben in Lodsz.

He walked slowly down the center of the jetty, avoiding the slippery moss. Medium-size waves — too small to coast, but big enough to slap against the jetty and shoot upwards — sprayed him. Midway to the jetty's end, he knelt and put his hands in the ocean. It was perfect — cold enough to do the job, but not to drive him towards the shore. He began to push himself up, but his right foot slipped and, when he tried to regain his balance, his left foot slipped also, hurling him down on the soaking wood. Somehow, his right foot ended up in the center of a slapping wave. Why the hell hadn't he removed his shoes? He felt pains and cuts all over, but didn't try to itemize them.

He got up and made it to the far end of the jetty where he turned for a final look at Rockaway. Except for a few seagulls at the ocean's edge and the speck of a human figure on the boardwalk ten or so blocks away, there was nothing but miles of empty sand and boardwalk.

But, in the ocean, twenty yards from him, between strips of foam, he saw a man's fedora floating. The hat rose to the top of a wave and dropped back to where it had been. It was like the fedora Max wore. Paul imagined a man beneath the hat, trying to stand in water that was over his head, too panicked to do anything except exhaust himself further. Paul would rescue that man. He would do a perfect dive from the jetty, a short crawl, grab the man in a hair hold, and then swim sidestroke as he rode the tide in.

Paul was a lifeguard. He was the son of a man who taught lifeguards, who died young because he chose to swim far out, before returning to his son and the shore. Life was the legacy left by his father — not shit-covered diamonds. How could he let the ocean deny him a new Reuben Hartman or a wife who would no longer perform Wagner?

He would get to the airport early and clean up.

CHAPTER 15

The Pan Am arrival area was crowded — suitcases, luggage carts, greeters pressed against each other — but no one stood near Paul. He was at the center of a circle of people who, except for a little girl, looked away from him. "Mommy, look at the funny man," the girl said in a loud voice. "His coat is white and sandy. He has a red face." The circle around Paul widened.

He had seen his image in the men's room mirror, and knew he looked a bit like a bum, a bit like a clown, and a lot like a lunatic. His face was streaked with red, probably from his bloodied palms and fingers. His fall on the jetty must have been worse than he had thought. His coat and pants, shapeless wet blankets, were flaked with bits of seaweed and splotches of white, probably salt that had stuck to him when the ocean sprayed over the jetty. His right shoe — the one that had been doused by a wave — was curled up around his foot, while its still shiny left mate could have been worn to court. Atop the wreckage, his perfectly blocked fedora, which he had left on the beach while he walked along the jetty, sat incongruously on his head. Although he had tried to wash the blood from his face and scrape the sand from his coat, nothing short of a shower and complete change of clothes could make him presentable.

Orchestra members (easy to identify because of their instruments) began coming through the Customs door. Paul stood on his toes to search for Sibyl. He didn't see her, but he did see her flute case in the hand of an enormous man. Paul recognized Boris instantly — the gay giant at the Ten/Four Gallery who had tried to entice Sibyl to London four years ago. Boris's almost-red beard was now short and trim, but all of his body bulk remained, along with a puppy-dog gaze of devotion toward the young woman who appeared at his side.

The woman had to be Sibyl, but Paul could discern only traces of the fifteen-year-old girl whose eyes and flute had glistened together. Like Ruthie, who had gone from a kewpie doll to a ghost, Sibyl had become a shadow, her face sallow and tense, her hair stringy and lusterless. Was this the wife who had haunted him? Yes — she was wearing Max's ring.

Sibyl pulled on Boris's sleeve and, when he bent down, whispered something into his ear. Boris moved his lips towards her cheek, but Sibyl backed away. For a moment, they stared at each other, and then Boris went through the customs door. She had cast him aside.

Paul moved quickly in front of her. The moment he had been anticipating for weeks was now here, and now he felt no desire to touch her. She looked at him with something like hunger, pulled him to her, and pressed her thighs against his. Her tongue jabbed at his lips.

What was going on? They were often affectionate in public, but passion had always been private. "I want you too," Paul said, "but we're in the middle of an airport."

Sibyl smiled a too-wide, toothy smile Paul had never seen on her. "I just can't wait." Her voice was throaty, an almost comical imitation of Lauren Bacall.

Paul didn't know what to make of her strange behavior. He said only, "That's two of us."

She stepped back, stared at Paul's curled shoe, then raised her eyes slowly towards his streaked face. A luggage wagon nearly crashed into her, but she seemed unaware of it.

"A long story," Paul said. "Let's wait until we're home."

"Wait until after. . . ." Sibyl flashed her toothy smile, and then solemnly said: "I want us to have the baby we lost."

Bullshit! Paul thought. *Not we. Not lost.* But no matter what was going on inside her, they each now wanted the same thing. Time to keep silent.

* * *

Neither of them spoke until they were on the Belt Parkway, past the two bridges to Rockaway and surrounded by marshes, more than half way to Brooklyn Heights. Before them was Bay Ridge with its blocks of semi-detached wooden homes and small factories; to the front and beyond Bay Ridge was the Manhattan skyline. It was a better view than from Rockaway.

"When did you first notice me at the airport?" Sibyl asked.

Paul knew what she really meant: Did you see me with Boris?

"When you came out behind Paul Bunyan." Sibyl pulled her shoulders back. He had to be careful. "I'm sorry, I don't really know him. Why did he go back into Customs?"

"He had to clear some instruments." She sighed. "He's a complicated person. Now that he's discovered he's Jewish, he's talking about making *aliyah.*"

This was the first Hebrew word she had ever uttered to him — a good sign.

"Moving to Israel?" Paul elevated his eyebrows. "Quite a step for someone who just figured out he was Jewish."

"I'm just accepting the fact that I'm Jewish. Maybe we should take a trip there, but that's not at the top of our to-do list." She put her hand on the inside of his thigh.

She had an agenda he could not fathom. But he had an agenda too. Later, after Little Reuben was conceived, they could each open up to the other.

* * *

As soon as they entered the apartment, Sibyl threw her flute case on the couch and put her arms around him. Paul forced a laugh. "It'll be more fun if I put the suitcases down. Still more fun, especially for you, if I take a shower."

Sibyl grabbed his crotch, something she never did until they were well into foreplay. "I want a baby." The desperation in her voice frightened him but, if he asked what was going on, her mood might change. Her hand moved in circles over his pants. "Where is it?" she asked. Her laugh was even more frightening. He put the bags down and led her into the bedroom.

Where was it? Ever since he first saw her playing the flute behind her grandmother's screen door, she had made him hard. For over ten years, the slightest physical contact — a brushing of lips, fingers against fingers, sometimes just thinking about her — was enough. And now, the urge wasn't there and his body might fail him.

But failure was unacceptable. This was no different than anything else he ever wanted — high grades, Boy Scout merit badges, first-rate draft opinions, a ruling against Olymp. Concentration. Effort. More concentration and more effort because he owed it to so many. True, one child couldn't compensate for Hitler's or Paul's own victims, but it was much more than no child.

The two of them worked at it with ant-like determination, going over each other from top to bottom, kissing, licking, sucking, gently nibbling, using every possible erogenous part of their bodies and every stimulation they had ever employed. At one point, Sibyl stared at the numbers on his arm before saying, "You can explain it after." Finally, he was almost ready. No longer was he the fifteen-year-old boy who had to hide his erection behind grocery bags but, with the help of Vaseline, he managed to get in and to stay there until, seconds later, he came. They pulled away from each other and lay on their backs.

"I'm sorry I had this problem," Paul said, and then decided that a final bit of bullshit would be kind. "It's got nothing to do with you."

"It's not you either. I couldn't get moist. Sometimes these things just happen."

He rolled on his side away from her. If not now, when? "A distant cousin of mine died today. Maybe murdered, maybe suicide, and it might be partly my fault."

She gasped, and the mattress jiggled as she sat up. "Murdered! Suicide!"

"His name is Asher Hartman. He was in Auschwitz — a Holocaust survivor."

"You never told me you had relatives who were survivors. Just the opposite."

He rolled onto his stomach. We thought he was dead. I met him only once."

"You never told me about him."

Was she accusing or searching for understanding? "It was just before you went to Seattle. A long story involving a lot of people."

She put her hand on his shoulder and, almost immediately, removed it. Paul pushed his head into the pillow and bit the pillowcase.

"What do you mean, a lot of people? Is this the first time you're telling me any of it?" The mattress bounced. She must be standing. And she *was* accusing.

"For you to make sense of it, I have to start at the beginning."

"You're mumbling into the pillow."

He should have drowned himself.

Without looking at her, Paul sat up and swung away from her until his feet were on the floor. "Oddly enough, it goes back to Wagner," he said, staring at his toes. The nails needed cutting. "In 1948, a few months before we met, Asher Hartman's brother—"

"1948!" she exclaimed as Paul was about to say the name he had carefully kept from her. "1948. I can't handle hearing it at this moment." Her voice became calmer. "Maybe after we take showers and get a bite to eat — after we make love again — then would be a good time."

She would try to understand. He would cut his toenails in the shower.

The phone rang. Sibyl answered and gasped. "My God, Lisette! . . . Cuba!"

Her sister must be calling about their father. Bernie had told him that Maurice was in Cuba doing something stupid. There was a revolution there — Castro trying to overthrow Batista. Maurice was *putz* enough to get in the middle.

"Mom thinks what?"

Paul heard her put down the phone, and he turned towards her. Thank God she had put on a bathrobe.

"Lisette wants to talk in private. Could you hang up when I'm on the kitchen phone?"

He did what she asked, and then looked at himself in the bedroom mirror, — a fuck-up who couldn't jump off a jetty or get it up. But at least he could be clean. He showered, without washing off the Auschwitz numbers, cut his toenails, and dressed in khakis and his lifeguard tee shirt. Then he lay down to wait until it was time to tell the toxic truth.

* * *

He dreamed about Ruthie's painted face spinning around the silver bowl of shrimps, and then he heard his mother's voice mixed with sobs: "Dead, murder, suicide, the cops won't say." *Shut up*, Paul wanted to scream but sleep enveloped him like glue. The voice continued: "The police want Paul to tell them what happened. And they're afraid some people want to hurt him." The words gave way to sobs and then resumed. "He's got to go someplace safe until he pulls himself together . . ."

A nightmare. He had to force himself awake and, with effort, he managed to open his eyes. But the voice went on: "Jack's cousin, Walter. You never met him, but—" Paul sat up. His mother was in the living room on the other side of the wall.

He slipped on his loafers, opened the door and saw his mother and his wife sitting shoulder-to-shoulder on the couch, gaping at him. His mother had to leave. Sibyl had to learn the truth from him alone — to realize that the deceptions were forced on him and were over his objections. "Ma, Sibyl and I have to talk alone."

His mother took his wife's hand and said, "I'm so glad the two of you are together again." Then, her tone suddenly switched from saccharin to anxious. "But I'm worried, Paulie. You weren't yourself yesterday, and Sibyl told me how you looked at the airport."

Paul reached behind him for the bedroom doorknob and squeezed it as hard as he could.

"Walter thinks you should come right to his hospital. It's Thanksgiving weekend, but one of the top men there will see you right away. Jack's outside in Bernie's car."

Paul didn't trust himself to speak. Jack taking him to Walter in Bernie's robin's-egg-blue Lincoln — he'd rather dive off the jetty straight into Auschwitz.

"It's for your safety, too," his mother implored. "Whoever was mad at Asher could be mad at you too. And if you're in there, nobody outside will know where you are. By the time you leave the hospital, maybe Bernie could calm them down. And when everybody's calm, we can talk about what you should say to the cops . . ." Her eyes moved to Sibyl and then zeroed in on Paul. "I think you know what I mean."

Paul knew. Questions from the police about Asher could lead to Max and the diamonds. Whether or not his mother cared about him — and she probably did — she was concerned about covering her own behind, and Jack's and Bernie's, even poor Ruthie's. He had to be coached to bullshit the police and obstruct justice — another crime.

Sibyl, Paul saw, was glowering at him, her eyes narrowed, her body tensed forward, her neck longer than it had ever been. "What the hell are you so mad about?" he challenged.

"Paul! Don't talk to your wife like that. She's very upset too. Her father—"

"Your father what?" He returned Sibyl's glare.

"Lisette says he's in Cuba, maybe in jail," Sibyl hissed. "And that you could have prevented it. She thinks Faye got him to be a front for the mob in some smuggling, like she did with the first Mr. Faye. Lisette says . . . She—"

"Lisette says what?" Sibyl seemed to know what happened at Borough Hall, and he would meet it head on.

She spoke slowly. "She says if you would have just told him three words — *Three words!* — he wouldn't have had to crawl back to Faye and none of this would have happened."

Bullshit, Paul thought. But even with all that was going on, he couldn't use profanity with the two most important women in his life. He was, after all, wearing the lifeguard shirt. But if he didn't assert himself now, the two of them would eat him alive. He would take responsibility for a lot, but not for Maurice. "Ba-lo-ney," he said, pausing between each syllable. "I told your father I would try to help him. He didn't have to run back to Faye."

"Bernie says —" his mother interjected.

Paul turned towards her. "Stay out of this," he said deliberately. "You walked out of my life when you went to Rochester." She shrank back from him. He was amazed at what he had said, but he needed the truth to restrain her. "This is my home, not the apartment where you dumped me with your father, and he treated me as if I didn't belong there."

"I asked her to come when she called and was so worried about you," Sibyl said, her voice now shriller. "And when she got here, I told her about my father trapped in Cuba, maybe because of you, and she started to tell me what you never told me — the brothers, the diamonds. I was trying to piece it together when you came in here foaming like a maniac."

Paul was on the edge of the Atlantic, the tide coming in fast, the waves rising. It wouldn't stop, yet he couldn't move. But he was a lifeguard. "Did she say I wanted to tell you everything on the day we met but that she told me not to because people, including her, might go to jail?"

"That's not fair, Paulie. Not fair." His mother's voice rose into a shriek that ran down his spine. "If you would have asked me again later, I would have said, tell her. She's your wife."

"Like hell you would have. It was dirty money and—"

"You took it, and if I was late, you let me know — even on *Yom Kippur*."

"How much money?" Sibyl demanded.

"He never even said thank you."

"Did my father ask you to help him?" Sibyl asked.

"Your father wanted me to commit a crime, and I told him I thought I could help him lawfully. I never told him no, just that I needed time to think, and—"

"She's your wife, Paul," his mother scolded. "She deserves an explanation."

Paul closed his eyes. He had to fill his mind so he wouldn't hear them. He would do long division: Asher's number; divide 53928 by two and keep dividing it until it approached zero. It would never get there, and he could keep going forever. 26964 and 13482 came quickly, but then the voices broke through.

"He always was nice to you." Sibyl's voice.

"It's her father. You, if anybody, should know what that means." His mother's voice.

"You told me the tuitions came from your father's insurance and from stocks. Did you tell me the truth about anything? How could you kneel and put that diamond ring on my finger?"

Paul opened his eyes and saw his mother wiping away tears. She spoke to him softly and with understanding. "I know you're upset because of the miscarriage. Sibyl told—"

"Miscarriage!" Paul exploded. "Not a miscarriage. She had an abortion."

His mother's mouth opened wide — a silent scream.

"She murdered our baby. Your grandson. Daddy's namesake. Without telling me."

Sibyl was on her feet. "Another one of your lies. Maybe the worst ever."

Paul pictured the curved mirrors in the Rockaway Playland Fun House turning everything upside down. For ten years, he had been the Emperor of Bullshit, and now, when he tells the truth, Sibyl usurps the throne.

"Paulie, you should apologize to your wife."

Paul clenched his teeth, but his mouth wouldn't stay closed. "Why aren't you ever on my side? *Ever!*"

His mother fell back against the couch as if he had struck her. Sibyl strode to him, thrust her face close to his and announced defiantly, "I won't hear any more of your lies!"

Paul was stunned. She was taking deception to heights he had never approached.

Sibyl pulled his hand off the doorknob. "I'm going to call and find out if there's anything new about my father." She went into the bedroom, slamming the door behind her.

Paul's mother pointed at his arm. "What's that?" she asked. "A five; a three. Two lines of them! Two-seven; two-eight." She pressed her lips together in thought, and quickly opened them. "I remember. How could anybody forget? They were always close." She nodded her head slowly, then abruptly stopped. "How could you do that? They were in the camp, not you!"

"You told me not to look at the numbers but I couldn't see anything else."

His mother sat straight up. "Oh my God, Paulie! I didn't want to put Max and you in the same room, but he was Daddy's cousin and he had no place else to go. How could I know you'd be so upset by the numbers? Please see Walter. For your own good — and mine too."

Paul looked directly at her. She had once been beautiful and had given birth to him. He walked over to the couch. "You're my mother," he pleaded. "Why won't you believe me about the abortion?"

She stood up, pulling down on his shirt, and spoke into his chest. "No self-respecting married woman would do that. It's a crime — a sin too. Come with me to see Walter now."

"Mom, that's my only lifeguard shirt left. It can rip."

"You were a lifeguard like Daddy. I know," she nearly sang. "He would want you to come with me. You can wear the shirt. Walter swims, too."

Paul separated her fingers from the shirt. "I'm leaving, Mom. You stay here and worry about me. I guarantee you Sibyl won't worry for a second."

He grabbed his old Navy pea coat in the front closet, but where would he go? Either the Saint George Hotel by the Clark Street subway station, or back to Sixty-fourth Street. *Please God, let her be pregnant, and don't let her kill this one too.* His mother was tugging on his shirt from behind. "Paulie, please! Everybody knows you wanted to do the right thing. Walter says there's no stigma in getting help from a doctor when you're going through so much."

He turned around and saw her head bobbing aimlessly — a drowning woman who had lost control and hope. But the waves were too high and he couldn't save her. At most, he might save himself. But he couldn't pull away from her while she was tugging on his lifeguard shirt from behind. If he did, the shirt might rip.

He reached back and grabbed her wrist, then turned around quickly and their bodies collided. Before he realized what was happening, she was sprawled on her back on the Danish rug she and Jack had given them as a wedding gift. He knelt by her and was momentarily paralyzed by what he saw — her skirt up to her thighs, blue veins under her stockings. He had to help his mother up from the floor, and he put his hands under her neck.

"No!" his mother screamed, but she was screaming past him, not at him.

A sudden pain in the back of Paul's skull made everything red. "Let go of her, you monster!" Sibyl shouted from behind him. He struggled to keep his eyes open and to stand up. If you collapse in the transport, you'll die, and someone will take your clothing.

Another pain in his skull. The rug became a brown and blue wave tugging him under, but he managed to turn around.

"You put my father in a Cuban jail! If Batista or Castro don't kill him, the mobsters will. And what are you doing to your mother!" The flute case was raised for a third blow.

Just like the guards with their clubs in Lodsz. But he wasn't being loaded on a transport. Somehow, he managed to get up and pull the case from her. Should he beat her to death with it or just break her fingers, the way Asher's were broken, so she could never again go on tour?

He had to leave. He dropped the case and stumbled past his mother out the hallway door. He couldn't wait for the elevator — Jack might be in it. The door to the building's internal stairs was just a few feet away and, dizzy as he was, he could hold onto the railing.

The staircase door was thick and didn't respond to his push. "Paul, Paul!" his mother called. "Paul, Paul!" Sibyl echoed. *Schnell, Schnell* or they would send him to Creedmoor. He pressed his shoulder against the door and pushed with all his might. This time the door flew open lurching him forward as the stairs rose to meet him. God they were steep. Lots of them, all cement, straight down to the third floor without any turn or break. But he was wearing his lifeguard shirt and would be safe. The walls were green, or maybe blue, colors of the Atlantic spinning and changing on a rough day. He could coast them like a torpedo the way his father had taught him. But he tripped over his own feet and no longer knew where his limbs were.

If he were going to kill himself, this wasn't the way to do it. He tried to grab hold of the railing and get his feet below his head. But his hand slipped from the railing and his body became a jumble of unrelated parts. He felt his legs hit every step except for the last few where they went into the air before smashing against the third-floor door. Everything blazed into pain, but he felt a particularly sharp pain in his right leg. Or was it his left? Then nothing hurt.

CHAPTER 16

First, there was only black — his senses had shut down. Then came a mild pain that mounted steadily until the black was shattered by his own cries. Then came the needle and a euphoria that slowly dripped into grogginess until the black, followed by pain, returned. He was aware of the cycle repeating, but that was all.

When he wasn't in bed, he was strapped to a narrow hospital table and wheeled — men in front, men behind, all looking concerned and competent. Into an ambulance (or was it a hearse?); up and down hallways; under monstrous machines that hung from the ceiling and slid above his legs, stopping every few seconds to click and flash; in and out of cavernous windowless rooms where people wore white masks over their faces and he was plunged into dreamless (and, he assumed, deathlike) sleeps; in and out of a smaller room where, for a moment, he thought he saw his mother's sad face. Once or twice, when they lifted him from the table, a piercing pain tore through his body and, while he screamed, he comforted himself with the thought that euphoria should soon arrive.

To the extent he could think, he focused on only one thing: What was the name of the table on which he was being wheeled? If he could just come up with that name, he would then be able to recite the multiplication tables and everything would be all right.

Gurney! It finally came to him. He opened his eyes and saw that both of his legs were encased in plaster. On one side of the bed, wires came out of a blue box with jumping dials and blinking lights. He moved his head and saw that the dials moved with it. On the other side of the bed, a pole held a clear bag of clear fluid that dripped into him through a clear tube and a needle planted in his forearm where he had penned the Auschwitz numbers. He strained to see whether the numbers were there, but his arm blurred. Next to the pole a gray woman dozed in a chair. He recognized his mother, and then he closed his eyes. When he opened them, she was gone.

He studied the scene in front of him: pale arms without numbers, a white hospital gown to just below his hips, white plaster from the gown to his toes and, just beyond the bed, a white wall. It was the opposite of swimming in the Atlantic where the waves changed colors as they rose and fell, his body moved freely, and he smelled salt water instead of antiseptic.

There was one good thing about his condition: They were leaving him alone, and that was precisely what he wanted — to be done with all of them and all of it forever. No questions, explanations (true or false), blame, forgiveness, or understanding, and as little of the past as possible. Whenever he sensed his mother in the room, he kept his eyes shut. As far as he was aware, nobody else came to visit him.

But finally, when he awoke from a real sleep, he saw her sitting at his side with her eyes open. "You're going to be all right, Paulie," she said. It was the first words he had absorbed since he tried to escape her and Sibyl's crow-like calls to him in the hall ("Paul! Paul!" "Paul! Paul!") just before he flung himself against the stairwell door and down into a chute of pain. "You're brain's not hurt, and with the operations you had — the best foot surgeon in the world — you're going to walk like it never happened. You'll dance a *kazatsky* again like at your wedding." She tried to smile.

"Go away," he told her. These were the first words he uttered since she fell to the rug in their apartment.

"Sibyl and I told the police the truth: It was a big misunderstanding. I fell, but she thought you knocked me down. You tried to help me up, but she thought you were choking me."

"Go away." Paul closed his eyes.

"Nobody thinks Asher's your fault," she said, more urgently. "Everybody knows you wouldn't want to harm a cousin who's already suffered so much."

Paul opened his eyes.

"Ruthie's going to go very soon. Maybe you can call Bernie and say how sorry you are for getting sick at the party. Maybe you should also talk to a doctor about how upset you are. Walter can arrange for one of the top men here to see you."

This time he'd make her hear him. "Go away!" It was as much effort as he had expended since he threw his weight against the hallway door.

She covered her face with her arms.

She wasn't going to leave, so he would leave instead. Pushing up with all his strength, he raised his back a few inches. Now the legs. Another push, but nothing moved. He tried to flex his knees and then his thighs to see how much breathing space the doctors had left him, but he felt neither plaster nor space. His scream drove his mother from the room.

Seconds later, he was surrounded by people in white. A nurse was wiping his brow with a cold cloth, and a dark young man, not much older than himself, was taking his pulse and talking sternly. "We can't give you any more morphine, not even a Demerol, for another two hours. Dr. Cole is afraid you'll become addicted."

The young man's necktie blocked much of his nameplate, but "M.D." was clear, and Paul asked him, "Are my legs there? I can't feel them."

The doctor's dark brown eyes laughed. "I guarantee you they're there. I saw the two of them myself, both the inside and the outside." The doctor patted him on the shoulder, and Paul could read the whole nametag:

Arthur Meltzer, M.D.
New York University Hospital

Meltzer! The name meant something. But what? Forget *gurney*. If he could only remember *Meltzer*, then everything would be all right.

"What happened to me?"

"A lot." Dr. Meltzer raised his head, and the one nurse still in the room left. Meltzer closed the door, and sat down in the chair where Paul's mother had been.

"Two broken legs. They should heal, but you won't be walking for a while. You needed a pin in your left ankle and a plate in your right tibia. Left tibia and right femur were broken too, but closed reductions were enough for them."

As Dr. Meltzer spoke, Paul's encased legs came to life — itching, but not too much; some sweat, but not uncomfortable; a tingling in his toes; different pains, more in his left ankle and right calf, but all of them manageable until the next shot.

Dr. Meltzer shrugged, raised his palms in wonderment, and resumed his summary. "Your head got banged up too, although the police aren't sure how. Amazing there's no permanent injury any place. After time does its healing and, subject to a few memory tests, you'll go back to conquering the legal world. How did you manage such a fall?"

The tension in Paul's chest eased. He took a Kleenex from the box on his night table and wiped his forehead. It felt good to do something for himself.

"I'm Dr. Meltzer, an orthopedic resident."

Paul remembered. According to Asher, a world-class violinist named Meltzer went to the Auschwitz gas because his playing would have exposed Max as a second rate fiddler. But he said nothing to Dr. Meltzer.

His thighs began to itch badly, but he couldn't get his fingers under the plaster.

"Try not to think about the itching," Dr. Meltzer said. "If it gets really bad we can give you something, but right now, we're interested in subtracting drugs, not adding them."

"How long will I be here?" Paul swallowed, bracing himself for the worst.

"Six, seven more weeks. Then you'll have to go someplace where there will be somebody to take care of you, close to round the clock and where there is easy access to a rehabilitation facility. You're pretty much helpless with two broken legs. Your mother said you and your wife just separated — I'm sorry — and that she'll tend to you up in Rochester."

Paul recalled a book from high school, *Ethan Frome*, in which a man crippled by an accident was cared for by a bitter woman. "I'm not going to Rochester, and I don't want my mother visiting me." It came out harsher than he had wanted, but it had to be made clear.

Dr. Meltzer walked to the foot of the bed and stood there silently. Paul tried to see himself through the young doctor's eyes. It wasn't pretty — an immobile grayish-white mass unwilling to accept his near-total dependency and ungrateful to those who seemed to care about him. So be it. He wouldn't further demean himself by trying to justify himself.

"It's a long story, and I won't put myself on trial for doing what I have to do."

Meltzer looked directly at Paul. "I've spent a lot of time with your mother and . . ." He stopped speaking, then shook his head and continued in a lower voice. "I'm training to be an orthopedist, healing bones and bodies — not getting mixed up in families. But I have to tell you this: Tomorrow, I'm rotating off of this service to hand surgery. If I had to stay here, I'd find it hard to be one of your doctors. I'll leave instructions that you're to have no visitors, including your mother, unless you expressly approve beforehand."

"Thank you."

* * *

Done, Paul told himself as soon as Meltzer was out of sight. *Family gone. Rockaway gone. Good.* Now he would make the break complete: *Abandon the law!*

In addition to taking the fruits of Max's diamonds, he had caused Asher's death and violated his oath. To save his and his mother's skins, he would soon have to lie to the police. No matter how noble his future, he could never be the lawyer described in the dean's orientation speech — one who had a high calling and practiced a noble profession. In his own eyes, and in the eyes of the dean, he would be no more than a shyster chasing a buck — *Treyf.*

As soon as Paul made the decision, he reversed it. Aside from the faded memory of his father, the law was the only thing he still loved. He would try not to agonize over what had happened.

He called Judge Webster for answers to three questions: Was he still the judge's clerk? Would the judge still recommend him to Justice Brennan? Would he still help him get a good job in private practice? Vivien put him right through.

"How are you?" the judge asked, mechanically, and Paul foresaw a "no" to each of his questions.

"I'm healing but it will be a while before I can come in."

"I know that," the judge boomed. There was no hint of concern in his voice. Sibyl, through Priscilla, must have poisoned his mind. "The police are investigating the death of a man named Asher Hartman, apparently your cousin, and the disappearance of a disbarred lawyer whose name I forget — taught securities at Brooklyn Law School."

Fenichel was the name, but Paul wouldn't say it. He shouldn't know too much. Asher had probably followed Paul's suggestion that he ask Fenichel how he could sell the information (ultimately, misinformation) Paul had whispered to him — "Olymp will win."

The pains inside of Paul's casts returned — an hour ahead of schedule, two hours before Demerol. He hadn't considered the obvious question the judge would ask: *What did your cousin and you talk about?*

Paul had to seize the initiative — convince Judge Webster that he was forthcoming and hiding nothing — that he had nothing to hide.

"Asher Hartman appeared out of the blue — everyone thought he was dead — on a Saturday in October, and we had lunch together. That was the only time I ever saw or spoke to him."

"I'm not conducting an investigation, and you don't . . . I mean . . ." The judge was stumbling over his words. Paul, for once, could control their conversation.

"My cousin asked—"

"Maybe you should retain a lawyer," Judge Webster said.

"I don't need a lawyer. My cousin asked me who would win the Olymp appeal and I refused to tell him." That had to be the story.

"Why didn't you report this? His asking you was a crime." The judge's voice was uncharacteristically soft.

This time, the truth and fuck the consequences: "My cousin survived Auschwitz, and there was no way I would do anything that might put him in jail."

"I'm sure you understand this means I can't recommend you to Justice Brennan," the judge said in his normal foghorn voice. Paul said nothing, and the judge continued. "You'll stay on the payroll with full insurance coverage but, since you're going to be immobile for the foreseeable future, I will need to get a replacement for you."

So be it. No job with Judge Webster. No job with Justice Brennan. The overbearing bastard certainly wouldn't help him find a job with a future in a white-shoe law firm. "They're coming in to give me a shot," Paul said, and it was a lie.

* * *

The periods of severe pain grew shorter and, several days after his talk with Judge Webster, Paul was able to get himself around in a wheelchair. Each morning and afternoon, Oscar, the Jamaican attendant, would root him on as he slid onto the chair from his bed and, with two casts leading the way, rolled himself into the patients' lounge. ("Go Papa Paulie-Paul, go! Don't let those big-fin Buicks get ahead.") In the lounge, he wheeled himself to the floor-to-ceiling, wall-to-wall plate-glass window, looked out at the East River, and lost himself in reading — *The New York Times* front page to back page, after starting with the obituaries, where he never found Ruthie's name; Proust; Mickey Spillane detective stories; *The New Yorker*; anything laying around.

In mid-December, three weeks after he had broken his legs, as he sat in the lounge struggling with a seemingly endless sentence of Proust, a young breathless nurse ran to his wheelchair in short steps. "Mr. Hartman, two men insist on seeing you. I told them you weren't to have guests, but they just walked into your room and now they're coming here. Should I call Security?"

Jesus, Paul thought; it was the guys who killed Asher. "Call the police."

Bernie swaggered in. Eyes riveted on Paul, he walked to the wheelchair, trapping the nurse between his mass and Paul's casts. Jack, a few feet behind Bernie, looked as uncomfortable as the nurse did.

"You're killing your mother," Bernie said. "Isn't Asher enough? Isn't it enough Maurice rotted in a Cuban jail — almost died — because of the smuggling you forced him into? I had to go to Havana two days after Ruthie's funeral to clean up the whole mess. Risked my own ass in the middle of a revolution. You owe me big time, buddy. But, for now, all I want is you should see your mother."

Bernie didn't frighten him. His legs were already broken and, if Bernie killed him, he'd be spared the future.

"I didn't know Ruthie died. I'm sorry. I really liked her. She —"

Bernie reached around the terrified nurse and clamped Paul's mouth shut. "Don't ever talk to me about Ruthie. She died on the day you threw your mother out of the hospital. There were six notices in the *Times*. I thought that even you would call with condolences."

Ruthie, Paul realized, had died while he was too groggy to read. But he couldn't speak and, no matter what he said, Bernie wouldn't believe him.

Still holding Paul's mouth shut and blocking the nurse with his body, Bernie asked, "What are you?" With his free hand, he twisted Paul's ear, then whispered into it: "I'm sure you've got the Switzerland key. But that can wait until you get out and I give you the bill for saving your father-in-law's sorry ass. Now, just be a *mensh* for once and see your mother."

Bernie released Paul's mouth, and turned to leave. The nurse ran into the hallway. Jack wasn't in sight.

* * *

A special delivery letter arrived the next morning. It was handwritten.

> Dear Paul,
> I'm sorry how Bernie acted, but I got no more
> control over him than you.
>
> I'm coming to the hospital tomorrow afternoon
> (18 Dec.) and I'm asking you to see me as a favor,
> like you asked me for a favor when I talked to you
> about being a slave for Olymp even though I
> didn't want to.
>
> Nobody knows I'm coming.
>
> Sincerely yours,

Jack Roth

After what Jack did to help other Olymp slaves, Paul couldn't refuse to see him. But once Jack left, he didn't owe a thing to any living person.

He waited by the large lounge window. Jack sat down on the couch in front of him without speaking or offering to shake hands; he put his hat in his lap, but kept his overcoat on. They were alone, except for a one-legged man in a wheelchair at the other end of the room.

Paul stared at Jack's fedora. "Take off your coat," he urged. "There's a rack by the door."

"I'm sorry about what happened yesterday," Jack said to his hat. "I came with Bernie because I wanted to stop him from doing what he did, but then I saw that would've meant a fight. I'm not afraid of fighting Bernie — I'm a lot stronger and faster than I look — but your mother would find out and get even more upset. Still, I'm ashamed. What he did, what I did, made me remember something from twenty years ago with some Czech Nazis."

A new survivor's story, Paul thought. When it was over, his stepfather, like his cousin Asher, would ask him for something. But he had to listen.

"I know the professor told you I was some kind of hero," Jack began, "but the truth is I was just another scared Jew who didn't fight back." Jack's chin dropped to his chest. "At the end of September in 1938, just after the Munich treaty where England and France gave Hitler the Sudetenland — that's where we lived — the Czech Nazis started going after us for real."

Jack described his friendship with a young man named Nach Morganstern, "a little guy who married an Orthodox girl and then went the whole way — big black beard, black hat, strictly *kosher*, always carrying a book of *Talmud*." He told Paul that, on the way home from work, he passed an alleyway in which three Czech Nazis in Gestapo-like uniforms were tormenting Nach. They threw Nach's book on the ground; "I heard one of them tell Nach to take out his Jew dick and piss on the book. I'm sorry to talk like that, but that's what they said."

Jack knew one of the Nazis, Hugo Vogel. The two of them were boxers who had trained together in the same gym and drunk together in the same beer hall. "I wasn't what you call a nice Jewish boy," he said. "That was before both places told me to keep out because I was Jewish.

"'Leave him alone,' I shouted to Hugo. He came down to meet me on the street. 'Don't be a fool, Kobi,' Hugo says. That was my boxing name. 'There's three of us, and that fairy will be useless in a fight. You go away, and I'll make sure your friend don't get hurt. The Sudetenland's in the Reich now, and I'll watch out for you. You're different than the rest.'"

Different? Paul asked himself. What difference does *different* make? To Hugo, Strummer, and Ty Martin, all Jews were the same.

"I asked Hugo if I could trust him, and he squeezed the back of my neck friendly-like."

Jack's not at all like Asher, Paul thought. "And then?"

"Then?" Jack repeated the question just as Asher had. "Nach hanged himself that night. He was the first Jew in Teplice that the Nazis made a suicide."

Without meaning to, Paul rolled his wheelchair a half turn back, away from Jack.

"Only Hugo and the two others knew I was there, but I told your cousin Malke. She and I were seeing each other. Not too serious, but not not serious. The next day she said she was breaking up with me, and we should tell everybody it was because I wasn't so interested in music, but the real reason was she was going to Russia in secret to train for the resistance. I told her I would go with her, but she just shook her head no. When they rounded up people for Auschwitz, I was sent to Olymp. I guess Hugo arranged it. Some bargain."

Paul rolled the wheelchair closer to the couch. "There *was* nothing you could do."

"Your mother said the same thing, and I'll tell you what I told her: I could have tried. From Nach's funeral, I went to the cemetery and swore on my mother's grave that, no matter what, I would always try to help another Jew. I didn't help you yesterday, but most of the time I did. It turned out pretty good what I swore because, by helping Max, I got to meet your mother again and I got some reason to keep living besides paying back for Nach."

Sweat rose on Jack's neck above his overcoat, and Paul pleaded, "Take off your coat, please." This time, thank God, Jack did.

As Paul watched this decent man return from the coat rack, he realized that this might be his last chance to learn more about the death that would haunt him for the rest of his life. "Tell me about Asher," he asked as soon as Jack was back on the couch.

"You should tell me. You know more. You couldn't have lied to Asher on purpose. Bernie knows a lot about Asher, but I try not to talk to him."

"I was surprised Bernie went to Cuba so soon after the funeral."

"Who wasn't surprised? Pine, Pincus — like me, two names — I guess he's still your father-in-law. He got arrested in Cuba for smuggling, probably because he didn't *schmear* the right people, and Bernie thought it was part his fault for making introductions."

"Please tell me about Asher, not Bernie," Paul interrupted. "Jumped or pushed, and why?"

"You never let me finish." Jack paused, but Paul had nothing to say, and Jack continued: "Nobody knows, except maybe Frieda Greenberg and she disappeared. She and Asher were going to get married and she might have been afraid for herself. All I know is Bernie got involved — he might have even gone to see the professor you spoke to. Bernie told Asher to forget about what you told him. Isn't that what you told me? Maybe Asher got the message too late. Maybe he didn't believe Bernie. I don't know. Maybe if you had just spoken to Asher, he would have understood. But I called you to see if you wanted to talk to Asher, and guess what? You hung up. I don't understand why you wouldn't talk to him."

"That's a hard question. I think about it a lot, but I just can't answer on the spot." Paul turned his wheelchair away from Jack and, through the window, he saw a lonely tugboat creeping north between patches of ice on the East River. Beyond the tug, a big electric "Pepsi Cola" sign lightened the gray sky over Long Island City.

"Why?" Jack asked.

From the Queensboro Bridge on Paul's left to the Williamsburg Bridge on his right, there were, except for the tug, three miles of empty water. Incredible.

"Why?"

How could Jack understand the judges on the Harvard walls or the power of Paul's assurance to Judge Webster? "I can't answer why because I don't understand myself. And what difference does it make? Asher's dead." Paul gripped the large wheels of his chair and started to propel himself out of the lounge. "I'm not cutting you off again, and I'm sorry about the times I did, but the pain's starting up and I have to go to bed."

"Don't go," Jack said. Paul paused. "There are two more things. Important."

Paul turned the chair back towards the couch.

"Do you want me to make sure Bernie stays away from you?"

"Why would he listen to you?"

"He won't, but he'll listen to your mother if I ask her to talk to him."

"He does what he wants."

"Not if she talks to him."

"You mean because he's so grateful my parents helped get his father out of Germany?"

"Yes, but that's only part. Bernie will listen to your mother because he's been in love with her since they were kids in Czechoslovakia, even more since they spent so much time together taking care of Ruthie."

Paul's stomach churned. Nobody should have to learn about his mother's love life.

Jack waited while his statement sank in, and then added, "Very respectful because he loved Ruthie, too." He smiled to himself. "A lot of men have been in love with your mother, and I'm one of them. I don't want her to suffer no more."

Paul glanced out of the window. There were now three barges on the river. How could he break with everything if Bernie were after him?

"Ask her to talk to Bernie," he said.

"Call her soon. I don't want her to feel she has no son."

Jack was bargaining, but he meant well.

"I can't see her; it would end badly for both of us." He wished he could reach out and squeeze Jack's shoulders — let his stepfather feel his compassion. To Paul's surprise, Jack reached out to him, leaning towards the wheelchair and clutching Paul's hands with his own.

"I agree you shouldn't see her for a long time, but that's no danger. We sold the store — the closing's in two days — and we're moving to El Paso next week."

"Texas!" Paul flinched. The one-legged man at the other end of the lounge put his index finger in front of his lips. There was now a baby asleep in his lap, and a young woman at his side. Paul hadn't seen them come in.

"No, El Paso, Czechoslovakia," Jack said and, for the first time in Paul's memory, he smiled. "It's to get away from Bernie.

"He was almost glued to your mother while Ruthie was dying. At the funeral, he insisted that she sit next to him, but your mother wouldn't do it unless I sat on the other side of her. Then, on the day he got back from Cuba, he showed up in Rochester out of the blue. He said he would make us partners with him in this Valley Stream jewelry store near his house in Woodmere. So, I followed your mother's suggestion and called Morty Koppel, one of the Olymp slaves in that picture I think you saw. His brother owns Dollar Most stores all over the country, and I got a job managing El Paso." Jack squeezed Paul's hand again. "So call her there. No big deal."

"It'll end up with her crying."

"It doesn't have to if you're careful what you say."

He was relentless, like Bernie outside the China Dragon, demanding to be told the outcome of the Olymp case.

Jack continued: "I told you I didn't know why Bernie was always so mean to you, but I do know, and your mother agrees." The saint was going in for the kill. "He never got over that she picked your father instead of him. But it's more than that. No matter how much money Bernie made, it was dirty. Your father, who was smarter, got more respect. He's jealous of him through you. And you went to all those fancy schools. Add it all up, plus whatever happened with your father-in-law; plus Asher, which I don't understand; plus Thanksgiving; plus throwing your mother out of the hospital — count that twice."

Paul yanked his hands free.

"Call your mother."

"I thought you swore to help Jews."

"Your mother's a Jew. Why do you always have to make things hard for yourself?"

Why? Paul asked himself, and nodded yes.

"Good," Jack said. "I told you there were two things. Wheel your chair next to me so I can talk in your ear."

Paul saw that Jack and he were now the only ones in the lounge, but he did what Jack had asked. Jack cupped his hands, and spoke into Paul's ear. "The New York City cops came to see us at the store."

Jesus, Paul thought. Once again, the inevitable hadn't occurred to him.

While Jack rambled about the interview by the police, Paul's pain mounted. But he had to listen or his own meeting with the police could be a disaster. He turned his wheelchair back towards the couch so that Jack and he faced each other directly.

"What did you say about the Olymp case?"

Jack answered and, as he had been taught in his trial practice course, Paul followed up with a series of pointed questions intended to elicit specific facts about the Rochester meeting. Jack's answers made Paul confident that what Jack and his mother had told the police could be reconciled with what Paul had told Judge Webster — that Asher had asked who would win the Olymp case and Paul had refused to answer. It would be bullshit, but plausible bullshit.

"Did you tell them I spoke to Asher only once?" Paul asked.

Jack stood. "Are you conducting a trial here? Am I doing okay? I'm not an idiot."

"I'm sorry. I'm only trying—"

"No sorry. No thanks. You're my wife's son, and I believe in family. You got two broken legs, but you're still the smartest boy in the class and you'll do fine. Just treat your mother nice, and I'll take care of Bernie." He left.

* * *

A hand-delivered envelope from "Isaacs and Kushner, Attorneys at Law" was on Paul's pillow when he returned from his meeting with Jack.

> Dear Mr. Hartman:
> I am the attorney for your wife, Mrs. Sibyl Pine Hartman. As you are aware, irreconcilable differences have arisen between your wife and you warranting a prompt dissolution of the marriage. I think it would be in the interests of all concerned for you to retain a matrimonial lawyer and to have him contact me promptly so we can discuss the best means of terminating the marriage and protecting the rights of all parties.
>
> While I understand that you may be disabled, I urge you to give this matter the immediate attention it warrants.
>
> The above is without prejudice to any of my client's rights including, without limitation, her right to commence criminal and/or civil proceedings relating to your recent conduct.
>
> My messenger will wait in the event that you wish to reply in writing today.
>
> Very truly yours,
> Gerard T. Kushner

Paul framed a one-sentence response: *Dear Mr. Kushner, The irreconcilable differences arise from the fact that your client killed our child and then tried to kill me.* But he then thought better of it. Instead, he wrote:

Dear Mr. Kushner:
Come to the patients' lounge on the eighth floor at 10:30 a.m. or 3:30 p.m. tomorrow. I'll be the one wearing two full leg casts. Since I will do whatever is necessary to have your client out of my life, I won't need a lawyer other than myself.

If you bring your client or any family member, or if you even imply that I injured or threatened anybody in any way (which I did not), we will not meet.

Sincerely yours,
Paul C. Hartman

It was drizzling the next morning, and Paul saw Kushner reflected in the window as he entered. He was a little round-faced man, probably in his fifties, weighed down by a thick briefcase in one hand and a gray plastic carrying case in the other. Kushner stood alongside Paul's wheelchair.

"I understand you had quite an accident, Mr. Hartman."

"Can we get right to the point?"

"I'd like to play you a tape from your wife. It's very candid and, as there may be litigation and you may attack her reputation, there are no copies. It will be destroyed this afternoon after you hear it."

What Kushner said, Paul realized, was extraordinary and, possibly, unethical as it foresaw the destruction of a tape which would be relevant evidence in any trial. Perhaps he should retain a matrimonial lawyer. But that meant money he would need for his recovery. Whatever was next in his life, Sibyl had to be out of it quickly and completely. He would listen to Kushner and the recording.

Paul sat in the wheelchair alongside the bed, his legs stretched out past the bed; the tape and portable Ampex recorder were on the floor next to the closed door, and Kushner sat on a chair in between with his briefcase and overcoat on his lap. When they were as settled as they were going to be, Paul said, "Just play it." His mounting anger frightened him.

Sibyl's voice soon filled the room. "I'm communicating with you by tape, Paul, so you'll know this is me and that these are my considered wishes."

It was her voice, but the words were Kushner's. From the day she first seduced him with "Waltz of the Flowers," until the evening she clobbered his skull, neither of them had said "I'm communicating" or "considered wishes" to the other.

"I'm sorry our last meeting was so awful and that I lost control so completely. On top of everything I learned, I was thrown when you said I had an abortion. Priscilla Webster said you agreed to say it was a miscarriage — what I was telling everybody."

Paul realized she was right. On that horrible night, following a day that began with news of Asher's death, he had simply forgotten his talk with Mrs. Webster. But he wasn't going to apologize for speaking the truth to his lying wife and to his mother.

"But there's no point in dwelling on that," Sibyl's voice continued. "I didn't tell you the whole story that night. I did have an abortion before the tour, but I was pregnant when we got back, and I wanted to go to bed with you quickly so that everyone would think you were the father and the baby was legitimate. My lawyer has the results of a rabbit test I took in Brazil so you can see this is so. I planned to end the marriage after the baby was born, but when I learned how you had misled me since the day we met, I couldn't wait that long. Boris is the father —"

"Boris!" Paul erupted. He had exercised enough self-control. Kushner shut off the tape, and Paul spoke to the Ampex player in a lower voice. "Boris is a faggot, and you're a lying whore. It couldn't be someone Hitler would have killed along with the Jews. It must be Smith or a Nazi who came to hear you play Wagner." He thought of naming Strummer, but that would be a sign he needed Walter.

"Try to stay calm," Kushner urged.

"Try to stop telling me what to do. Turn it back on, although she won't top that one."

As if she had anticipated Paul's outburst, Sibyl's voice said, "I know I told you Boris is a homosexual, but life isn't so clear-cut, and he's the only one it could be. I'd like a divorce as soon as possible so that Boris and I can get married, move to Israel and start off on a clean slate with our baby — discover the Judaism we never had."

Paul felt his jaw opening. To scream or laugh, he wondered, and managed to close it.

"Boris inherited some money, and we're going to open a music store in Haifa with an aunt he never knew existed. Don't laugh at the prospect of my settling in Israel, but—"

"I'm not laughing! Who's the *real* father?"

"Mr. Hartman, please just listen. This is important."

"Turn it off or I'll do it myself even if I have to ram my wheelchair into you."

Kushner turned the tape off, and Paul said, "Bottom line: I want a divorce too, but my understanding is that the only ground for divorce in New York is adultery."

The tape, Paul realized, was more than enough evidence but, even if Kushner didn't destroy it, the procedure would be nasty and would hold him back in the world he had to escape. And if credibility became an issue at the trial — *She told me she had an abortion in Seattle; I told him it was a miscarriage* — Kushner could cross-examine him about his ten years of lying to Sibyl. And God knows where that could lead.

"Am I right about New York law, Mr. Kushner?"

"Unfortunately, yes, Mr. Hartman." Kushner spoke with calm authority now that they were discussing his field of expertise. "I'm on a committee that's trying to get New York to adopt no fault divorce, but that's not going to happen for a long time, if ever."

"So how can we to do it? Nevada?"

"Mexico," Kushner answered. "She can fly to San Diego with the signed papers, go to Tijuana and have the whole thing done in a matter of days. Hundreds of couples have done it."

"I'll sign."

"She wants a religious divorce also — it's called a *get* — but that can be done right in this room with three rabbis holding a court. It will make their lives much simpler in Israel."

"I'll sign that too, but only if she doesn't show up. Get thin rabbis so they can all fit in my hospital room."

Kushner tried to stand, but there was too much on his lap and he gave up. "Mr. Hartman, you have a brilliant law school record, but you're totally inexperienced and seem to be treating this as a joke. I urge you again to get a qualified matrimonial lawyer."

"Mr. Kushner, if you give me the papers right now, I'll probably sign on the spot. If you don't . . ." Paul pointed at his casts. "If you don't, I have a lot of time to figure out a payback that will make her as miserable as she's made me. You, too, if you destroy the tape. A lot of people saw you carrying the tape player into my room." Paul pulled his lips into a smile, and Kushner opened his briefcase.

* * *

Exhausted by the meeting with Kushner, Paul took a nap. When he awoke, two detectives were sitting in his room. *You're ready for this*, he assured himself, and he was right. He had anticipated all of the detectives' questions, and had silently rehearsed his responses. From Asher ("I wouldn't tell him what the judges decided, but how could I report an Auschwitz survivor, a cousin, to the FBI just for asking me to do something I didn't do?") through Sibyl's attack on his head ("I rushed towards the stairs because I was afraid that if she came after me again, one of us might get seriously hurt."), it couldn't have gone more smoothly. However his life might change, he would continue to prepare everything thoroughly.

The next morning, four black-suited rabbis appeared — three with short beards and one, the scribe, with a long-beard. Paul told them his name in Hebrew (*Peretz Chaim ben Reuven Moshe*), said what they told him to say, signed what they told him to sign, and didn't ask to have any of the Hebrew or Aramaic explained. When the oldest rabbi asked if he would like to say a prayer, he answered, "Please go."

Before year's end, Paul had two divorce decrees, one in Spanish, the other in Hebrew. He could read neither one.

CHAPTER 17

"You need to do some planning," said Mrs. Stern, the Orthopedics Department social worker. Paul knew she was right. It was early in the New Year; he had been in the hospital for over a month, and he would be discharged in a few weeks at a time when he would still be in two casts and require near-constant care. But, after a lifetime of planning everything, he could not address the subject.

Stern: The name accurately described the woman in the doorway to his hospital room. Had she ever slouched, smiled or let her eyes wander? Had the family name been changed from Severe? She was tall and thin — like Willa, as Paul imagined her — and when Paul undressed the social worker with his eyes, everything under her tailored suit seemed as straight-edged as an examining table.

"Are you listening to me, Mr. Hartman?"

"Yes," Paul said, though he wasn't.

"You don't seem to be a candidate for a PINS proceeding."

"I'm not," Paul quickly responded. He remembered PINS, Persons In Need of Supervision, from his bar review course. If a person couldn't manage his own life, the court could appoint someone to manage it for him, often a close relative. "I'm fully competent."

"Then I suggest you face reality. If you're refusing to have anything to do with your family, as I've been told, then your limitations leave you few options. I spoke to your mother. She's willing to take care of you at her new home in Texas. If that's not satisfactory to you, she'll come back to New York. If you reject her offer, you'll need a nursing home with access to rehabilitation services."

Paul took a deep breath. "Please keep my mother out of it. I'm sure Dr. Meltzer told you I'm an ungrateful monster, but neither of you knows the family history."

"I know how to do my job, Mr. Hartman." Mrs. Stern entered the room and placed some brochures on the night table. "These are some nursing homes that might be suitable. I don't know what your financial resources are or whether they'll have a bed for you. Let the nurse know when you're ready to discuss them. I expect to treat you in a professional manner and to be treated courteously in return."

* * *

The smiling, mostly white-haired residents pictured in the brochures reminded Paul of the grandparents in his first-grade "Dick and Jane" reading primer. He wondered, as he had in P.S. 42, whether there were people who actually looked like that — certainly not in Arverne. He wouldn't find them in one of the homes proposed by Mrs. Stern, because the fees were more than he could possibly afford.

Then, as if by a miracle, he received a letter from Kushner enclosing a surprisingly large check. Sibyl had sold everything they owned, and was forwarding half the proceeds. Kushner's letter reported that the diamond engagement ring had been returned to Paul's mother. *Good,* Paul thought. It was the only one of Max's diamonds he had actually seen and, on Sibyl's finger, it had been a near-daily reminder that he had benefited from the Holocaust.

Kushner also wrote that Lou Fabrizio wanted to buy Paul's Buffet clarinet. *Perfect.* The first gift from Max would mark the end of Max.

Paul started to write a thank you note to Sibyl, care of Kushner, but he couldn't get beyond the first two words.

Now, he told himself, the time had come to confront the unpleasant facts he had been avoiding: He was alone, with no home, no plans and both legs in casts up to his hips. Awful, but self-pity could only cripple him further. It could lead him to seeing a psychiatrist (Walter himself?) or even being subjugated to a PINS proceeding. If the survivors could confront their problems, so could he.

He needed someone to talk to — someone with no connection to the diamonds who, unlike Mrs. Stern, cared about him as a person. Following Mrs. Stern's advice he forced himself to face reality: He had been close to nobody other than Sibyl and his grandmother. If there was an exception, it was Chip. Since the day Paul screamed his mother out of the hospital room, he had thought of calling him. But if he spoke to Chip about job options or wanting to meet another woman (Willa?) or even about rehabilitation, he might be crossing a line that would turn him from a friend to a pushy Jew.

Why hadn't Chip reached out to him? Following Talmudist tradition, Paul answered his question with a question: Who would want to assume the burden of a needy Jewish fuck-up?

But within a day after he faced reality, Chip appeared in the hospital room doorway. Not quite a miracle, but a delightful surprise. Paul felt himself break into a smile. "Am I glad to see you!" He pressed his bed's elevation button and, when he was sitting nearly straight, pointed at the two casts, "They're not contagious, so you can come in."

"Judge Webster said you were refusing company and didn't want calls."

"Not entirely true, but close enough so I won't refute it."

"My grandmother's down the hall. She broke her hip and got even more confused. How could I be in her room and not come to see you?" Chip shook his head. "You look terrible."

"Thanks. Let's talk in the lounge where there may be patients who look even worse."

Chip stepped into the room and nodded towards the wheelchair alongside Paul's bed. "I assume you don't want to be pushed."

"Would you want to be pushed?"

"Of course not. But I don't know whether you want to talk about what happened."

Paul was moved by Chip's concern. "I don't want to lie, and I can't tell you the truth. I'll just say that if I never see Sibyl again, it will be too soon. I don't even want to hear her name."

"That's why I brought a pocket backgammon set. I'll teach you and then beat you."

"I'm ready for something new, but don't count on beating me for too long. I've got endless hours, to study backgammon books. They'll be easier to follow than Proust."

"It's good to see you haven't changed." Chip walked to the wheelchair. "Is it safe to sit?"

"Usually."

Chip dropped into the wheelchair, then tossed back his head, almost like a horse, so his unparted silky hair flowed straight from his forehead to the rear of his neck. "I have an idea that might interest you." He didn't wait for Paul to respond. "If you're not tied to New York, you might want to consider a job at Knox and Black in Boston. It was my father's firm, and he thinks you might have an opportunity there."

"Ty Martin's firm," Paul blurted out. "They won't even interview Jews."

"That's almost the point." Chip leaned toward him. "They have to change. Many of them want to change, and a lawyer with your ability and openness might be ideal."

"I'd be their Jackie Robinson."

"I never thought of it that way."

"Jackie Robinson took a lot of crap."

Chip seemed flustered, and Paul said, "I'm sorry, Chip, it's just a . . ." He made himself slow down. "I'm not sure I could handle another dose of Ty Martin."

"That's the rest of the point. Ty's not there anymore. He's at Foley Square right now completing the remainder of your clerkship. Some people just aren't cut out for private practice, and Ty didn't help himself by showing his prejudices."

Chip sat back in the wheelchair. "You'll be a breath of fresh air at Knox and Black. I don't think you'll have a rough start like Jackie Robinson, and I'm sure that, just as with him, it'll work out well for everybody."

Paul shook his head. "What irony — Ty and me switching jobs. Let me think."

"Don't think too much."

Asher had said almost the same thing, that Jews think too much. "Thanks, thanks a lot. I'd like to look into it."

Chip nodded. "Three members of the B&K Executive Committee will be in New York this weekend for a wedding, and they'll probably come over to see you. Polish up your casts. My father and Judge Webster have already spoken to them."

"Your father doesn't know me."

"But he knows me and respects my judgment."

"And Judge Webster?"

Chip shrugged. "I don't know what happened, and I don't want to know, but Judge Webster told my father and my father told me — which he shouldn't have done and I shouldn't repeat — that members of your family may be the subject of some investigation, and that even though you have a lot of family loyalty, he's sure you didn't do anything wrong. He says you're the ablest clerk he ever had." Chip raised his eyebrows. "I was his clerk for a while, and I wish I could tell you my father disagreed."

"Family loyalty?" Paul shook his head, but said nothing else.

Chip shrugged. "How about backgammon in the lounge? Five minutes in this room and I'm desperate to get out. I can't imagine how you feel."

But instead of getting up, Chip sat straighter in the wheelchair. "There's one other thing. Nancy and I are going to San Francisco tomorrow — her father's getting an award at Stanford — and my sister's coming down from Boston to feed our cat and keep an eye on our grandmother. Would you like to meet her?"

"Willa?"

"I have only one sister." Chip suddenly looked uncomfortable.

It was too much too soon — and too frightening. Sibyl had been Paul's entire romantic experience. He had never even dated another girl. Paul recalled the pictures of Chip, Willa and their mother in Nantucket where, according to Chip, the family had owned a house since before the Indians. Paul simply didn't belong there — at least not yet.

"Thanks I appreciate it, but I need too much right now." He gestured at his casts. "My life's in turmoil. No, my life's a blank slate with no chalk. Maybe later, when I have a job and . . ."

Chip ran a hand through his hair. "I'm doing it for her, as well. She, too, needs a lot — baby dead, husband gone. Fact is, you both might really need the same thing — a fresh start with somebody different and kind." He ran his other hand across his forehead. "Wow. I'm not good at this kind of thing. Maybe we should just play backgammon."

Paul faced reality: He had no place to go. Willa knew people in Boston, and she played the flute. And those long legs!

"Thanks. Ask her to drop by. I'm not going anyplace."

* * *

The next morning, a young woman — it had to be her — was standing in the doorway where Chip and Mrs. Stern had stood. She smiled tentatively, and Paul was suddenly aware of how helpless he was. But maybe that was for the best. Let her see him improve.

"Paul?"

"Willa?"

She was tall, probably a little bit shorter than Paul if he could stand up, but maybe a bit taller if she would stand straight. Her long legs were shapely under a tight-fitting skirt; her breasts were small, but soft and round; her blondish hair, worn pageboy style, curved nicely over her high cheekbones — a Modigliani portrait.

"Thanks for coming." Paul waved her in. "It's not much but it's mine." Willa looked apprehensively at the wheelchair, and Paul said, "Chip loved sitting in it. I had a normal chair, and I'll ask them to bring it back if you come again."

Willa took the three steps to the wheelchair and held out her hand over the bedrail. It was cool and smooth with long thin flutist's fingers. How could he not compare? He released her hand and, with an exaggerated grimace, she sat in the wheelchair.

"We've seen each other several times, but I don't think we've ever spoken," she said. Her voice was soft and cultivated, the sound

Sibyl's mother tried to emulate when she wasn't carping about someone. He told himself to stop the comparisons.

Paul didn't remember Willa, but it was a time for kindness. "At concerts, I think."

"The first time was at Town Hall in Manhattan, over ten years ago, just before we moved back to Boston. I had the flute solo in *Peer Gynt* that Sibyl thought she deserved. It was the one piece I played better than she did."

Shadowy bits of that evening emerged in Paul's memory — Sibyl pouting; Maurice attributing Willa's solo to her family's connections; Mrs. Pine being awful in every way possible. He remembered, more clearly, being dressed as if he were going to his *bar mitzvah* and being afraid there would be no time to neck. And, with perfect clarity, he remembered returning home and finding Jack at the kitchen table with his mother.

Willa half-smiled. "During intermission, one of the cellists said how cute you were and that you seemed more nervous than the soloists. Then Sibyl said all of your clothing was new because you wanted to impress her mother."

"Ever the striver," Paul said, and Willa's half smile disappeared. Paul raised the back half of his hospital bed as far as it would go. "I know we have Sibyl in common, but I don't want to talk about her. Ever. I won't go through the whole history, but . . ." He pointed at his casts, and let his anger show. "One for each time she banged me over the head with her flute case. But nothing compares with her aborting our child without even telling me she was going to do it."

Paul shut his mouth, but too late. He had just met Willa, and he was telling her what he had never told anybody. But, if not now, when? And if not her, who? Would he tell Cousin Walter, who wanted to commit him to Creedmoor, or Mrs. Stern, who wanted to ship him to El Paso, or even Chip who was embarrassed by the little Paul had disclosed?

"I'm sorry," Willa said.

"I told my mother about the abortion — nobody else — and she didn't believe me."

"And I'm not going to tell anyone, and I do believe you."

They sat in silence without moving, and then Willa folded her hands in her lap. "If I ever remarry, I don't want children. I can't go through what happened to Billy ever again. It's called fibrocystic disease." She pronounced the name of her son's condition in awful wonderment, as if she had never uttered them before. "It's genetic and stopped his lungs from working. Horrible. He was gone within two weeks after they figured out what it was. Right here in this hospital — seventh floor, beneath my grandmother's room. Will couldn't deal with it. He moved out three days after the funeral, and I went back to Boston."

"I'm sorry." Paul wished he could take her hands or hug her, but the maneuver was too complicated. He wondered what else he might say. Chitchat would profane her loss and, if he told her anything about his own plight, it would have to be everything.

"Do you play cribbage?" Willa finally said.

"Chip taught me backgammon yesterday."

"I have lots of memories of losing to Chip in backgammon."

"So now I can lose to you in cribbage. What is it with you —" Paul cut himself off.

"Us WASPs?" Willa raised her eyebrows teasingly. Her smile, which was tentative at first, quickly grew.

"Anytime I start getting familiar with people — the Websters, Chip, you — someone suggests a game I never played."

"That's how we stay in control — and it's a good way to avoid conversation." She pushed herself up from the wheelchair. "There's a cribbage set in my grandmother's room."

* * *

Oscar intercepted Paul and Willa outside the lounge.

"Sorry, Paulie-Paul, but I have to take you away from your new friend. They're gonna cut down your right cast to below the knee. I know it was supposed to be tomorrow, but sooner is better for you."

To Paul's surprise, Willa rested her hand on his shoulder. The long fingers felt good. "How long will it take?" she asked.

"Hour, maybe less if there's no hurry-up-and-wait," Oscar answered. "No pain, no big deal compared to what they already done to him." He turned the wheelchair around and pushed Paul in long strides towards the elevator. Willa matched his pace. The elevator door opened, and Oscar ran towards it.

"I'll wait," Willa called behind them.

"We got an empty elevator, so I'll tell you like it is," Oscar said in his musical Jamaican accent. "Once you can bend one knee and your arms get strong, you'll be ready for crutches school," The elevator doors closed. "They'll teach you everything you thought you knew — walking, climbing stairs, on and off the toilet, wiping your ass standing up. Don't think it's easy on crutches. And they don't teach this, but if you got a good woman, you can do love. Things like busses, and getting really clean by yourself—" Oscar laughed and pushed Paul out of the now open elevator door. "Forget it, man — you'd be better off in a limbo contest. Unless you got a patient woman." Oscar stopped pushing and put his head next to Paul's. "It's not my business," he said without any lilt in his voice, "but your friend, I saw her with her grandma. She got patience — class too."

"Thanks for telling me," Paul said, and they both laughed.

* * *

As soon as Paul was resettled in his bed with a pillow under his newly liberated and surprisingly white right knee, Willa entered the room carrying a Bergdorf shopping bag. "Oscar told me you'd be up and around on crutches soon, so I ran out to get something to celebrate." She held up a bottle of champagne. "The bag's camouflage."

"We better not. The staff's mad enough at me as it is."

"Why are they mad at you?" Willa seemed perplexed, but then she shook her head. "I'm sorry, I shouldn't pry."

"You better put the bottle back in the bag and slide it under the bed." *Damn*, Paul thought. He was giving her orders. She'd never come back.

Willa knelt, and Paul turned his eyes to the wall so he wouldn't look down her blouse.

"I'll give the champagne to Oscar." Willa said nervously. "He's been—"

"No!" Paul barked, and immediately regretted his interruption. "Word will get out, and the head nurse and social worker, lots of the staff will give me an even harder time."

"I'm sorry. Maybe I should go."

Paul turned his eyes back to her. "Please stay." He stretched his hand under the bed rail, but couldn't reach her. "I'm sorry if I sounded harsh. I agreed to let medical students watch the cast removal. They made me a stage prop. I hope they treat the cadavers with more dignity."

With a few swift graceful movements, Willa stood and put the cribbage board on Paul's stomach. He seized her hand.

"The staff's angry with me because I won't let my mother visit." Willa cocked her head. "And why won't I let her visit? I'll try to explain, although I don't know the right place to start. If I start with my father, I might cry. So I'll start with my Cousin Max, really my first cousin once removed. He had numbers on his arm from Auschwitz."

Willa, standing motionless between the wheelchair and the bed, nodded. "I saw pictures of the prisoners' arms in *Life* magazine. I know, but I really don't know."

"Neither do I. Nobody who wasn't there can really know." Paul paused and the room began to blur. "Five-three-nine-two-seven. My mother told me I shouldn't look . . ."

He pointed to the wheelchair and said, "Please sit." She did.

He neither planned nor listened to what he was saying. He left out nothing except his now-gone passion for Sibyl. When he did mention Sibyl, however, Willa interrupted: "Except for that one Town Hall Concert, I spent years playing second flute to Sibyl. I don't want to be her replacement."

Paul took her hand and squeezed it. "You aren't; you won't. I don't want to talk about her either." He raised Willa's hand to his lips and kissed each of her fingers.

When he started telling her about the night of his fall, he was drenched in sweat. He finished by saying, "My mother believed Sibyl instead of me about the abortion, and she was trying desperately to put me in Creedmoor. Why? All I ever wanted was to do the right thing, but I was never sure what that was. It's awful how that night ended — awful except you must believe me that I didn't touch anybody."

"I believe it," Willa said. "I believe everything. I don't see how you could have done anything differently. Maybe, with perfect hindsight, you might have told Asher what you learned in New Haven. But you did give your word to Judge Webster."

"Come closer and kiss me," Paul said — or pleaded. He knew it was too soon and too much — or maybe too little. Yet, the moment seemed to require it.

She closed the door to the hallway, came back to the bed and, with her eyes open, bent over to kiss him. Paul felt none of the devouring passion of his kisses with Sibyl. Willa seemed to feel even less. But, he assured himself, this was only the beginning.

Willa straightened up and spoke in an almost trance-like voice. "We've both been through a lot, and we know what Chip is trying to do. He's not very subtle."

"We don't need subtlety," Paul said.

"Perhaps, but before things go farther, I want to be as honest as you've been."

"Honesty: I'm not used — "

"Just listen to me. Okay?"

"I'm sorry."

Willa's neck, Paul realized, was much longer, more swan-like, than Sibyl's. "I don't want to talk about Will any more than you want to talk about Sibyl, but I could tell from that night at Town Hall when some of the girls were teasing Sibyl, and later, when I saw the two of you at different musical events, that there were strong physical feelings between you."

Paul wanted her to stop. The past could only make the present more difficult.

"I never felt that way towards Will. He said — I never told anybody what I'm telling you now. He said that my coldness was one of the reasons he started drinking." She was close to tears. "I think he might be right."

"Why did you get married?" Paul asked in as kindly a tone as he could manage.

Willa tilted her heard towards the ceiling, just as Paul's grandmother used to do. "You don't know my father. We got married because we were a perfect match and were supposed to get married. Will and Willa — it was ordained. I thought the physical part might be better after the knot was tied because I wouldn't have to worry about protecting my sacred virginity. But it was awful. So quick — wham bam. No feeling. No tenderness. Almost as if I wasn't there — and, usually, I wasn't." She seemed exhausted.

To Paul's surprise, Willa's description aroused him. Sibyl and he had long loved making love. It wasn't enough to save their marriage, and Sibyl was now gone. But Paul had learned much about a woman's wants and pleasures and, with patience and tenderness, Willa and he could also share the joys of their bodies.

"Please come over to the bed and hold my hand," he asked.

"Okay," she said in a voice so low he could barely hear her.

They held hands on his abdomen. "We don't know where this is going," Paul told her, "but you call the shots. If the time comes, I'll try to show you that things can be better than wham bam. End of pitch."

Willa kissed his cheek, then took the champagne bottle from under the bed and clutched it against her chest. "I'm going to take this into the bathroom and pop it open and pour us each a paper cup. You can do whatever you want with yours, but I'm drinking mine."

"And then teach me cribbage," Paul said.

That evening, Paul tipped Oscar three dollars (a violation of hospital rules) and asked him to tell Mrs. Stern that he would like to be discharged to a nursing home in Boston.

RUBY

1980
In Transit

CHAPTER 18

The typewritten envelope in the center of Paul's desk was marked "PERSONAL" and postmarked Tel Aviv. It had no return address. Aside from distant relatives he had never met, Sibyl was Paul's only connection to Israel. He hadn't heard from her since 1959 when, in his hospital room, her tape-recorded voice proclaimed that she was carrying Boris's baby.

Paul picked up the letter opener. Then he put it down and tore the envelope open. Inside was a column clipped from the August 14, 1980 *Jerusalem Post*, entitled "**MUSIC NOTES.**" The second paragraph was circled in red:

> **GALILEE QUARTET** — The Galilee String Quartet announced that in September, Ruby Hartman, a 20 year-old violinist from Haifa, will be temporarily replacing Yehoshua Spiro as one of the Quartet's violinists while Mr. Spiro recovers from elective hand surgery. Miss Hartman, who previously performed under the name Yael Pinkus, was a finalist in the Young Mozart contest (sometimes called the World Prodigy Prize) at last year's Vienna Music Festival. She is spending this summer at the Tanglewood Festival Institute in Massachusetts, USA, where she is the Leonard Bernstein Fellow in the master class and concertmistress of the Tanglewood Student Orchestra.

Paul sat down on his desk chair, an heirloom given him by Willa's parents when he made partner at Black & Knox, and read the clipping again. The violinist calling herself Ruby Hartman had to be the child of Sibyl's infidelity. Willa had learned through the flutists' grapevine that Sibyl had named her daughter Yael; Pinkus was Maurice's family name before he changed it to Pine. Obviously, the girl had the good sense to reject the names of both the oafish Boris Kendal and her sleazy grandfather.

A righteous fury ignited inside him. Whether or not Sibyl's daughter was a prodigy, she could not be allowed to masquerade as the child he would never have. Even in its feminized form, the name she had commandeered belonged to real Hartmans — his father, his great grandfather, Max's murdered son, his own aborted child, and to countless forebears going back countless generations.

Paul would go to Tanglewood on Sunday, two days from now, to stop the profanation of one of the few remaining ties to his Jewish past. Sibyl or the imposter had sent the article to entice him there, and when they found him (or he found them), he would urge Yael to stop using his family's name. If necessary, he would ask one of his litigation partners to bring a lawsuit to enjoin her from using it. He, himself, would research the legal issues and draft the strongest complaint possible.

The girl could not have barged into his life at a more trying time. Willa was about to announce publicly what she had told Paul in June — that she and Diane were in love and would soon establish their own home, confirming rumors about Diane that had been whispered since she was a girl, and enabling Boston wags to say that Paul had the distinction of marrying two flutists and being cuckolded by both. On top of that, his two most important clients — Granville Turner III, Willa's father, and Johnny Cheung, who had enabled Paul to become a millionaire several times over — were about to go to war with each other, requiring Paul to make some difficult decisions.

Staring at the *Jerusalem Post* column, Paul resolved that, no matter what transpired at Tanglewood on Sunday, he would go forward with his scheduled trip to Hong Kong in September. Eli "Brad" Bradford, the Black & Knox Managing Partner, had asked Paul to explore the possibility of the firm opening an office in the Far East. Paul was his choice for the assignment because, over the years, he had demonstrated an ability to work well with Asians, including Johnny, Johnny's Hong Kong backers and several Japanese and Korean companies starting to do business in the United States.

The Hong Kong trip would allow Paul to be far away from Boston when Willa and Diane made their announcement, but it also offered an opportunity for a broader escape. If Paul ran B&K's Hong Kong office, or struck out on his own, or joined another firm in that city, he would rarely be with people who knew that his wife had left him for a woman. There would be an opportunity for new friendships and, perhaps, romances in a place where he wouldn't often feel like the other — like the New York Jew who, with help from his father-in-law, made it big in a firm dominated by Boston Brahmins. Although he had achieved great professional and financial success at B&K, Paul never quite felt he belonged there. He suspected that, like Ty Martin, some of his colleagues — particularly ten or so excessively polite and formal partners — resented both the professional respect that was now Paul's due and the social changes he personified. He was not a Jew trying to elbow his way in. He had arrived, but was still not one of them.

Paul started to read the *Jerusalem Post* article again, but sensed a presence looming over him. He looked up and was shocked to see Granville Turner III, all six-foot-four of him, leaning over his desk — the desk that had once belonged to Granville Turner II. Nobody outside of the firm, even its most important client, was allowed to roam the firm's hallways unescorted. There was no one in the world, except for Diane, Paul less wished to confront.

"You must get Willa to change her mind," Granville declaimed. "I've chartered a helicopter so we can go to Nantucket and you can talk sense to her before she carries this stupidity further."

Paul waited a moment to compose himself before replying. "I spoke to her — more than once. It made no difference."

"I've always been suspicious of that Diane, starting when she was a little tomboy. Hanging around Willa this whole summer, trying to get her to be something she's not. How long have you known about this nasty business?"

The question, Paul realized, had at least three parts. How long had he known that Willa was sexually attracted to women — or, at least, Diane? How long had he suspected it? How long had he hoped it? He had suspected since his earliest days in Boston when, despite determined efforts by each of them, sex with Willa (he could never think of it as making love) was primarily a chore. There was rarely an afterglow — only relief that it was over for at least another week. From time to time, he had almost hoped Willa was a lesbian so he couldn't fault himself for her failure to respond.

Diane was often the butt of jokes in the Harvard Club locker room and, given her mannish dress and gait, Paul had simply assumed she was a lesbian. In the early seventies, it seemed to him that Willa and Diane sometimes exchanged private smiles, but Diane moved to New Mexico in 1974 and Paul stopped thinking about her until last summer, when she returned to Boston and seemed to be wherever Willa was.

"Willa told me two months ago," Paul answered Granville, "on the day she left for the Island. That's why I haven't gone there. It's not possible to change her mind, and I'm the last one in the world to try."

"It might be possible if you told her you would abide by your marriage vows and give up the foreign hookers Johnny gets for you."

Granville didn't stir, but Paul felt as if his father-in-law's massive hands were pushing against his chest. Although Paul had gone to great effort to keep his affairs private, Granville seemed to know about both Ella Ku, who had returned to her home in Taiwan, and Lana Adimov, a Russian-born naturalized American citizen whom Paul began seeing after Ella left. Both women had responsible positions at Concord Memory, Johnny's company, and neither was a hooker in any sense of the term. Paul wondered how Granville would react if he learned that Willa had suggested Paul see Ella.

Granville leaned closer. Paul smelled his cigar-smoke breath. "You may be ready to give up on Willa, but I'm not. I'm not asking you to come to Nantucket. I'm telling you."

Paul fought two competing urges: to stand up and meet Granville's eyes; to shrink back. The powerful man had always treated Paul civilly — sometimes even warmly — and with a respect that had grown over the years as Paul became one of his principal advisors.

"I can't discuss our personal lives. Willa wouldn't want me to."

"Then let's discuss your professional life." Granville stood to his full height. He was as imposing in 1980 as he was in the picture of the 1928 Harvard crew he captained. "Your client and pal, Johnny, forgets what he owes me. Concord Memory exists for its stockholders, including me, the second biggest. It's not his private laundry with you as the number-one coolie. If you can't get him to back down, I'm going to knock him off his rickshaw."

Paul made himself speak slowly. "Keep in mind what the three of us have accomplished since I brought Johnny and you together and we launched Concord. I can suggest a compromise that —"

"Tell me in the helicopter," Granville interrupted. "But remember that the only compromise I want is you back with my daughter and Johnny's head on a platter. I'm sick of that damn Chinaman ignoring me."

The final straw. It was Bernie on Montague Street — another big man trying to bully him. If the King of the Boston WASPs was sick of that damn Chinaman, he must also be sick of the Chinaman's coolie-Jew. In any event, Paul was sick of him.

Paul looked at the newspaper clipping on the desk. "You better speak to Brad."

"I'm going to Mr. Bradford right now."

Paul kept his gaze focused on the name "Ruby Hartman" until Granville was gone.

* * *

As soon as Granville was out of sight, Maria called on the intercom to say that Johnny was here early. Could Paul see him now? The answer was yes, as it always was for Johnny and for Granville.

For sixteen years, ever since Johnny Cheung was a Harvard Ph.D. candidate in applied physics tinkering with magnetic tape in his parents' basement, Paul had always been available for him as a lawyer, a business advisor and, arguably, a friend if Johnny was capable of friendship. Whenever Johnny and Granville had simultaneous demands on Paul's time, Paul simply worked longer hours. Willa had told him, "With you, Johnny comes first, my father second, and I won't rank myself." She was smiling, but she wasn't joking.

Johnny and Granville had each sent Paul a great deal of business, referred other clients to him and helped him become a rainmaker. Only four of B&K's forty partners took home a larger share of the firm's profits than Paul did, but that was not the principal source of Paul's wealth. The Concord Memory stock he bought at the company's founding (with money borrowed from Willa and Granville) and continued to buy over the years kept soaring higher. There was more than synergy between Johnny and Paul. Each fed off the other's inquisitiveness and intellectual energy. When Johnny, in preparing a patent application, described a new way of recording electronic information on magnetic tape, Paul, who had only a rudimentary understanding of the physics, asked simple but probing questions which enabled Johnny to appreciate how the invention could be refined and expanded. When Johnny asked Paul to explain the rationale of a Delaware law concerning classes of common stock, the two of them reconsidered Concord's financial structure and came up with a plan of reorganization that enabled Concord to reduce its overall taxes. And, besides their joint efforts being productive, they had fun.

Johnny strode into Paul's office. Dressed like the brilliant physicist he was — frayed loose collar, unfashionable black knit tie, slightly soiled and knotted too low, tangled black hair — he nonetheless had the demeanor of the driven entrepreneur he also was. He came directly to Paul's desk and leaned over it just as Granville had, but he seemed to take up only half the space. "The shit's not only hit the fan, it's flying right at us," he said. "You were right. We have to do something fast and potent."

Paul understood him perfectly. For weeks, Johnny and he had been holding confidential merger negotiations with General Data Corp., a company that was much bigger than Concord Memory and which, like Concord, made computer memory devices, primarily state-of-the-art magnetic tapes which stored electronic data. GD had offered a price which Johnny called "fair," but the sticking point was Johnny's role in the merged company. Johnny wanted to be in charge of all research. GD wanted him to do whatever its president wished. Granville wanted Johnny to take GD's offer and disappear. He, unlike Paul, thought that Johnny's brilliance was overrated and that Johnny would be disruptive in any company he couldn't run dictatorially. Paul believed that Concord's most valuable asset was Johnny's brain, and that the merged company would not thrive without it. Nevertheless, since he was the lawyer for a company whose largest stockholders (Johnny and Granville) were at odds, he felt obliged to remain neutral. He predicted that GD would make a hostile tender offer if Johnny didn't budge; it would stop negotiating with the company and offer to purchase Concord stock directly from Concord's shareholders.

"You think GD will make a hostile tender offer?" Paul asked.

"Soon after Labor Day."

"How do you know?"

"You don't want to know how I know."

Paul tensed. "Johnny, I can't ethically represent you if somebody's feeding you confidential inside information."

"Climb down from your pulpit, Paul, and remember I need you." Johnny dropped his voice. "Granville's shooting off his mouth where he can be overheard. There's going to be a war between Concord and GD, and your father-in-law's on the side of GD. Whose side are you on?"

"Yours," Paul answered without hesitation. His heart thumped as he said it.

"Good. Now, let's come up with a strategy to kill the bastards."

A half-dozen thoughts darted through Paul's mind, but one pushed to the fore. "First, I have to leave B&K. If you and Granville are on opposite sides, the firm is going to represent him which means I can't represent you and stay as a partner. Conflict of interest." Paul felt perspiration under his shirt, but he was pleased with himself. He would resign as a professional son-in-law before he stopped being a son-in-law.

"Good again. B&K's no place for the sons of a clockmaker and a laundryman."

For the first time in weeks, Paul felt like smiling. Johnny's "laundryman" father owned the biggest linen-supply service in

Metropolitan Boston. But he said nothing; Johnny's talents did not include the ability to laugh at himself.

Bradford was speaking on the phone with his Nantucket plumber. He waved Paul into a chair and then paid him no attention. As Paul sat before the brilliant lawyer who had offered him a job during their first meeting at the hospital, and who had then gone out of his way to advance Paul's career, he felt the full impact of what he was doing: He was leaving behind an enviable law practice he had worked relentlessly to build, as well as many colleagues he enjoyed working with. He had to be crazy. But it would be crazier to remain at B&K where any face could become a mask hiding what its wearer was really thinking — that the pushy New York Jew, who had catapulted his career by marrying into the Turner family, had gotten his just desserts when his wife left him for a dyke and he lost his guest membership in Brahmin Boston society.

"Are you all right?" Paul heard Bradford ask.

"I'm trying to recover from back-to-back meetings with Granville and Johnny."

Bradford did not hesitate. "Granville's made me aware of that. Your primary loyalties should lie with the law, your family, the firm and yourself, not with John Cheung. Do you think Cheung has loyalty to you? Granville, who has played no small role in your success, would be the second to say that you deserve everything you've gotten." Bradford fixed his grey eyes on Paul. "And I'd be the first. Before I even met you, I convinced the Management Committee that we should make you an offer because of what Judge Webster and Chip Story had said, and — let's not beat around the bush — because the time had come to have some Jews in the firm. You seemed the ideal person to start with. It was one of the best decisions I ever made."

Paul suddenly realized that Bradford resembled a silver-haired, silver-tongued Ronald Reagan. "I appreciate everything you've done for me," he told Brad, "but I can't abandon Johnny. We've been together — almost partners — since the beginning. The name Concord Memory was my suggestion."

Bradford's face reddened, and he scowled in uncommon anger. "You don't have to work for or against either one of them. B&K will represent Granville, and you have nothing to do with the dispute. We've researched the ethical issues, gotten an opinion from the chair of the Bar Association's Ethics Committee, and there should be no problem." He paused and breathed in deeply through his nose. "As Managing Partner and your friend, I'm asking you to stay."

Paul was moved, but his answer, he realized, had to be no. After twenty-one years, he couldn't just say, *I resign*. Yet, if he opened up to Brad — if he alluded to the fact that he was ashamed of Willa leaving him for Diane — his mentor might regret having fostered the career of an emotional Jew. Brad, however, made it easy.

"You've come a long way," he went on, "and you're accepted, as you should be, as an able lawyer, a personable fellow and a member of the Turner family. If you straighten out your personal life and time does its healing, that shouldn't change. Don't get mixed up in a takeover battle. You're not like the lawyers in that field. Sure they're smart and shrewd, but they don't have the esteem you've earned and want to keep. Hostile takeovers is a dog-eat-dog New York practice. Why follow Cheung out of the firm? He's from a different world than we are."

We? Paul asked himself. *Who's my we?*

"Dog-eat-dog," he echoed Brad. "I guess K&B's practice is just the opposite."

Brad clenched his jaw and stood. "You'll be called about transferring your matters."

* * *

Paul went directly to Concord's office. By the time he arrived, both he and Johnny had reached the same tentative conclusion: Concord's best course of action for defeating any attempt by General Data to take it over might be for Concord, itself, to seek to take over General Data — have the minnow swallow the whale before the whale swallowed it. Concord would do this by going around GD management and offering to buy a majority of GD's shares directly from GD's shareholders — a "preemptive hostile takeover." After the two men locked themselves in Johnny's private office, they concluded that Concord would have to borrow five-hundred-million dollars in cash to make the offer. But they also concluded that Granville, who wanted Concord sold to General Data, would make it difficult for Concord to borrow much in the United States. To counter this, Paul suggested, and Johnny agreed, that Paul would try to raise most of the money through Johnny's backers in the Far East — the Cheung family, its banks, partners, and friends — who had profited from Concord's meteoric rise or who regretted not investing with Johnny sooner. If Paul could accomplish this, the minnow could triumph.

That evening, Johnny and Paul flew to New York for weekend meetings at the offices of Berman, Lieberman & Callahan, a law firm that specialized in hostile takeovers. It had been formed ten years earlier by mostly Jewish lawyers who hadn't been hired by, or hadn't made partner at, establishment firms. Even for New York lawyers, they were aggressive, hard-working and expensive. Johnny loved the name. "Berman, Lieberman and Callahan — the sound of street fighters. I wish they could add an Italian name. Too soon for an Asian name, but that's coming."

By Saturday afternoon, Lew Berman, Johnny and Paul had assembled a team — lawyers, investment bankers, investigators, a public relations firm, and a stockholder-solicitation specialist. Paul would leave for Hong Kong next week, but Johnny made it clear that he wanted Paul's role to go beyond financing. "I want Paul to be in on all significant decisions and have the final judgment call on all legal questions," Johnny announced. "With telephone and telexes and nobody sleeping, it's doable." Mike Colin, the Berman lawyer who would be in charge of day-to-day operations, agreed that Paul should head the legal team to the extent it was feasible to do so from Hong Kong. He had looked up to Paul since they were both Columbia freshman.

Paul had never experienced anything quite like the meeting at Berman — the sheer number of people and specialties; the stream of wisecracks ("Don't bend over if he's behind you." "Stay under sixty until you're sure he can count beyond that."); the decisiveness; the endless arrival of Chinese take-out and two-inch thick delicatessen sandwiches; the irreverence, near condescension, towards the establishment law firms. Mike Colin dismissed Judge Webster's old New York firm, which regularly represented GD, as "like a dinosaur, but with less imagination." Unaware of Paul's connection to Black & Knox, one young Berman lawyer said, "Those Boston stuffed-shirts are too genteel for this. We'll be filing with the SEC, while they're still agonizing over split infinitives."

The crack about B&K, Paul thought, was not entirely fair, but it had some merit. He would ignore it. Why dampen the near-euphoric atmosphere? The mostly Jewish lawyers in the room were preparing to beat the *goyim* who hadn't hired them, and they were having a good time doing it. Max, who never smiled, would be smiling now.

At seven that night, when the group was discussing the agenda for Sunday, Paul pulled Johnny aside and told him he couldn't attend the next day's meeting. "Something personal's come up which I can't discuss. It will make me unreachable most of tomorrow."

Johnny smiled. "Take care of it. Maybe you'll be less jumpy when it's behind you."

* * *

By the time his shuttle landed at Logan, Paul was grateful to Johnny. Whatever awaited him at Tanglewood, his immersion in the takeover would give him something to think about instead of the WASP woman leaving his life and the two Israelis trying to break into it.

Lights were on in the Beacon Hill townhouse he still shared with Willa. He almost hoped she was there — and she was.

She was standing in the foyer, lean and stylish in the blue shift she often wore over a bathing suit. It had been nearly two months since he had seen her. Should he try to kiss her? They had never given up their hello, goodbye, and goodnight pecks.

She didn't approach him.

"What's wrong?" Paul asked.

"*You're* wrong!" Her brow wrinkled in exasperation. "You're rushing into something crazy that you'll regret, and I came back here to try to get you to think."

Her hair had been lightened by the sun and was almost blonde again. He could sense the scent of Nantucket salt water and light perspiration that had rested on her bare arms earlier that day. There was nothing masculine about her. Why was she here? To urge him to stay at K&B? To suggest they continue their lives together, including their affairs — she with Diane, he with Lana? He knew he had to part from the firm and from Willa, but he was overwhelmed by the prospect of losing both — of, once again, having to build a new life.

"Let's talk in the library," she said, and Paul followed her. The room, which was mostly furnished from her grandmother's estate, was what Bernie's decorator must have had in mind when she assembled his Woodmere homes. Paul loved it. The picture of his father's swim team was on the fireplace mantle next to the picture of the 1928 Harvard crew. If he could only think calmly, he might come up with a way to reorganize their lives without losing all of this.

Willa sat in the easy chair, and Paul sat on the couch across from her. A good arrangement.

"Brad came over to the beach house. He and my father feel they were too rough on you and that you're acting out of anger. Maybe I was too rough when I told you about Diane, and that made you huffy with them. There's no need for you to leave the firm — just have nothing to do with the dispute between my father and Johnny. Brad can build what he calls a Chinese wall around you. Chip's father, who wrote the ethical rules, says there's nothing wrong with it."

"A Chinese wall to keep out the Chinaman," Paul said.

"What are you talking about?"

"Your father called Johnny a Chinaman."

"So what? You can say a lot about my father, but you can't say he's a bigot. He's an equal-opportunity snob who looks down on everybody. You're one of the few exceptions. Johnny would be another if he didn't disrupt the world my father grew up in."

She was right, Paul realized, but Granville was tangential, and he said nothing.

"Think it over," Willa continued. "I've taken a job at Devon Academy teaching music, and Diane and I are buying a house there. Little chance of our having awkward encounters if you stay in Boston."

"I've given Johnny my word."

"He has no sense of loyalty to you, to anybody."

Paul wanted to deny it, but the facts were disturbing. Johnny's original collaborators were gone with little to show for their joint efforts. Ellen Ko had told him that Johnny's wife, who had returned to Hong Kong with their daughter, was living in near poverty.

"I'm rich because of him."

"And he's many times richer because of you and my father. Johnny's a genius — we all know that — whose done some remarkable things, including controlling you."

"Your father called me Johnny's number one coolie."

"It's more subtle than that." Willa tilted her head back and closed her eyes, then opened them. She seemed to be gathering strength. "I never imagined I'd tell you this, but I can't let you blow up everything you've built." She shrugged. "Remember what happened seven years ago during the Yom Kippur War? Do you remember?"

October 1973 — Paul remembered vividly. He had been almost paralyzed by news reports that Israel might be destroyed. He nodded at Willa.

"You went into a daze, and I asked you if you were anxious about Israel. You said you didn't want to talk about it." Paul nodded again. "I was worried, and when Maria said you weren't taking phone calls I became even more worried, and I tried that night in the bedroom to . . . to be what I wasn't . . . to do things I never . . . ."

Paul looked away from her. "Let's not talk about it."

"Just say that I tried to comfort you and failed." Willa ran her tongue over her lips, and then said, "I'm sorry."

She waited a few seconds before continuing. "Anyway, the next evening, I went to a musicale my mother was hosting for Boston Symphony patrons. I tried to get you to go, but you were glued to the TV

and flipping the radio dial for news. Johnny was there — Diane, too."
Willa began to speak haltingly. "Diane and I had started to see each other
that fall. Very discreetly." She rolled her eyes. "Some *discreetly.* We were
talking to each other near the bar — small talk — and Johnny walked up
to us and . . . It wasn't a smile, more of a smirk. Then, without a word, he
winked at Diane, then at me, and walked away."

Paul cursed Johnny silently — he knew more about Willa than
Paul did. Perhaps Brad and Granville were right about him. But Paul had
chosen to represent Johnny and was central to his strategy. Anything less
than the total commitment he always gave would be unprofessional. It
would mark him as a vacillator who couldn't be counted on.

Willa leaned forward. "My father always suspected that Johnny
used private detectives to spy on people and, when I asked you, you said
something about lawyer-client privilege."

"I can't reveal my talks with a client."

"Well, I can reveal my talks with him," Willa snapped.

Shut up! Paul wanted to scream. He would soon fly halfway
around the world to do battle for Johnny, and he needed no more doubts
about his client's integrity and motives. But a lawyer shouldn't run from
facts.

"What did he say?"

"Before I went home, when I was coming out of the bathroom,
Johnny was waiting for me in the hall, and he said, 'Ella Ko has eyes for
Paul.' 'Why are you telling me that?' I asked. I felt I had to do something
or he would tell you about Diane. I was so upset that the whole thing
might come out that when Diane was offered a job at a museum in Santa
Fe, I urged her to take it. She stayed there till last summer. Almost six
years. Diane felt—"

"I remember you mentioned Ella Ko at breakfast," Paul
interrupted.

"I told you that someone at Concord said Ella had eyes for you,
and that I promised to keep the name confidential. You just crinkled your
nose. Anyway, Israel started to do better in the war, and you became
almost your old self. I don't know when you started to see Ella, and we
never talked about it even though it was far from a secret."

Paul remembered the day well. He had gone directly from
breakfast to his broker, and arranged to anonymously contribute
$720,000, half of what was then his personal wealth, to the Yom Kippur
War Campaign of the Combined Jewish Philanthropies, using a cashier's
check on a Utah bank so it couldn't be traced back to him. (In Jewish
tradition, eighteen or *chai* signifies life and luck; there were thirty-six

people, two *chai*, in the wedding picture on his parents' bedroom wall; his 1973 gift was 40,000 *chai*; he walked into Ella Ko's office in Concord's accounting department at eighteen minutes after noon.)

The next month, on the fifteenth anniversary of Asher's death, he went to say *Kaddish* for his cousin at a synagogue in Lowell where nobody knew him. After that, Paul recited *Kaddish* for his father, Max and Asher several times a year at the Lowell synagogue, and he made anonymous annual contributions of $1,800 to that synagogue and $18,000 to the Combined Jewish Philanthropies. He compared himself to the Marranos in Spain, the Jews who converted to Catholicism to save their lives, while continuing to practice Jewish rites in secret. His anonymity, he assured himself, wasn't intended to hide his support for Israel, but only to escape being hounded by people and organizations he wanted nothing to do with. He had left his family for a life with Boston aristocrats, but he had stayed a Jew.

He also remembered Lana Abramov, Johnny's administrative assistant, running up to him in the Concord parking lot soon after Ella had returned to Taiwan. Lana's car wouldn't start; her dog had to be walked; would Paul be an angel and . . . . Granville was right; Johnny had been his procurer.

"Brad wants to come see you tomorrow," Willa said.

"Impossible tomorrow," Paul managed to mumble.

"Why?" Willa asked. "Can't Johnny wait for once in your life?"

"It's not Johnny."

Willa sighed loudly. "I feel badly about what you're going through, but I'm not going to play twenty questions."

Paul waited a long moment pondering whether to show this woman who was shattering his life the article about the younger woman who might make it more difficult to put back together. *Why not?* He had to confide in somebody. He took the *Jerusalem Post* column from his inside jacket pocket and handed it to her.

Willa read and raised her eyebrows. "Young Mozart Prize finalist! That's beyond talent."

Paul stood by Willa's chair. "It's obvious that, when the Boris hoax collapsed, Sibyl lied to her a second time about who her father is. Probably said it was me because there were too many candidates. Even if Yael Pinkus is the new Yehudi Menuhin, I'm going to Tanglewood to find out what's going on and stop her."

Willa took his hand. "Perhaps she is your daughter." Paul just stood there. He couldn't focus on the possibility. "Why would Sibyl lie?" Willa asked.

"To keep her skills honed."

Willa broke into a grin, and Paul suddenly understood what Sibyl was doing.

"She doesn't want her daughter to be branded a *mamzer* — illegitimate."

"A what?"

"I'm not an expert in Jewish family law, but if your father wasn't married to your mother, you're a *mamzer*." Paul felt the words just spurt out of him. "It's worse than being illegitimate in America because in Israel, where the ultra-Orthodox rabbis control this kind of thing, religious law is the law of the state. There are severe restrictions on who a *mamzer* can marry, the legitimacy of their children. It's a curse for life and for generations."

Willa was frowning, but Paul was wound up and couldn't control himself. "Yael must have figured out that the fairy her mother married couldn't be her father, so Sibyl designated me — the husband when Yael was conceived. Anyone else would make her a *mamzer*."

Willa yanked her hand free. "You may be too agitated to appreciate what you're saying, but 'fairy' is offensive. In fact, your whole theory is. My father's more tolerant than you are. You should realize that, as freakish as we are, homosexuals can have children just like the real people do."

Was this a new Willa, a suddenly strong and sensible woman, or was she simply repeating Diane? It made no difference — Paul needed her. He needed somebody!

"I'm scared — *terrified!* — about going to Tanglewood tomorrow," he heard himself say in a tremulous voice, admitting to Willa what he had, until now, not acknowledged to himself. "It could reopen everything I've tried to forget. Will you come with me — make sure I don't say or do anything stupid?" *Don't leave me all alone*, he thought of adding, but then he might sob?

Willa stood up. "You know that's a terrible idea. Sibyl and I never liked each other, and my being there would make things even more difficult. Besides, a real estate broker is showing us houses in Devon tomorrow." She smoothed her hair.

Paul felt desperate. She was really leaving him. "Stay here tonight so we can talk in the morning about what I should say in Tanglewood. You stay in the bedroom, and I'll stay down here."

"Diane and I are leaving early for Devon, and we're staying with her mother. Of the four parents, she's the closest to accepting us."

Willa held out her hand. "We can shake goodbye."

Paul took her hand. "So long as neither of us squeezes."

They shook hands and Willa went to the front door but, before opening it, she turned back. "Good luck tomorrow. You've been very kind to me. Try to be kind to Sibyl if you see her, and to her daughter, whatever her name may be, but most of all, to yourself."

Paul nodded. He didn't trust himself to speak.

CHAPTER 19

Paul searched the crowd on the huge impossibly green lawn for a place to put down his blanket. There were a few small patches near the Music Shed, but he chose a spot in front of the cement path to the restrooms. This would be a good place to be found or, if he decided to make his own search, to look for Sibyl and Yael. Of course, Sibyl might be unrecognizable. He had never seen a picture of Yael.

He opened the program to the names of the Boston Symphony musicians and did not find Hartman, Pinkus or Pine. Not surprising; whatever-her-name was only a student. He turned to the end of the program and found, "Student Orchestra: *** Concertmistress — Ruby Hartman." Its final performance would be tomorrow evening. The name-robber would have to perform without him in the audience.

He lay flat on the blanket and, for an instant, felt that he was again entombed in plaster as he had been two decades earlier. He doubted the opening pieces would free his mind from the people who had taken possession of it — not only his wives, his pseudo-daughter, his untrustworthy client/friend and overbearing father-in-law, but also the swarm of Boston Brahmins (many in today's Tanglewood audience) who would soon be mocking him as the cuckolded interloper he was. But the music immediately absorbed him and he actually enjoyed the brightness of Mozart's Overture to *Idomeneo*, as well as the dreamlike evocation of tides in Debussy's *La Mer*. When the music stopped and the intermission chatter began, he remained still. If he were to be found, it would happen without his doing anything.

But he had been laying in the sun for close to an hour and, after a few minutes of watching a variety of bare legs flicker around him, he sat up. Humming to himself, he tried to recapture the mood of *La Mer* but, suddenly, without warning, his heart became a timpani playing forté and enveloping all around it.

Sibyl was on the cement path, a dozen feet away, staring at him. His stomach clenched, unclenched, clenched. He had to calm himself or he would collapse in front of her. If only the timpani would stop.

He was standing beside her on the path, although he had no recollection of getting up from the blanket. Why, he wondered, was she wearing this strange costume — the peasant skirt, the open-toed sandals, the square toenails — and why had she puffed out her face and padded her hips. But it was her. Take away some pounds and decades, brush the hair straight back, add a flute and here was the fifteen-year-old girl he had kissed on the boardwalk. Trade the flute for its case and redden her eyes, and she became the fury who had tried to split his skull.

She briefly smiled, then drew in her lips. "I was wondering whether you'd come." Her legs were slightly apart, her hands sturdy on her hips.

"Did you send me the *Jerusalem* . . .?"

Her lips were shaking and her face had turned gray. *Be kind*, Willa had urged, and he asked, "Are you all right?"

She took several deep breaths and looked at the ground. "Yes." She swallowed. "I have my opening speech prepared, but after twenty-one years I have to first say I'm sorry about that night. I didn't mean to hurt you so badly. I thought you were —"

"What would you have done if you did intend to hurt me? Save your apology." She flinched, but she deserved it. "Look, Sibyl, or whatever they call you in Hebrew —"

"Tsipora."

To his surprise, Paul remembered some Hebrew and Bible. "Look Tsipora, Little Bird, Moses' wife — your mother must love you having a Hebrew name — whatever you want, you're not going to get it if you harp on the past. What *do* you want?"

"Can't we have a civilized conversation?" she pleaded

"Like last time? No!"

With broad swipes of her forearm, she wiped her nose and then her eyes. The old Sibyl would have never done anything like that, but this was Tsipora.

Paul watched her eyes move up and down his body.

"Why are you studying me? Am I a tractor you're thinking of buying for your kibbutz?"

She smiled. "I haven't lived on a kibbutz in years. I live in Haifa above the music store I own. You look terrific, and I've gotten so heavy. Are you still swimming?"

"At least three times a week. I came in third in . . ." *Fishes swim.* "Can you just tell — "

"Is your wife here?"

For a moment, Paul didn't know who she meant. She was his wife, or she would have been if she hadn't betrayed him. "You know her name." Sibyl's new round face reddened as if he had slapped her. "We're separating." He couldn't believe what he had just said. Sibyl was the last person in the world he should be open with.

"I'm sorry," Sibyl said with seeming sincerity. "When did things start to go bad?"

Paul realized that he was staring at her low-necked blouse. "I didn't come here to talk about my marriage — either one of them. Can you just explain why your daughter's using that name?"

A white-haired woman with a cane in her hand and a brace on her leg was standing behind Sibyl on the path, waiting for her to move. The woman frowned at Sibyl and limped around her.

Sibyl covered her eyes with both hands. "I can't explain here."

The question Paul hadn't strung into words burst from his mouth. "Did you tell her she's my daughter?" He feared whatever she might answer.

"I'll tell you everything," Sibyl said, "but it's too complicated for a yes or no in the middle of ten thousand people." The audience was beginning to return to the Music Shed or to their blankets on the lawn. "There's a place we can talk during the Ninth — past the Hemlock Gardens before the Rehearsal Stage, a cottage they use for storage. I'll meet you at the bench in the back. I'll tell Rivka I'm going to sit with some people I know from Juilliard."

"Rivka?"

Sibyl arched her eyebrows. "She's never been easy. When she stopped being Yael, she gave herself new names — Ruby in America, Rivka in Israel. She's a dual citizen. She's always mad at one of her countries. Sometimes she's mad at both."

"You're not bringing her to the cottage, are you?"

Sibyl shook her head no. "I want to try and explain everything first. Make it easier." Her face and voice dropped. "And so maybe the two of you will hate me a little less, although I still think I did the right thing."

Be kind. "I'll be there."

She started towards the Music Shed, striding like a gladiator off to battle.

* * *

The cottage with its peaked roof had the shape of a summer bungalow on Sixty-ninth Street. The bench, with its wooden slats and iron arm rests, reminded him of the one on which they sat when they first kissed on the boardwalk. He wondered whether she had picked this spot to unnerve him. If so, she was succeeding.

He focused on what was in front of him — Route 183, and beyond it a few white buildings, a dirt road, endless trees, and a water tower atop the highest hill. It bore no resemblance to Rockaway. There were no people in sight. He spread his blanket out in front of the bench, and sat on it. Her story couldn't take more than fifteen minutes, and he'd leave as soon as she was through — miss the heavy traffic and fly from Boston to New York on tonight's last shuttle. In his head, he tried to refine the purchase offer that Concord Memory would make to the GD stockholders — what percent cash, what percent new stock — but he couldn't concentrate.

Applause came from beyond the cottage. The orchestra must be in place and the concertmaster making his entrance — unless it was a concertmistress, like whatever-the-hell her name is. The musicians tuned, and there was more applause; Seiji Ozawa was entering. Almost immediately, Beethoven's Ninth began. Ozawa wasn't wasting any time. Sibyl better get here soon.

Paul had heard Beethoven's Ninth a half dozen times at Tanglewood, and he had heard it often years earlier in their Morningside Heights apartment when Sibyl, then a Juilliard senior, was writing a paper on it. He had always been conscious of the fact that the composer was a German, but one who was a democrat, not a proto-Nazi. Still, portions of the piece were a Germanic call to action, and last year, sitting in the third row of the shed between Willa and Granville, he heard the boots of Obersturmführer Strummer coming to get him. "Are you all right?" Willa had whispered in his ear, and he had replied by smiling.

Strings and a few winds played softly — a gentle dawn. But temporary. The introduction would grow louder, become almost violent. Fortunately, Paul recalled, that was several minutes away — plenty of dawn for him to brace for the storm of sound ahead. He lay down on the blanket and, after barely a minute of dawn, Beethoven's storm broke, every instrument going at full force, the timpani and his heart booming together. The dawn was much shorter than he remembered. He shouldn't be lying alone at the periphery of Tanglewood. He should be at Johnny's side in the Berman conference room.

Sooner than Paul anticipated, Beethoven's dawn returned and, although his skin was clammy, he had survived the first storm. How could he, the first Jewish partner in Boston's most prestigious law firm, let himself be reduced to jelly by music when his cousins had survived Auschwitz and his stepfather had maintained his humanity before the hell of Olymp's furnaces? Strummer's boots be damned. But when would Sibyl get here?

The Ninth went back and forth between turmoil and calm. He became increasingly apprehensive about the climax to the fourth and final movement when the "Ode to Joy" would evoke a mass of swinging arms and striding legs marching in unison. Notwithstanding its title, the "Ode" summoned a Teutonic crusade. There could be only one explanation for her not being here: She was trying to soften him up so he would admit paternity and help finance her daughter's musical career

The third movement began with a contemplative, almost ethereal melody, and Paul stared at the sky. A large white cloud covered the sun. What does it look like? He asked himself. A fat goat, he answered, the one Abraham sacrificed in place of his son Isaac. And Isaac went on to marry Rebecca whose Hebrew name, Paul recalled, was Rivka. He stood up abruptly, folded the blanket once, and then let it drop to the ground; it would slow him up.

When he reached the front of the cottage, Sibyl was approaching him, her arms and legs moving as if "Ode to Joy" were playing in her head. She was perspiring.

"Where were you?" Paul growled.

She stopped and raised her chin and eyes mockingly. "You forgot your blanket."

"I assumed you weren't coming."

"Rivka insisted I meet some of her friends. This morning, she won't talk to me, and now she wants me by her side every second." Sibyl put her hand against his bare elbow, apparently without thinking. "Let's go to the back. We should both be sitting."

Paul pulled his arm away. "Sitting on a bench that could have come from the Rockaway Boardwalk? Behind a building that could've been a bungalow on Sixty-ninth Street? What are you setting the stage for?"

Sibyl looked directly at him. "Don't be crazy. That kind of bench is in every park in the world. And, except for a pointed roof, I see no resemblance to the Sixty-ninth Street bungalows."

Paul felt the music recede as he followed her to the back of the cottage. Good — he wanted to ignore Beethoven so he could focus on what she was saying. But he had to know when the "Ode to Joy" was approaching so he could get away before the Teutonic call and her terrible tale might combine to overwhelm him.

She sat at one end of the bench, he at the other, and for a while — perhaps ten seconds, perhaps two minutes — they listened to the Ninth in silence. Paul kept his mind empty for whatever was coming.

"She's your daughter."

He hadn't thought it, at least not in words, but he wasn't surprised to hear her say it. His mind was chaos — belief, disbelief, fear, joy, hope, fury, God knows what.

"So is every twenty-year-old in Tanglewood."

"You don't believe me."

"I wouldn't believe you if you said you were lying."

"You're treating it like a joke."

There was a sudden dissonant blast from the orchestra. Machine guns, Paul thought. "Some joke. It would be hard to think of anything less funny." He stood up.

Sibyl grabbed his wrist. "Please hear me out — lives are at stake."

"I owe her nothing," he said, but then sat back down.

The orchestra was repeating earlier themes — probably the beginning of the fourth movement. Paul pulled her fingers from his wrist. "Tell me why I should care about your daughter, and don't repeat I'm the father. Your lawyer played me a tape about that. He offered to produce a rabbit test showing you were pregnant in South America."

"You should care because she's a human being who wants to find out where she came from — to connect."

"Some of us want to disconnect." *Be kind.* "Is there some test to determine paternity?"

"Only to rule certain men out when there are rare blood types. That's not the case here. But because of the dates of the abortion and my periods, it could only be you."

"What about the dates of your . . ."

Inside Paul's head, words wrestled to come out — *your whoring, your being with someone, your you-know-what.* "I don't know what to call it," he finally said.

"Call it a . . . " She paused. "I was going to say *mistake*, but I love her too much."

Paul wanted to be kind but that could make him an even bigger fool. "How can you expect —"

"Do you want to make accusations or do you want to learn what happened?"

He looked straight ahead. "Start with your tape recording."

"I have to start with the abortion."

"You told my mother it was a miscarriage."

"I thought you didn't want to rehash the past."

"Start wherever you want."

He felt her slide away from him. "It was the worst experience of my life." She sounded sincere, but then so does any good con artist. "Not just the grubby doctor's grubby office or the three locks on the inside of his door — I kept counting them — or the fact that it was illegal, but I was . . ." She seemed to be speaking more to herself than to Paul. "I know people don't feel that way about abortion anymore, but this was 1958. And it was my baby, our baby. Reuben." Her voice was quivering. "Years later, when your mother was in Israel, she told me —"

"You met my mother in Israel?"

"Alone," Sibyl answered hurriedly. "If Yael were there, they both would have had questions. You should visit your mother —"

"Don't tell me should. Maybe I should have stayed in Boston today."

"I'm sorry." Sibyl blew her nose. "You don't need my shoulds. I don't need yours."

"Go ahead."

"I felt as if I had sold my soul — two souls — to play in an orchestra." She was crying softly. "It affected my playing — the *neshome* wasn't there."

Paul resolved to listen in silence until she was done or the approach of the Ninth's crescendo became unendurable.

Her story rambled between South America in late 1958 and Israel during the next twenty-one years. Dates and places blurred in Paul's mind. As with Asher, he was afraid to learn more than he could handle, and he was almost deliberately inattentive until she said that Reginald Smith added Wagner to the repertoire. "For the first time in my life, I'm thinking about being Jewish. Boris was the only one I could talk to especially after the Wagner brawl when he decided to accept his Judaism, whatever that means. He gave me *What the Jews Believe* to read — it's by some Reform rabbi — and also *Exodus* by Leon Uris."

She tugged on his shirt collar from behind. "You knew all about the religion and the struggle to create Israel. Why didn't you tell me?"

"Why didn't you ask?"

She released Paul's shirt. "We played our first Wagner, *Tristan and Isolde*, at a matinee. But it wasn't me playing, just my fingers and lungs." Paul turned towards her and saw that her body had sagged. He fought the urge to slide closer.

"Back in the hotel, I somehow ended up in the elevator with Reg alone." There was no expression on her face. "He said I didn't look happy playing Wagner. I don't remember what I said — something dumb I'm sure — and the next thing I knew he was trying to kiss me. I pushed him away, and he said that Dr. Vorse wouldn't object to a kiss." She laughed sadly to herself. "Dr. Vorse did the abortion."

She paused, as if waiting for Paul to speak, but he couldn't.

"I told him that if he touched me, I would push the elevator alarm button. We both got off at the same floor and turned different ways in the hall. I knew my job would be over when the tour was over. Over. After all I did to our marriage, to you, to our baby — over."

"And then?" Paul slid as far away from her on the bench as he could.

"And then I told Boris the whole thing at dinner. He said Reg would exploit any musician he didn't desperately need, and that he was thinking of moving to Israel to try to become more than just his genius cousin's faggot flunky. We went to his room for a drink. He cried. I cried. We tried to comfort each other, and all of a sudden — I don't know how it happened. Afterward, he was more upset than I was. Only once."

Paul had no idea of the supposed date and place. "Once?"

"Only once."

"Anybody else on the concert tour?"

"No. You don't realize how upset I was by the abortion and by that last awful night with you. It was years before I got involved with a man again. Dov and I were going to get married, but . . ."

"What happened?"

"He died in the Yom Kippur War."

Paul felt the air shoot from his lungs. While Dov gave his life for the Jewish people, Paul gave money in secret and said *Kaddish* in a synagogue where nobody knew him. His memories swirled like the ocean during a storm — his father, Reuben Hartman, volunteering to parachute behind Nazi lines; his five-year-old cousin, Reuben Hartman, whose face was eaten by rats; his cousin, Malke Hartman, a partisan hero. And now, Paul Hartman, frightened by Beethoven, terrified of Wagner, hiding who he was.

"How did Dov die?"

"Killed on the Golan. A musician, but a tank officer too. Every Israeli's at least two things. That's when I gave up performing and started to get fat."

"I'm sorry," Paul said, and immediately wondered whether Sibyl was playing the Jewish death card — the trump of trumps — to manipulate him, just as Asher had.

Manipulate him for what? he asked himself. Legitimacy (or the appearance of legitimacy) for her daughter? Money? Or, perhaps, she wanted to resume the romance of their youth. Whatever it was, he had to be wary.

Behind them, trumpets were calling to something and, as if they were calling to her, Sibyl sat erect, ready to advance with the music. "I was sure I was pregnant by Boris in South America. I knew the feeling. I wouldn't have an abortion. One is too many, and she was going to be born." Sibyl nodded in agreement with herself. "I was sure it was a girl too, and that if she was illegitimate, a *mamzer*, it would mean the destruction of four lives. So when I got to Kennedy — Idlewild then — I knew I had to get right to bed with you, so you and everybody else would think you were the father and she wouldn't be a *mamzer* even if we got divorced. I was afraid the baby would come out a red-headed giant, like Boris, but I had to take that chance." She shook her head. "Poor Boris."

"Try to stay on point," Paul said.

"It's painful to tell."

"And to listen."

Her head bobbed in agreement. "I knew in the airport something was terribly wrong with you, but I couldn't ask anything because I thought I was pregnant and we had to get it done. I just never imagined such a difficult night."

Beethoven's Teutonic finale was approaching. It would arrive when her story reached the nightmare of his near-impotency, his mother on the floor and Sibyl's assault upon his head. Paul shoved his hands in his pockets so he couldn't cover his ears.

"I went wild when I learned about . . . your cousins . . . your deceptions." Her breasts heaved. "Wilder when Lisette said you might be responsible for our father being in Havana . . . in jail. Over the edge . . . " She seemed close to sobbing. "And then, when I thought you were trying to choke your mother . . ." Her voice became calmer. "I think I now understand how you were in an impossible . . . ."

She gripped his arm. "For all that was good in our years together, look me in the eyes."

He did. Her old sparkle wasn't there, but the pure brown was, along with a sadness and weariness new to him. "I'm sorry," she said, and they both dropped their eyes.

He became aware of the music again. The two main vocal themes had come together — women answered by men. The Ninth was universal, not German, nothing to be afraid of. *Be kind —* but where would that lead?

"Now you look me in the eye," he told her. She did, and this time he saw only wariness. "You said in the tape that you had a rabbit test showing you were pregnant in Brazil."

"You don't know Brazil." She smiled to herself. "Or how much I wanted you out of my life. I did think I was pregnant when I got back, but I hadn't seen a doctor yet. If you had asked an obstetrician some obvious questions, told him the abortion date, you would have learned that it was almost impossible for me to become pregnant in South America so soon after the abortion, and absolutely impossible for a Brazilian rabbit test to show anything."

"Sorry," Paul said, "but I didn't have an obstetrician at the time — only an army of orthopedists who hated me for refusing to see my mother."

"You research everything. I was sure you'd research this."

"Maybe I wasn't that interested in becoming an expert on how my wife . . ." He stopped in mid-sentence. Any ending would be unkind and could terminate their talk before he had an opportunity to protect his father's name.

"The tape and the forged rabbit test report — written in Portuguese, even . . ." Sibyl paused. "They were Boris's idea, but I went along because I knew that if you thought you were the father, especially if it was a boy . . . " Her voice drifted off.

Paul looked up. Traffic was crawling on Route 183. "Please get done."

"Boris and I wanted to start a fresh life in Israel with my baby."

"A fresh life," Paul heard himself mutter.

"A fresh life," Sibyl snapped back. "The same kind of fresh life you tried to build a few months after us, except we moved to the new Jewish state and you moved to old WASP Boston. My oh-so-Jewish ex-husband became a Turner. My mother couldn't believe it. She would have sacrificed her two children — me first — just to have your new mother-in-law say hello to her."

True — nasty, but true. "Bullshit! You go back and forth about who the father's supposed to be. How can I believe anything you say?"

"I don't expect you to believe me. Look at her and you'll know."

"That's *narishkeit.*"

"Remember your parents' wedding picture? Better, the picture of your mother wheeling you in a carriage in Czechoslovakia?" Her hands moved with her words — Tsipora from Haifa, not Sibyl from Neponsit. "Look at Rivka and compare. Taller, hair straighter — but one face. And her all-consuming ambition — it could only be your genes."

A child who was as beautiful as his mother, who shared his drive and would be there for him in three years, when he turned fifty. As close to a pure Reuben as possible.

A baritone thundered the "Ode to Joy" theme. "Can I see her without meeting her?"

"Where are you parked?"

"South Lot."

"Stand by the Lion Gate, and we'll walk toward you," Sibyl said. "After you see her, if you want me to introduce you, cross your arms. If they're not crossed, we'll walk by. But on Tuesday, she's coming to see you no matter what you say or want."

"What does she know? Tell me quickly. The traffic is getting —"

"Boris broke down and told her the basics — that he's not her father and you are. She figured out the first part years ago. And while she was in El Paso, she decided to change her name to Ruby Hartman, to join her real family, she says."

"I have to go." He got up from the bench and walked away without looking at her.

"Will you wait at the Lion Gate?"

"Yes." He kept walking.

"Can I get hold of you at the office tomorrow?"

"Yes."

Less than an hour with her, and the lies were flowing again.

* * *

The chorus made its final entrance. It would get louder and faster as it advanced to the crescendo. He had to move quickly, but if he ran, he'd be conspicuous.

When he reached the Lion Gate, the music erupted into a mushroom cloud of sound. A hundred voices, a hundred instruments, the "Ode to Joy" consumed everything around him.

Not everything. Somewhere near the patch of trees he had just passed, a husky female voice was battling to be heard through the music. *"Abba! Abba!"* — one of the first words he had learned in Hebrew School while his own *Abba* was alive — Father! Father!

"Abba! Abba!" He stopped. She was less than two swimming-pool lengths away, holding her skirt above her knees and running too quickly for him to examine her face. She was not nearly as thin as the Sibyl from Rockaway, not nearly as heavy as the one from Israel. He turned towards the parking lot and ran. She would never find him in the rows of cars.

"Abba! Abba. Zot ani Rivka. Rivka." Paul remembered *ani* — I, me. *"Tichakeh li."*

He heard his father above Beethoven: *Body straight; only move your head. Mouth above water, air in. Mouth below, air out.* Who had taught his father? And whom would Paul teach?

"Abba! Abba!" He had gone out on the jetty but saw the fedora and hadn't jumped.

"Abba! Zot ani Rivka." The Beethoven chorus joined her. It *was* an ode to joy. He didn't understand the words, but Asher fit the music to life: *Take turns on each other's shoulders.* Max elaborated: *Get air from the top of the boxcar.* Then Jack: *Shovel, keep shoveling — but don't lose your humanity.* Finally, his father: *Opportunities!*

"Abba, it's me. Ruby. Ruby!" English with a Hebrew accent. Beethoven's crescendo of crescendos filled the air. "Your daughter. Please, allow me to speak with you. Ruby!"

While Paul ran, the music stopped and the audience erupted into cheers — almost a continuation of "Ode to Joy." Maybe she *would* look like his mother.

"Abba. Papa!" Nobody had ever before called him that. "It's me, Rivka. Ruby."

Paul stopped and turned toward the voice and the cheers. Ruby, Rivka — what difference did it make? — the girl calling him *Abba* was barely 30 yards away. Her smile seemed familiar.

"Zot ani Ruby," she said again.

His response came to him instinctively — *Zot ani Abba* — but that would be irrevocable and he couldn't speak. Still, he couldn't stop his arms from opening halfway.

They hugged awkwardly and Paul quickly dropped his arms. He was conscious of her breasts pressing against him.

They stepped back from each other, and she said breathlessly, "I must hurry. We are rehearsing for tomorrow's student concert, and I may not be late." She smiled broadly and then, suddenly, her mouth opened into a gape, and she took another step back. "You are here." She seemed surprised. "I am here." Her lips parted, then closed, then parted and closed several more times. "I plan so much, and now I don't know what to say."

He looked over her head at the crowd heading towards the parking lots. Soon, someone he knew would see the two of them talking. "I must hurry too."

"Ima says, like me, you rush all the time." Her smile was electric. "I will come see you in Boston on Tuesday."

"I may be in New York."

"I will go wherever you are." She took both of his hands. Her fingertips were hard. "New York — so you can't come to the concert tomorrow." She shrugged. "No difference — a student orchestra. You'll hear me with better musicians. I'll call you tomorrow."

"I may be —"

"Don't worry. I'll find you." She kissed him quickly on the lips, and said, "Tuesday." She turned and, waving as she dashed, ran into the exiting crowd. *"Shalom, Abba!"*

She had to be his daughter, hurrying off to work like that. *Shalom Rivka*, he thought of shouting, but he could no longer see her.

CHAPTER 20

Tuesday — two days from now.

He had to see her because they could be father and daughter and, without the other, each would be incomplete.

He couldn't see her because, whether she was his daughter or not, she would bring all of it back.

He couldn't name her in his thoughts: Ruby? Rivka? Yael? The Name Robber? Sibyl's *mamzer*? No — too callous. Sibyl's daughter? No — implies *mamzer*. My daughter? Not yet, maybe never. Each name bore an implication he didn't want to consider.

As soon as he was on the Mass Turnpike, he realized there was only one way to deal with the young woman he couldn't name: Leave for Hong Kong on Monday.

Then a name came to him: *Sheyn Meydel* — Yiddish for Lovely Girl. It seemed to fit the exuberant violinist who had pursued him while shouting "*Abba.*"

But not so fast. In addition to being a talented musician, she might be a talented actress after his money. And, if she were a *Sheyn Meydel*, how could he justify fleeing from her? He settled on plain *Meydel* — no adjective and no implications — because he had to settle on something, and he reaffirmed his decision to leave the U.S. tomorrow.

He stopped at the Howard Johnson's near Exit 10 and called Johnny at the Berman office.

"It's Paul."

"Thank God. I need you. Come to New York now, and leave for Hong Kong tomorrow. We have to raise the bulk of the Asian money in a hurry since many of my relatives are leaving for Singapore next week to celebrate my *po-po's*, my grandmother's, ninetieth birthday. You're the one to do it. A lot of those guys have dealt with you and, every time they did, they made a lot of money. They think you're pretty smart and honest for a *gweilo*."

Johnny was saying precisely what Paul wanted to hear. It was too good to be true, but this was no time for suspicions.

"Also," Johnny continued, "if we're going to get the jump on GD, key decisions have to be made in the next twenty-four hours, and I want you in on these decisions. The Berman lawyers are smart, and our investment bankers make sharks look like goldfish, but none of them know my business like you do. And all they care about is their fee."

Johnny had arranged everything. A private plane would fly Paul from wherever he was to New York; Johnny's chauffeur would drive Paul's car to Boston; a first class seat had been reserved on Pan Am Flight 4 leaving New York Monday evening; a suite had been booked at the Mandarin Oriental Hotel in Hong Kong Central; Johnny's New York tailor would supply Paul with a complete wardrobe (including two suits) until he could shop in Hong Kong; Concord's treasurer would pick up Paul's passport and bring it to New York. Once in Hong Kong, Johnny's cousin Wang would make sure Paul had everything he might need, from a swimming pool for exercise to an expatriate American lawyer to do research and draft documents. Johnny had even arranged for bilingual business cards to be printed in raised lettering as soon as Paul chose a title for himself. Paul picked "Senior Vice President – Special Projects." It sounded important without being specific.

Paul could no longer control his suspicions. Johnny, with the help of his detectives, probably knew about the *Meydel* and was trying to ensure that her sudden appearance didn't diminish the Number One Coolie's ardor for the takeover battle. Perhaps the detectives had been snooping on Paul since 1973 (or earlier), when Johnny engineered the affair with Ella Ko.

"One more thing," Johnny said. "Lana's coming down tonight also — to make sure everything's coordinated."

Paul flinched. His suspicions about Johnny's manipulations became a certainty. Contrary to what he had assumed, Lana Abramov, Concord's Russian-born Director of Administration, might not have been suddenly attracted to him when Ella returned to Taiwan. Like Ella, Lana might have been carrying out a delicate assignment from her boss — keeping Paul a contented member of the Concord team by giving him what Willa couldn't give.

"Let Lana come tomorrow. I don't need help in complicating my private life."

"Okay. I just don't want you brooding about whatever's upsetting you."

"Let's talk about financing," Paul replied. "Barron's reported yesterday — I read it on the shuttle from Washington — that Granville brought a libel suit against Keene National Bank on Friday. Keene might welcome the idea of helping to finance his upstart adversaries."

"Keep thinking, baby. That's why I put up with you."

* * *

Alone in Berman's conference room on Monday, the packed luggage provided by Johnny's tailor in the corner, his passport in his new jacket, a phone in front of him, Paul asked himself whom he had to call before leaving. For a moment, he had trouble breathing. The answer might be nobody.

He certainly couldn't call either of the women he had married or the *Meydel*. They were the reasons he was leaving today. He couldn't call his mother — they spoke only on their respective birthdays, neither of them saying anything that might upset the other. Today, a call couldn't last thirty seconds without one of them mentioning the *Meydel*.

He couldn't call Jack or anyone else from his Rockaway life. Paul had moved beyond them all too successfully, and had made himself no more than an unpleasant memory.

Lana had said goodbye to him a few minutes earlier in the hallway outside the conference room when she whispered in his ear, "Thanks for not seeing me last night. Alex and I are going to give it another try — this time in Chicago. Good luck in everything. *Everything!*" She stepped into the ladies room before Paul could respond.

That left two people, and he really did have to speak to them — Marie Lupo, his secretary, and Chip. But before calling, he had to stop feeling sorry for himself.

He surveyed the conference room. The walls were hung with pictures of Native Americans. What did American Indians have to do with Berman lawyers or takeover battles, except for the unintended irony that the Indians, themselves, were taken over? At least the oil paintings in the smaller and darker B&K conference room — eighteenth century Boston and the firm's nineteenth century founders — had some connection to some of the firm's lawyers (not including Paul). But why compare? Why think of anything except the takeover and the challenges of Hong Kong?

The conference table before him was huge, light, and shaped like a surfboard. He imagined himself lying naked on it as it rose from its marble supports, sliced through the wall-to-wall window, and glided with him to wherever it would go. Then he picked up the phone.

* * *

When he told her that he had resigned from the firm and would be working for Concord Memory for a while, Marie gasped. "Take me with you," she pleaded. "You're the nicest boss I ever had. You came to my mother's funeral. You sent flowers when Agnes gave the valedictorian speech at Saint Rose." Paul could recall none of this; he thought her daughter's name was Rose.

"Wherever I end up, I'd love it if you came with me," Paul replied, "but that may not be with Concord or in Boston. As soon as anything is firm, you'll be the first to know."

"I appreciate it."

"For the next few days, only Mr. Cheung will know where I am. As soon as things settle down, I'll give you a number, but keep it to yourself. Above all, if anyone says she's my ex-wife or my daughter, tell her nothing."

"Ex-wife? You mean — I heard a rumor, but I don't gossip. Daughter?"

"She says she's my daughter. It's too much to explain."

"I don't want you to explain."

"Thanks, Marie."

* * *

Now, the call to Chip, his half-brother-in-law, his best friend, perhaps his only friend. The call could be awkward, even painful, but things might come up while he was in Hong Kong and, more important, the prospect of total isolation was too frightening.

Although Paul and Chip spoke often and trusted each other totally, they almost always avoided, or circled around, emotionally charged matters. While in the hospital, Paul told Chip the entire story of Max's diamonds — from seeing 53927 across the bedroom until seeing his own legs encased in plaster. Chip had replied with reassuring but neutral words, and neither of them ever again mentioned the subject.

Eight years later, when they went with their wives to Bermuda to celebrate Paul's election to partnership in B&K and Chip's tenure in Brown's Chemistry Department, Chip told Paul on the beach that he suspected Nancy was having an affair with a justice of the Rhode Island Supreme Court. "Just like my own father had an affair when he was first appointed to the Massachusetts Supreme Court," Chip had said. Paul had wanted to respond in some meaningful and helpful way, but he was shaken by Chip's candor, and he couldn't get beyond platitudes — "What about a marriage counselor?" In the airport, the next day, Chip asked him to "forget what I said on the beach — it will work out." That Sunday, they went to a Patriots football game together, got drunk on beer, and had a terrific time.

Paul whispered into the telephone even though he was all alone in the Berman conference room. He was going away, he told Chip. He couldn't say where or for how long, and he would be mailing Chip a power of attorney to act for him "if Willa needed papers signed for our investments or if she wanted to sell the brownstone or anything else."

"What!" Chip exclaimed. "I'm both overwhelmed and flattered, but I know enough not to ask for details."

"I have no plans beyond finishing the job I've undertaken. The big secret, which is probably a bit silly, may not last very long."

"Willa told me about the *Jerusalem Post* article. She thought you would want her to."

"I doubt she's my daughter." Paul kept his voice even and soft.

"What's her name?" Chip asked.

The predictable question took Paul by surprise. The temporary name he had chosen — *Meydel* — and those he had considered revealed unflattering sides of him. "That's complicated," he said, and then felt an urge to talk about Willa. Not just to change the subject, but because Chip, who had brought Willa into his life, might help him come to grips with Willa's startling decision.

But how much did Chip know? And how could Paul tell him that his sister was a lesbian and much of their marriage a pretense? Paul's hands shook slightly, but he had to try.

"Did Willa ever tell you that . . . tell you she was . . . ?"

"A lesbian?"

Paul nodded his head, then realized Chip couldn't see him.

Chip answered the question left hanging. "I don't think she ever thought about it until Diane moved back to Boston last summer. The world is changing."

Chip's answer shocked Paul. Johnny and his detectives knew of Willa's affair with Diane in 1973, before Diane left for New Mexico. Willa's husband and brother had been kept in the dark — or had kept themselves in the dark — until the two women were ready for a public announcement. But no useful purpose would be served by filling Chip in.

Paul chuckled. "The world is changing. Why can't I change with it?"

"You're one of the changers — the Jackie Robinson of the Boston legal establishment. One of my doctoral students is outside."

"I'll call when I get a chance. But I just want to . . . " Paul's throat began to dry. "I owe Willa a lot. When we . . . " Again, he found it hard to speak.

"You've been a good husband to her. She was close to a breakdown when you met. Wherever you're going, whatever you're doing, come home soon."

Home? Where's that?

* * *

Paul sat on the upper level of the 747 listening to the pilot's pre-takeoff announcement. "We'll be aloft in a few moments for Pan Am's non-stop service from JFK to Hong Kong. We'll take off to the east, bank to the south, and then fly northwest, giving you a breathtaking view of Manhattan on this glorious summer afternoon."

It wasn't until then that Paul realized precisely where he was. To his right, thirty-or-so yards beyond the tarmac on which his plane sat, was Jamaica Bay and, beyond it, Rockaway peninsula. He tried to bury himself in GD's recent filings with the Securities & Exchange Commission but, when the plane rose and banked, he looked down at the ground.

Like a gnarled finger poking into the blue-green Atlantic, the peninsula emerged from Long Island, and ended twelve miles to the west, at Breezy Point, where Jews couldn't live. All of it glistened in the late August light. He only had a few moments before the climbing 747 would leave it behind.

The beach was the easiest to identify — twelve miles of white, spotted with bathers catching the end-of-day sun. The railroad trestle and two bridges over the bay — how many times had crossed over them? His last crossing had been over the Marine Parkway Bridge, the nearest to Breezy Point, on the Thanksgiving Day Asher died. There were apartment houses which hadn't existed then, as well as large fields of gray just before the beach, where white bungalows and summer rooming houses had once stood. He recalled a *New York Post* article his mother had sent him: Miles of Rockaway beach blocks had been demolished to make way for an urban renewal that had never been funded.

One landmark still stood out as the plane rose and turned — the six-story smokestack next to P.S. 42 on Sixty-sixth Street, the elementary school he attended for more years than Columbia and Harvard combined. With the smokestack as a reference, and Rockaway growing smaller by the second, he counted jetties to the east — two per street — and picked out the one from which Max jumped in 1948 and where Paul, himself, stood in 1958, ready to follow his cousin until he saw the floating fedora. He next tried to identify the beach at Sixty-ninth Street where he swam with Daddy on their last day, but the jetties were now blurred with distance, and Rockaway was almost gone from view. Next time he would look there first. No! There would never be a next time.

He was sure of only two things: He didn't want to reach Hong Kong and he didn't want to return. As for the *Meydel*, he wanted to find the right name for her, and this, he realized, would require a degree of serenity he did not now possess. For a while — at least until Hong Kong was behind him — he would try not to think of her.

CHAPTER 21

As promised, Wang provided a pool, and on evenings when his meetings with potential investors were over for the day and Johnny's New York takeover team was getting a few hours' sleep, Paul swam laps at the Ladies' Recreation Club, half way up Victoria Peak. The water was a needed break from not only the meetings, but also from the hours Paul spent editing documents sent by telex or by DHL's new overnight delivery service and from the intense strategy phone calls — whether the offer to GD stockholders should be revised, or a lawsuit brought, or a press release issued, or a dozen other things — that often pulled him from sleep before dawn.

Towards the end of his third week in Asia, as he stood at the side of the pool, Paul noticed a young woman with an apparently perfect body and a clearly perfect stroke swimming in the far lane. He was reluctant to swim next to her because they might end up racing, which would wind him before he completed his forty minutes, but the only open lane was alongside her.

She was swimming away from him when he dove in and not moving as fast as he had thought. He didn't want to race but, once in the water, his adrenalin took command and he paced his stroke so as to catch her halfway back. He did, and then swam faster so as to pass her. She kept up with him. He swam still faster and, again, she matched his pace. He didn't have to prove he was the fastest one in the pool, particularly when he wasn't, so he slowed up. And there she was, still head-to-head. He slowed up some more and she flipped her body over and now matched him with her backstroke. He closed his eyes, told himself he was swimming anchor in a neck-and-neck freestyle relay, and gave it all he had. When he reached the shallow end, he would leave the pool — forget the forty minutes. Johnny had called at 2:00 a.m. and he would take a nap to recover. But when he got to the end, she was there, breathing calmly.

"Your stroke's not smooth enough." Her accent, strange but not unfamiliar, made Paul uneasy. She was a bathing beauty in miniature, reminding him of the Barbie doll Chip's daughter held on her lap when he last visited Providence. She pulled off her bathing cap, revealing a non-

Barbie-like mixture of brown, blonde and silver hair, defying anyone to guess her age.

"Let's get dressed and have a drink," Paul suggested. No time for delay. Johnny or Wang or a half dozen other people could call at any moment.

"Finish your laps first. I watched you yesterday, and I'm sure you do at least forty minutes. I'll be in the Terrace Lounge."

"I'm Paul Hartman." He held his hand out above the water, but she didn't take it.

"You're Johnny Cheung's Boston lawyer." She licked the pool water from her lips. Like Sibyl behind her grandmother's screen door, she knew all about him.

"What's your name?"

"Ann Weiss."

"Weiss?"

"A German Jew meets a Czech Jew in the Ladies' Recreation Club pool in Hong Kong. It sounds like the beginning of an anti-Semitic joke."

"I'll cut back to thirty-five minutes." Paul pushed off towards the deep end.

* * *

As Paul approached her table in the Terrace Lounge, Ann stood and held out her hand. It was much smaller than Sibyl's, even smaller than his mother's, and Max's engagement ring would have fit her without having to be enlarged.

She wore a low-cut, seemingly silk blouse and a gold necklace with a dangling pearl directing his eyes downward toward what he was sure would be a perfect cleavage. As they each sat down, he was aware that, depending on their respective postures, he might be able to see that cleavage, and he focused on her face. It was lovely, but seemed almost sculpted — high cheek bones and straight eyebrows that framed her small grey eyes; a slightly jutted curved chin, and a small undramatic nose which Paul could only think of as *goyishe*. Her light skin was smooth and tight. Had she had plastic surgery? *Stop*, he chastised himself. Why, when he felt so completely alone, was he looking for imperfections in an attractive Jewish woman he had just met? He should live for the moment, because it might be all they had.

"What else do you know about me?" he asked her.

"Only what Danny Lee told me yesterday when we sat right here and watched you swim. How you were two rooms apart in the Columbia freshman dorm. How he would have flunked out without your critiquing his papers and coaching him through calculus. And how he envied you for having such a pretty and talented girl friend."

"Let's leave her out of it."

"I'll leave out stuff also." She smiled. Her teeth could have been an ad for toothpaste.

"He said the friendship cooled because of the Korean War — that you got angry when he said President Truman committed treason against America and Free China when he wouldn't let General McArthur use the atomic bomb."

"I remember it all vaguely," Paul said. He would keep to himself, as he always had, his clear memory of that awful weekend in 1958, when Maurice Pine was desperate for money to pay his mob debts and Paul had toyed with the idea of asking Danny for a loan.

"I thought Danny worked in Singapore."

"He did so well there that they brought him back to run the main bank here. When he told me about you, I asked him to introduce us, but he said Johnny would doubt your loyalty if you got involved with the Lees. The families have been feuding since before the British came."

Paul resolved to get together with Danny — but not today.

"How did you end up here?" he asked.

"I was about to ask the same question."

"But I asked first," Paul rejoined. He wanted time to think about what to hold back. But her story so gripped him that he thought of nothing except the little girl who had evolved into this captivating woman and whose life, like his, began with fleeing from the Nazis — only in opposite directions.

While Paul's family fled to the west in 1933, shortly after his birth in Czechoslovakia, Ann's family fled to the east in 1938, shortly after her birth in Berlin. Unlike Paul's father, Ann's father denied everything happening outside his comfortable sitting room — "'They're not the real Germany,' he insisted." — until, on *Kristallnacht*, the synagogue across the street was burned to the ground and a brick crashed through their sitting room window. Clutching her tiny baby and pulling her husband by his worsted lapel, Ann's mother bribed their way onto a boat for Shanghai — a city where seventeen-thousand North European Jews (mostly Germans) were tolerated by the Japanese occupiers and assisted by the Committee for the Assistance of European Jewish Refugees and by a well-settled Iraqi-Jewish community.

The Weiss Family had it better than most European Jews in Shanghai, because Ann's father was a dentist in the Japanese Army dispensary. They left Shanghai when the Japanese did, afraid that their neighbors, both Jewish and Chinese, considered them collaborators. Until they reached Hong Kong, Ann had never heard a word of English. There, she saw who was in control, and she devoted herself to learning the language. "It turned out I was talented at languages," she said matter-of-factly, "but I could never get the accent right."

That was it. Her accent was part German, part British, and part Asian — a mongrel composite, like Asher's. But Paul wouldn't tell her about Asher — the full story could end everything before they left the table.

"Your turn," Ann said.

Paul pictured Asher, and said: "I'll skip the Holocaust, because I don't want to lie, and I can't tell the truth. I'm between lives, but not yet between wives. My present wife . . . the second . . ." Paul's throat itched. "I can't talk about that yet. It's over. My first wife . . . That's complicated."

She put her hand on his wrist. "Talk about it when you're ready. Any children?"

Paul was perspiring. "Complicated. I keep saying that. Maybe a daughter. I just can't believe anything my first wife says. Do you have any children?"

"A son in Singapore. Eric pays him not to see me."

"Eric?"

"My husband. We're getting divorced. He's in England now. He says he needs a bigger country — and a bigger woman."

Her hand was like a small bird, a *tsipora.* "He's crazy," Paul said.

"We're second cousins. We were both named Weiss, and everyone assumed we'd get married."

A thousand years ago, Paul recalled, Willa had said something similar about her marriage to Will. He had to be careful. Honest talk about either of his wives or about the *Meydel* could make him less appealing to Ann. But how could he start out with anything less than candor? Look what that led to with Sibyl.

"The fire clinched it," Ann continued. "When I was eighteen, my face became disfigured in a kitchen fire — bad burns and broken bones — and Eric's father sent me to London for reconstructive surgery. He paid everything. You can spot some of the signs if you study my face closely as you did when we first sat down." She looked at Paul directly and arched her eyebrows.

Paul felt himself blushing, but managed to say, "You're hard not to look at — and I mean that in a good way."

"I hope you do. I work at it." Ann nodded.

"Anyway, sending me wasn't an act of spontaneous generosity. The fire was in Eric's parents' apartment, and it was partly his mother's fault. Besides, his father was grateful because my father had gotten him digitalis from the Japanese Army dispensary for his heart condition — a risky thing to do during the occupation."

"Family members have to help each other," Paul said and, again, realized he was blushing. How could he toss her this banal homily — what Bernie had said when he demanded that Paul tell Maurice the outcome of the *Olymp* case?

Ann, to his relief, ignored it. "We were married soon after I returned from London, when Eric approved my modified face. Everything was fine until my Chinese became fluent and I became a local celebrity for organizing a mostly Chinese water ballet troupe. I knew I shouldn't marry him, but who else was there if I wanted Jewish children?"

A Jewish child with Ann — the prospect left Paul almost breathless. But what could he say? He wasn't ready to be as open as she seemed, and another platitude would be two too many.

"Dinner?" he proposed, and Ann replied, "There's this wonderful floating restaurant, Mother Fish — no menu, just whatever the chef caught that day. Only four tables, but they'll put in one more for us."

After dinner, they went to Ann's apartment. Paul was afraid that if they went to his hotel suite, the phone would ring and he would pick it up.

He woke while Ann was asleep next to him, and looked at her in wonderment. Plastic surgery or not, her face was, quite simply, beautiful. How had he gotten so lucky?

Johnny? he asked himself. The possibility shook him. Perhaps Ann was another inducement from Johnny to keep him laboring faithfully. She was replacing Lana who had replaced Ella whom Johnny had snuck into Paul's life when the Number One Coolie was distressed by Israel's Yom Kippur War and his own incomplete marriage.

He would go back to the Mandarin and call Johnny. No, he would shake Ann awake and ask her point blank. Neither. If he asked the question, this glorious night might never be repeated. He went to the window, looked down on the Hong Kong harbor, calmed himself, and decided to do nothing.

Fortunately, Ann resolved the issue a few hours later when, fully dressed in a modest suit, she woke Paul and said, "One thing before I go to the office. If you're thinking of tying your career to Johnny, let me introduce you to some people who really know him, including his ex-wife. You'll find out it's a terrible idea."

Hooray! Paul wanted to shout. She wasn't carrying out an assignment for Johnny. But he couldn't even hint at his concern, and said, "I've known him for sixteen years."

"You haven't known him in Chinese."

Paul didn't know what she meant, and he didn't care. They arranged to meet that evening.

* * *

Ann made him feel as if he was physically in the Far East. Before her, he often saw himself as a moviegoer transported from his seat into and out of scenes of Hong Kong showing on the screen. He was engaged in complex business transactions, but they rarely seemed real.

He attended seemingly endless meetings with endless relatives of Johnny, along with their bankers and partners, but Wang did the bulk of the talking. After Paul made his presentations and Wang translated, the conversations were mostly in Chinese. Although Paul knew he had to stay alert to furnish details or respond to doubts, his mind was back in his Rockaway bedroom listening to the Yiddish of the adults as it seeped in from the kitchen. Occasionally, when his head numbed, he would whisper in Wang's ear and demand to know what was being discussed. Although Wang resented this, the other men in the room usually welcomed Paul back into the conversation.

Even when the Asian men in the room — only men — were fluent in English, Wang would sometimes translate. "Why does he do that?" Paul asked Ann.

"Wang's a *sha qua*, a *dumkopf.* I hate using German, but that's the best word. He's making himself seem important by keeping the white man, the *gweilo*, outside."

"Why does Johnny put up with him?"

"You don't understand China."

When Paul looked out the window of whatever Hong Kong Central skyscraper he was in and saw the streets below, with their rickshaws, paper lanterns and smoking food carts, and the crowds of people wearing everything from bowlers and business suits to coolie hats and black pajamas, the scene seemed more of a mechanized diorama than actual city life. When he raised his eyes past the streets, across Victoria Bay towards New Kowloon, the number and variety of boats — junks, san-pans, yachts, Coast Guard cutters and God-knows-what — were unreal; if they were jammed in Jamaica Bay, port to starboard, bow to stern, there wouldn't be enough space to hold them.

Now, with Ann, Paul began to feel as if he could belong. She seemed to know everybody — the businessmen he dealt with, waiters, street vendors, traffic cops, even some rickshaw pullers. One ancient rickshaw man who had helped Ann's father fix up his first Hong Kong dental office on Des Voeux Road, and who had been doing odd jobs for the family ever since, offered to pull them to Ann's apartment on Victoria Peak. "Half price," he said, "so you can tell Dr. Weiss that old man Sohn is still strong."

Paul politely declined. "I can't have a human skeleton cart me around like he's a pony," he said to Ann. Then he told her about Jack's *Befreite Olymp Sklaven* picture.

Ann's face went from smiling to somber. "You may be right. I always thought of them as part of the Hong Kong atmosphere, but they're people."

Walking with Ann in the crowded streets, Paul became even more aware of the spices and cooking smoke that overwhelmed the sea air. "Do you know what Hong Kong means in English?" Ann asked him.

"Fragrant Harbor," Paul answered. "It's the first sentence in my Berlitz guide book. My entire Chinese vocabulary."

"It doesn't have to be that way. Chinese is no harder to learn than Hebrew."

Paul put his arm around her, but said nothing.

* * *

A week after he met Ann, when Paul's work in the Far East seemed close to done, Johnny called him at Ann's apartment. It was two in the morning.

"Keene Federal just pulled out. Granville made peace with them, and that was part of the deal. Bottom line: We're at least twenty million short. Do you have any ideas?"

Paul sat up, naked, and put his feet on the floor. Ann, also awake, propped herself against the bed backboard. As always, she was wearing boys pajamas, which made her seem even more feminine.

"How did you know where I was?"

"We've milked the Cheung cow dry and, without a replacement for Keene, our tender offer can collapse."

"Are you having your detectives follow me? The way they followed Granville? If so, I quit right now."

"Don't be ridiculous. You're the only person I trust. Half of Hong Kong sees Ann and you at the Ladies' Recreation Club pool and at restaurants nobody can get into. I'm worried about you, Paul. Wang says that at a meeting at Freeman's you just got up from the table and stared out the window. He had to call your name three times to get your attention."

Paul couldn't recall the incident. He gave little thought to the impression he made on the men in the conference rooms. Why should he when he rarely felt himself actually with them?

"Wang's a useless pain in the butt. Can't we find somebody more professional?"

"He's my cousin," Johnny answered. "What do you know about Ann Weiss?"

"I know she wants to go back to sleep."

"Very funny. Eric Weiss, her husband, probably understands the Hong Kong financial world as well as any *gweilo* can, and she's not far behind him. See if she has any ideas."

"Do you trust her?" Paul turned towards Ann, and she smiled at him.

"Not entirely, but I'm desperate, and she's discreet."

"How much is Johnny short?" Ann asked as soon as Paul put the phone down. Although they had made love twice that night, her serious expression aroused him.

"At least twenty, and it will have to come from Asia. Any ideas?"

"Eric's doing to me here what your father-in-law's doing to Johnny in America—cutting me off from my usual backers. But maybe . . ."

She paused and, almost simultaneously, they each said "Danny Lee," Paul as a question, Ann as a suggestion.

It was a long shot, Ann told him. "The feud between the families is bitter. After World War Two, they each accused the other of collaborating with the Japanese, and they both might be right. Way beyond my father's filling Japanese teeth. Let me see the financials."

Paul fished papers from his briefcase, and started to explain, but Ann waved no. "Just let me read." After about ten minutes, she handed them back. "You do nice work. What's Johnny's phone number?"

"I'll call him from the living room," Paul said.

Ann waved no again. "We'll speak Chinese. There are things I can say better in that language, and some history I'd rather you not know just yet. Let me have the number."

She sat in the brocaded easy chair in front of the drawn blinds and dialed. "Johnny? Ann. Long time." She switched to Chinese and her voice seemed to rise an octave.

Paul let himself stew while Ann's Chinese came faster and grew angrier. Once more, Paul's mind traveled to Rockaway and to sitting in his bedroom while the adults in the kitchen isolated him with a foreign language. Suddenly, she switched to English. "Okay. That makes sense. You tell Paul, and he'll call Danny."

She held the phone out, but now it was Paul's turn to wave her way. "If I'm going to be the messenger boy, just give me the message so I can deliver it and leave."

Ann's face dropped. "We'll call back," she said into the receiver, and hung up. She stood and started to unbutton her pajama top.

"Don't get undressed." Paul forced himself to lower his voice. "I'm sick of being the provincial American who's excluded by language."

Ann crumpled into the easy chair. She took up less than half of it. "We didn't have to speak Chinese," she said apologetically, but then sat up straight. "No, I did have to speak Chinese — to let you know what I should have let Eric know when we were kids — that I refuse to be any man's little helper, his concubine. I may look like a doll, but I am not. That's why when you tried to show me up in the pool, I had to make it clear, even before you knew my name, that I wasn't anybody's toy."

Paul realized that he was standing in his underwear gaping at her. "Whew!" he finally said. "I don't know whether you're apologizing or chewing me out, but I won't complain any more about people speaking Chinese in Hong Kong. Just promise me that if we talk to Danny together, it will be in English."

"Speak to him without me. He's grateful to you, and you have an attractive proposal."

"I'll call him in the morning. Now go back to unbuttoning your pajamas."

* * *

Thirty-eight hours later, Danny signed a thirty-million dollar loan commitment on behalf of his family's bank. Concord now had enough cash to offer to buy a majority of GD's shares directly from GD's stockholders. Paul telexed the news to Johnny at four p.m. Hong Kong time, and Johnny called him minutes later.

"Congratulations," he said. "Remember my gratitude when you send your bill."

But Johnny, being Johnny, had more on his agenda. He wanted Paul to fly immediately to New York. "The war with GD is far from over. The Berman lawyers are good, but Lewis Berman isn't available except to pat me on the head, and Mike Cole doesn't have the little extra that you and Lew do. Come back and take full charge of the legal front. The Berman boys will swallow their pride for a big fee; they're *shylocks*."

Shylocks! Paul clenched his teeth and allowed silence to convey his anger. Finally, he spoke. "I'm going to stay put a while." He would let the question of *What next?* lie fallow along with the *Meydel's* parentage.

Johnny wouldn't accept Paul's decision. He used temptation ("Name your fee."); appeals to ego ("Show everybody you're up there with Berman."); guilt ("How can you walk out on me when I need you so badly?"); and, finally, mockery ("Are you being pussy-whipped?").

Paul hung up. The next day, he moved into Ann's apartment at the top of Victoria Peak, had all calls routed through the concierge, and told him to put through no calls from America.

* * *

The trip to Hong Kong had been a great success. He had completed a challenging job from twelve time zones away and raised over five hundred million dollars. On top of that, he had played a central role in devising strategy and preparing key documents. He had met and was living with a captivating woman in an exciting city and, together, they had reached peaks of passion he hadn't experienced since the early days of his marriage to Sibyl — a woman who had empathized with him as he told her the full story of Max's diamonds and the *Meydel*, and who seemed to believe sincerely that, except for his fleeing the *Meydel* without a word, he had done nothing wrong — a woman with whom he could live a life of love.

Then why did he feel anxious and empty, as if he hadn't lived a full life? The answer was all-too-simple: He felt that he hadn't lived a full life because that was the fact. From striving to be valedictorian in his P.S. 42 graduating class, through learning how to climb stairs with two casts, through persuading Danny Lee to lend the last thirty million dollars, his life had been driven by his father's message on their last day together — *Opportunities* — and by a relentless To-Do list: work and determination, then more work and determination, with some breaks for sex and swimming.

But never spontaneous pleasure — never just letting things happen. He owed himself some true time off before focusing on his next job and the right name for the *Meydel*. He literally wrote a new two-item To-Do list: "Hong Kong and Ann."

There had to be limits: Nothing illegal (except he might try marijuana), and nothing he couldn't report to Ann (no exceptions). He couldn't endanger what was so good.

He bought a Fodor's travel guide, which was more detailed than Berlitz, and set out to see every site mentioned — gardens, parks, museums, temples, docks, beaches, even tanneries. But most of all, he walked without a clear destination through the British colony's mixture of East and West. He marveled at the coolies who looked like coolies and carried loads no human being could carry, and at the Japanese businessmen who seemed to see nobody in the crowds that thronged around them. As he walked, he would buy food from street vendors without asking what it was and, no matter what he had eaten, he would stop for a large lunch, including beer and wine, at whatever Asian or European restaurant he happened upon. He would hop on and off trams almost at random or take hand-driven san-pan water taxis, instructing the drivers by hand signals to meander around Victoria Harbor or through the floating homes off of Aberdeen. On several mornings, he got off the water taxi in Aberdeen to swim in the China Sea and loll on the beach. When lost or tired, he would take a taxi, but never a rickshaw.

After lunch, he would wander some more, return to Ann's apartment for a drink and a nap, or swim at the Ladies Recreation Club. His swims became less frequent once he realized that, even with Ann's lessons and his improved stroke, he would never match her speed. He stopped swimming completely after some teenagers sitting across from him in the sauna laughed at his nascent, but noticeable, potbelly.

He and Ann would usually have a gourmet dinner, often at Mother Fish or another floating restaurant, followed on most nights by some kind of public entertainment. Paul wanted to go beyond Western concerts and theatre and, with Ann as his cultural guide, he tried everything — Chinese opera, lion dances, puppet shows, and nightclubs of all types. On several weekends, they went "junking," taking an all-day cruise on a lavish yacht owned by Danny or one of his relatives; Paul was usually tipsy by lunch and asleep in a deck chair by dusk.

On days that Ann worked late, he took the Star Ferry across Victoria Bay to Kowloon. Bells would ring and Chinese deck hands in blue sailor suits would screech out unintelligible directions as the green-and-white ferry plowed forward, jostling boats of all sizes and shapes in its wake. Throughout the seven-minute trip, his fellow passengers, almost all Chinese and wearing every conceivable form of Western and Eastern dress, seemed primed to charge from deck to shore. For the first time in his memory, Paul had no urge to join the rush — he wasn't striving. Instead, he sat serenely near the bow, pleased that he had no destination and could exit with ease when the mood struck him.

One cloudy afternoon, he decided to explore Kowloon without a guidebook and to walk up Nathan Road, the main street, past the Peninsula Hotel, until he found something different — the real China. But even well beyond the Peninsula, Nathan Road remained too Western and commercial, and he turned left at Boundary Street simply because of its name. After one more turn onto a street that seemed to have no name, Paul felt totally removed from the excitement of Hong Kong Island. But this couldn't be what he was looking for — it was too dull. He saw nothing but two long rows of almost identical five- and six-story apartment buildings with a few nondescript shops at street level. The buildings were mostly brownish-gray cement and, to a lesser degree, grayish-brown cement. The clothes of the people in the non-terribly crowded street were equally dull. The only bright color was the red tee-shirt of a little boy who wore nothing else and who pointed at Paul — the sole *gweilo* in sight — until an elderly woman pulled him into one of the buildings.

Paul walked away from Boundary Street looking for something different but, despite trying three more streets, it was more of the same. He decided to go back to Boundary Street, and realized he now had no idea where it or he was. He'd have to find someone who spoke English.

A moped approached, the first motorized vehicle he had seen on this particular street. The driver, a thin young Chinese man (perhaps even a teenager), wore a western suit and, to Paul's amazement, a fedora with the brim bent over his forehead.

The moped stopped with a screech, and the young man jumped off at Paul's side The hair showing below his fedora was dyed blood red — both clownish and frightening. His suit was shiny and broad-striped, the jacket hanging to his mid-thighs — a zoot suit from the forties, a mobster from a high school production of *Guys and Dolls*. Paul's elbows pulled back and he squinted uneasily at the unexpected sight.

"Can I help you?" the young man asked.

"No, I'm just walking around," Paul answered, as evenly as he could manage.

"No American just walks around Yoman. I think you want something and you're lost. You're surprised I have American accent?"

Paul nodded.

"I worked for U.S. Army in Tokyo, translating Chinese newspapers — for Major Hugh Jackson. You can trust me. Not a slicky boy."

Paul looked over his shoulder. The street had gotten more crowded.

"You don't have to look how to get away. With me, you're safe. I'll take you back to Nathan Street on my moped. To the Peninsula Hotel if you want."

Paul turned to the man. Was his smile inviting or sinister? "No, I like to walk."

"Okay, you're the boss. You know what you like." He pointed to a dusty street-level shop about twenty yards away with large baskets of grain lined up outside it. A young woman stood in the doorway wearing high heels and a raincoat. Even from this distance, he could see that her eyelashes curved down and up like a fishhook — as frightening as the young man's blood red hair, and not at all clownish.

"You like that?" the man asked. The woman opened her raincoat. She wore nothing underneath.

Paul turned away. "No, no, that's not why I came here."

"You can look. No harm. You want a date?" The man paused for an answer which Paul did not give. "You know why you came here? Maybe you like a young boy? Chinese, Korean, English possible. No American today; maybe tomorrow. All very clean."

"No." Paul wanted to leave, but he stayed put. "I'm not . . . I have a girlfriend — a lady friend."

"Chinese girl?"

For a moment Paul had to think. "Small like Chinese. She speaks Cantonese fluently."

The young man beamed and ran his hands through his hair. "Then I help you make a party. Something you never did before." He pointed at the buildings around them. "Not here. A nice place on Victoria Peak. Luxury. You know Victoria Peak?"

"I'm staying there." Paul wished he could shut himself up.

"Perfect! I should have realized. We have clients there. Important people."

Paul held his hands up, palms facing out. "Stop!"

"No, no, nothing in a hurry," the young man said, soothingly, while shaking his head from side to side. "First you talk to your lady friend — the *gwei-mul* who speaks Cantonese. I can make a party special for just you two plus the pretty girl in the raincoat if you want. She can bring her twin sister—something really special. After, you and your girlfriend will love each other even better." The young man held out a business card conjured, it seemed, from the air. Paul put it in his back pocket.

"We bring food and drinks — free. And, come close." He beckoned, and Paul complied. "I can get you any kind of drugs. High quality. Where are you staying on Victoria Peak?"

Paul spun around and walked away as fast as he could.

"No, no," the man shouted from behind him. "Don't go that way. Dangerous street for a *gweilo*. You'll get hurt." He sounded alarmed.

Paul halted and the man was immediately in front of him. He looked concerned. "I'll take you to a taxi. Maybe I rushed too much, but you seemed like a nice man who wanted to try new things. I have a better idea. Will you listen?"

The streets seemed to point in every direction. "What's your idea?"

The man spoke rapidly as if he were afraid Paul would leave again. "If you have time without your girlfriend, I make a party for just three people — you, the girl in the raincoat, Lilly, and her sister, Lola. Nobody will know — an experiment. Then, if you like it, we can make another party and you can bring your girlfriend. Tonight would be perfect because regular clients, an ambassador from South America and his wife, very cultural people, had to go home suddenly and just cancelled. Don't eat before because we'll give you the best Chinese dinner you ever had. Plum wine they make in my village — you never taste anything like that."

Paul wanted to walk away, but in which direction should he go? "Let me think about it."

"I'll walk you to a taxi. Five minutes on safe street. And we won't talk. I see you don't like pressure talk."

The young man kept his word; he led Paul to a street he hadn't seen before where three cabs were lined up in front of a building that seemed to be a bank. As he opened the taxi door for Paul, he said, "I apologize if I made you uncomfortable but, if you want a party tonight, you have to let me know soon. Lola is going away tomorrow, and other clients might call."

Why not? Paul asked himself when the taxi turned on Nathan Road — particularly tonight when Ann would be staying at the hospital with her mother who had undergone cataract surgery that morning. He had promised himself a brief period of spontaneous pleasure, and two

Chinese girls at once, an erotic but harmless experiment, would be no more than that. How would they do it? He felt an erection starting.

He certainly couldn't report the orgy to Ann. But neither of them had made a commitment, and it would only be this once. God knows her sexual history. She had invited him to her apartment on the night they met. She — alone, or with her husband, or with some group Paul couldn't imagine — might have gone to special parties.

He had been a good boy long enough: Faithful to Sibyl while she was unfaithful to him; faithful to frigid Willa while she was doing whatever she did with Diane; and, since Ella Ko, he had practiced serial monogamy or something close to it. Never a party for three or anything else out of the ordinary.

He told the driver that his plans had changed and to let him off at the Peninsula. There, he went directly to the lobby phone booth to call the boy pimp and arrange a party of three—Lola, Lilly, and himself—as soon as possible, with high quality marijuana. (He hoped he wouldn't be asked to define "high quality.") He closed the phone booth door tightly and took the card from his pocket. One of the sides was printed in English:

373-322
Personal Guide
Hong Kong Beyond the Tour Books
Ma Ho-Yan ("Max")

Max! He must be hallucinating. He turned the card to the Chinese side, then back to the English — "Max." He knew that Chinese who deal with English speakers often adopt English nicknames — Johnny, Danny. But why this name?

Was it a coincidence or an omen? It made no difference; Paul couldn't possibly call the Chinese Max. That would return the Czech Max to the center of his mind and add a fourth to the party. *Shanda, shame,* the First Max would condemn. *For this, I left you diamonds.*

In "Pinocchio," boys who buttered their bread on both sides and played jacks instead of studying turned into donkeys. In America, a pot-bellied lawyer who wallowed in women would not command respect in conference rooms. Paul went to the men's room, ripped the new Max's card into small pieces, and flushed it down the toilet, just as he had dropped cousin Max's note in the ocean. From there, he went to the Ladies' Recreation Club where he swam for sixty minutes and then ate a dinner of cottage cheese and fruit salad.

Still, he was not yet ready to focus on *What next?* or the *Meydel*. When Ann called in the morning to report that she had arranged full-time nursing care for her mother, Paul proposed they take a trip. "Show me the real China," he said.

"The real China," Ann laughed. "There are a hundred, maybe five hundred, real Chinas, but they all have one thing in common: Even though the Cultural Revolution is over, it's a police state. Let me call a friend in Beijing and see what can be arranged. I'll be home by noon."

But at noon, as she was about to make the call, the concierge delivered two envelopes. One was a telex from Maria: "Call me immediately. There are some calls you should know about. One is urgent." It was midnight in Boston, but Paul reluctantly picked up the telephone.

"The urgent call is from, Professor Story," Maria reported. "He said to call, no matter the time." The others messages were from Johnny ("He said you should see yesterday's Asian edition of the *Wall Street Journal*. The takeover battle is over — thanks to you, a wonderful outcome."); John Bradford ("I'm sure B&K wants you back. So do I."); and Lewis Berman ("I bet he's going to offer you a job in New York. Please don't take it.")

He told Ann he would call Chip now. The others could wait.

Chip got right to the point: "Willa and Diane bought a house in Devon. They're having a housewarming next Saturday — more of a coming out party. Kind of gutsy of them, I think."

Paul suspected what was coming next, and dropped himself onto the long couch in Ann's living room, while Chip continued. "Willa would like you to be there. She feels funny asking you directly, so I volunteered. I know it won't be easy, but if you can publicly accept what they're doing — or, at least, act as if you do — it will . . . I can't spell it out."

Paul knew he had to attend. Willa and Chip had literally helped him into a wheelchair when he left the hospital in two casts, and they opened doors in Boston that he wouldn't have dared to knock at by himself. "Who else will be there?"

"Lots of people you know. You'll be asked what you're doing — your plans."

"I'm weighing options."

"By which you mean none of your fucking business."

"I never heard you say that word before."

"The world is changing. My mother, our mother, will be there. She's trying to convince herself that what Willa's done is for the best, but she has a way to go. If you came it would help. Granville, I don't know. Can I tell you something confidentially?"

"You don't have to ask."

"My mother told Granville she would leave him if he didn't come. That would be terrible because, in their own ways, they like each other. Granville's a vast improvement over her first husband, my father, but that wouldn't take much. He never said that he would or wouldn't come. But I think he would if you go. He'd just be following your noble example."

"I don't know if it's nobility or Jewish guilt, or just gratitude to Willa, but I'll be there."

"I'm not surprised."

Paul visualized Chip's kind smile. "Should I anticipate any surprises?"

"Priscilla Webster — Judge Webster's former wife, Puck."

Paul sat up straight. "He won't be there, will he?"

"No one's seen him in years. Willa has the job Priscilla retired from."

"Anything else I should know?

"Yes. I used your power of attorney to sell the Beacon Hill town house with Willa. A good price, but I assume you don't want details."

Now, he didn't even have a home address. "Not yet."

"If you need a place to stay, Nancy's parents' house in Newport is empty. You could have complete privacy or our company whenever you feel like talking. You can walk on the beach and relive your Rockaway childhood."

"Thanks, but the last thing I want to do is relive Rockaway. Besides, sand is the only thing Rockaway and Newport have in common. Marie will send you my itinerary."

* * *

Paul opened the bedroom door. Ann was sitting on the bed naked, with a Chinese newspaper in her lap. "There was an envelope for me too," she said. "I can't go away for a while, and I'll tell you why. But first things first." She threw the newspaper to the floor.

When they were through, they lay on their backs, sweaty and silent, until Ann said, "You start." They pulled the sheet over themselves and turned towards each other.

Paul told her about his talk with Chip, and Ann agreed he should go back for the party. "I'll miss you, but she helped you when you needed her and, if you go, it will solve two problems."

"Tell me."

"My mother doesn't like the nurse, and I may have to spend some time there."

"What's the second problem?"

She closed her eyes. "Gregory, my son. He sent a telegram. He's coming to visit from Singapore in two days. I haven't seen him in nearly a year — his father's doing — and I don't know what to tell him about you ... about us. He's very prudish when it comes to my behavior, although not when it comes to his father's or his own. The Chinese are centuries behind in their views of women, and the most Chinese of all are the *gweilos* who were born here."

Paul leaned over and kissed her eyes. "I'll move out tomorrow, but stay in Hong Kong till the last minute so I can meet Gregory and — "

To Paul's relief, Ann interrupted him. "Let's not talk about Gregory until you and I have ... We've never discussed the future."

"We can start now."

Paul put his hands on her shoulders, and felt her tremble under the sheet. A little bird, a *tsipora*. "Let's get dressed and talk in the living room," he said.

* * *

They sat on the couch, several feet from each other, and Ann began: "I can see you have no talent for debauchery. You've got to be doing something positive and challenging, and Hong Kong is the place ..."

Ann seemed transformed. Now, she was more than a *tsipora* — she was a hummingbird and bumblebee combined. Focused and determined, she moved closer to Paul on the sofa and pitched the virtues of Hong Kong — why it was made for him, really for them together. With a magnificent view of Hong Kong over her shoulder, she argued her case: Paul should be an American lawyer in Hong Kong, working with her to represent both American companies who wanted to do business in China and wealthy Chinese who wanted to invest in America. She reached into recent history, to Nixon's 1972 visit to China, and then began to chronicle the American companies who had already established outposts. She grew more excited as she spoke, and stroked Paul's forearms. He shivered.

"Ideally, I'd like us to be business partners — equals, not like Eric who always tried to keep me down. Just imagine the opportunities here, with our complementary skills and backgrounds, especially if you learn some Cantonese. I know a wonderful teacher for you." She ran her fingernails along the hairs of his arm. "And whether we end up being a permanent couple, an occasional fling or past lovers, we'd have a lot of fun and make a lot of money."

Opportunities, she was saying to him on Victoria Peak, just as Paul's own father had said *opportunities* to him by the Atlantic. But his father wasn't talking about amassing wealth. "Each of us already has a lot of money," Paul told her, "and I might get more depending on how the takeover ends."

"Your idea of a *lot* and mine aren't the same. Besides, I just enjoy making money as an end in itself. Outside of being in bed with you, it's the most fun there is."

Paul opened his arms to her but she pulled herself back from him. "I'm not giving you the whole story." She raised her chin enough to remind Paul that, like her nose, it had been reshaped. "The partnership I want is more than business and bed."

Suddenly, she was standing. "Hong Kong isn't just commerce and hedonism. There are real families leading real lives. An active Jewish community for over a hundred years."

Now her ebullient analysis of business opportunities gave way to a determined cataloguing of Jewish organizations and activities: Hadassah, Israel Bond Drives, Young Judea, Introduction to Talmud, — she could have been describing the Rockaway of his youth or the synagogue outside of Boston where he secretly said *Kaddish*. He had a flash of insight: *Jews survive, because they keep doing the same thing every place.* He was appalled by his thought. It was *they*, not *we*.

"I like the idea of going back to organized Judaism," he told her. "That's how *we* survive." He stressed the *we*, but her mind was elsewhere.

"There's something else," she said, and he heard hesitation in her voice. She looked down for a moment, and then directly at him. "I'm forty-two, and the odds are against it but, strangely enough, the doctor thinks my size might help. If you come back and you agree, I want to throw away the pills. Maybe this time I'll get motherhood right."

The moment called for *Yes!* — to settle everything and sire a real Reuben or Ruby. But reason pleaded for time. And the *Meydel* . . .

Ann rescued him from trying to complete the thought: "Don't say anything before you leave. I've sprung a lot, but I've been thinking about it since Danny told me about you. Before we even met, you sounded like somebody I might like to connect with permanently. And when you couldn't stop staring at me at the Ladies Recreation Club — I'm used to being stared at, but not with such appreciation — and seemed so overwhelmed by my pajamas, I was pretty sure." Ann looked down at him. "I was sure when you refused to ride in the rickshaw, and I became absolutely positive today when you immediately agreed to go back for Willa's party."

Paul started to stand, but Ann shoved him back onto the couch. "Right now I want to call my travel agent and make sure you get the highest priority."

"Tell her to get me back to Hong Kong as quickly as possible."

* * *

He telexed Chip to accept the invitation to stay at his in-law's house in Newport. That meant flying to Providence, and there were two ways to get there — Hong Kong directly to JFK (with a refueling stopover in Los Angeles) where he would change planes for Providence, or Hong Kong to San Francisco where he would change planes for Chicago where he would change planes for Providence by way of Cleveland and Philadelphia. He chose the longer route. Flying into JFK might mean flying over Rockaway.

CHAPTER 22

Paul woke with a start and, instinctively, threw his forearms across his eyes: They were driving on the wrong side of the road! At any second, they would crash head-on into a car going in the opposite direction. "Driver!" he shouted, and then realized where he was — in a Hong Kong taxi en route to Kai Tak Airport, away from Ann and towards Willa's awful party. As in England, which would continue to administer Hong Kong until 1997, cars drove on the left side of the road. He would never adapt to it. *Wrong!* He would adapt easily because that would be part of his new life with Ann.

He dreaded the flights awaiting him — hours upon hours with no work to occupy him. He'd be too agitated to sleep or read, and would be at the mercy of uncontrollable thoughts concerning Ann, the *Meydel*, and the "RESIDENCE" question on the U.S. Customs Form.

If he could think like a lawyer, the right decisions would become clear. One issue at a time, and Ann before the *Meydel*. Ann was awaiting his answer to her proposals, and would interpret delay as ambivalence. He had already rejected the *Meydel's* pleas for a father/daughter relationship by fleeing from her; some further passage of time shouldn't aggravate the pain he had caused or the hatred she must feel towards him.

Once on the plane, he would list the reasons for and against a commitment to Ann and, with her, to Hong Kong. Two reasons *Against* occurred to him in the cab: One — Everybody in Hong Kong drove on the wrong side of the road. Two — He might bump into Hong Kong Max, along with Lilly and Lola, on their way to a special party in Ann's apartment.

As his cab approached the terminal, he could come up with only one reason *For* — her boys pajamas. Who needs reasoning beyond that?

He knew he wasn't thinking and wouldn't be able to think on the plane. But so what! Thinking was irrelevant. His parents, despite money and health problems, had a good and loving marriage. Had either of them made a list when his mother cried at his father's *bar mitzvah*? They were in love, and there was nothing to think about. He knew from the past four weeks (it seemed so much longer) that life with Ann could be wonderful

— every bit of him felt it. He knew from more decades than he cared to estimate that life without her would be a void filled mostly with work.

From the check-in counter, he went directly to the phone in the Clipper Lounge to call Ann and tell her yes to everything — Hong Kong business partnership, domesticity, Cantonese lessons, and a diligent, yet joyous, effort to have a child. He would do her two better — marriage as soon as they were both divorced, and an adopted child if she didn't conceive. But he didn't lift the phone from its cradle. Gregory, who was due to arrive home in a half hour, might be early, and Ann wanted to be the first to tell her son about Paul. If Paul's call frustrated her wishes, she'd think him no better than Eric — another man determined to dominate her.

Thirteen hours later, after Ann had ample opportunity to tell Gregory whatever she wished to say about Paul, he called from the San Francisco Airport Clipper Lounge.

"It's Paul, darling. I know it's early there, but I have something important to tell you."

"I have something, too."

As Paul said, "My answer," Ann said, "Eric called," and Paul stopped speaking.

"He wants to get together again, and he made all the right promises. Gregory, like an emissary, laid the groundwork. If I say yes, he'll go back to school in Hong Kong."

Paul tried to speak calmly. "Do you believe Eric's promises?"

"Do I believe him?" Ann paused. "He'll try, but it won't last." She made a sound Paul couldn't decipher. "I have more memories of him from when I was young than I have memories of my own parents. I remember him on the boat from Germany even though I was an infant and we were on different boats. The sad fact is we're part of each other."

"What did you tell him?" Paul asked, then wished he could take it back. He was interrogating her instead of telling her that he loved her and they would build a future, not be ensnared in the past.

"I told him I'd think about it." She seemed to choke back a sob. "If you were in Hong Kong, I might have said no, but you—"

"You told me to go!" Paul looked around to see if anyone had heard him, but saw only a dozing matron at the other end of the lounge. What time was it? What day?

"You didn't have to listen to me!" Ann replied with a frightening vehemence.

"I'm coming right back."

After a brief silence, Ann said, "I'm sorry, darling. You should go to the party. It's the right thing."

Paul was relieved — they had each said "darling."

"It's on Saturday and I'll come back on the first plane — that night if there's a flight. I won't return any of the calls I told you about."

"That's crazy. Why burn bridges before you know where they lead?" Her tone was now crisper and less emotional, more British and business-like. "Each of them is a powerhouse and, if we become partners in Hong Kong, each could help us get business."

He, too, must be more business-like. "When is Eric arriving?"

"Not for at least ten days. He has an arbitration in Geneva."

"I'll be there before him."

* * *

Devon was a bit beyond the peak of its New England fall foliage. Half the leaves above its wide streets and on the surrounding Berkshire hills were gone, and most of the remainder were closer to brown than to red or gold. But the autumn blaze was easy to picture, and the small commons across from Willa's new clapboard house was almost as green as the Tanglewood lawn had been when he encountered the *Meydel*.

He would do what he had to do — get through today so he could keep his appointments in New York (burn no bridges) and beat Eric to Hong Kong.

The handwritten sign taped to the front door, just below the wooden American eagle, was bordered by small drawings of red hearts and tiny photos of the heads of two little girls. Paul recognized Willa. The other, a round-cheeked cutie-pie, bore no resemblance to the stolid fifty-year-old who Willa apparently loved. The sign announced:

WELCOME TO OUR HOME
Just Walk In
W & D

Paul pushed the door open. Would he be met by all-too-jovial slaps on the shoulder, or embarrassed faces turning away from him? The foyer was empty and, in the room beyond, a few narrow-shouldered men stood with their backs to him at the far side of a table holding platters of food. The central platter featured a large pink ham with a white bone running through it and cloves scattered over its surface. A carving knife and serving fork each leaned against its sides, like crossed swords at a military wedding.

He would not eat it.

After a lifetime of consuming *treyf*, and years of keeping his prayers and donations secret, he would affirm his Judaism. The gracious WASPs at Willa's party who had tried to treat him as a Turner wouldn't notice what he did or didn't eat but, for Paul, it was a personal statement — a new beginning.

The outside door opened and closed behind him and, seconds later, he felt familiar long fingers on the back of his neck. Why was Willa coming in from the outside? "Thank you, Paul," she whispered in his ear. He turned around, and she kissed him quickly on the cheek. "I'm glad you're here," she said with enthusiasm. "Your support means a lot to us. You helped increase the turnout and I just got back from ordering more champagne." She patted him on the shoulder. "Don't look so lost."

"Not lost," Paul replied. "Only trying to orient myself."

She wore a long, billowing skirt and a peasant blouse — a new type of outfit for her, but similar to what Sibyl had worn at Tanglewood. Ann would never dress like that.

"I'll orient you. You're at my new home with my new partner, and I appreciate it." She took his arm, and led him into the dining room. The men standing by the table nodded at him. Willa stopped and again whispered in Paul's ear, "When my father learned you were coming, he said he'd come."

"Is he here?"

"Almost," Willa sighed. "He tripped over a curb yesterday, and now he's home recovering from wrist surgery. He sent flowers and he called to—"

"A Freudian slip," Paul interjected.

"That's what Diane said."

They both stood there, hands at their sides, in silence. Several passing guests uttered greetings. Then, Willa said, "I understand you have a girlfriend."

Paul nodded. He didn't want to talk to Willa about anything except the divorce. They had to agree on the basic terms quickly so Ann could appreciate his determination to marry her.

"She's lucky," Willa added. "What's she like?"

"She's . . . " Paul faltered. A candid answer would have to include Ann's passion.

"She's nice. Different. A German Jew . . ."

Willa raised her head and hand to greet someone walking behind Paul, and he stopped speaking. This wasn't the moment for a refugee story.

When he again had her attention, Paul said, "I have meetings in New York — what I might do when I become an adult again. From there, I'm going right back to Hong Kong."

"Meetings with whom?" Willa dropped her voice. "I'm truly interested."

Paul had an urge to touch her, but that might revive unhappy memories.

"Three meetings on Tuesday," he said. "First, Brad. He's my friend again, just like you predicted." They each nodded. "We're having breakfast with two London solicitors about B&K opening an office in Hong Kong."

"And?" Willa asked. "I bet the other two meetings are with Johnny and Lew Berman."

She was right, and Paul realized he didn't want to discuss either man with Willa. Johnny and Lew were *nouveau riche* upstarts — neither of them Christian, one not even Caucasian — who were pushing aside the establishment WASPs, beating the *goyim* at their own game. To Willa, they were the "other."

"You're right," he told Willa, "but we should talk about us. Can we get together at Chip's on Monday to work out the divorce details? Neutral ground with someone we both trust, but you should have a lawyer. Everything should be amicable, but there are a lot of matters to resolve."

"Okay. Are you going to see your daughter before you leave? I'm sure you know she's performing in New York tomorrow night."

The *Meydel!* "Is that why you and Chip got me to come back?" Paul felt the sting of his words, but Willa shouldn't have sprung this on him. He looked at the buffet table, and saw that the ham was nearly gone.

Willa stood at her full height — at least as tall as him. Her eyes burned in anger. "I'm not going to tell Chip you said that." She barely moved her lips. "This party's about Diane and me. It's not about you and your tumultuous marriage to . . ." She didn't complete the sentence.

Paul felt his face drop. "I'm sorry. It's just—"

"I don't know anything about Sibyl's daughter," Willa said more kindly. "Priscilla Webster says she's wonderful and that you're the father. You deserve a wonderful daughter."

Paul doubted he deserved anything wonderful. The ghost of Asher wouldn't think so. Nor would Jack, nor his mother, nor more people than he cared to recall.

"I don't know if I'm up to seeing her. If I want to make a life in Hong Kong, I've got to get back there soon. And if I want to remarry and have a child, which we might like to do, you and I have to get divorced. But I do want to know what's going on."

Willa told him she knew only what Priscilla had related to her earlier in the day — that the Galilee String Quartet was performing at Town Hall tomorrow and returning to Israel on Monday. "Priscilla heard them at Smith earlier this week," Willa continued. "She thought they played beautifully, especially Ruby. . . . Now, don't make a face. That's the name she uses and everybody accepts. . . . Priscilla can tell you what's going on, and she's here."

Paul lost any will to resist, and he followed Willa through the dining room and living room into a small sitting room. Several people nodded as they passed — Brad Bradford, the somber pianist who sometimes accompanied Willa when she played at St. Mark's Episcopal Church, two young men he knew from someplace who were self-consciously holding hands.

Three women were sitting on a Victorian couch. He recognized two of them — Diane and Willa's mother, Meg Turner, the woman he must no longer think of as his mother-in-law. The third, a thin old lady with a thick blue vein running from the back of her right wrist to her elbow, had to be who she was supposed to be — Judge Webster's wife, twenty years older than when he had last seen her, but looking at least a decade beyond that, thanks to the weariness around her eyes. Something terrible had happened to her.

Diane and Willa's mother were on their feet as soon as Willa left him at the couch. Diane bent over and spoke into his ear. She smelled of burning leaves. "You're a *mensh*."

It was the first Yiddish word ever spoken to him by a Brahmin. He wondered if it was a compliment or a reminder that he did not belong among them?

Willa's mother patted the back of his hand and whispered into his other ear. "Thanks for coming, Paul. It can't be easy for you. Willa and I will come up with an excuse for your leaving early." She smiled slightly. "Take a look at Granville's flowers in the foyer before you go."

Now he was sitting alone with Priscilla Webster on the couch. Nobody was within ten feet of them, but she spoke softly.

"You look wonderful," Priscilla said. Her eyes closed halfway.

"Am I the father?" The question just burst out.

Her eyes closed all the way. "Sibyl says you are."

"What did she tell you in 1959, before she moved to Israel?"

The sensation of ice, so cold it burned, enveloped his fingers. She was touching him.

"Nineteen-fifty-nine? So much has happened since then." She released his hand. "Sibyl and I were both so upset. Me with my two sons in India and their father in a perpetual rage. Sibyl, afraid she had permanently crippled you, not knowing what to do about the baby or where to go. She told me something about her periods and rabbit tests — New York, South America, dates. Very confusing. I didn't try to understand. I don't think she even knew then what was true and what wasn't. But I believe what she tells me now. And Ruby . . ." She took a deep breath. "They visited me several times, and I went to see them in Israel once. Interesting country — I hope it survives. Ruby stayed with me last week when the quartet played at Smith. . . . Nobody else could be her father."

They sat without speaking for some long seconds, and Paul thought nothing. Finally, Priscilla spoke. "You better get some ham before it's gone."

"I don't eat ham anymore."

"I baked . . ." She looked at him and seemed to grasp the import of what he had said. "Don't you want a daughter? Someone so . . . straightforward . . . talented."

"That's not an easy—"

"It is easy."

How had she gotten so thin? "I'm sorry about your sons."

"I never talk about it, and I always think about it."

Her face seemed to shut down. After a long moment she opened her eyes. "Everybody knows Robbie died in India and Clay disappeared, but I told only two people the details." She sounded as if the words were scratching her throat. "Not details. I told them what I know, which is far from everything. I told my sister and Sibyl. I don't know why, but, from the day we met in Vermont, Sibyl and I had a special feeling for each other."

Sibyl? Paul asked himself. Was there a side to her he had never appreciated?

"Clay was in India — he hadn't written in months — and Robbie was on parole in McLean Hospital. Clayton couldn't stand the thought of a Stag Weekend without a son there to shoot his guns with, so he tried to get Chip to get you to go. I told him not to, but he never paid attention to me."

Paul didn't want to recall that terrible time, but Priscilla was recounting what she had told only to her sister and to Sibyl. She seemed thin enough to belong in *Befreite Olymp Sklaven* picture. *Absurd*, Paul told himself — grouping a dowager with Jewish male slaves. But when they are all emaciated, don't the differences between them pale? He had to pay careful attention.

Priscilla continued: "Then, all of a sudden, Robbie was in India, too. Very serious — a parole violation. Clayton went crazy. No son of mine is going to blah blah. I pleaded with him to think about the boys, not his he-man pride, but he had this lunatic plan."

Priscilla's description of the plan was disjointed, but Paul was able to piece the parts together. First, Judge Webster hired an international firm of private detectives who located the sons in Varanasi, India, a holy city on the Ganges. Then, he began to pull strings, call in favors and, in India, spread cash.

As soon as he learned where his sons were, he met with Attorney General Victor Ohms, a friend from the New York law firm where they had both worked, and Ohms agreed to have the United States Department of Justice commence a proceeding in India to extradite Robbie to Massachusetts as a fugitive from justice and a parole violator. Within a few days after that meeting, the necessary papers were prepared, Robbie was arrested by the Varanasi police, and the extradition proceeding was brought. If the proceeding succeeded, as Judge Webster fully expected, Robbie would end up in a Massachusetts jail where a judge, who was a friend of Chip's father, would commit him to McLean until he was "cured," meaning, Priscilla explained, "until he would obey his father."

Priscilla shrugged. "The old boys' network moved full steam ahead and Clayton went to India to supervise the whole thing." Her voice dropped. "It worked perfectly until they found Robbie dead in his cell." She seemed shocked by what she had said. "Clayton went into a stupor, and he didn't object when the ashram had the body cremated and the ashes scattered in the Ganges. So, we never learned how he died: Murder, suicide, some bizarre Hindu diet. Who knows?"

Priscilla's head rolled forward; her chin seemed to slide between her collarbones. She seemed exhausted. "Clayton's older sister brought him from Varanasi back to her home in Maine. I don't think he's ever left there. I never saw him or spoke to him again." Priscilla shook her head. "And as for Clay, my older son? He disappeared off the face of the earth."

Paul didn't know what to say. "Thanks for telling me," he finally uttered, but he didn't know what he meant.

Priscilla's lips pulled back into a quarter smile or a grimace. "Sibyl was wonderful to me," she said. "When I returned from India the second time, she and Boris and Ruby — Yael then — came from Haifa to stay with me in the brown house right across the Commons from here." She looked directly at him. "I could tell, just tell, that Boris wasn't the girl's father. He and Sibyl never looked at each other, and he was afraid to touch the baby. How could you not pick her up? She was the cutest and brightest little thing. The only time she sat still was when we played music on the phonograph — classical records. When she moved her head you could see she was part of the music, the harmonies, the changing keys."

"Why are you telling me this?"

"Because I love Ruby and she needs you." Priscilla gave him a fierce look. "I don't know how a parent can give up a child."

"Thank you," Paul said again. He looked at his watch. He had twenty-eight hours until The Galilee Quartet's New York concert — plenty of time to return to Newport, pack for Hong Kong, travel to New York, hear the *Meydel* perform, and decide for himself whether she was a virtuoso and he was her father.

CHAPTER 23

The Galilee String Quartet was performing at Town Hall where, thirty-two years earlier, Paul first heard a live orchestra. Sibyl had played second flute and Willa (he later learned) had played first flute. Nothing but coincidence, Paul assured himself but, as he opened the taxi door, he saw a man clothed in prison stripes standing in front of the hall holding a handwritten sign:

BOYCOTT
WAGNER
Hitler's Inspiration
Respect the 6 Million Martyrs
Simon Schlussel — Auschwitz No. 54313

That number, 54313, was within 400 of Max (53927) and Asher (53928). This man, Simon Schlussel, could have arrived on the same transport as his cousins. How could Paul walk by him as if the two of them were unconnected? How could he not ask him whether he knew his cousins? But that would invite questions from Schlussel: *How are they? Are they alive?* Only one answer would be candid: *They survived Auschwitz, but not their encounters with me.*

And, if he spoke to Schlussel, he couldn't ignore his sign or Wagner. Wouldn't he have to say, *My daughter's in the quartet?* And if Schlussel went into a tirade about Jews playing Wagner, wouldn't Paul have to defend Ruby?

Paul froze in his tracks — one foot on the curb, one in the street. He was thinking of her as his daughter, Ruby. Good. He accepted it.

It was as simple and quick as that.

And, although he knew from an obstetrician whom he had called earlier in the day (a roommate of Danny Lee at Columbia) that there was no scientific way to prove or disprove this strongest bond of blood, he would accept her as his daughter without qualification. If Ruby sensed any reservation, she might reject him as he had once rejected her.

A taxi honked, reminding Paul that he was blocking access to the curb. He stepped onto the sidewalk and, like most of the people entering the concert hall, walked around Schlussel, casting his eyes firmly on the crowded entrance and keeping the survivor's angry prison stripes out of his view.

Schlussel's extreme hatred of the Nazis was understandable, Paul thought, but his objection to the Galilee performing a Wagner quartet was not. If Wagner composed chamber music, which Paul doubted, an Israeli quartet wouldn't be playing that music in the world's largest Jewish city. But, the first thing Paul saw in the lobby was a poster announcing the evening's program: the quartet's third number would be Wagner's "Siegfried Idyll . . . adapted by Moshe Levi," the first violinist. Schlussel was right.

Paul didn't know the piece but, no matter how martial it might be, even if it evoked Obersturmführer Strummer, the SS officer who had defecated the diamonds that helped pay Paul's tuitions, he had to overcome any temptation to flee.

He went to the seat he had carefully chosen — Row W on the far left, next to the wall. With eight people between him and the aisle, bolting during the performance would be virtually impossible. If the quartet sat as it was pictured in this morning's *Times*, his daughter — yes, he now fully accepted it — would be facing away from him.

Electricity shot through him when she walked on stage. Among the quartet members, she stood out as the only female, the only blonde, and decades younger than the other three. And she resembled his mother. She was not quite as pretty — Ruby's nose was slightly bigger and her hair less golden — but both women had the same light eyes and thin upturned lips, and their features blended into a balanced whole. The girl exuded a vitality that made Paul think of his father running into the Atlantic. He was anxious for the music to begin so he could sway along with it.

Paul remembered the first piece, "Beethoven's Quartet in C Minor, Opus 18, Number 4." Sibyl had played it at weddings while he was at Harvard, and she practiced it at home regularly. As Moshe Levi swayed with the melody, Ruby swayed with the violin harmony. Her playing was clear and pure, perfect support for whichever of her colleagues was taking the lead. Paul tried to dampen the pride swelling inside him; the music genes could have come only from Sibyl.

The piece ended with what seemed to be a gypsy dance and, amid the applause, Paul felt an urge to leap to his feet and exclaim to the exuberant woman next to him, *That's my daughter.* But it was too soon; he had silently acknowledged the tie only a half hour ago. Besides, the woman might ask him questions he couldn't answer. But, to himself, he said, *I'm kvelling, schlepping nachas,* using Yiddish phrases that meant (he believed) feeling extreme pride in a child — phrases he hadn't heard in well over twenty years. He was pleased that he had accepted her as his daughter before he experienced her artistry.

Tonight he would meet Ruby backstage, apologize profusely — *There's no excuse, I was just afraid* — and go with her for a drink, or coffee, or anything else she wanted. Any place. It had to work because they each wanted it to work and they both deserved happiness in their family lives.

Before going to bed, he would call Ann and tell her that they could start with a family of three. Or four, if Gideon accepted him. Soon to be five, if their lovemaking proved half as fruitful as it was pleasurable. Any number would be better than his present family of one.

The second number, "Elegy," by David Schiff, unnerved him. It was a modern piece he didn't quite appreciate or understand, and he watched Ruby closely, trying to imagine how the music spoke to her. He didn't want to associate his daughter with such dissonance, but he wouldn't discuss the piece with her until each of them was comfortable with the other.

At intermission, he decided to take a brief walk on Sixth Avenue to calm himself for the Wagner that was coming and the meeting with Ruby that would follow. But there was Schlussel still picketing by the entrance. Paul considered approaching him and then remembered how back in 1958, when he had planned another calming walk, he had been pulled to Asher at the bottom of the courthouse steps, initiating a sequence of events that had destroyed much of his life — another reason to avoid Schlussel.

But Paul saw three young men who were not avoiding the survivor. Dressed in black leather pants and jackets, with caps that seemed modeled on an SS uniform, they were standing at attention a few feet from Schlussel, their right arms raised at a forty-five degree angle, giving the Nazi salute. The tallest of them held a comb under his nose, imitating Hitler's mustache. They were shouting something and laughing. A policeman stood by impassively.

"What are they shouting?" a voice asked. It was the woman who had sat next to Paul in the concert hall.

"*Heil, Heil,* like in *Heil* Hitler," a male voice answered. "I asked the cop to stop them, but he said they were just kids fooling around and that if the man in stripes had a First Amendment right to picket, they had the same right to make fun of him."

Paul had to do something. Even if the Nazi imitators were not threatening Schlussel, he could not allow the Holocaust to be mocked. He hadn't dealt with the First Amendment or public disorder statutes since he moved to Boston, but he was confident he could sound knowledgeable enough to convince the cop that he had a duty to make the young men move on. And if that didn't work, he could confront them himself and exercise his own free speech rights.

Jack had been ashamed he had not come to the defense of his Orthodox friend who was being assaulted by Nazis in the Teplice alley; Paul would not be ashamed here. He started to march towards the survivor and his tormentors.

He felt two taps on his back. He pivoted and faced a dark, tall, stern young man in a smooth, black suit. A hint of even blacker hair shadowed his shaven head.

The man handed him a single sheet of paper. "For you."

Paul's hands shook as he took it. He welcomed the opportunity to look away from the man's face:

Mr. Hartman:

Please leave the concert. Your presence makes it difficult for me to play. Also, do not try to see me or speak to me. You have rejected me once, and that is enough. Yitzhak, who will give you this note, is providing security for the Quartet, and I have asked him to keep you away from me.

R.H.

Paul knew he shouldn't be surprised, but he was. He hadn't rejected her. He had left for Hong Kong instead of keeping his appointment with her because, with his life in uproar on every front, a sudden Israeli daughter was more than he could handle well at that time. By nature he was not, he told himself, a coward. Yitzhak would confirm Paul's courage to Ruby once he realized that Paul was no ghetto Jew who wouldn't fight back. He was a tough Jew who, like Yitzhak, would stand up to anti-Semites.

He looked into Yitzhak's dark eyes. "Those boys are picking on an Auschwitz survivor. I'm on my way to stop it. Why don't you come with me?"

"I think you should go home," Yitzhak said impassively.

Paul held Yitzhak's stare. "I'm going to speak to those kids and the cop, and then go back to hear my daughter. Nobody's —"

Yitzhak's index finger shot up towards the side of Paul's neck. Paul saw only a blinding white light. The pain sped from below his earlobe to the back of his cranium.

"I think you should go home."

By the time the white light softened, Yitzhak was gone. Paul could make out Ruby's note on the floor next to his feet. He left it there.

He didn't go back to the concert hall, not out of fear, he assured himself, but because he didn't want to interfere with Ruby's playing. He remained in the lobby to hear his daughter play Wagner and, whether Yitzhak approved or not, to meet her at the end of the concert.

Surprisingly, Wagner calmed him. "Siegfried Idyll" was, as the program described it, a soothing conversation between four strings. While Moshe Levi's beautiful violin presumably led the conversation, the harmony provided by the other violinist, presumably Ruby, sounded at least as beautiful.

The audience applauded at the end, but not nearly enough. Didn't they appreciate the beautiful rendition they had just heard? And, no matter what the audience thought about Jews performing Wagner, shouldn't they applaud the musicians' courage in taking a principled stand?

Paul wanted to enter the hall to shout *Brava!* But that would upset Ruby who still had one more number to perform. As that piece, *Quartet Number 3 in B-Flat Major*, by Brahms, began, he was too edgy to stand in the lobby any longer. He would now go outside to talk to Schlussel and confront the hecklers — show everybody, the dead and the living, but mostly Ruby and himself, that he was a strong committed Jew.

There was, however, no sign of Schlussel. Wagner was over, and the concert was, once again, pure music. Paul walked around the block and then went to the stage door, a few feet west of the lobby entrance, to wait for Ruby. The hell with Yitzhak. If he attacked Paul again, he would merely make Ruby appreciate the depth of her father's determination to see her.

The stage door was open, and the policeman who had watched Schlussel and his tormenters stood beside it, as bored as before. Good, Paul thought. The cop would keep Yitzhak under control. Paul went up to him, prepared to say, *I'm waiting for my daughter, she's one of the musicians*, but then he saw Yitzhak in the doorway with his arms loosely folded over his chest. He seemed more bored than the policeman.

If Paul tried to speak to Ruby here, the result could be disaster, a public incident that would humiliate both of them and strengthen her resolve not to see him. He had to find another path to her.

Priscilla! She would help him. She had to – there was no one else.

He turned from Yitzhak, and hailed a taxi.

* * *

Entering his hotel room at The Plaza, Paul was racked with urgency. He *had to* see Ruby before she returned to Israel. If it did not happen now, it would never happen.

His large corner room had a dizzying view of Fifth Avenue, the perimeter of Central Park, and the horse-drawn carriages awaiting tourists along the park's edge. Paul shut the blinds.

On the bed before him were the suitcases Johnny's tailor had purchased for him hours before he first left for Hong Kong. Paul put them in the closet.

He sat at the mahogany desk, and he called Priscilla. "It's Paul Hartman. Ruby won't see me. You convinced me to see her. Please get her to see me."

Her response was silence.

"Two lives are at stake."

More silence.

"She wants her real father — her real heritage. Why else would she pick that name?"

Finally, Priscilla spoke. Her voice was stronger than in Devon. "She called me this afternoon crying about how you cast her aside this summer."

"Allow me one slip. I've tried to do the right thing, like coming to the party."

Again, silence.

"I wasn't going to see her until you said that you don't understand how a parent can give up a child." Paul paused to let his words — really her words — sink in. "It's not good for a child to give up a parent either."

"I don't want to cause her more pain," Priscilla said.

"There won't be more pain. If she lets me, I'll try to be a good father."

The desk chair was suddenly hard and narrow. He had to get to the bed. But if he put down the phone, even for a few seconds, she might hang up.

"*Teshuvah.*"

The word, almost whispered, surprised him. For a moment, he wasn't sure which one of them had spoken, but it couldn't be Priscilla. He hadn't heard the word *Teshovah*, or even thought it, since long before he came to Boston.

"What did you say?" Priscilla asked.

Why not? Paul asked himself. Nothing else was working.

"*Teshuvah*. It's the Hebrew word for repentance. But it's more than repentance. It's a central concept of Judaism — trying to make the world whole. Even if, like most Israelis, she's not religious, Ruby will know what it means."

There was more silence, but now it was a relief. Priscilla was judging his sincerity, and she would realize it was total.

"I'll call her and then call you," Priscilla finally said. "Don't make me sorry I did this."

"You won't be," Paul replied but, as he spoke, the phone clicked at the other end, and he didn't know whether Priscilla had heard him.

CHAPTER 24

Following Priscilla's directives, Paul arrived at Charing's on Madison Avenue at ten minutes before eight. Although the restaurant was serving only breakfast, its tablecloths were white linen and the waiters were freshly tuxedoed. On the wall alongside the maître d's stand was the picture of a familiar dignified woman in a blue-feathered hat sitting at a heavily laden table and smiling politely as a tall man in tails and white tie served her a slice of cake. The label below the picture reminded Paul who she was — "Queen Elizabeth the Queen Mother." The man facing Paul from behind the stand was the man in the picture. His attire was, again, impeccable – *suitable for the Queen Mother herself*, Paul thought.

Paul had planned to hand the maître d' ten dollars and request a table at the nearly empty rear of the restaurant. But the Queen Mother and white tie made him reconsider. Granville would probably give the maître d' nothing. Bernie would give him twenty. Before he could decide, the maître d' said, "How many, Sir?" Paul replied "Two," and the maître d' led him to the very table he had in mind. A good start, he thought.

While he waited, Paul sipped black coffee and tried to read the *Times,* but he couldn't get much beyond the headlines. He realized that planning was, at best, pointless, but couldn't help himself. Should he start with *I'm sorry* or *I'm glad?* Extend his hand to her or lean forward to kiss her? Nothing seemed right. At eight-ten he felt an urge to urinate, but how could he not be there when she arrived?

He checked his watch again and, when he looked up, she was there, as abruptly as Sibyl had appeared at Tanglewood. The maître d' seemed to be asking her something, but she walked around him. As Paul stood and spread his arms, Ruby, grim faced, sat down across from him without removing her coat. Paul dropped back into his seat. She didn't want to touch, and he couldn't blame her.

She nodded and said, "So this time you came. Should I thank you?"

"I won't try to apologize for the unforgivable, but I . . . was . . . I wasn't . . ."

"Wasn't ready then?" she suggested. "That's what *Ima* and Priscilla said you'd say."

It hadn't occurred to him that, like Asher, she would control the conversation. He needed time to compose himself.

"Are you ready now?" she asked. Paul felt a steady pressure pushing against his chest. "Do you want to be my father?" He managed to nod. "Because I *am* your daughter. We didn't ask for . . ." Now it was her turn to leave a sentence hanging.

Up close, he saw that her eyes were light blue, the color of Bernie's Lincoln. He should be wary of her. She stared at him with an intensity approaching hatred. Very wary.

The maître d' came to the table. "May I take your coat, Miss?" His English accent was almost as strong as that of the Chinese bankers in Hong Kong. She didn't seem to hear him, and Paul waved the maître d' away.

"I'm sorry, sir, but we must maintain our dress standards."

Their meeting would end before it began. "You have to give him your coat, Ruby." It was the first time he had called her by that name — by any name.

To Paul's relief, she did as asked. She was wearing the simple black dress she had worn for the concert last night, but now there was an oval cameo pinned just below her throat — the silhouette of a woman in a Victorian dress.

"Did you wear that pin last night?" Paul asked when the Maître d' was beyond hearing.

"No," she said. "*Safta* gave it to me."

"Who?"

"*Safta*; Hebrew for grandmother, Grandma. Your mother."

Paul stared at it, shocked. The cameo was his mother's prized possession — a gift from her *Safta*, his great-grandmother, Ruby's great-great-grandmother, who had died on the transport to Terezenstadt. He had to change the subject. "I was surprised you played Wagner last night."

She leaned towards him over the table. "You object to Jews playing Wagner?"

"A vicious anti-Semite, a Nazi before there were Nazis."

Why was he throwing Max's condemnation at her — perhaps, Max's exact words — when, at last night's concert, he had thought it admirable for the quartet to play Wagner? Sure, she was a precocious condescending kid, but their meeting shouldn't start with an argument — particularly when he had no strong views.

"Are you the champion of the Jewish people telling me something I don't know? I'll tell you something." She paused, and Paul struggled to hold her stare. "We won; they lost. We have a proud, free, open country, and they're trying to hide in South America like rats. Moshe Levi says the music belongs to the world, and we have more right to it than the Germans."

Later, he would think about this, but now he couldn't capitulate. "Don't a lot of survivors agree with me?"

"Moshe doesn't and he was in Buchenwald, but Cousin Malke does. I think you know who she is." Paul recalled the name, but not much more. "The cousin of your father," Ruby went on, "who was a famous partisan and a hero in Israel because of what she did in the Mossad."

Paul's memories concerning Malke, whom he had never met, started to trickle in: In 1958, intending to help Asher get Malke out of a Russian political prison and into Israel, he had disclosed to Asher that Olymp would win the patent case Paul was working on, and he suggested a way Asher could use that confidential information to obtain cash for bribes in Russia. That disclosure to Asher, which was unlawful and ultimately erroneous, led to Asher's violent death as well as Paul's total break with his family and background.

He hadn't expected that Ruby, who had yet to be conceived when all this happened, would add an additional Holocaust survivor to the ghosts already tormenting him. He looked at her stern gaze across the table, and wished he were back in Hong Kong.

Ruby sat straight. "Malke is organizing a big demonstration against us next week at the amphitheater in Caesarea where we're giving a concert that includes 'Siegfried Idyll.' *Ima*'s not coming because of the Wagner, but at least she's not going to picket like she first said she would. The amphitheater is where Romans used to slaughter Jews. Should we not go there or not play Verdi or stop eating spaghetti?"

Paul tried to imagine the conversations among Ruby, Malke and Sibyl. Would Sibyl have given her own views about performing Wagner? Certainly not the Sibyl from Rockaway, but the Tsipora from Israel, who came into being when she beat at his skull, would have spoken up.

They must have argued — raised voices, fists slammed against the table. No slammed fists, Paul corrected himself. They were musicians who wouldn't endanger their hands.

Ruby's body relaxed. "Caesarea is my last concert with the Galilee before I go back in the *Tzahal*." She sounded almost wistful.

"In the what?"

"The Army. You don't know anything about Israel, do you? I completed my two years compulsory service, but I volunteered to go back to play with the *Tzahal* Symphony — I might become concertmistress — and organize chamber music concerts for soldiers at the front, help soldiers form their own chamber groups. If you are as rich as *Ima* says, I may ask you to contribute money." She smiled for the first time.

"Where's the front?"

"In Israel, everyplace but, right now, especially Lebanon."

What Ruby was telling him was more than Paul could absorb. Thankfully, a waiter was standing over them with menus. Ruby took hers, glanced at it, pointed, and said, "This one."

"The full classic English breakfast, Miss?" the waiter asked.

"Yes." She grimaced, and Paul realized she didn't know what she would be getting.

"For the third course, bacon or sausage, Miss?" the waiter continued.

"Both."

Paul was stunned.

"For the fourth course, kippers or deviled kidneys?"

"What are kippers?" she asked Paul.

"Some kind of salty fish, I think."

"Like lox?"

"No Miss," the waiter answered. "We don't eat smoked salmon in the morning. Perhaps you might find the kidneys more to your liking, although they are a bit spicy. I can get you some poached haddock if you prefer."

Ruby gave the waiter a surprisingly broad smile and said, "Kippers *and* haddock." Her eyes now sparkled. Maybe she was as pretty as her grandmother.

"Sorry, Madam. I shouldn't have—" The waiter blushed and turned his head towards the empty table alongside them.

Paul loved her. No wonder the English couldn't stop the Jews from creating Israel.

The waiter composed himself and asked Paul, "What can I get for you, sir?"

"A half grapefruit and black coffee."

Ruby looked at him, surprised.

"I'm on a diet."

"You shouldn't be on a diet. You look fine."

"You shouldn't be eating pork."

"Why not?"

The waiter stood by the table, pad in hand.

"Why not? Because you're a Jew."

She leaned over the table at him again, just as she had when he questioned her playing Wagner. "Eating pig doesn't make me not a Jew any more than playing a pig's music does. I was born in the Jewish homeland. I speak the Jewish language. I breathe Jewish air. And I'm going back into the Jewish Army. I'm not a Diaspora Jew who has to show who I am to anybody, including me." She leaned back in her chair. "I'll make you a bargain — you eat a real breakfast and I won't eat pork. I almost never eat it anyway."

Paul turned towards the waiter. "The full breakfast with kippers, no meat. Same for her." He turned back to Ruby. "Why did you pick this restaurant?"

Ruby didn't respond until the waiter was gone. "*Ima* said everybody you know in Boston is English, and you're used to this kind of food."

"*Ima* doesn't know what she's talking about. She's accusing me of trying to pass."

"Pass?"

"Acting like I'm a Christian — a *goy*. I've never done that. I never will." Quickly, before Ruby could respond, he asked, "Is this the kind of restaurant you expected?"

"I came here yesterday with my other *Safta,* Grandma Evelyn, for tea."

Who? Paul asked himself, and then realized Ruby was talking about Sibyl's mother.

"She wants me to move to America, but Israel is where I live, where I'm going to do my music, and have children."

"Do you have someone to marry?"

"Yes, but he doesn't know it yet." Light seemed to bounce from her smile.

"You're very sure of yourself."

She stopped smiling. "Where I come from and what I plan to do, I have to be sure."

Her certainty, even if it might be bravado, unnerved him. "Do you know there was an Auschwitz survivor picketing you last night?"

"Simon Schlussel?" She wrinkled her nose. "Why should I pay attention to him? If he cares so much, why doesn't he come to Israel to fight Arabs instead of fighting Jews in America? Why doesn't he change one of his names so the initials aren't SS? Malke, I care — she's a fighter. I told her victims don't play Wagner, and free Jews play who they want. Do you know what *Safta* Ida said about playing Wagner?"

Paul felt himself perspiring.

"She said only I could decide what was right for me about Wagner, but if I played it in Caesarea, she and Papa Jack would come."

Ruby dropped her voice. "Family should hear me." Then, she spoke in her normal voice. "Why don't you go see her in Texas? I'm sure your father would want you to."

Now it was Paul's turn to lean over the table. "We made a deal about breakfast. You don't tell me what to do and I won't tell you what to do."

She shrugged. "You can tell me whatever you want, but I'm going to make up my own mind what I do."

She wasn't his daughter. She wasn't anybody's child. Like the *golem* manufactured from clay and prayers in a Prague synagogue by a medieval rabbi, she was created unnaturally and would soon try to destroy both the synagogue and her maker.

Then suddenly, Ruby's lips parted imploringly, "I love Wagner's music, but I want to show respect for Malke. If I don't play Wagner, they won't let me play anything. Spiro's hand is better and I'm just his substitute even though a big critic wrote I play better. They're giving me one final night in Caesarea because I'm going back in the Army — the next day, in fact. They agreed to feature me in the last piece, Ravel's *Quartet in F Major*. It's very difficult — a lot of violinists won't try it, but Moshe says I can do it. I'll get reviewed."

"I think you should play."

"I already decided I would."

She looked at him defiantly, but then her lips quivered and she turned away.

A scared kid, Paul thought. *Bravado trying to hide fear.*

Her mother would boycott her performance. Malke, whom Ruby admired, would publicly condemn it. Her grandmother — his own mother — would come from Texas, but that was a poor substitute. Perhaps he should call Sibyl and urge her to attend. Perhaps he should go.

"I would come to the concert too, but —"

"I didn't ask you to."

"But I want to get married. A Jewish lady from Hong Kong. You'd like her. And if I don't get back soon, a lot of things could go wrong."

Ruby's eyes narrowed. "I don't want to hear about your women! I'm going to the toilet." She pushed back her chair, just as the maître d' and waiter arrived with a shining serving cart. The waiter turned his head to follow her, but the maître d' stood as still and straight as a lamppost.

Paul took out his wallet, and handed them each a twenty dollar bill. "I apologize. My daughter's upset. We may be here a while, and I'd like as much privacy as possible."

* * *

"I never cry," Ruby announced when she returned. "Even after they blew up the bus in Nahariya and my best friend died and I started to play *Eil Malei Rachamim* at her funeral . . . The rabbi waved his finger and tells me you don't play the violin at a funeral, but I played and everybody cried — even the rabbi. Everybody except me. Now, two days in a row I cry like a baby. But no more." She ate a bit of porridge, made a face, and put down the spoon.

"Tell me about yourself," Paul said in a low voice.

"First I'll tell you about you."

He had humored her enough. "You're twenty years old. Don't be such a know-it-all."

"I was twenty-one in August. Born nine months to the day after *Ima* came back from South America and you broke your legs and, *Ima* finally told me, something happened in between." She flashed her full smile, but then looked at him earnestly and placed her hand on his forearm. "Look *Abba*, since I met you at Tanglewood, I've learned a lot, especially about the diamonds — some things you don't know."

The diamonds! Max's diamonds! Paul didn't want to discuss them with anyone, most of all with Sibyl's daughter. But he said nothing, lest their first day together be their last.

She told him she had spoken to all the living actors — his mother, Jack, Sibyl, Malke, Bernie (described by Ruby as "this old man in a wheelchair who's living with *Safta* and Papa Jack in a house he built for the three of them in Texas"). By telephone, she had talked to Frieda Greenberg, Kelly's widow, who was now living in the same Warsaw convent where she had been hidden during the war. With the help of the history student she expected to marry, she had also done research about Auschwitz at Yad Vashem, the Holocaust Museum in Jerusalem, where archives of the camps were maintained, and she had interviewed some Auschwitz survivors. She echoed much of what Asher had told him two decades earlier about the camp — the extra food for the orchestra, the high quality of its music, the mounting hatred between the brothers. The survivors, she said, had trouble telling Max and Asher apart, although they all agreed that at least one of the brothers ran the orchestra. A survivor who worked in the infirmary was sure the brothers were twins who had died on the operating table while SS doctors used them as guinea pigs in medical experiments.

Long ago and far away, Paul thought. Hearsay — what somebody told somebody told somebody. None of it would hit the gut like Asher recounting the rats at Max's son's face, or Max's few words about thirst and drinking from puddles "where maybe the dogs went," or Jack's description of the heat in front of Olymp's furnaces — "twenty degrees hotter than hell." Soon it would be nothing more than words and numbers, having little to do with anyone he knew.

"It's impossible to figure out what exactly happened," Paul said when the waiter left after serving the kippers. "With six million dead, the details seem less important."

"But the details are people," Ruby replied between forkfuls. "Sometimes I think maybe both brothers ran the Auschwitz orchestra. When Max conducted, Asher played first violin. When Asher conducted—"

"No, no, Max played the violin."

"No," she retorted with conviction, "I'm sure. Everybody told me. Asher played the violin. Max was a pianist, and when he wasn't conducting, he played the xylophone."

Absolutely sure and absolutely wrong, Paul thought. How could he believe anything she reported? Still, he shouldn't be harsh, even in his thoughts. She was trying to become part of a newly-found family that had been decimated by the Nazis and by her own father's determination to separate himself from that family. And she must be shaken by what she had learned about her own origins. At least Paul had always known who his parents were and that they had conceived him in love. And his own father, far from fleeing his child, had reached out to Paul for one final swimming lesson before dying.

"Did anyone tell you about a safe deposit box in Switzerland where Max and Kelly might have put some diamonds?" he asked. "I threw away one of the keys for it."

"I know all about it."

At some point, he would have to tell her that such assertions of certainty could come across as arrogant. Shouldn't a father correct his child?

To Paul's amazement, Ruby reached across the table and took his hand. "*Safta* said she should have listened to you and not kept the diamonds secret." Ruby squeezed his hand hard. "You must call her. Everybody should make up. Jews have too many enemies to fight in their own family."

Paul, afraid he would break down, summoned up words, "There's no point in imagining a world in which we didn't keep the diamonds secret. Everything would have been different. I would have gone to different schools. My mother wouldn't have met Jack. I wouldn't have met your mother." He stopped abruptly because he was about to say, *You wouldn't have been born.*

Ruby shook her head no. "*Safta* said you would have been a big success no matter what." She squeezed his hand again. "I'm proud you threw away the key."

He needed her to be his daughter — to help him overcome the shame of the diamonds. But he couldn't let himself cry on her shoulder. "You're covering too much too fast. Let's talk about you now."

"Don't you want to learn what happened with the diamonds in Switzerland? You asked."

Resigned, Paul nodded.

Ruby looked over Paul's shoulder, and spoke steadily without pause, as if she were giving a well-prepared lecture. "Malke, because of her work with the Mossad, was owed favors by Swiss intelligence, and between that and a smart Jewish lawyer from Zurich, the bank opened the box for them. They shared it, fifty-fifty between Malke and Frieda because they were the closest relative of Max and Kelly who got the box in the first place. They didn't want it for themselves — too much blood — so they gave it to good causes."

Paul felt as if a Hong Kong coolie's load — one he had been carrying for over thirty years — had been lifted from his back and shoulders.

"Frieda gave hers to the nuns, who hid her," Ruby continued, "and Malke gave most of hers to Yad Vashem. The rest, she bought me a Guarneri violin — I can't tell you how expensive."

The Buffet, Paul thought. "Give it back to her," he said to Ruby urgently. "It's from the same blood and filth. I'll get you a better violin."

Ruby plunged ahead. "I told Malke no, I don't want it, but she told me that beautiful music played on a beautiful violin by a relative born in Israel would be the best memorial to her family, they all loved music so much. I put it in a safe in a Haifa bank, and I'm going to perform on it for the first time at Caesarea."

Now or never, Paul told himself. He took a deep breath. "Did Frieda tell Malke how Asher died — whether it was suicide or murder?"

"No. Malke said there are things you don't say and questions you don't ask."

"Asher told me he needed my help in getting Malke out of Russia and, in one way or another, that led to a lot of bad things. When Asher told me that, Malke was actually in Israel. Did he know that?"

"I don't know, *Abba*," she answered gently. "Malke never talks about how she made it to Israel. Her son was sick — his name was Reuben, you know." Paul winced. "On the way, or just after they got there, he died. *Ima* says that after losing two husbands and so much family and so many comrades in the partisans, her son's death nearly broke her. So nobody asks about that time."

Paul felt a sudden need to breathe fresh air away from this stage-set of a restaurant, this monument to a world that had passed. Enough Reubens and losses and *Imas* and *Saftas*. The day was too beautiful and Ruby's smile too infrequent. He needed to be with his daughter in present time. "Let's go to The Bronx Botanical Gardens," he proposed, because it was the first thing that came to mind. "I'll rent a car and afterward I'll drive you to JFK. When's your flight?"

"Midnight tonight, but we're being interviewed by *Newsweek* at six. Let's go to Rockaway instead. It's on the way to the airport."

Paul felt his chest clench. "Why there?"

"It is where you and *Ima* met — the place of my . . . I can't think of the English word."

"Origin?"

"My origin."

"It's changed. Arverne, where I grew up, was torn down for urban renewal."

"When were you there last?"

"Before you were born," he answered. Maybe later, on the boardwalk, he would give her a full answer — *On the day Asher died and you were conceived.*

"Well, when we see it, you can tell me what it was like so I can see my origin. But I have to ask you something." Her mouth smiled, but her eyes betrayed anxiety. "When you go to rent the car, will you disappear again and leave me waiting?"

Paul took his passport from his jacket pocket and handed it to her. "Security."

"How do you know that I won't disappear? Like father, like daughter."

"Because you're stronger than I am."

Now, her eyes smiled along with her mouth.

* * *

Paul had never heard of Ruby's hotel, The Wales, at Madison and Ninety-third. It was out of the way, small and nondescript, but that might be the whole idea — easier to maintain security. She was standing on the sidewalk outside the hotel entrance, looking glum and waif-like, carrying a violin case. Her luggage, she had told Paul, would be shipped through by the quartet's manager. Before getting in the car, she handed him his passport. "I almost hoped you would disappear again so I wouldn't have to say I'm sorry."

Paul reached for the violin case, but she wouldn't release it.

"What's wrong?"

"I'll explain later when I won't cry and make myself a bigger fool." She held the case on her lap with both hands. It was shabby and dull, not shiny like the one Max had carried.

When they reached FDR Drive, Ruby said, in a flat voice, "I'm sorry."

"What for?"

"I called Malke because you thought I got it mixed up — which brother played what — and she told me you were right: Max, the violin; Asher, the piano. Why didn't you tell me?"

"You seemed so sure."

"Sure?" she said mockingly. She pulled the violin case into her stomach. "The only thing I'm sure about is the violin. For nearly all my life, I don't know who my father is, only who he wasn't. That boy I said I was going to marry, he's not going to. Boys don't like me. I make them nervous."

"I can't imagine boys don't like you."

"Imagine."

Paul was afraid she would resent words of comfort or assurance from him — dismiss them as insincere platitudes from a near stranger — and, for a few moments they sat in silence until Ruby said, "Malke asked about the Town Hall concert."

"And?"

"When I told her we played Wagner she got hysterical. Then I got emotional too. I told her I just want to play my music and live my life without that history getting into everything." Ruby shook a fist in the air. "I'm sick of them — victims, heroes, all of them — making me feel I owe them something. I don't."

The FDR Drive was surprisingly uncrowded, and Paul put his right hand on her shoulder, but she shrugged it off, and he returned his hand to the wheel.

"Did she say anything else?"

"She said that, even though I'm her only blood relative left, she would make me sorry if I played Wagner in Israel."

Paul felt anger building inside of him. But was it towards Malke or himself? "I'm her blood relative, too."

"She said that, for Jews, you died when you became a *goy*, and I should say *Kaddish* for my father." She looked straight ahead. "I don't want to say *Kaddish*. I just found you."

Paul had no words. Even if he could somehow hug her while he was driving, she might rebuff him. Instead he pushed the radio "ON" button. A piano was playing. "What is that piece?" he asked her. Ruby didn't answer.

The music stopped as they entered the Brooklyn Battery Tunnel, but the silence between them continued. When they exited and the radio came back on, an orchestra was playing a piece Paul recognized but couldn't name. "Listen," Ruby said. She smiled slightly. "It's Debussy's 'Afternoon of a Faun.' The New York Philharmonic. Nobody plays it like they do. In a minute there's a flute solo. Julius Baker. There'll be a long C-sharp. *Ima* says no flutist makes as pure a C-sharp as Julie." She sat in a contented trance, absorbed in the music, just as Priscilla had described her when she was an infant — Yael. How had he become so lucky?

At the end of the piece, the announcer confirmed what Ruby had said, and Paul turned the radio off. "You were right about them. The Max and Asher confusion was an aberration."

"What's an aberration?"

"Forget it. There are a few things I want to ask you before the Rockaway ocean air transforms me into God-knows-what. When did you find out I was your father?"

She answered without pause, as if she had been waiting to be asked. "Malke figured it out, but it didn't take Mossad. Then Boris told me the whole thing. I thought *Ima* would kill them both, although it would be hard to kill Malke. I don't respect you became a *goy*, but you seem like a nice man and maybe you'll come back."

"I never became a *goy*, but let's not argue." They were near the exit for Rockaway.

* * *

From the Marine Parkway Bridge, he saw sailboats on Jamaica Bay for the first time — not just rowboats and motor boats. Beyond the bridge, the beach was whiter and wider than he remembered, and the unusually calm Atlantic glistened in the sun. He wondered whether Ruby could swim. Could she coast waves? They would buy bathing suits and he would teach her. But even his father never went into the ocean in October.

"Is this how it was when you met *Ima*?"

"The beach seems wider." He wouldn't mention sailboats. Willa had a forty-foot sailboat, and Paul had occasionally sailed with her. But Ruby didn't want to hear about his other women, and he certainly didn't want to discuss his second marriage with her.

"Are you okay, Papa?"

Paul realized he had been shaking his head. "Fine. It's emotional taking my newfound daughter to my old home." He felt compelled to say more. "I started out on the wrong foot, and I wanted today . . ."

He cut himself off. They were leaving the bridge, and although Rockaway had numbered streets and was barely half a mile wide, he might get lost if his emotions took over.

From the corner of his eye, Paul saw Ruby make two tight fists. "Do you think you might come to the Caesarea concert next Sunday? It would be nice to have a parent there." She was working to keep her voice steady.

A bright light flashed behind Paul's eyes for each of the specters who would confront him in Israel — his mother (now *Safta*), Jack, Sibyl (now *Tsipora* and *Ima*), Malke (the heroine ready to say *Kaddish* for him), maybe Bernie in his wheelchair. And Ann, who wouldn't be there, could easily be lost forever.

"Forget it, forget it," Ruby said. Paul wondered how long he had been silent. "I know it's impossible on such little notice. I shouldn't have asked. I shouldn't have."

"I want to. I want to." (Why were they both repeating themselves?) "It's just I have so much going on in Hong Kong."

"I understand. I understand. You don't have to explain."

"Maybe I can come next week."

"I told you, I'll be in the Army then. I told you. But come even if I can't see you. How can you be a Jew without going to Israel, at least to visit if you're not ready to live there?"

Paul willed himself to ignore her urging and just drive.

"Papa!" Ruby almost shouted, and Paul stepped on the brakes. "This is *Ima's* street — One-four-four. You're driving past it. Are you all right?"

Paul released the brakes, backed up quickly and turned sharply to the left.

"You are upset," Ruby said. "Do you want I should drive? I drove a truck in the Army."

"No, I'm fine. Besides, it's a rented car and I'm the only driver who's insured."

But he wasn't fine. He was lost on a small street he had been on hundreds of times. Nothing seemed familiar. Modest homes, smaller than Willa's and his brownstone, had replaced the mansions he remembered. On the lawns, plaster Madonnas had replaced plaster black jockeys. More American flags flew than on the Fourth of July. Should he have turned right instead of left?

"I think it's that one over there." Ruby pointed to a house coming up on their left. "*Ima* said it was Four-two-five One-four-four Street."

That was the address Paul remembered, and "425" was the number on the bird feeder hanging above the porch. But this wasn't it. The Pines' house was bigger, with yellow brick, a peaked roof and a screened porch. Or was that Bernie's first Woodmere house?

"*Abba!*" Ruby exclaimed. His eyes shot from the bird feeder to a little girl playing hopscotch in the street. The car screeched to a halt, and the girl ran towards Sibyl's house.

"We should go," Ruby said in a controlled voice. "Maybe Rockaway was a bad idea."

"No, you should see Arverne. I should see it, too."

* * *

As he drove east on Rockaway Beach Boulevard through Rockaway Park, Paul was aware they would pass the very spot where Asher was found dead across from the Jefferson Arms Hotel. He stared straight ahead, looking away from street signs and buildings, until he stopped for the light at One-hundred-sixteenth Street, beyond the Jefferson Arms. Now it was safe to relax — even to compare this 1980 street with what he remembered.

In 1948, reeking with aftershave, and on the bus to Sibyl's house for the first time, he had gotten off at One-hundred-sixteenth to scrub away the smell at Kitty's Luncheonette on the corner. Then, the street was a mélange of well-kept white ethnic stores — Jewish, Irish, Italian — and white ethnic customers. Kitty's, or whatever that space might have been over the past two decades, now had no sign identifying it and was covered by corrugated iron. The iron was covered with graffiti — the top half with a slashing sketch of a black fist. Maybe his memory was flawed and Kitty's had been one store away from the corner where an overhanging sign now announced, "TAXI SERVICE — ATLANTIC CITY BUS."

Paul looked down the street towards the boardwalk. Most of the people seemed to be Black or Hispanic, a dramatic change from his Rockaway years when nearly everyone in sight — whether a shopper or beachgoer — was a white ethnic. He recognized nothing. Several of the signs were in Spanish.

"Is this like you remember?" Ruby asked.

"Yes, basically," Paul lied. The truth — that the skin colors on the street had changed and the stores were unrecognizable — was too complicated. She might think he was a bigot. "By the boardwalk, there was an open air movie theater your mother and I went to. Then, they built a nursing home there where my grandfather died." He stopped himself from saying what was on his mind, and then decided to say it. "I hated him."

"I think *Safta* felt the same way," Ruby said.

Had he realized this? Paul wondered. How could he have missed it? But those questions were for another day. The light had turned green, and they drove into Irish Town.

There were still bars flying Irish and American flags, but most were boarded up and many of the flags in sight, unlike the flags of his youth, were frayed. The beach blocks still had bungalows and sand in the street, but the sand seemed gray, and the bungalows even grayer. And there was something else — something was missing. For a moment, Paul couldn't figure out what it was, and then he heard himself gasp. The Rockaway Playland roller coaster which had dominated the landscape for miles and years, and which he had ridden with his father, had disappeared. Gone! Who could have taken down the structure that defined Rockaway? At Ninety-eighth Street, he saw the answer: All of Playland was gone. The acres of rides and games that Paul had stared at from the boardwalk on the night Max died were now smoothed brown dirt surrounded by a tall barbed wire fence. There was a sign on the fence but, without stopping, Paul could only make out the words at its top — "URBAN RENEWAL SITE."

"*Abba*! *Dai*! Please stop! You're driving crooked. We will have an accident."

"No, I'll be careful. Arverne's thirty short blocks away — right after Hammels."

But, Paul soon discovered, there was no Hammels. Where, in the Hammels of the 1940s and 1950s, there had been boarding houses and bungalows on the beach blocks and slightly decrepit two-family houses on the bay blocks, there were now blocks and blocks of unremitting rubble extending into Arverne — wood, stucco and cement, everything smashed, nothing cleaned up.

Three buildings stood amidst the wreckage. To his right, on Eighty-fourth Street, Saint Rose of Lima Catholic Church and Temple Israel, looking as he remembered them, appeared to have been divinely spared. Less than a mile ahead, he saw a brown structure that had to be Congregation Derech Emunah, his *shul*, where he completed six years of Hebrew School, became *bar mitzvah*, and faithfully attended Cub Scout, Boy Scout and Teen Torah meetings. He remembered the day of President Roosevelt's death when, within an hour of the radio announcement, he and hundreds of other Arverne winter people spontaneously gathered there for a memorial service. How dare Malke call him a *goy*. But another memory tainted it all — praying in Derech Emunah on *Yom Kippur* just before his mother gave him cash proceeds from Max's diamonds.

"They've knocked it all down," he said, "everything I was going to show you."

"When is the rebuilding to occur?"

"I suspect there are no plans. If there were, there would be a sign and a fence."

She gestured at the rubble. "And when did they knock it all down?"

Paul remembered the article his mother sent him. It had been on his bureau when he returned home from a party celebrating Concord Memory's first public stock offering — the day he made three hundred thousand dollars and three civil rights workers (two Jewish, one Black) were killed in Mississippi. "Nineteen-sixty-four," he answered.

"Sixteen years? In Israel nothing is destroyed without getting rebuilt right away."

"Stop being so —" Paul cut himself off. Near the boardwalk, four emaciated dogs, mouths open, tongues hanging down, were running through the remains of the bungalows.

"Are these dogs wild?" she asked.

"I don't know, and I don't want to find out."

"How can this be permitted? In Israel —"

"Good God Almighty," Paul mumbled to himself, and Ruby laughed.

"I was going to say, in Israel we have wild Jews." She looked again at the rubble, and then said consolingly, "This must be sad for you. I'll play something on the boardwalk to make you feel better. I did that in Army hospitals."

A beautiful thought, but a terrible idea. He might cry. "I'm not sure we should go on the boardwalk. The dogs —"

"They're running away from us. We can get back in the car if we see them."

Foolhardy, Paul thought, but he said nothing. She was flaunting her Israeli toughness, which meant he couldn't be a weak Diaspora Jew.

He turned the car onto Sixty-ninth Street where his father had collapsed on their last day together. "Right on this corner, when I came here with my father, your grandfather —"

"My *Saba*."

"Your *Saba*. On the day he died, there was a butcher shop here with a sign in the window: 'Send a Salami to Your Boy in the Army.' The rhyme made it almost funny."

"What's funny? In Israel, every boy's in the Army — every girl . . ." Her mouth suddenly opened wide, and she pointed ahead at three black boys on the boardwalk. "I don't like the way they look, *Abba*. They're big."

In the rubble on Paul's left, a few feet from where they were driving, the bungalow with the gold-star flag had once stood. And, on the road beneath them, Daddy had collapsed and then disappeared. Paul stopped the car.

"Turn around, Papa. This isn't my best violin, but it's worth a lot."

Paul felt as if he had been taken over by a force deep inside of him. "I never told anybody everything that happened that day. If I don't tell you now and here, I never will."

"Okay, but turn the car around and keep the motor running so that we can get away fast. *Ima* told me the town where you lived isn't safe anymore."

Paul did what she had asked, and then began: "We walked here, right here, in June of 1944, a few days after the Allies invaded Europe. I was ten years old but I see it all so clearly. My father, Reuben, your *Saba*, was upset he wasn't fighting in the war . . ."

He told her everything he could remember — the gold-star flag, the swimming lesson in the ocean, how his father had suddenly gone white, and his own failure to do what he had promised his mother — to run to a telephone and call the police immediately if his father didn't feel well. Ruby's eyes moved anxiously back and forth between him and the boys on the boardwalk, but he didn't hurry. He had held the story inside himself for too long. He finished by saying, "I lied to my mother about exactly what happened because I didn't want her to think I was responsible for his dying. But she thought it anyway — and maybe she was right." He tried to swallow, but his throat was too dry.

Ruby let her fingers rest on the back of his neck. "*Safta* told me about that day, too." She looked directly at him, and Paul felt his teeth might chatter. "She knows you think she blames you, but she never did. He couldn't have lived much longer, no matter what, and she blames him for dying so young. Stubborn — he wouldn't listen to anybody or let himself act like he was a sick man." Ruby smiled. "You know, after all these years, she still loves him even though Papa Jack is so wonderful. You're lucky to have parents who loved each other."

Paul let his teeth chatter.

"There's more," Ruby said. "*Safta* said you think it's your fault Max and Asher died, but it's not your fault. You didn't want to hurt anybody."

Ann, Willa and Chip had told him the same thing, and he had been unable to respond to any of them in words. With his mother speaking through his daughter, it was even more difficult.

"Don't you think so, Papa?"

As Paul struggled for a response, Ruby looked again toward the rear of the car, then suddenly screamed, "*Abba!*"

Paul jerked his head around and saw the three black boys on the boardwalk backed up against the railing by three large enraged dogs. He could almost feel their fangs. Angry growls filled the air.

"Let's call the cops," he said. He would take action, not like on that day with Daddy. But as he said it, he heard a bang and, almost immediately, one of the dogs collapsed and the others tore away, running to the west, where Playland used to be. The boy nearest the fallen dog had a pistol in his hand. Paul pressed down on the accelerator and, with a screech of the tires, headed towards Rockaway Beach Boulevard.

At Sixty-sixth Street, he saw a roofless building standing across from Derech Emunah, surrounded by rubble. It was where his family's grocery store had been, where Sibyl had called to order pot cheese she didn't want so Paul could deliver it to Ruby's great-grandmother's house and Ruby's parents could meet.

"Origin," Paul said — the first word between them since the dog was shot. "The building we're passing is where —"

"No more," Ruby interrupted. "I know enough. It's over. *Maspeek*, we say in Hebrew."

Maspeek, Paul repeated to himself when they passed Sixty-fourth Street, where Max had drowned and where, hours before Ruby's conception, he had come close to following him.

"We should be at Kennedy in a half hour," he said.

CHAPTER 25

German filled the air: "*Wilkommen an bord auf dem Lufthansa flug, non-stop dienst von New York nach Frankfurt.*" It was a man's voice — deep and resonant, yet also soothing. So different from Strummer's barking commands on the death march from Auschwitz — *Schnell. Keep going. It's only two more dead Jews.*

Paul felt ridiculous. He was comparing the pilot's voice with the voice of an SS Oberstrumführer he had never heard or seen. He had lived a life dominated by the Holocaust, although he hadn't experienced a moment of it.

It was ironic that his first trip to Israel would be on a German airline — Lufthansa's overnight flight to Frankfurt, where he would change for another Lufthansa flight to Tel Aviv — but Ruby's El Al flight was full, and this was the quickest way to get there.

Four hours earlier, as he dropped Ruby at the JFK Administration Building, where the Galilee Quartet was being interviewed for a *Newsweek* article about Israelis playing Wagner, she told him that "Malke said playing Wagner on the Guarneri would be like peeing on Auschwitz ashes. So," Ruby continued, "as soon as I get back, I'm going to take the Guarneri out of the safe and give it back to her. Too much blood and filth on the diamonds that paid for it, and too much she's bossing me around like she does *Ima.*" As she got out of the car, Ruby blew Paul a kiss. "*Shalom, Abba.* Come to Israel soon."

She was gone, a violin case swinging at her side, before Paul could respond, which was fortunate because he had no idea what to say about the Guarneri or Max's diamonds. He had to think and, like a good father, give her his reasoned opinion — soon and face-to-face.

And then the idea came to him — or, more accurately, it leaped from the back of his mind where Ruby had planted it. He'd go to the Caesarea concert because, for the first time in his life, he had a child who craved his support.

And go as soon as possible. The concert was less than a week away – not much time for Ruby to rein in emotions that might otherwise interfere with her performance, or for Paul and *Safta* Ida to begin growing the mutual trust they had never shared.

Besides, as Ruby had pointed out, if he really was a Jew, it was about time he went to the Jewish homeland.

The only problem was Ann. In two or three days, Eric would arrive in Hong Kong, probably with their son, and urge her to give their marriage another try. She had told Paul that her answer would be no, but that it would be easier to say the word if Paul were five minutes away, rather than half way around the world.

Ann would understand why, at this juncture in Ruby's life, Paul had to be there for her. If she couldn't understand this, if she needed Paul to be literally at her side to resist Eric's pleas and promises, her commitment to a life with Paul couldn't be that strong.

There was no time to debate the matter. His father didn't debate whether to leave Czechoslovakia. Paul drove directly to the JFK Holiday Inn to rent a room where he could make the necessary calls in private.

First, he would call Ann. No! First he would buy his plane ticket so that Ann would appreciate the strength of his desire to be there for Ruby.

As soon as he had reserved the Lufthansa flights, he called Ann but was told by the maid that she had taken her mother to the doctor and would be in her office "soon."

He called Maria and asked her to cancel the meetings scheduled for the next day: "Mr. Bradford, Johnny and Lewis Berman. Tell them I've recently discovered that I have an Israeli daughter who's in the center of a controversy there and needs me right away. I'll call from Israel to explain and set up new appointments for when I come back." It was close to the truth with one exception: He might not come back.

He then reached Ann and, when she picked up the phone, asked what her mother's doctor had said. He, unlike Eric, would be concerned with whatever concerned her.

"There's nothing life threatening," Ann answered, "but enough issues to make it dangerous for her to be alone. Did you see . . . Have you settled the name question?"

"Ruby. My daughter's name is Ruby." It felt good saying it. "You'll like her, and she'll like you. Her quartet's playing Wagner at a big concert in Caesarea next week. Very controversial. There will be picketing led by one of our cousins who's a genuine hero. It could be nasty, and Ruby's mother's not coming. Ruby asked me if I could come. She's going back in the Army the next day."

Paul paused, hoping Ann would make it easy for him, but she was silent.

"I'm at the airport now — on the way to Israel. I was going to ask you if you could meet me there, but I guess with your mother—"

"My aunt is coming to visit from New Zealand. Maybe she could come a few days earlier. And I was going to meet with Eric on Wednesday or Thursday so I could tell him no to his face. God knows what he'll say if I'm gone, or how he'll try to alienate Gideon from me even more. But I can't let Eric's spite control what I do. Let me make some calls." She emitted a sound which could only be a sniffle.

"If you can't meet me in Israel, I'll fly to Hong Kong immediately after the concert."

"Is that sensible?"

"Sensible is overrated, and I'm sick of it," Paul answered her.

Ann laughed between sniffles — she might be crying. "You have to support your daughter, and I want to support you."

Sitting in a Boeing 747 on a JFK runway waiting to take off, Paul realized that two months ago he had been sitting in another 747 on the same runway — possibly in the same spot. Then he was en route to Hong Kong — running away. Now he was going to Israel by way of Germany, and from Israel, he would go to Hong Kong, either with Ann or to meet her there — running *forward*. But he would make no comparisons and he would plan nothing. *Just live it.*

Following the pilot's direction, he lowered his shade for takeoff, but once they were airborne he raised it. How could he not look at Rockaway?

He saw a peninsula, the outline of a bridge and a few lights, but it was a dark night, and he wasn't sure which peninsula it was — Rockaway or Atlantic Beach or Long Beach or some other extrusion from Long Island. He thought he could make out the Rockaway Playland roller coaster, but then recalled that Rockaway no longer had a roller coaster. *Maspeek*, Ruby had told him — Gone. Was that good or bad? It made no difference. *Maspeek.*

He looked down at the endless Atlantic, the ocean that had drowned Max and pushed his father's heart beyond its capacity, but had also brought him to America and given him both the joy of coasting and the peace of floating. For a moment, while the plane ascended, he made out a few stripes of white foam, and then they were gone. The Atlantic, with its ever-changing colors, now showed none. Except for the lights of the plane, he saw nothing but blackness — black air over black water — like the dark that had enveloped him during his first days in the hospital.

But the black, he knew, was temporary. In Israel, he would land in daylight.

**THE END
of
MAX'S DIAMONDS**

ACKNOWLEDGMENTS

My thanks to those who helped me try to get it right:

David Groff, poet and independent editor, guided me through every step of this novel. His ability, sensitivity, integrity and simple love of language make me happy I launched this second career.

Mary Barto, the flutist, who reviewed or contributed to all of the many scenes concerning music; Jessica Kirzane, a Columbia Ph.D. candidate, who filled in the Yiddish and checked the Holocaust and war scenes for veracity; my former partners, Yvonne Chan and Jamie Horsley, who bridged the gap between my memories (or fantasies) of Hong Kong and the realities of that unique city; and Dr. Danielle Spratt who, during the novel's early stages, answered whatever question I had quickly and accurately.

Suzanne McConnell, Fiction Editor of *Bellevue Literary Review*, worked with me on several pieces of fiction, which, for the moment, are on the shelf. Most of what I know about writing fiction, I learned from her.

I am also indebted to Yvonne Goshorn, Eileen Levin and Millie Gonzalez who took pages of scribbles I could barely decipher and turned them into a readable manuscript.

Special thanks to my children, Susan, Mark and Ben, who supported my career change and were there with encouragement, advice and, most important, love whenever I needed it; and to Steven Drachman of Chickadee Prince Books, whose close reading, generosity, and commitment to the promise of the independent press have improved this novel and made the publication process a pleasure.

And Judy Greenfield, my love, soul mate and wife for more than fifty-eight years – we were partners in every word of this as in everything else. Her singularly insightful and careful reading made this a much better novel than I could have written without her. Thanks are not enough.

Jay Greenfield
December 2015